THE RUNAWAY BESTSELLER OF THE WEST!

"FAST-MOVING, VIVIDLY WRITTEN, AND RICH AND AUTHENTIC IN DETAIL . . . This sweeping historical novel could be to Colorado what Edna Ferber's bestselling GIANT was to Texas. Skillfully plotted . . . a happy addition to Western literature. Mark the name Brundy. You will be hearing more of him!"

The Denver Post

HIGH EMPIRE

CLYDE M. BRUNDY

AVON
PUBLISHERS OF BARD, CAMELOT, DISCUS, EQUINOX AND FLARE BOOKS

HIGH EMPIRE is an original publication of Avon Books. This work has never before appeared in any form.

AVON BOOKS
A division of
The Hearst Corporation
959 Eighth Avenue
New York, New York 10019

ISBN: 0-380-00040-7

First Avon Printing, June, 1974.
Sixth Printing

AVON TRADEMARK REG. U.S. PAT. OFF. AND
FOREIGN COUNTRIES, REGISTERED TRADEMARK—
MARCA REGISTRADA, HECHO EN CHICAGO, U.S.A.

Printed in the U.S.A.

In memory of Louise,
who read these
first pages,
smiled, and said—*write!*

HIGH EMPIRE

PART ONE

1880–1881

Chapter 1

The house was known as Swope's mansion. In the gray December twilight of 1880, its two-storied, square massiveness was yet unsheltered and unscreened by the maple and elm trees that later would soften its harsh and uncompromising lines. It had been finished the previous summer and at once darkened by brown paint which would preserve its timbers, but doom forever the hopes of Lance Ainsley that this house, the largest yet built in Horace Greeley's Union Colony, would bring to the Colorado frontier a simplicity and charm of architecture. Why could it not be like the homes so well remembered from his childhood in the plantation lands of Louisiana?

This was Jared Swope's house. Passers-by, pausing to stare, agreed it was just the kind of house that banker Swope would build. A home large enough to lend assurance of its owner's prestige in the colony—and to provide, at minimum cost and on the second floor, separate quarters for his daughter, Emily, for Lance Ainsley, the fiddle-footed surveyor she had married, and for their two children, Caroline and Shawn.

Snow had begun falling in mid-afternoon, sweeping across the plains on a northwest wind. In gathering darkness, Caroline Ainsley walked through ankle-deep whiteness toward her grandfather's house. The collar of her plaid coat was drawn snugly about her throat; her mittened fingers thrust firmly into her pockets out of the cold of the storm. It was a rare thing for her to be allowed out late. Only her seventh-grade teacher's insistence that she attend the final rehearsal of the Christmas program had wrung consent from her mother, Emily Ainsley, for Caroline to walk the three blocks alone as darkness approached.

The graveled walk led past a vacant lot. She stopped, kicked stubbornly at the snow, then made a fox-and-geese circle of the lot. When the snowy ring was trod to her satisfaction, she strode to the center, faced into the wind, and let white flakes fall against her face. Before and below her were the few business blocks of the town, laid out with broad and straight streets that led quickly into the sagebrush and loneliness of the encroaching prairie.

A half mile farther north was the river, the Cache la Poudre, flowing eastward clear and cold toward its meeting with the South Platte. Caroline remembered the Platte, and its great wide valley up which the wagons had brought her and her family to the colony—to Greeley. She turned to face west and hoped for a glimpse of the mountains lost in the stormy darkness. Yet in her mind's eye she could see them, the vast and wonderful sweep of snowy peaks marching for two hundred miles along the horizon. In morning sunshine, they always seemed close enough to touch. A week earlier her father had promised that in the spring he would take her to the mountains. She smiled, knowing that Lance Ainsley was not one to break promises; some warm morning they would leave with a picnic basket and fishing poles tucked in a spring-wagon drawn by her father's team of matched bay horses.

Thoughts of her father caused her to turn and gaze wistfully up the gentle slope of the hill leading southward. Through veiling snow she could see the swaying gas lamp in front of her grandfather's house. Beyond this, the lights of the town dwindled quickly into black nothingness. She knew there were other lights and another town beyond the hill. It was a town whose name she must never mention at home, a town that Grandfather Swope said was damned by rum and harlots.

Defiantly she lifted her head, then firmly spoke the forbidden name aloud: "Evans ... Evans ... Evans." Moments later she circled back to the walk, studied a pine wreath tied to a post with wind-whipped red ribbon, and walked swiftly homeward.

She entered by the kitchen door. House cleaning had

12

been an all-day affair in preparation for Christmas and Grandmother Swope would be in no mood for having snow tracked into the parlor. By yellow lamp light she removed her coat and overboots and placed them in a closet. She turned, and was momentarily silhouetted against a glistening white wall. It was the shadow of a twelve-year-old girl, tall and thin, with an erect and proud bearing.

She had never been at home or at ease in this house. She sensed that she had never been really welcome here, carrying so indelibly as she did the likeness of the man that Jared Swope had come to detest above all others. She touched her black and shining hair which was combed back simply to hang in two long and plaited braids falling midway to her waist. She was indeed Lance Ainsley's daughter. She had his dark hair and his gray, steady eyes, and her face, glowing with a clear loveliness born of the outer cold, was intense and intelligent.

The kitchen was warmed by a fire banked in the cook stove. Now the room was filled with mysterious and hunger-sparking odors that told of baking and roasting. She hesitated, torn between desire to raid the pantry and knowledge of the wrath such an act would bring down upon her. With a quiet sigh, she turned instead to a stubby pump mounted above a tier of cabinets at one end of the kitchen. This inside pump, one of the few in the colony, was a mark of Swope distinction. She drank deeply of the cold water. No outer traces of her anger and resentment were evident as she moved with sure, firm steps into the living room and under the gaze of those already there.

Her eyes, adjusted to brighter light from two flower-bowled kerosene lamps as she examined the square, high-ceilinged room. The massive furniture was too closely placed and crowded against walls papered with a design of grapevines climbing into shadows above the lamp glow. Floors of milled pine were strewn with hooked rag rugs.

Midway up one wall a painting of the Royal Gorge was encased in a huge gilded frame. The striking painting was conceived more from rampant imagination than reality, and revealed a turbulent, green river flowing between cliffs narrowing in sheer and dizzy heights. The painting always

13

fascinated Caroline. Her conception of the Rocky Mountains, that mystic, snow-crested ridge off to the west, where she had never been, was based largely on the painting. She was staring at the canvas when her grandmother's voice cut the quiet and semi-gloom of the warm room.

"For heaven's sake, Caroline. Sit down and stop gawking." Florence Swope turned in her rocking chair and peered over steel-framed spectacles. She was short and heavyset. *Fat* was the word Caroline used in moments of lesser discretion and out of hearing. Grandmother Swope's hair, fading from brown to white, was done in a bun and held by amber-hued bone pins. About her shoulders was the black, knitted shawl that was her constant companion from first frost to green grass. Her blue, slightly protuberant eyes masked both baffled inner resentment and resignation.

Caroline watched her lift one foot tentatively from the hot guard rail of the heating stove as she glanced toward the younger woman seated on a ladder-backed chair. "Emily, we'll have to get the child something to eat." Noting that her daughter was already rising, Florence Swope settled back in the rocker, picked up her Sunday School quarterly, and began reading.

With her mother's hand on her shoulder, Caroline turned back to the kitchen. Her gaze moved across the closed doors she knew led to the parlor, that carpeted, dusted, and polished room strictly forbidden to children except on special occasions. She was aware, too, of another room opening off the living room, a smaller one known only as Grandfather's library. He would no doubt be there now, warmed by the only fireplace in the house, and bent over papers carried home from the bank.

Downstairs there were also two bedrooms, more elaborately furnished than those on the second floor. Caroline preferred those upstairs where she had a small one to herself. Her five-year-old brother Shawn still slept in his mother's room. She thought of it as *Mama's room*, for her father seldom remained overnight in this house. She had heard heated, bitter discussions punctuated by such words as *ingrate* and *ambitious fool* from Grandfather Swope, and the low-spoken, unsure protests voiced by her mother.

14

Minutes later, seated at the kitchen table spread with a red-checked cloth, Caroline ate hungrily for a time, then cupped her chin in an open palm and looked steadily at her mother. "Mama, I like the Christmas play and songs. Do you suppose Papa will be there—at the program?"

"I'm sure he will be, Caroline. Now take your elbow off the table and finish supper. It is nearly bedtime."

Caroline raised her fork, then lowered it as wistfulness gathered in her eyes and voice. She carefully studied her mother. "I don't like the dress you're wearing," she said bluntly.

Emily Ainsley's reply was guarded. "It's a good dress—and clean."

"It's drab and baggy. I liked those you used to wear. Remember that red one with the puffed sleeves ... the one you wore when Colonel Adams visited us back home in Louisiana? It made you beautiful."

Her mother glanced nervously toward the silencing door between the kitchen and the base-burner where Florence Swope sat reading. Her face softened, shedding time and worry. Traces of pink enlivened her cheeks. "That was a wonderful dress, wasn't it?" she breathed.

"You were the prettiest lady there. Papa said so." Caroline was silent a time, then added, "I wish our dresses for the Christmas play were pretty like that, not just black and gray robes."

Emily Ainsley straightened and the glow receded from her face. "Don't ever let your grandpa hear you say anything like that. Hurry now ... to bed."

Caroline rose from her chair and again looked into her mother's face. "Mama," she asked thoughtfully, "what is a whorehouse?"

The question brought Emily to her feet. Amazed incredulity opened her mouth and eyes. "Caroline," she gasped. "Child, where do you hear such things?" She walked quickly to the living-room door, as if she might block with her tense body the possibility of words leaking through.

Caroline's eyes remained calm and questioning. "I heard Grandmother say it herself, Mama. She was talking to Mrs. Snyder. She said no woman from Evans could join the Ladies Aid, because over in Evans they have

15

several—" Her words were cut short by the quick alarm with which Emily covered both ears, then spoke sharply. "Caroline, be still. Listen. Someday, when you're older, you will understand such things. Just forget all about it now, and think of your schoolwork. Do you know your lines perfectly? You'd best go upstairs now. And . . . and Caroline, please go up quietly tonight?"

The first rays of sunlight two days later brought Caroline awake and conscious of the fact the storm had passed. For a time she lay snuggled between cotton blankets, knowing drowsily that this day was important. Then realization hit her. There would be no school; at night would be the Christmas program. She began humming the song the girls of her class would sing.

Suddenly wide awake, she slid out of bed and dressed in the chilliness of the room. Minutes were spent before a mirror as she brushed her hair to shining orderliness. Her humming became a clear-toned song when she descended the stairs and began the morning chores her grandfather insisted she always perform.

As the hours wore toward evening, she moved often to the window to peer anxiously into the street. It was up this street that Lance Ainsley, driving a team of matched bay horses, would surely come to take his family to the program.

It was unusual for her to have free hours, but today Florence Swope, engrossed in last-minute preparations, paid scant attention to Caroline. Toward dusk, as Caroline stood expectantly before the window, she noticed that the wind was rising sharply. A light snow swirled through the street as though racing to seek shelter for the night.

She was still beside the window when a carriage stopped outside, and Jared Swope alighted. Her grandfather never walked home from the bank. Usually a business acquaintance would drop him by, or a livery rig was scheduled for the short trip if no other means were at hand.

As he opened the wooden gate, he glanced up, his eyes sweeping across the house and fastening briefly upon the window and Caroline's face. She sensed that she should turn and go upstairs before he entered; tonight she would not do it, for her father was coming and she was not going to miss his arrival.

Jared Swope entered through the parlor, removed his coat, then rubbed his hands before the heating stove. "Caroline, come here," he said abruptly.

Her face whitened as she moved toward him. Her stomach tightened; she wondered if she was going to be sick. It was always this way when she confronted her grandfather. She had become fearful of this man, but her fear was tinged with hatred. She was scarcely aware that her feelings, stamped clearly on her face, would arouse to higher pitch the smouldering anger within him. Hers was the Ainsley spirit; it must be humbled or broken—if not in her father, then in this child who stared steadily toward him.

His hand streaked to her shoulder, holding it in a painful grasp. Caroline looked into his heavy and reddening face, seeing dark and blazing eyes that contrasted strangely with the sandy hue of his beard and the fringe of hair beneath his balding head. His loud and slightly nasal voice boomed across the room.

"I warned you to keep away from the windows ... not to stare out at everyone like a common slut."

"I wasn't staring at anyone, Grandfather. I was watching for Papa."

"Don't talk back to me." His grasp grew tighter as he shoved her toward the kitchen. "I'll break you of this Ainsley insolence ... strap some Godly respect—"

They moved through the kitchen door, and were confronted by Emily Ainsley. She moved quickly between them to face the livid-faced man. "Father—stop. What on earth is it this time?"

"Father, what is it?" he parroted. "This girl can disobey me ... stare out at important people ... sass me. All I hear is *Father, what is it?*"

Caroline felt her mother break the painful grasp upon her shoulder and wheel her about. "Go upstairs, Caroline. Get ready for the program. Be sure and fold your costumes in the box. Stay in your room until your father arrives."

As she turned to obey, Caroline cast a long and contemptuous look at Jared Swope. Her face was white. Her

17

gray eyes were filled with unspoken thoughts as she slowly entered the living room and ascended the stairs.

Half an hour later she heard the tinkle of bells, and knew that her father was outside. This was the moment for which she had waited, had put on a green-and-white-plaid dress, and for which she consulted the mirror many times.

She picked up the small box in which her costume for the play had been placed, then moved to her bedroom door. In the hallway she hesitated. Moments passed ... then on tiptoes she went to another door leading into a small room adjoining her own, opened it, and moved about in the darkness to locate and open an old and battered trunk. Then her hands searched downward through layer after layer of packed clothing.

When the sound of Lance Ainsley's voice drifted up to her, she came down to meet him. The costume box was nestled tightly under her arm. She had taken time to tie it with red string in her own room.

Her descent of the stairs quickened to a reckless rush, for, as she had known he would be, her father was waiting with outstretched arms. As she leaped into his embrace she was aware of many things—of his dark-brown suit, of the wide expanse of white shirt front, of a maroon necktie that spoke jauntily of the holiday season. Her face lifted eagerly for his kiss; she had seen him less and less often during the past weeks. There was fulfillment in this moment.

Then he stepped back to run searching eyes upward from her toes. Anyone watching would have marveled at their similarity. The years had been kind to Lance Ainsley. No gray strands marked the carefully parted blackness of his hair. He was six feet tall with a thin suppleness that found expression in his smoothly coordinated movements and physical power. Below a high forehead, lively gray eyes added expression to his words.

"I'll swear, kitten, you grow an inch a day. And look at that dress; it wasn't nearly so lovely until you put it on. Hurry, get your coat. We've little time."

She was moving from him as her mother came from the kitchen, leading five-year-old Shawn. Caroline was glad they were all together and by themselves in the room. She

18

sensed that her grandparents had left earlier for the school. Jared Swope never greeted his son-in-law. Their infrequent meetings were at the bank. The bank was Swope's domain, offering an aloof and commanding position from which he preferred to contact Lance Ainsley.

As she pulled her coat collar snug about her, Caroline saw that her mother and father were standing face to face, with few words passing between them. Lance lifted his son into his arms, but the boy strained away, poking out imploring hands toward his mother. To little Shawn, this tall, immaculate man was becoming a stranger. The Swope house was Shawn's world; and, oddly, the smallest of the Ainsleys had become the captor of his grandfather's heart.

"We'd best be going," Emily said. "Lance, will you come here after the program?"

"I'm afraid not, Emily. There are men in town from Denver who will be waiting for me. It's important."

"But this is the holiday season. The children—"

"And this is Swope's mansion," he replied. "Remember? Why add fuel to a fire already out of control? You can all ride home in Swope's carriage."

Emily Ainsley flushed; her words grew strained. "A holiday family . . . a holiday wife. Where is this leading us, Lance?"

"I hope to God it leads anywhere," he said, "away from this house and this life."

"Where would it be better?" she responded coldly. "Father offered us security here. A settled life for you and for me . . . for the children."

"He offered *you* those things," Lance persisted. "For me he had use only when he needed a surveyor at starvation rates, except for an occasional, grudging handout because he is too proud to have his daughter live the life I provide for her. You haven't seen him recommending my work, or introducing me to any of his business friends."

"All that will take time."

"I haven't time for eternity."

Silence fell between them as they left the house and moved to the shining black buggy where the bay team awaited them.

Unalterable facts weighed upon them. At his wife's insistence, Lance had left a small but growing surveying and engineering business in Louisiana shortly after Shawn was born. With his wife and children, he journeyed to Horace Greeley's Union Colony of Colorado, where Jared and Florence Swope were determined their daughter must live. Life seemed to go well and the future to hold promise for a surveyor who could lay out land boundaries, town-site lots, and irrigation canals and lateral routes.

It was inevitable though, that differences should arise between Jared Swope and his son-in-law. Swope would tolerate no happenings or circumstances that might impede his drive toward wealth. As a boy, growing up in a small Pennsylvania town, he had known abject poverty. Only with his marriage to Florence and with control of her inherited money had the opportunity opened for greater wealth and the respectability he was sure it would bring. Horace Greeley's widely published and discussed call for colonizers had seemed to be his big opportunity. The colony would be a farming area of cheap but potentially valuable land. A bank would be needed. Shrewdly managed, it could lead to a position of dominance and power. Jared answered the call, loaded wagons with family possessions, and moved westward. His wife laid down only one firm stipulation. If she must leave the East and her lifelong friends, Swope must persuade their daughter who lived in Louisiana with her husband to agree to accompany them to the western frontier.

Lance Ainsley's reluctance to leave Louisiana, and the promising future of his growing engineering firm, gave way before the flurry of letters exchanged by Florence Swope and her daughter. Wouldn't a newly developing area offer endless opportunities? The Ainsleys' two young children would have an assured future. Emily would be near her father and mother, who could aid the young couple in establishing a worthy home and community prestige.

Within a few weeks Lance Ainsley agreed to the venture; the three generations joined forces in the small, strictly-run colony beside the Cache La Poudre River.

Lance soon was frustrated and somewhat bitter. The Greeley Colony was puritanical in its concept and laws

20

and looked askance upon the free and pleasant mode of living under which Ainsley had worked and passed his days and nights in the South. Liquor was forbidden in Greeley; card playing and horse racing were held to be cardinal sins. An anathema to most colony residents was Evans, the older settlement a few miles south. Only a stretch of open prairie and the barbed-wire fence of the colony offered physical separation of the communities. In beliefs and values and ways of daily conduct the two villages lay a world apart. Greeley's colony offered the sobriety of churches, debating forums, and hard farm-based work; Evans—catering to cattlemen, railroad builders, and adventurers—provided saloons, dance halls, and the pleasures of sensuality.

Work was available for a competent surveyor in the colony and on farms rapidly expanding across the adjacent prairie land. From the day of Lance Ainsley's arrival, it seemed to Jared Swope that his son-in-law's time and skill should be devoted to Swope interests, and there should be no reason to pay a member of his family the rates an outsider would demand. He spoke often of "family interests" and priorities. Lance's income was adequate for little more than a portion of household and family expenses, so he sought outside jobs. The best were found among acquaintances made in Evans.

Despite a deteriorating relationship, it was to his father-in-law that Lance came, flushed with excitement, after a two-day trip eastward along the South Platte River.

"Jared," he said enthusiastically, "I've been running some surveys north of the river. A tributary creek comes in from the north through a basin. Water can be diverted from the Platte and stored in the basin. Some grading will have to be done and a half-mile earth fill built. A reservoir there will hold enough water to irrigate thousands of acres along the Platte Valley. We can buy that land cheap."

Swope listened in an impatient, disinterested manner, then said, "So you've been down the Platte dawdling and dreaming while I needed you. I've taken over a half section in Pleasant Valley, three miles from town. Needed boundary lines run. It's in farms that money will be made,

21

not through some impractical scheme out in the sand and sagebrush."

A growing anger drove the eagerness from Lance Ainsley's face. "Then you won't even listen . . . or look over the plans I've sketched?"

Swope shook his head. "I haven't time. Besides, the funds of my bank can be put to better use than financing a dam Hell-and-gone away from Greeley."

Ainsley rose from his chair. "Then I haven't time to run surveys on a foreclosure farm. Get yourself another man, Jared. And you'd better be prepared to pay him the going rate."

Anger rode Swope's reply. "That'd suit you fine, wouldn't it? Sluff off my work and have all your time for daydreams—and for helling around in Evans. Playing cards and drinking while I provide a roof over your wife and kids."

"I've an idea I am capable of providing another roof for them," Lance said coldly.

"Are you?" Swope smirked. "Ask your wife, my daughter. She went to the swamps of Louisiana with you once; she's not likely to again leave her mother and me—and what we can provide."

Within two weeks Lance Ainsley completed detailed plans and cost estimates of the reservoir, intake ditches, and canals of the downriver project. Within a month, and with the assistance of friends in Evans, he secured a promise of financing by Denver capitalists. Pending the drawing of necessary legal papers, the deal was bound by a handshake.

Jared Swope lost no time in getting in touch with his son-in-law. His approach was friendly and expansive as he leaned forward to place his hand on Lance's shoulder. "Perhaps I was a little hasty about the reservoir project. Needed time to think it over. I think I can persuade the bank directors to go along with us in financing this and acquiring the farmland. I've drawn up papers."

"Without consulting me?" Lance replied in astonishment.

"Of course, I knew you would want to keep this in the family. For ourselves . . . Emily . . . the children."

"That was what I had hoped for originally, Jared, when I came to you."

"Now is a good time to wrap it up," Swope said, grinning.

Lance rose and stared down at his father-in-law. "There'll be no time to wrap it up, Jared. My commitment, my promise, has been made to H. A. W. Tabor and others in Denver."

"There's been no legal arrangement yet, has there?"

Lance was silent for a time, wondering how deeply the ruthless mind and finagling of Swope had delved into his affairs. Finally, he said, "You're asking me to throw this your way, to break a promise—to renege on the agreement I made in Denver?"

Swope's eyes narrowed. "Business is business, hog eat hog!" he rasped. "Emily would want—"

"Leave my wife out of this," Lance replied heatedly. "She is capable of speaking for herself."

"Now, now, Lance. Let's take a family approach to this."

Lance moved toward the door. "The family approach was made quite some time ago. Now it's time for honor and self-respect. Sorry, Jared. The answer is *no*. The Denver agreement will stand." He hesitated briefly, studying the florid face of Jared Swope, then added, "If you have any idea of going it on your own, or with friends, forget it. Preliminary surveys have been filed with the secretary of state in Denver . . . enough to establish a priority—in my name."

From that moment Jared Swope detested his son-in-law. Had it not been for Florence, he would have been delighted to see the Ainsleys depart from under his roof . . . especially his twelve-year-old granddaughter, Caroline, whose appearance and spirit reminded him of Lance, the stupid, inept son-in-law who had "betrayed" him.

The ride to the school program began for Caroline with a numbness born of the words she had overheard. This was the first time her parents had ever quarreled within her hearing. From the seat between them she suddenly reached out an arm, linking it in the one with which her

23

mother was holding the small boy, Shawn. Her other arm soon snuggled into that of her father. She drew both of them toward her.

Within seconds, she sensed a subtle change come over them. Abruptly Lance Ainsley's clear baritone voice filled the street with "Silent Night, Holy Night." Caroline joined him, and then heard her mother catch up the tune. From graveled and planked sidewalks people turned to listen. It seemed that even the tiny harness bells joined in.

They drew to a stop before the school steps. Lance Ainsley handed the reins of his bays to an attendant, and helped his wife as she quickly inspected her children and stepped from the rig. He lifted Caroline and little Shawn down. Then, with a very special bow to those watching, he escorted his family inside.

There were few empty seats. The largest room of the school, from which desks had been removed and chairs crowded in, had drawn members of practically every family of the colony. An uncertain, flickering glow was cast from a dozen wall-bracketed kerosene lamps backed by polished glass reflectors.

A third of the room was given over to a heavily curtained stage, which was entered from an adjoining room. To one side of the stage stood a tall and shapely spruce tree, festooned with yard after yard of popcorn and cranberries, and bearing the few ornaments available in the town. There were many small candles which would be lighted later when the Christmas treats were to be handed out after the program ended.

With a quick, excited kiss, Caroline left her seated family and disappeared into the hallway to join her classmates. The red-tied box was still beneath her arm, and she held it tightly.

Emily Ainsley glanced about, acknowledging the waves and nods of friends and neighbors. She noticed that her husband had steered them to a row of seats several rows behind Jared and Florence Swope. Curiously, she watched Lance Ainsley place his coat and hat across two vacant chairs in an attempt to reserve them. He noted her puzzled gaze.

"The men from Denver ... they'll be here. I wrote

them not to miss it, that my daughter is a member of the cast."

"How ridiculous, Lance. Grown men—from Denver—at a children's school program. Little tots reciting, and forgetting, verses."

"What else," he asked bitterly, "has this brave, new, sanctimonious colony to offer?"

Later two men entered, greeting Lance Ainsley and taking the seats he reserved. Emily acknowledged the introduction, but the names of these strangers were drowned by a fourth-grade recitation.

She turned her attention to a tableau given by half a dozen boys which depicted the journey of the Wise Men from the East. As it ended, and the curtains were drawn for a change of homemade scenery, she became aware of a murmur of screened curiosity across the crowd. More and more of them turned for quick glances at the strangers beside Lance. She wished she had caught the names of these men. Any stranger among the well-acquainted members of the colony would be the object of notice and quick glances.

The curtains drew slowly apart; the room quieted. Emily Ainsley leaned forward. On the stage in semicircle stood the seventh-grade girls in black-and-gray costumes. She quickly scanned their faces. Caroline was not in her place. An elderly teacher, seated at the piano, glanced questioningly toward the door at the stage's rear. Seconds passed. Emily tensed as a restless shuffle marked the audience. Suddenly the door opened.

Caroline entered—not as a black-and-gray-draped schoolchild. She wore a dress that was red ... and with sleeves ending with a broad flare just below the shoulder. At the side was a giant white bow which gathered in inches of excess waist. Because the dress was too long, Caroline held a portion of it gracefully in her arm.

There was a loud and discordant bang of piano keys as the teacher's ten stiffened fingers dropped upon them. Caroline ignored the sound and walked slowly forward to take her place in the center of the group. The girls tittered nervously and excitedly as they made way for her. She acknowledged them by a toss of her head. The long braids had been combed out and the ribbons discarded. Her black, shining hair cascaded over her shoulders.

A moment later her voice struck the first high and clear note of a song. A voice joined hers ... another ... and another. The piano player picked up the melody. The seventh-grade girls—and Caroline Ainsley—were singing.

As the song ended, Emily turned quickly to lay her palm over her husband's mouth. Lance Ainsley had laughed in a sound that rang aloud through the hall. Then she turned quickly toward the stage. Caroline had stepped forward and was singing a spirited Christmas song of the Louisiana Negroes. The room was silent—entranced by a child, a red dress, and a spiritual.

It was the older of the strangers alongside Lance who came to his feet as the song ended. His voice echoed throughout the crowded room. "My God, the child is beautiful!"

With tightly clenched fists against her cheeks, Emily turned to her husband. "Who is that man?" she demanded.

Lance Ainsley's eyes were sparkling. "That, my dear, is H. A. W. Tabor."

There was only one act of the program remaining, a Christmas carol with all students on stage and in which the audience was asked to join. For this number, Caroline did not appear. Emily rose and edged her way toward the hall. She ran quickly to the next room toward a portion that had been curtained off as a girls' dressing room. Abruptly she was confronted by Mrs. O'Brien, the seventh-grade teacher who was pulling the red dress over Caroline's head. Her glance toward Emily was coldly furious. "Mrs. Ainsley," she hissed, "why did you let this happen? This girl ... this brat ... has disgraced all of us. The class. The school. The colony."

She paused, thrusting the wadded crimson silk into Emily's hands. "Take this! And take your daughter. It's ... it's ... intolerable."

With numb lips and shaking hands, Emily hustled her child into her plaid dress and her coat. Caroline seemed oblivious of the hovering fury of Mrs. O'Brien. About her quietness was a distant and dreamy tranquility, an inner satisfaction born of knowledge that for minutes she had been the star of the show. Emily sensed her daughter's triumph. The seething tumult of her own thoughts relived the moment of Caroline's appearance, the clearness of that one voice above all others, the rhythmic spell that had been cast upon those in the overcrowded room, and the booming voice of Denver's most celebrated millionaire ringing its approval through the hall.

Even now, as she listened to Mrs. O'Brien's final words, *"She won't enter this school again until the board decides,"* Emily was aware of an undeniable truth. Caroline was beautiful. Her act was the one lovely and captivating moment of an otherwise dull and boring program.

They would have left the building, to stand in the outer wind and snow awaiting the Swope carriage, if their way had not been blocked by Lance and by Mr. Tabor.

"Saints have pity," Emily murmured inwardly. "Will this trial never end. What a time and place to meet this man. I must look like Banquo's ghost." She lifted her hand in greeting as Lance presented the illustrious and fabled lieutenant governor of Colorado. She would never remember what words she spoke.

"Lance," Tabor was saying, "I know now why your daughter is so lovely; I've met her mother." He held her hand. "Mrs. Ainsley, your child has given me the most enjoyable moment of this trip. You're wasting her here in the colony. She belongs in Denver. Bring her there for schooling. I insist."

"You're very kind," Emily whispered. "I hope we do meet again." A moment later she reached for Caroline's hand. She had caught sight of Jared and Emily Swope moving purposefully toward the outer door. She knew that this was a night of trial.

Lance stooped to gather Caroline into his arms. "Kitten," he said softly, "you shouldn't have done it. But, by god, I'm glad you did." He turned, lifted little Shawn, and placed him in Emily's arms. "Take good care of our girl and boy, Emily. Better go now. The banker mustn't be kept waiting. I'll see you tomorrow; it's a promise."

The ride home in Jared Swope's curtained carriage was silent. Only the sounds of plodding hoofs, snow-tortured

27

wheels, and Jared Swope's short and rasping breath contested the wind that had quickened into a gale.

Caroline went upstairs at once. Next to her room she could hear her mother putting Shawn to bed. It was quiet downstairs. Her grandfather would be stabling and unharnessing the team.

She sat down, stiffly erect on her bed. More minutes went by. There was the distant sound of a clock tolling ten. There was the sound of her mother going downstairs, and of muffled voices. Quietly she waited.

"CAROLINE! Come down here!" The words, high-pitched and menacing, tore through the silence of the house and beat upon the door of her little bedroom. "You hear me, Caroline? Do I have to come get you?"

She rose and moved dully toward the door. For a moment her clenched hands lay against the door and her forehead pressed against them. Then she was walking the stairs one by one. Her small, even teeth bit her lip savagely. Her palms were sweat-beaded and lifeless.

Jared Swope waited near the bottom of the stairs. He was coatless and had torn the tie from his shirtfront. In his hands was the long and tasseled carriage whip. His reddened face was a blazing background for his narrowed and furious eyes.

For an instant Caroline glimpsed her mother across the room. She started to speak, to cry out. The words died in a low gasp as her grandfather arced the whip backward and brought it slicing against her upthrust arm. She stumbled backward, and fell against the stairs. Then the lash was upon her again and again, biting through her clothing. She regained her feet, only to have the whip descend across her cheek.

Emily ran quickly across the room, seizing Jared Swope's arm. "No, Father. Not that way. Not on her face."

He turned and thrust her from him. "Get the hell out of my way, Emily. I'll take the devilment out of her this time." The whip swept down again. Caroline dodged blindly from its torment. It cracked down upon the banister and broke in two. In utter frenzy, the grandfather seized the two lengths and flailed the child, neither knowing nor

28

caring that blows were now falling upon her from the heavy butt end of the whip.

Caroline fell dazedly across a chair as her mother tried to tear the whip from the man's hand. "Stop it. Stop it, I tell you! You'll kill her!"

He shoved Emily away. "Keep out of this or take both of your brats and get out of this house."

Then again he struck. He was doing more than punishing a child. He was pouring out his wrath against Lance Ainsley.

Florence Swope entered calmly from the kitchen and brought an end to it. "Keep it up, Jared. Just keep it up. You can kill her, you know—*and they will hang you.*"

Jared Swope gave the whip a final and brutal swing toward the child now lying still on the floor. For a moment he towered above her. The battered and raveled whip ends slid from his grasp as he walked slowly into his library and closed the door.

Emily lifted her daughter onto a chair and wiped a wet cloth across the white and agonized face. Dark and ragged welts were forming on a shoulder. She knew that Caroline would carry scars of this night for a long while, possibly a lifetime.

Abruptly Caroline drew away from her, then staggered to her feet. "No," she moaned. "Don't touch me. You let him do it. You could have stopped him. If Papa had been here—" She moved with quickening steps toward the outside door. "My father. I . . . I want my father."

Emily reached out, and attempted to hold the child. Caroline eluded her and jerked open the door. She half-ran and half-stumbled from the porch. Within seconds she had disappeared in the thick, wind-whipped snow. Emily called frantically, listened, then called again and again as she moved to the yard gate and toward the street. There was only the hushed roar of a building storm.

Emily Ainsley turned toward the house for help. At the porch she fainted and fell heavily against the door.

In the moment of her escape, Caroline ran quickly around the house, sped by terror of her mother taking her inside again, of having to spend the night and the future in

29

Swope's mansion. The snow was ankle deep. She was without boots or coat. To this she paid no heed. The wind was cool and the snow soothing against her bruised face and body. She knew that she must flee, must run as fast as her legs could speed her from this place of hatred and horror.

Beyond the barn and across a vacant lot, a street lamp came dimly into view. She crossed over to the opposite side of a street to avoid it. Then she walked swiftly eastward where the buildings were thinning.

This way lay the road to Evans up the hill to the south. She knew the street of its beginning, and had been warned never to go this way alone, never after sunset, and never to venture beyond the crest of the hill. That crest, marked only by a barbed-wire fence, was the dividing line and barrier between the stern and orderly and church-steepled colony and the unknown outer world.

All warnings lay in pain and chaos behind her now. At the edge of town, she stopped for a moment, gathered directions, and sought the snow-mantled course of the road she must follow. Then she walked swiftly on, enveloped by the loneliness, the night, and the fury of wind-lashed whiteness.

She was cold and frightened. Tears that she had failed to shed under her grandfather's lash came like a blinding flood. Even as she sobbed aloud, she continued steadily along the trail. Unbroken by buildings, the wind was a harder and steadier blast. Only the infrequent dark patches of frozen earth from which snow had been whipped kept her on the road.

She ran, but within minutes stumbled and fell headlong in the trail. She struggled to her feet. Her breath came in sharp and torn gasps. She glanced back, hoping to glimpse a house or a light. There was only the storm-filled darkness and the surge of wind about her. Again she ran.

Then she was thrown back to fall upon the snow—she had plunged headlong into a barbed-wire gate. She vaguely sensed her whereabouts. She had reached the colony fence, the point where she would enter an untrodden and unknown land. She sat still for a time, then crawled beneath the bottom wire of the gate. It would be all right now. Out here, beyond another ridge, or perhaps down a long and gentle slope, she would come to lights ... to warmth ... to the arms and the love of her father. ...

She rose, and again moved down the frozen roadway. Numbness had crept into her feet, across her lips, and upward from her fingers. Her pace slowed to plodding and then wavered and faltered. Had not there been low embankments, she would have wandered from the road. Now there was no sense of direction, no prodding urgency. The whiteness of the road was a broad and gentle river on which she was gliding, high atop a brightly painted boat. Her mother sat near, proudly erect and smiling in a red and beautiful dress. She felt the warmth of Lance Ainsley's great hand clasped about hers. She peered into his face as he lifted her onto his shoulder in bright and warm sunlight.

Caroline fell forward in the snow. The wind fluttered the green checks of her dress and the dark cascade of hair at her shoulders.

When a freighter's wagon rumbled nearer and nearer along the road, she heard neither the frightened snort of the horses or the amazed but gentle curses with which the driver climbed from the wagon and lifted her into his arms.

Chapter 2

After Lance Ainsley bade his family good-bye and saw them homeward bound in the Swope carriage, he rejoined Tabor and the mining king's companion, Elkins. He sensed that they had attended the Christmas program only through courtesy and to allow him to be with his family for a part of the evening. They asked him to drive them to the Union Hotel, the colony's only hostelry, and to join them there for a time, after which they wished to return to Evans with him for the night.

They gathered in a small and scantily furnished room, the best the small hotel could offer.

"Gentlemen," Elkins said, "before we enter into the matter at hand, I believe a bit of cheer and warmth would be in order." He handed a silvered flask to Lance. It made a circle twice before they settled into conversation. H. A. W. Tabor lost no time in coming to the point of the meeting.

"Lance, you realize, of course, that two or three years of construction work will be necessary before the down-river irrigation project will be completed and begin to pay off?"

"I have thought of that," Lance answered. He wondered if these men had become wary of their deal.

"What are your plans meanwhile . . . during the building?" Tabor continued.

"Likely I can find jobs to get me by—provide for my family."

Tabor studied him with a probing gaze. "We have a deal, a sort of opportunity to offer you. Bob Elkins is from Cincinnati. He is interested in some properties on the Western Slope at Aspen. So am I, indirectly. Would you want to work for us there?"

"You mean give up our downriver project?" Lance asked uneasily.

"We are prepared to buy you out—either for cash or have you keep a percentage. Others can handle the dam building and canal layouts. We need you at Aspen."

Ainsley lifted a polished boot onto the bed, then studied the snow whipping past an uncurtained window. A perplexed frown knitted his forehead. "Why me?" he asked. "I know nothing of mines. Besides, neither of you knows much about me." He turned to Tabor with a slow smile. "Except that you and I played poker together a couple of times at the Windsor Hotel in Denver. I recall that I lost."

"You sure didn't lose much." Tabor laughed.

Lance rose, thrust his hands into his pockets, and strode

thoughtfully across the room. "What do you offer for my share of the irrigation project?"

Lance emitted a sharp whistle when Elkins quoted the figure. "That's sure fair enough, but would you have steady need for a surveyor in Aspen?"

"Maybe not a surveyor," Tabor said, "but plenty for a skilled engineer. We need an honest man who can be depended on to represent us, one who can think and act on his own."

Lance looked at them with level and uncompromising eyes. "I'd have to call the shots as I see them, not from a ten-page memorandum. If so—maybe it's time I shake the colony dust from my heels. Will there be accommodations for my family?"

"As soon as they can be built," Elkins assured him.

"And the salary?"

"You're not apt to find a better offer—anywhere."

"When should I be ready to leave?" Lance asked, and smiled.

"Not later than mid-April," Elkins replied.

Lance nodded, listening to H. A. W. Tabor's chuckle. "Unless the flask is dry, we can seal us a deal. Then if there's a stick or two of wood for this potbellied stove, we can iron out the details."

"Gentlemen," Lance said quietly, "you've honored me."

They left the hotel and made their way to a livery stable where Lance had given his bay team a respite from the storm. None of them cared to spend the night in Greeley. Lance assured them that to the south was a game in which their wits could be matched with cowmen and land speculators.

At the snow-banked livery stable, they soothed the ire of a dozing hostler with the emptying drag from the flask and a gold piece.

"Take it easy over the hill in this storm," he warned. "Only rig I've seen headed Evans way in the last hour or so was a freighter. Likely he'd have bedded here all night, except he was hauling a coffin for some cowpoke who got himself killed off."

Lance drove slowly and was glad that only about three miles separated the towns. The wind had eased, and was followed by a heavier snowfall. The bay horses traveled this way often; their inborn sense of direction took over.

It was shortly past midnight when they pulled up in front of the Prairie Star Saloon in Evans. The street was now a snow-packed expanse between two short rows of rough, false-fronted buildings. Unlike at the colony, there was considerable night life here with men moving about. Light spilled from a dozen haunts of merrymakers; occasionally the hum of conversation was punctuated by a shouted greeting, an exuberant yell, or the excited laughter of men and women.

Holiday gayness was upon the town. Brave but scanty efforts had been made to decorate the street. Humped against the storm, half a hundred saddle horses and teams, whose less concerned owners had failed to stable them, waited for those inside to finish with the business or pleasures of the night and come to claim them.

Far off the muted whistle of a railroad engine roused a dozen dogs to a barking and howling response.

Lance turned his bay geldings over to the care of a Mackinaw-coated old man. Then the trio entered the Prairie Star, blinded momentarily by the brightly-lit room. Lance was greeted by a dozen men and girls at the bar and the tables. His welcome was warm, carrying a note of friendship and respect. For Tabor and Elkins, the nods and spoken words were guarded. People stood a little in awe and uncertainty in the presence of H. A. W. Tabor, an awe born of the legend of his wealth and power. Elkins was accepted as the great man's companion and as a stranger.

They walked the length of the large, street-fronting barroom, where they were greeted by the owner, a portly and red-mustached man wearing a candy-striped shirt and flowing black tie.

"We've sort of been expecting you, gentlemen. Right this way ... second door to the left, Lance. All set up for a game, and it's quieter and warmer. First drinks are on the house. Whistle if you get hungry; likely we can scare up a steak or so."

Lance glanced with interest at the half-dozen men already seated about a green-velveted table. Two of them were from Greeley, where their businesses in the growing colony were destined to make them wealthy. He dropped a hand to the shoulder of each.

"Amos . . . Tom . . . do your mamas know you're out and howling tonight?"

The older man grinned ruefully. "If they do, we'll sure as tarnation hear about it when we get home. Lady luck better——"

"Are we going to talk or play cards?" The query, from a leather-faced and leather-coated individual, caused Lance to laugh. "Hi, Jim," he said in greeting. Then he added. "Mr. Tabor . . . Mr. Elkins . . . this is cow-poor Jim Daley from downriver. If the snow gets too deep, he can furnish enough cowhides to cover the road to Denver. What brings you up this way, Jim?"

"I'm headed for Denver in the morning with a beef shipment. But damned if I don't think we'll still be talking come train time." The cowman paused, looking toward Tabor. "I'd rather shut up and win me a silver mine," he added.

As they settled into chairs, H. A. W. Tabor stared firmly back at the rancher. "Fair enough, my friend. Now me, I could use, say, five hundred steers. Suppose you deal first."

Lance picked up his first hand of the game, riffled it quietly, and studied the faces of the men about him. Abruptly his thoughts were broken by excited voices up front in the saloon. "Wonder what's up?" he said.

The cowman, Daley, glared at him. "Hell's fire. You know what's up—it's my jack of diamonds."

It was Elkins who took the first pot. He was pulling it toward him when the door opened quietly and the proprietor entered, bearing a tray of glasses.

"Sorry about the commotion," he said. "Seems like some freighter coming in from Greeley found a kid—a girl—about frozen and lying in the road. They've got her over at Maude Selby's place. The doctor's been working on her quite a spell."

All eyes turned to him in disbelief and concern.

"Who is she?" Jim Daley asked. "Someone from Evans?"

"I don't think so. One of Maude's barkeeps just came

35

in. Nobody that's over there with the kid ever remembers seeing her. She's in bad shape ... out in this storm and didn't even have a coat or boots on. She's a tall kid with long, black hair. Had on a green-and-white-plaid dress. Been unconscious all the time."

Ten seconds passed before Lance Ainsley's memory gathered and exploded. The cards slipped heedlessly through his fingers as he rose to his feet. "A plaid dress," he murmured. "Green and white. Great God Almighty—it can't be. No ... no ... it isn't Caroline!"

Before Lance could leave the room, H. A. W. Tabor was beside him. "Wait, Lance. I'm going with you."

Every man was on his feet.

"You mean it may be someone you know?" Jim Daley asked in a low and strained whisper.

"It may be his daughter," the younger Greeley player answered. "I know her. She fits the description."

It was a block and a half to Maude Selby's bawdyhouse. Lance Ainsley sped toward it at a pace that left the others panting behind him. He slammed through the door and into view of three girls seated alone and graven-faced in the downstairs parlor.

"Where is Maude?" he shouted. Then, neither awaiting or hearing their startled replies, he leaped the stairs three at a time.

Midway down the hall a door was open, spilling out lamp light and low voices. For a moment he was rooted there. His stare encompassed the two women and a black-suited, gray-thatched man bending over a wide, brass-steaded bed. His gaze fixed on the child. He entered and dropped to his knees beside the bed. It was the white and tortured face of the child he had sent home in Jared Swope's carriage.

His hand moved up, dazed and trembling, to brush a shining, unruly lock of black hair from her forehead. His eyes were wide with terror as he turned them to the doctor, who was firmly pulling him farther away from Caroline's face.

"How is she, Doc? Will ... will she live?"

"Easy, Lance ... easy. She needs all the air she can get." The older man studied Lance's face. "No need now

36

to ask who this little girl is. We're doing all we can. It'll take time to know—hours, maybe days. How did this happen?"

"I don't know," Lance answered. He looked slowly about the room as though searching vainly for an answer. "I don't know. But Christ knows I'll find out—tonight!"

The doctor held a glass toward him. "Drink this. You'll need it. And stay here. Nothing that you can do, or find out tonight, will help her. Except maybe to pray. Now, get out of the way . . . get out of this room. I've got work to do."

It was Maude Selby's cool, firm hand that slipped into Lance's and led him toward the door. "Come along. She's in good care now. Better than you or I could give her. Doc isn't going to leave her side." She turned to an older woman. "Stay here, Vera. I'll be back if you need me. I'll tell Ellen to lock the front doors. This establishment is closed—indefinitely."

Across the half-filled downstairs parlor lay an expectant and uneasy silence. The house girls had quietly left. Friends and townspeople had heard what had happened and had come with offers of help and sympathy.

H. A. W. Tabor and the rancher, Jim Daley, broke off a low-voiced conversation. They knew at once that Lance's daughter lay upstairs.

"How is she, son?" Daley asked.

"Not good. Maybe by morning. . . ." Lance's words trailed off as a mug of hot, black coffee was thrust at him. He drank it in silence.

H. A. W. Tabor led him to a large leather chair. "Ease down, Lance. I'll have doctors on the way up from Denver by morning or I'll arrange a special train for her to Denver."

Lance grasped and held the older man's hand. "Thanks," he answered softly. "I doubt she could stand the trip. Doc is pretty capable. He'd probably welcome help; he'll have other people needing him."

The two Greeley men who had followed from the card game moved closer. "We'll be getting back to the colony; likely they've got everyone in town searching for her."

They halted in leaving as Maude Selby moved to Lance's side and spoke. "Lance, Doc didn't waste time or words to tell you. The child has been beaten. That towel on her cheek hides a cut like a bullwhip lash would make; her shoulders and her backside are nothing except welts and bruises." She paused, then knelt beside him, her face twisted with fury and disgust. "Who? Who would do such a thing?"

Lance Ainsley stared at her in unbelieving horror. "Are you sure?" he demanded.

"I should know. I undressed her."

Realization crept into his face. His lips tightened to a rigid, white line; his gray eyes darkened to ruthlessness and savagery.

"Jared Swope—her grandfather—did it. What kind of a damned fool have I been to leave her in his house?" He struggled to gain his feet. Friendly hands pushed him back.

"But your wife . . . her mother . . . wasn't she there?" Maude persisted.

Before he could answer, footfalls thumped on the stairs, and the doctor came down. His shirt sleeves were rolled and his thin, graying hair awry. Lance met him at the bottom steps.

"You can go up and look in now. She's beginning to move about. Don't expect much. The fever's coming in; she's out of her head—delirious."

"The beating—will it——?"

The old doctor shook his head. "We can take care of cuts and bruises, and the frostbite—luckily there is not much of that. But, Lance, I'll not fool you. We may not pull her through. This is going into lung fever."

From the third step, as he ascended the stairs, Lance turned to the two men from Greeley. "Take a message up to Swope's mansion for me. Tell my wife that Caroline is with me, sick and under a doctor's care at Maude Selby's in Evans. Tell her I said to come at once. Then tell Jared Swope that I'll be in to see him—after I know whether my child lives. He'd better pray that she does live. If she dies . . . if she dies . . . I'll kill him."

From a vast and encroaching whiteness, Caroline Ainsley felt herself fighting in pain-wracked and terrible desperation. Her eyes opened momentarily and fixed upon light pouring through an open window. She would have turned her head, but the agony of sudden and uncontrollable coughing was upon her. Billowing clouds of nothingness again engulfed her in that moment of recognition on New Year's Day, 1881.

For a long time she drifted between light and darkness. There would be the hot, sun-drenched fields of Louisiana, or the reaches of calmly flowing water where a boat moved lazily toward another town. There were moments with her family. Then it would darken. Cold—terrible and cutting cold—would envelop the sun and the river. She would run through snow and wind from some terrifying thing that pursued her.

There were the times of music, when she had been tucked in bed, only to creep out and move to where she could peer at the crowd gathered aboard the *River Queen* shouting and clapping their hands in approval as the gaily uniformed band played, and men and women on a wide stage broke into song. But this dream faded, and the sound became a high-pitched and angry voice beating upon her. *Caroline, come here! I'm coming up after you!* She would scream out her loneliness, her pain and her terror.

The twilight shadows of January 11, 1881, were gathering across the plains and the mountains of Colorado when she first realized she was awake ... and thirsty. For a time she lay still, staring at a lampshade from which gaily colored strands of beads were hanging. Gradually she sensed more of the room. Her eyes closed wearily, but soon reopened. Her head turned slowly and tentatively; she saw the woman seated at her bedside reading a paper. "Who are you?" she asked.

The words, scarcely more than a whisper, caused Maude Selby to whirl about. "Thank God," she said. "At last——" She moved quickly to the stair landing. "Lance ... Lance, come up here. Quick."

As he approached the room and noticed the eagerness

of Maude Selby's smile, Lance experienced a surge of reassurance. It was as though shafts of sunlight were piercing the shadows under which he had lived in recent days. Maude stood in the hallway, holding the door to Caroline's room open. "Go to her, Lance. Don't tire her. She is quite weak, but she's awake and conscious. Call me if you need me."

He stepped quietly into the lamp-lighted room. Caroline was not aware of his coming until he stood beside her bed, leaned close, and placed his hand softly upon hers. She was thin, pale, and quiet. On her face and in her drowsy expression were marks of the ordeal through which she had passed.

"Kitten," he said at last, "do you know me?"

She looked at him solemnly with full recognition. "Of course, Papa. I saw you last night at the Christmas program. Remember?"

He lifted her hands and pressed them against his cheeks. What purpose would it serve to tell her that many days had passed since Christmas, that the fever had almost swept her from him. He knew that his own face was tired and gaunt from sleepless nights and interminable days as he had watched her sink so far from him, and then slowly, ever so slowly, fight back to life and awareness.

Her tongue slid over parched and cracked lips, and she said, "I'm awfully thirsty."

When she had sipped from the glass of water he held for her, she lay quietly, her brushed curls a dark and shining halo against the white pillow and the brassy luster of the bed. Her eyes roved the room in perplexity. "How did I get here? In this room? A lady was sitting by my bed ... who was she?"

Lance braced himself to answer, sure that in the next moment she would ask for her mother. What would he be able to say? Emily Ainsley had not come to her child, had not entered this room or this house or this town, as Caroline battled for her life.

"You're in Evans, kitten. This is the house of a friend of ours. You've been pretty sick, but you'll soon be well. The lady you saw owns the house and helped the doctor take care of you."

He paused and waited, but the dreaded question, the pleading of the child for her mother, did not come. Her eyes closed and she lay still and quiet for a long time.

"Papa," she said at last, "tell me about Louisiana . . . the river . . . the showboat. I've forgotten so much."

Before he could answer, he saw Maude Selby motioning to him from the doorway. "Of course I'll tell you, kitten—in just a little while. Right now you go back to sleep. Rest and get well." He stooped to place a light kiss on her forehead. "I'll be close by, all the time."

Before he reached the door, her lashes closed in tired contentment.

"Maude," he said, "she's going to be all right." The words were gay and confident.

"I'm glad, Lance," Maude answered simply. "So many people are going to be glad. You've no idea how many friends you have, or how they have been pulling and praying for your child."

He stood looking at Maude Selby, really seeing her for the first time in many days. Before him stood a woman in her early-thirties with calm and level eyes, eyes that in the dim light of the hallway carried faint flecks of green within their hazel depths. About her there had always been something of reserve and remoteness, both perhaps of some old, old pain.

Now, the reserve had dropped from her face, revealing compassion and a reflection of his own unburdened spirit. She was of medium height, with a well-rounded and preserved figure. The hint of softness had been disproven often to the dismay of men she had thrown bodily from this house. Lance suddenly remembered the ease with which she had lifted and turned and comforted Caroline during the days and nights when she had kept vigil at the child's bedside.

She had indeed kept her word about closing the brothel. It had become a hospital, devoted only to the care and comfort of one twelve-year-old girl. The only visitors had been friends who had come to offer help and then sit quietly and await the outcome. Somehow meals had been made ready, washing done, the stoves kept fired, and daily tasks carried on.

Suddenly he was tired, vastly and utterly weary. "Maude," he said uncertainly, "I have you and Doc to thank for a miracle. I'll say it better tomorrow after I've slept awhile."

"You've said it all now, Lance—your words and just seeing light and reason in Caroline's eyes again. Now I'd suggest you have a hot toddy and sleep the clock around."

A slow smile touched his lips. "When she's a little better and stronger, I'll arrange to have her moved. You've about put yourself out of business caring for her, Maude."

Maude Selby laughed as she started down the stairs. "You're darned right I'm out of business, Lance—to stay. Last week I sold this property to one of your Greeley friends who wants to tear down the house and build a lumberyard. Come warm days, when Caroline is up and walking, I'll be leaving Evans . . . leaving Colorado."

"But why, Maude? Where will you go?"

"The where part is easiest," she answered. "I'm going to San Francisco. Why? Well, let's just say that having your friends, such men as H. A. W. Tabor, that man Elkins, and . . . and Jim Daley about makes me realize the time I've wasted here." From the shadows of the empty downstairs, she waved gently back. "Now get some sleep—and for God's sake—shave!"

On an afternoon in early March when the cold had receded before a warm wind and snowbanks were shriveling before a bright sun, Lance Ainsley halted the bay team close to the porch of Maude Selby's place. He had spent a good part of the morning washing and polishing the buggy. Now it shone black and red in spotless splendor. He entered the house and moments later he reappeared. He carried his daughter in his arms and placed her carefully on the leather upholstered seat and drew a woolen robe about her. Maude Selby watched from the porch.

"Good heavens, Lance. I said cover her—not smother her." She waved and added, "Be sure and get her back here before the night chill comes on."

They drove at a swift trot down the muddy street, waving and calling out acknowledgment of the greetings tossed to them. Caroline sat upright. Her eyes shone with interest. "Do all of those people know us?" she asked.

"They know you, or know about you, kitten. Mind you keep covered."

They left the village and drove westward up a long and gently sloping hillside. There was a point where the road branched off to the best-traveled route leading northward. Lance was silent as they approached this junction, but he quickly studied his daughter's face. The northbound road led to Greeley. It was the one down which she had come fleeing through a night of storm and anguish. He watched her gaze turn for a time up the Greeley road. There was nothing he could read upon her face. It was as though she was a stranger gazing indifferently toward an unknown and uninteresting place.

Suddenly she cuddled closer to him. A smile played across her face. "Papa, can we drive up west, up the hill. Maybe we can see the mountains."

With a soft-spoken command he urged the horses straight ahead up a slope sprinkled with sagebrush and cactus clumps. "Sure we'll see the mountains," he said quickly. "There's a spot ahead about three miles from here where you can see about every mountain from Pike's Peak to the Wyoming border."

He realized that not once since she had come back to him from those tormented, fever-ridden days had she asked about her mother or her brother or her grandparents. He sensed that Caroline had closed a book on a chapter that had been useless and cruel beyond her comprehension.

In lazy afternoon warmth and prairie quiet, they drove on up the long, grass-matted slope. Ahead and far off, an ermine-wrapped peak thrust its crest into view.

The next day was Sunday. On that day Lance Ainsley walked firmly up the steps of Swope's mansion in Horace Greeley's Union Colony. He did not pause to ring the large, polished bell or to knock. His face was grim but not angry. There were words he had come to say. He wanted only to say them and to get out, to get away from this hulking brown house forever.

43

He passed through the gloom of the parlor, noting that every blind was tightly drawn and the furniture swathed in endless yards of protective gray cloth. Momentarily the urge flared within him to fling open the blinds and let sunlight pour into the room, to sweep the dustcloths onto the floor so that the furniture would be revealed in its mahogany grandeur. What, he thought, would sunlight, a few gay flowers, and some real laughter do for this room?

In the living room, Florence Swope sat close to the circle of heat cast out by the stove. She had been asleep. The black shawl was tucked tightly about her and her head lay against a white-crocheted piece on her chair.

Lance was well across the room when she opened her eyes and without the slightest movement spoke to him in a flat and expressionless tone. "So you've come here at last; I knew you would."

"Where is my wife?" Lance asked.

"Upstairs. Lying down with the boy. She's been poorly since that night. You'd better go up to her."

"Later," he answered, then glanced toward the closed door of Jared's library. "Is he in there?"

"Yes. He has been there all day." She paused, studying her son-in-law with a troubled gaze, then added, "Lance, get it over with quickly—this terrible thing between the two of you. That reservoir affair has caused him to hate you. But not all of the trouble came from that. Lance ... listen to me. You're a young man and strong. You could beat or even kill Jared. It would only make matters worse for you—for all of us."

"Florence, I must see him," Lance said firmly.

"Of course. But first you must know something. For a long time, even before you refused him the reservoir opportunity, Jared has been jealous of you. Don't look so surprised. It's true. Your way of life represents a lot of things he believes he has missed. He thinks life has cheated him. I know that most of all he has cheated himself. Many things—his bank, his stores, his power here in the colony—are ashes in his mouth when he sees you with such men as Mr. Tabor. Yes, he's envious, and has been for a long time."

Lance stood beside her and peered into her anxious,

44

desperate face. "All that may be, Florence. But why—in God's name, why—did he whip my child, beat her until she ran crazed and broken into a storm? Why didn't he come at me?"

"You weren't here, Lance, when his fury broke. Perhaps he is afraid of you. Caroline was here, looking and acting like you. The first blow or so may have been for her. Jared was upset about the red dress she took from the house and wore. Well, I was too; it's so small a town and people have vicious tongues. Maybe something entirely different was unbearable for him, seeing you with those wealthy prominent men at the school. They're men of a sort he has always wanted to meet, to be like, to enjoy their respect."

Florence fell silent. Her eyes closed and the lines of her face sagged tiredly. "Now you know, Lance," she murmured after a while. "Go on in. Likely he has heard you and is waiting. I will go upstairs and tell Emily you are here."

His father-in-law was seated at a massive roll-top desk. To his side a half-burned cottonwood log smouldered in a stone fireplace. Beams of afternoon sunlight fell across the room, through a large window. As Lance came forward, Jared Swope half-rose from his seat. His hand moved toward an ebony cane with a heavy silvered head. Stark and unmistakable fear swept his face.

Lance watched him and laughed. The laughter was low and mirthless. "Jared," he said, "you might as well forget that shillalah. If I were of a mind to, I'd take it away from you and break it over your mean, vicious head."

"Stay away from me," Swope breathed.

Lance dropped onto a stiff-backed sofa. "Sure. Sure I'll stay away from you. A long way. I haven't the guts for a whiff of you. But you'll listen. Shut up and listen to me "

Swope's dark eyes gained boldness. A rising tide of crimson worked upward from his collar and mottled his face. "There's nothing for us to talk about," he said. "You're never to enter this house again."

"Quite interesting," Lance commented. "Now . . . about my family."

The banker's hands trembled. "Emily is my daughter.

45

This is her home. She's not apt to traipse off with you again and leave all I can offer her."

Ainsley's eyes narrowed. "She will if I take my boy, Shawn."

Swope's head jerked back against his chair. His mouth opened. For a moment trapped bewilderment, akin to terror, lay in his eyes. "You can't take little Shawn. He's more mine now than yours. I can take care of him, educate him, set him up in business. What can you offer?" He hesitated, then continued with uncertainty. "There are laws. I'll . . . I'll fight you."

"Like hell you'll fight me," Lance snapped. "You are forgetting one thing—one person—the most important one just now—your granddaughter. Caroline."

Swope rose. He stood shaking before the fireplace. "That's really why you're here," he said. "Well, she deserved all she got."

Lance jumped to his feet. "Sit down you stupid old idiot. Don't talk about laws or what a child *deserves* to me. For days on end I watched my little girl fight and suffer, only inches from death, because of a beating you gave her. Whatever decision is made about my wife and my son will be made by Emily and me."

He paused and swept a contemptuous gaze over Swope. "With Caroline it's different. She is out of your house and your clutches. Probably you'll never see her again; for sure you won't if I can prevent it." Lance had unheedingly drawn closer to the banker, causing the older man to drop again into his chair and stare at him.

Lance Ainsley's words gathered the fury of a lash. "No, Jared, don't spiel off to me about law. That means witnesses, and by god I've got witnesses! Witnesses to the cuts and welts from Caroline's face to her feet. Some of my witnesses are men from this colony. Their names would surprise you."

"She was incorrigible; she drove me to it," Swope protested. He crouched low in his chair, as though to draw protection from the desk and to get beyond the menace of this towering, accusing son-in-law.

"You drove yourself to it, Jared. Now cut out the bullshit and be truthful with yourself." Lance was suddenly re-

calling Florence's words. "You beat a child to get at me."
He drew back, waited, then added, wearily, "Jared, it could all have been different if you had let it be. Perhaps we could have been good friends. I would have been pleased to take you a lot of places with me, to introduce you as my wife's father. But ... no—you had to make a whipping boy of me, scorn me and any of my ideas. That wasn't sufficient so you turned on Caroline. Why? Because she is my child and happens to resemble me in face and in build and in attitudes."

"Maybe," Swope said slowly, "we can still work something out, Lance."

"Not a chance, Jared. What's done is done. Now sit up. I have no intention of striking you. So listen. H. A. W. Tabor has offered me a good thing on the Western Slope. I'm going to take it, just as soon as spring breaks and we can travel. I'll not say any more about this whipping affair to anyone. Let it die, Jared. But remember this; keep it always in mind. I'm going to come after you where it will hurt the most—in the pocketbook. Someday, somehow, I'm going to shear you. I'll find out what sort of man you are when you're minus a bank and bonds and Swope's mansion. Yes, damn it, when you are broke!"

Without a backward glance, Lance strode from the room. Florence Swope stood near a window, toying aimlessly with the curtain. Her eyes followed him questioningly.

"That's over, Florence," he said. "I'll soon be out of your house and your lives."

"Lance," she answered, and her voice trembled, "go up to Emily. She is waiting for you. But before you leave, say good-bye to me."

Upstairs, he walked slowly down the hall and knocked quietly upon the bedroom door. Without waiting for his wife's response, he pushed the door open and entered. His gaze fell first upon a narrow bed where his tousle-headed son slept with an arm outthrust on the pillow. He was glad the boy was asleep and would be unaware of his coming.

Emily Ainsley sat stiffly on the edge of the larger bed where he had spent so few nights with her.

"How are you, Lance?" she asked.

47

"Tired, sort of washed out, Emily. I've just parted company with your father. It wasn't a pleasant affair."

Her next question came in a struggling undertone. "Where is Caroline? Is she better?"

Bitter words built within him. Suddenly they died unspoken. He had caught sight of her face in the lessening but revealing light of late afternoon. Lord, he thought silently, is this my wife? Is this Emily? In his memory were etched pictures of the lively, pretty girl he had married, of the proud and eager wife of those first Louisiana years. He recalled the last time he saw her. She was then young and attractive as she blushed beneath the compliments of H. A. W. Tabor at the Christmas program.

Somewhere in the time since that fateful evening three months past, Emily Ainsley's youth had fled. The face before Lance now seemed that of an older woman. It was hardened and masked. Something within his wife was gone; he sensed it would never return.

"Caroline is much better," he answered at last. "She is in Evans—with friends. I couldn't bring her."

"Don't, Lance. Don't try to explain. I have known for a long time that she is lost to me."

"You could have come to her, Emily. I sent word."

"Yes, you sent word. At first I couldn't come. I was quite ill myself. Later I . . . I couldn't face her or you."

"Emily, why did you let it happen? You could have put a stop to the beating Jared gave her."

Her head dropped forward, and she clasped her hands nervously. "I tried, Lance. Honest to God, I tried."

"But not hard enough," he whispered. "I can forgive you. But Caroline . . . I don't know. She has never mentioned you or your father since that beastly night." Lance moved to the smaller bed and ran searching fingers across his son's forehead. His gaze remained on the slumped figure of his wife.

"Emily, I'm leaving soon for Aspen. It's a mining town in the mountains. Caroline will go with me. You realize I could never again leave her here, even for a few minutes. I've been offered a good thing there. Maybe a new life, away from the colony and Evans. You're my wife. There should be a place for you there, too, with me."

48

Emily lifted her head and stared at him. "I have followed you before, Lance. What have we to show for it?"

"Perhaps not much . . . as you see it. Two fine children. Memories of wonderful times together."

"Memories aren't much to live on," she answered.

Lance was silent a long time. When he answered, his voice was tired but determined. "Emily, you could have come to Evans . . . to Caroline . . . but you were afraid. Afraid of what people might say, afraid of being seen in a wide-open town and in a sporting house. And I'm pretty sure you were afraid most of all that you might lose the precious shelter of Swope's mansion, and Swope prestige here in town."

"You're unfair, Lance. Unfair and wrong."

"No, Emily, I'm not wrong. I have sensed your turning from me for a long time. I just wouldn't bring myself to realize it could happen."

She rose and stood before him. Her face was stubborn and set. "I won't give this up—all that I have built since we came here, all that my father and mother have to offer. I . . . I won't lose it for myself or for Shawn."

His hands swept upward and lay gently on her shoulders. "Need we say more, Emily? Let's not part with a lot of cruel and senseless words." He drew her to him, holding her tightly as he kissed her forehead.

"Good-bye, Emily," he said quietly.

She stepped back. Amazement shone in her eyes. "You can't go like this. How about your things, your clothes and Caroline's that are here? It will take time to——"

"No. Let's not prolong this. I have nothing of value here. And Caroline . . . let's not hurt her deeper by sending things to remind her of what's past."

Lance turned from her. For a time he stood above his son and gently looked down. Then he walked from the room.

Emily Ainsley dropped to her knees, burying her head in the softness of the quiet and lonely bed as long shadows of the mountains crept eastward over the colony and engulfed Swope's mansion.

Chapter 3

On a sun-drenched morning in May Caroline Ainsley sat
on a peeled-pole hitching rail in front of the Prairie Star
Saloon in Evans. Her father stood beside her. For a long
time he had talked with Jim Daley. She first listened carefully. She was fascinated by the cowman's habit of squatting on his haunches and using a stick to draw endless
circles on the boot-stained boards of the walk. Talk turned
to land prices. She tired of it and looked about.

Spring was in the air. It dried the mud holes and
brought an enchanting greenness to the prairie slopes and
to the trees and shrubs of the town site.

This was the first morning she had been allowed out of
the house without a coat or bonnet. The sun's warmth
penetrated the smoothness of her blue percale dress and
seemed friendly and strengthening. She lifted her feet,
studying her knee-length black stockings and the glossy
sheen of her high-buttoned shoes. As she quietly looked
about, she was unaware that the passing days and the constant care of Maude Selby had brought again to her face
the clear glow of health. All that told now of the whip
lashes was a scar forming a small white cross low on her
right cheek.

Abruptly she turned again to look toward Jim Daley,
who was saying, "Sure, Lance, settlers are bound to come.
It's the sodbusting that has me worried. Turning prime
grass country into corn and potato patches."

Lance Ainsley's narrowed, thoughtful gray eyes were
fixed on the rolling hills northward. "You've reason to
worry, Jim. Perhaps those men up in the colony aren't our
kind, but they know what water and deep, rich soil can

50

produce. They're playing for keeps. Cowmen will have to reckon with them."

Daley spat into the street. "If they'd stay there—in Saint's Roost—we'd get by. But they ain't. This spring they're fanning out over hell's half acre and beyond, stringing barbed wire and putting a plow to every likely spot."

"They can't touch your deeded land, Jim."

"What deeded land?" Daley snorted. "I've got squatter's rights to maybe three sections, my home place down the river. Come roundup time we drive critters in forty miles in all directions."

Lance dug two cigars from a vest pocket, handed one to the cowman, and lighted the other before answering. "Someday, Jim, you'll have to move on—or turn to farming."

Daley came to his feet, disgust deepening the crevices of his wind-darkened face. "For a smart man, Ainsley, you sure talk foolishness. Me a sodbuster—hell!"

"Well, you can always move on."

"Sure," Daley scoffed. "Move on. Leave a spread I've fought twenty years to build. Put a few thousand cows in my pocket and shove off. I'm a gambler, but not that kind."

Caroline had listened in silence. Now she thoughtfully shook back her long braids. "Uncle Jim, you could sell your cattle and restock over on the Western Slope. Mr. Tabor said there's no end to water and grass over there. There's meadows where you could cut hay instead of wintering your cattle on short grass. The miners will need beef, so prices should be good."

Daley walked the length of the hitching post, then turned to Lance. "Maybe someday I'll do just that. I figure I've got a few good years left here."

Caroline looked squarely into the rancher's face. "When we get over there, Uncle Jim, I'll look for a place . . . a good one . . . for you."

"You do that, Caroline, and write to me." Daley placed his arm about her shoulder. "Likely someday we can be partners."

Daley squatted again and resumed drawing circles.

"Lance," he said after a time, "watch out for this girl; take good care of her. She's got more sense than both of us—now. When you heading out?"

"Mighty soon," Lance said. "Probably next week. I've in mind to go by way of Wyoming and see a friend of mine in the cavalry at Fort Fred Steele."

"Papa, who is he?" Caroline asked excitedly. "You never told me we'd go that way."

"I didn't plan on it myself until a couple of days ago. I got a letter asking us to come up. It's from Captain Brenton. He was with my father at Shiloh during the rebellion."

Jim Daley studied the point of his sketching stick. "Could you put off starting for about a week?" he asked.

"Sure," Lance answered. "But why?"

"Could be we can go up Wyoming way together. I've been thinking about doing some horse buying around Elk Mountain, close to Fort Steele. I'll take maybe five or six men and a couple of wagons. We can make it up there in a week or ten days from my place."

Lance grinned. "Jim, you're a fraud. Don't tell me you aren't making this trip except to see us well started."

"I said I need horses." Daley scowled. "They have good ones around Elk Mountain, and some creeks begging to be fished. Besides, your daughter and I have a business deal to iron out. Just tell me when you can leave, Ainsley."

Caroline answered as she slid down from the post. She stood firmly planted before the two men and said, "We can leave in the morning, if you have a place for us at your ranch while you get ready. I can pack everything this afternoon."

Jim Daley thrust out his hand to seize and hold hers. "Keep your pa out of the saloon and the card game. Make him help you. We'll be heading down river at sunup." He turned from the hitching post.

"Where," Lance asked, "are you going in such a hurry?"

Daley's answer came back over his shoulder. "I haven't got a pretty daughter to keep me from wetting my whistle and dealing a few hands of stud."

Dawn was but a blush along the eastern horizon when two loaded and tightly tarped buckboards stood in front of

Maude Selby's place the next morning. Jim Daley climbed down from his rig, to be met on the veranda by Maude, who waited for Lance and Caroline to finish their last-minute packing.

"Maude," the rancher said uncertainly, "I hate to think of coming back to this old town after you're gone. The place will seem mighty empty. When will you leave?"

She linked her arm in his and looked down the short and quiet street. "Tomorrow, Jim. Nothing keeps me here." In her words were hints of the unspoken fear of the silence and loneliness soon to envelop the house.

His strong callused fingers interlaced with hers. "Write me, Maude. And if you ever need——"

"Thanks, Jim. Thanks so much. I will write."

Jim Daley struggled for words. "Dagnab it, Maude. For once I'd like to talk like Ainsley or H. A. W. Tabor. Maybe then I could tell you . . . tell you that for my book you're the best woman ever walked."

She placed a frank unabashed kiss on his cheek. "You're quite a man yourself, Jim. Now don't say good-bye. Someday we'll meet again for a rip-roaring pinochle game." She stepped from him and walked toward the street.

"Ain't you waiting to see Lance and the little gal off?" Daley asked.

"I've said *so long* to them," she answered, her voice low and controlled. "My hanging around would only make it harder for them . . . for me. Jim, take care of them."

Maude turned and with no backward glance walked swiftly toward the Prairie Star.

An hour later the two wagons forded the South Platte river, reached its south bank, and turned eastward. The river ran wide, cold, and clear, hurrying from its birthplace in the high Rockies and wending its way through this wide and gentle valley across Colorado to its union with the North Platte, and later the Missouri.

The sun warmed the thin, clean air. Caroline threw back the robe in which she had been cuddled and cared for. There had been spring rains, greening the buffalo grass, the soap weeds, and the cactus clumps of each hillside. On every side were splashes of color formed by sand

53

iris, verbenas, and the small, dainty, and yellow blossoms that rose on stems like a shepherd's staff which she knew only as johnny-jump-ups.

Along the river, age-old cottonwoods budded. Willows formed a graceful tracery of green. A meadow lark trilled a morning greeting. Suddenly Caroline was completely happy. "I hope," she told Lance teasingly, "this trip takes days and days."

He tilted his broad-brimmed hat and smiled at her. "Kitten, you'll have plenty of traveling. It's just a couple of days' drive to Daley's ranch, but that's just the beginning."

Caroline studied the bay team for a time, then turned to wave and call out to Jim Daley who followed close behind. Her voice brought the raucous response of low-winging magpies and a colony of prairie dogs. She glanced about to spot them, aware of the width and the loneliness of the valley, of a clearness through which she could see almost into tomorrow and hear sounds unbelievably far away.

She slept for a time as the morning wore on. When she awakened, the buildings and fences had dwindled behind. Off south, a herd of cattle grazed the prairie slopes. She watched them in fascination. These were not the gentle milk cows she had often driven through the colony pasture. Instead they were shaggy and wild long-horns which carried the seared brands of pioneer ranchers.

Lance pointed to the rutted trail they followed. "You know who came this way, kitten?"

Memory was roused within her. "We did," she said. "With the wagons, a long time ago."

"Not only us. Before that there were explorers, trappers of the fur brigade. Later the gold hunters trekked this way, hell-bent for Denver and the diggings beyond. Yep, a lot of them, and supply wagons and cavalry units, and cattle herds seeking out new pastures. It's quite a route, this Platte River way."

"What do you suppose those first ones were looking for, Papa?"

Lance Ainsley scratched his neck, searching for words. "It's hard telling ... maybe they wanted to get away. To

54

be alone. To find out what was beyond the next hill. Who knows?"

"You should have been there," Caroline said, after a time.

"Me? Why?"

"Papa, you're one of them, just a little late. So am I."

The weather was sunny and brisk as they drove on. Gradually the mountains were lost to view and slipped behind endless grassy slopes. For Caroline, every mile of the trail, every bend of the river, seemed an adventure. With each passing hour she became stronger. She had reddened a little from sunburn and had begun to tan. Often she climbed down from the wagon and ran alongside, exploring for birds and animals, or for the traces of abandoned Indian camps.

Afoot, far ahead on the trail, she came to the crest of a hill, paused, and shouted delightedly. A huge and lazy bend of the river lay before her. Close to the water's edge were the corrals and the buildings of Jim Daley's home ranch.

She waited for the wagons, waved her father past, and climbed to the swaying spring seat beside Jim Daley. "How far have we come, Uncle Jim—from Evans?"

"About seventy miles, maybe sixty as the crow flies," he answered.

Caroline studied him in wonder. "You mean you have to go that far to a store?"

Daley smiled wryly, remembering the Prairie Star and other establishments that had beckoned him westward. "Well, not exactly, Caroline. There's closer settlements up north on the railroad. Fact is, I had business in Evans and wanted to check a couple of my cow camps out that way. Seemed a good idea."

Her dark curls pressed against his shoulder as she said, simply, "I'm awfully glad you were there, Uncle Jim."

They drove ahead and neared the buildings by way of level, open grassland along the river. Abruptly Caroline sat upright. Her gaze swept the wide river bottom lands. "I thought there would be lots of cattle here."

"Not this time of year," he explained. "In spring and

55

summer we graze on the open prairie miles from here. We save this grass, nearer home, for winter. Keeps the herds under our eyes when the blizzards come along."

Quiet for a time, she turned to him and said, in a low and thoughtful voice, "Know what I'd do, if this was my ranch?"

"What?"

"I'd put a fence all around this flat land. Then I'd take horses and scrapers and put a little dam out into the river and flood the grass. Make it grow belly high. Then cut it and save the hay for winter. My cows wouldn't starve in the snow."

Jim Daley stared at her with widening eyes. "God Almighty," he muttered to himself. "She remembers that from the colony. But why didn't I ever have sense enough to do it?"

Later, Caroline was to remember Daley's ranch as a place of low and solid adobe buildings, of corrals so endless that hours could be spent exploring them, and from which she could escape only by scaling the poles and moving directly toward the house, once she had located it. She remembered also the dozen rough-clad and gun-bearing men who seemed always to be at the table or riding in and out on sweat-caked, spirited horses.

There were only two women at the ranch, the fat and busy wife of Daley's foreman, and a Mexican woman who spoke little English but worked magic with sick animals. Caroline learned that Jim Daley was a widower. Years earlier, after a Comanche raid, he had buried his wife and son on a grassy river slope.

The first week Caroline learned to ride. At first Lance made certain she was set astride an old and gentle gelding that would walk or trot slowly about the buildings. On the second day she climbed down, slapped the old gelding gently away, and sought out Jim Daley. "Uncle Jim, I want a horse that runs . . . one that dances!"

Daley stood silent a while, slapping a broad and dusty hat against his leg. "Maybe you can't handle that kind of a horse. Your pa would skin me if——"

Caroline had climbed to the highest pole of a horse cor-

56

ral. "That one," she said. "The big black one with white hair around his ankles."

Daley snorted. "Why don't you learn to talk proper, Caroline? Horses have *hooves*. Them *white hairs* are fetlocks." He studied the nervous movements of the three-year-old black mare to which Caroline had pointed. "All right. Have the foreman's wife fix up some riding pants you can wear. We'll shorten the stirrups of a good saddle. Then tomorrow morning, if you can tell me what them *little hairs* are, you can take a fling at the mare—if Ainsley hasn't shot me."

The duel between the spirited horse and the determined girl was fought out on the ground of a river meadow at mid-morning. Caroline was thrown half a dozen times to sprawl in the grass and sand. Each time a badly jolted, skinned, and bruised girl picked herself up and climbed back into the saddle to try again.

An hour passed before a mutual respect and agreement came about between the black mare and the child. The mare's bucking and dancing turned suddenly to a controlled and swift-gaited gallop as Caroline petted the animal's sleek neck and guided her from the meadow toward a long prairie slope.

Minutes later Jim Daley rode out to follow. Caroline was resting her mare in the shade of a greening cottonwood and watching a small herd of grazing cows nearby.

"Those cows are springers," he explained. "They'll calf any day now. They came through the winter in bad shape, so we haven't driven them onto the short grass yet."

She nodded. For a time she peered closely at the herd. "Uncle Jim, what do you sell a cow for?"

"It all depends. Grass conditions. Market situation. We don't sell many cows. Mostly steers. Last fall they averaged out about nineteen dollars a head. I've sold them for a lot less."

"You mean you sell all of them that way ... by the head?"

"I always have. The buyers size 'em up and make an offer."

"Well, I wouldn't do it that way. I'd have scales and

weigh them—just the way they weigh beef when you buy it in a store."

Jim Daley was silent as the two rode back toward the corrals. Later that day he started a freight wagon eastward toward Julesburg. "Bring back the best damned scales you can find. Go clean to Omaha if you have to. Just don't come back without them."

In late spring of 1881 the high plains of Eastern Colorado were the domain of great herds of cattle that grazed the gently folded hills rising for a hundred miles toward the front range of the Rocky Mountains. Small settlements lay scores of miles apart. Most of them had sprung up along the South Platte River and the Omaha to Salt Lake route of the Union Pacific Railroad. Vast bands of buffalo had thinned before the onslaught of hunters who killed, wasted, and took only hides. Indian tribes scattered and were pushed into more secluded and inaccessible reaches of the prairies. Through this big and empty land a horseman could ride from the railroad village of Cheyenne all the way to the South Platte without sighting a ranch, a fence, or another person.

The short grass swept endlessly toward far horizons. Creeks wound down from the distant mountains or were born of springs that offer abundant, widely separated watering places.

Across this prairie land with its warm days and cool, quiet nights Caroline Ainsley traveled with eagerness and delight. She looked a hundred times a day toward the mountains growing even larger to the west. There were three rigs and half-a-dozen men in the caravan that Jim Daley had put carefully together. Lance Ainsley's buckboard, drawn by the matched bay team, held to center position with Daley's similar rig out front and leading constantly along trails left by cattle, buffalo, or antelope. A heavier wagon, bulging with bed rolls, the cooking outfit, and provisions brought up the rear. Strewn nearby were the mounted and armed men that Daley knew might be necessary for safe conduct through this frontier land.

Each day's travel was long, beginning before the sun rose, and ending only when darkness was near or upon reaching one of the creeks suitable as a camping spot. A small remuda of extra horses moved with the caravan for alternation of mounts from day to day.

The black mare was part of the remuda. To Caroline's joy she was allowed, when tired of the endless bouncing of the wagons to mount and ride. Even Lance Ainsley, after a day and a half atop the swaying wagon, had picked out a tall and rangy sorrel on which to ride part of each day, leaving his bays to the care and guidance of those who might swap with him.

Daley had chosen a route that led them into the mountains by way of the military post of Fort Collins, the settlement of Laporte, on Cache la Poudre River, and then up the mountain valleys to the stage station at Virginia Dale. They then would follow the stage route into Wyoming and to Laramie City, the first contact with the railroad and the route they would follow to the military post of Fort Fred Steele.

They stopped twice for a time at lonely cattle camps, and lingered while Jim Daley sought out and talked to his men in charge of herds grazing these outposts of his territory. Mail and supplies were left for the men.

The small caravan pushed farther westward.

At mid-afternoon of a day that had begun with drizzling rain and deepened to a steady gentle downpour, they came to a line of telegraph poles marching interminably from north to south, and to the railroad track of the line linking Denver with the Union Pacific's main tracks near Cheyenne. Lance knew that here they were not more than twenty miles from Cache la Poudre River, and that only the low-hanging clouds and the veil of falling rain kept them from sighting the Greeley Colony toward the south.

Caroline was wrapped in a black slicker and rode on the wagon beside him. There was no graded or established crossing of the tracks at this point. They were forced to use shoveled dirt to improvise a means of getting the wagons across the tracks. Lance said nothing of their whereabouts, talking only of the rain and of the mountains they neared. Caroline listened and then looked off south. Her gaze moved along the tracks leading into the distance and the storm.

"Someday," she said, "this will be farmland. The colony will spread out. Folks from there will homestead this part of the country and irrigate it."

"I suppose so," he answered guardedly. "By that time we'll be mining silver and helping build a city at Aspen."

At night the rain clouds moved eastward. The air was left cool and fresh, and the entire sky was washed and clean. Thousands of stars hovered above. For a long time Caroline lay awake. She traced the milky way, the dippers, and the planets that cast a pale and luminous glow over the prairie.

At sunrise she was up and about and helped with camp tasks. With the coming of morning sunlight, a gasp of amazed disbelief broke from her lips.

They had camped on a high, grassy knoll, chosen to avoid rivulets of water born of the daylong rain. Now she studied the panoramic view before her. A valley sloped gradually a dozen miles wide. The uplift of the land, the beginning of the foothills, rose tier upon tier to blend into the high mountains and the rugged spirelike peaks with their great snow fields gleamed rose-pink in the early sunlight.

Her father called to her. When she did not answer, he came to her side, encircled her waist with his arm, and smiled at her rapture. Together they scanned the big, beautiful country ahead. The high barrier seemed to spring from the earth far on the southern horizon and grow steadily higher, then to recede far off in some northern wilderness. Caroline knew that her dream would become reality. They would enter and ascend the Rocky Mountains.

"Wonderful, isn't it?" Lance said finally.

Her quick reply was breathless. "Papa, let's always stay in the mountains. Let's never leave them."

"Take your time, kitten. This is only the beginning. Beyond this front range are other and higher ranges, hundreds of miles of them, with great peaks, broad valleys, swift rivers. You'll see much of it before we reach Aspen on the Roaring Fork."

The days that followed were a magical time for Caroline. They entered the Rockies at Laporte through the natural gateway cut by the turbulent Cache la Poudre River. Jim Daley told her how the river had gotten its name from a French trapper who had hidden gunpowder in a cache on the river while seeking beaver pelts and adventure.

Caroline spent many hours with the cowman these days because the country was a new world to be explored, and he answered her endless questions. From Daley she also learned about cattle and horses and the wild game animals.

In forested country she sighted deer, elk, and an occasional bear. At placid beaver ponds the plentiful trout were easily caught. Avoiding the narrow canyons, they kept to the broad grassy valleys of the stage route that led northwestward toward Wyoming's Laramie plains.

All traces of Caroline's sickness had vanished. Lance Ainsley thought she had grown inches taller. From wind and sun she had acquired a slightly coppery hue of face and arms. She laughed easily even though there was an occasional pensive aloofness about her. These, he believed, were her moments of reflection and summing up, a private time and a private world in which it was best not to intrude.

He thought of her future. What sort of life could he make for her in a raw mining camp? The abruptly interrupted schooling must be resumed. H. A. W. Tabor, who had often come to Evans during her long sickness, had insisted that Caroline be sent to Denver. That could be decided later.

Already she had learned to ride well. Only the insistent warnings of Daley and his men kept her from speeding far ahead, racing up the trail to gain a crest, and sitting entranced as she scanned the distant shimmer of a peak or the green cloak of unending forests.

At Virginia Dale Stage Station, set in an encircling mountain park, they paused to pick up mail and to repair an iron wagon tire. The men wanted to tarry, but Jim Daley ordered the caravan onward. The Virginia Dale station was a hangout for the notorious Jack Slade. Daley had seen enough of Slade's devious ways at Julesburg to fill him with disgust and distrust. The wagons moved again in two hours.

They crested a divide and sighted a huge plain to the north. The level expanse seemed limitless though it merged with the mountains ringed about it. To the east lay Sherman Hill, the barrier up which the railroad twisted and then descended. Westward were the snowcaps of the Medicine Bow range. Here were the fabled Laramie plains. Now the caravan was near the railroad, Fort Laramie, and the route bearing northwestward around the rugged escarpment of the Medicine Bow range toward the distant North Platte and the military post at Fort Steele.

Fort Fred Steele, sixteen miles east of the hard-bitten frontier town of Rawlins, was a four-company garrison on a ten-mile-square military reservation. It had been established in 1868 to guard the Union Pacific Railroad's bridge over the North Platte River from molestation or wreckage by warring Indians. The wide and cold river ran northward through a narrow valley bordered by high vermilion-tinted bluffs.

It was a clean and well-ordered outpost made more accessible than most because it lay alongside the railroad tracks and the telegraph line. The personnel of the post preferred it to many others of the area. The river teemed with trout, and the wooded areas along its banks could be counted on for good deer hunting. On the higher slopes above the bluffs, elk and antelope were often sighted.

Caroline saw the fort shortly before noon as Jim Daley's three-wagon outfit plodded down a narrow canyon. A train had passed them minutes before, and now belched smoke in front of the depot just beyond a high and fragile-appearing bridge. She eyed the length and height of the weblike structure and the swift-flowing water beneath it. Erect in the buckboard, she clutched Lance's shoulder in excitement and concern.

"Are we going to have to drive across *that*—with the wagons?" she demanded.

"Of course not, kitten. Only the trains get over the river that way."

Caroline studied the broad expanse of water with unabated anxiety. "I guess we'll have to ford it," she sighed.

Lance shook his head. "It's too fast and too deep for any fording monkey business. Likely there's a ferry, where they will load us onto boats or rafts and haul us across."

Caroline's concern was eased, and she sat down. They were close to the river now. She scanned the fort beyond. In its center was the rectangular and clean-swept parade ground, marked at exact center by a high-masted flag that moved restlessly in a noontime breeze. Facing them beyond the parade ground was a group of two-storied buildings with massive sweeps of roof and stone chimneys. She knew these must be the officers' quarters. Nearer at hand, but well above the surging river, were large, well-tended buildings that quartered the troopers. On all sides other buildings, the storehouses, the shops, the stables, and the corrals sprawled about.

"It's a big place ... awfully big," Caroline marveled aloud. "Why do they need so many troopers here?"

"Probably because the country is so big. Spread these men out, and there wouldn't be one for every fifty square miles. Patrols ride out from here." Lance recalled details written in a letter from Captain Brenton. "These cavalrymen ride out on some mighty desperate and bloody missions. A lot of them don't come back. Remember a few months ago, Caroline, when Nathan Meeker from Greeley was killed in a massacre on the White River?"

She nodded and recalled how news of the massacre had been the talk of the colony for days.

Lance pondered her calm reaction to mention of the colony and added quickly, "This is the place from which troopers were sent out to find and punish the Utes. A lot of them were killed. Soldiering up here is a hard and dangerous business. There are uneasy Indian tribes in every direction."

Caroline's view swept over the high bluffs. "Maybe there's Indians up there and they will attack the fort."

"Not a chance," Lance answered resolutely. "There's too many men and too many rifles. Even cannon protect this place. I imagine you'll see Indians—some peaceful ones who come to trade furs for white man's trinkets and supplies."

They drew close to the water's edge. Abruptly Lance halted his team, gazed about, and with a sweeping arm motioned Jim Daley to his side. "Good Lord, Jim," he said. "Look over there in that patch of cottonwoods. There must be fifty wagons waiting to be ferried across. We'll be waiting here to next week."

Daley looked toward the grove, noting the array of canopied wagons, the campfires, and the bushes serving as clothes lines.

"Likely it's a wagon train headed out for Oregon country; they're traveling this trail pretty heavy this spring."

Lance shrugged. "Well, let's get over to the ferry and put our name in the pot." He strode to the ferry slip and spoke to the squat, ruddy-complexioned fellow who seemed to be giving orders. "Any chance of making it over with three rigs today?"

The ferry boss lifted a greasy felt hat, and drew his hand across his forehead, wiping sweat and grime.

"Five dollars a wagon; be here at midnight." He uncoiled yards of frayed rope from a giant drum and said, "What name do you want on the list?"

"Ainsley ... Lance Ainsley. I'm here to visit Captain Brenton."

The ferryman straightened and thrust out a big-boned hand. "Why the hell didn't you say so right off? The captain's been expecting you." He turned to the river, cupped his hands about his mouth, and let out a yell that caused Lance's ears to ring crazily. "You—over there!—send someone to tell Captain Brenton that his friend showed up. Shake a leg!"

He waited for acknowledgment from the opposite shore, then turned to Lance and Daley and men of the caravan who had gathered about. "Better unhitch and leave your rigs. We'll get them over later on. Carry a few things and walk across the railroad bridge. Careful of them danged ties. One slip, you break a leg."

A willow thicket a short way upstream was miraculously unoccupied. They drew the wagons toward it, unhitched the teams, and after letting them have their fill of river water, tied them securely to the trees. Two men watched over the outfits. With a light array of bags and boxes, they clambered up the steep, gravel-bedded slope toward the bridge.

At the abutment they were hailed by a blue-clad figure who moved with a broad grin and outstretched hand toward Lance. "Lance," he yelled, "you've been a darned long time getting here. How are you, boy?"

Caroline stood still. She eyed this stranger and noticed the smartness of his uniform, the gold-leafed insignia on his campaign hat, and the captain's bars across his shoulders. She turned to watch two troopers walking with measured pace and shouldered rifles across the bridge.

"Captain, we're glad to be here," Lance said. "It was great of you to invite us. This is Caroline, my daughter." As she acknowledged the captain's greeting, Lance said, "And I want you to meet Jim Daley and some of the men who took good care of us on the trip."

"Daley," the captain acknowledged, "I've heard of you. Welcome to Fort Steele. We'll get accommodations set up for all of you." Turning to the bridge, he acknowledged the salute of the two guards. "Help these men across," he said. "They're friends of mine." He lifted Caroline to his shoulder. "Don't mind a piggyback lift do you, Caroline? I'm more accustomed to high-stepping these ties."

In this way Caroline Ainsley crossed the high bridge into Fort Fred Steele, Wyoming Territory. She cast quick glances at the blue and rushing river far below and clutched tightly the neck of Captain Brenton, U.S. Cavalry.

Arrangement were made to quarter the men of Daley's crew in a small building near the troop barracks, but the captain insisted that Lance, Caroline, and Jim Daley become guests in his own home. "We've plenty of room," he insisted. "Our family is grown and away. Mrs. Brenton and I shake around in the house like two forgotten souls. We've looked forward to having company." He led them across the parade ground toward one of the huge and solid houses on officers' row.

The luxury of a hot bath and of her own well-furnished room upstairs overlooking the parade ground caused Caroline to realize what a welcome respite this was after the arduous life of the trail. Mrs. Brenton was a stranger for only a few moments. Her warm smile and happy laugh proved disarming and contagious. With her head tilted pensively, and a forefinger against her chin, the captain's wife sat on a pink-quilted bed and combed out the cascade of Caroline's black and lustrous hair.

"Something tells me," she said excitedly, "we're going to have exciting times while you're here, Caroline. This weekend there's an officers' dance. There aren't many young ladies here—even twelve-year-old ones. You'll be the darling of the ball. All the young officers will insist on escorting you. You do know how to dance, don't you?"

"I think so. I used to dance . . . with my father . . . that was an awfully long time ago."

"How exciting," Mrs. Brenton said, beaming. "After you've rested, Caroline, you must tell m℈ about it. Right now you make yourself at home and take a nap. Call if you need anything."

For a time Caroline stared into a large mirror atop a golden-oak dresser. A dance, an officers' dance—that would mean men in dress uniform and ladies in evening gowns. Memories swelled within her. Memories of a red gown with puffed sleeves and a long, flowing train, of a crowded schoolroom, of the words of a stranger. *"My God—the child is beautiful!"*

She rose quickly to her feet as her mind moved to block other memories of that night. She walked thoughtfully to a large window that had been raised to allow a breeze through her room. There was a painted shutter but no screen, so with palms firmly on the sill she leaned forward and looked about.

Below her the parade ground lay quietly in mid-afternoon sunlight. The flag barely stirred. Beyond the ferryboat moved cautiously across the river with a prairie scooner. Upstream were other buildings of the fort and of the adjacent town. A large and slow-moving raft approached. It was formed of hewn railroad ties lashed together. Captain Brenton had mentioned how this method was used to bring railroad ties downriver from the high mountains for use along the Union Pacific line.

She searched the countryside curiously. Far off a snow-crested peak towered. She recognized Elk Mountain, the wild and isolated area into which Jim Daley and his men would go to buy horses. It would be exciting to go up into the wild forests, but she surmised that she would be left behind. That would be all right, too; the fort would be exciting to explore. And there would be the dance. She began dancing in measured steps about the room. Suddenly she knew that she was tired and sleepy, and that the bed awaiting her was the most attractive notion of all.

Moments later she was unaware of the rumbling and creaking of an eastbound train. The hours passed and she slept on, not awakening when darkness came and Mrs. Brenton came into the room and covered her for the night, or when Lance and Jim Daley stood smiling in the doorway and then cautiously stepped into adjoining rooms.

The sound of a bugle and a volley of rifle fire brought her to her feet and again to the window in the early morning sunshine. The parade ground was now a place of color and action. The flag had been hoisted. Uniformed troopers faced it. Their horses wheeled into precise formation.

Before the formation and ceremony of reveille had ended, Lance came into the room and watched beside her. They saw the parade ground cleared of all except about forty troopers mounted on black horses. Off on one side to the north other horses waited, held by troopers afoot. They busily checked the rope hitches that held tarp-covered and tied packs in place. Lance read the question in his daughter's face as the black-horsed troops swung about into a long double file.

"Kitten, watch it closely. It's something to always remember. There's trouble out west and they're headed out that way on patrol."

"How long will they be gone?" she asked.

"Hard telling. Maybe a few hours. Maybe a week." His face grew grave, as he added, "Perhaps some of them aren't going to come back—alive. They're too well armed and supplied for a training jaunt. Likely some Shoshone or Ute war party is aprowl."

Caroline watched the patrol move toward the bend of

the river. A dust trail hung lazily in the morning air. "Is Captain Brenton with them?" she asked.

"No, not this time. He's just back a day or so from a rough patrol up toward Fort Casper."

Lance drew her from the window. "Say, you've reminded me. The captain and Mrs. Brenton are waiting downstairs. She's fixed enough breakfast for a threshing crew. Let's go."

As they ate, Caroline was conscious of Mrs. Brenton, who watched her with a studied and close gaze behind which lurked intense excitement. Mrs. Brenton turned and spoke animatedly to Lance.

"You men can have the whole house for talking or what you wish this morning. We're going shopping—Caroline and I."

"What on earth for?" Brenton asked. "We've enough food in this house——"

"Food? Who said anything about food. Over at Hugus's store they have some green yard goods, green organdy." Her gaze again measured Caroline. "Let's see. About six yards should do it." Mrs. Brenton smiled knowingly at her husband and silently poured coffee into Jim Daley's cup.

Chapter 4

John Hugus was the post trader at Fort Steele and his large, single-storied building was stocked with groceries, dry goods, patent medicines, items of hardware, and all the necessities of frontier life. Wagons came from a radius of a hundred miles and more—from isolated ranches, Indian villages, lonely mining sites, and smaller trading posts that drew on Hugus's place as a wholesale house. Often those who came in for supplies after days on the trail remained for several days. They were allowed to spread blankets on the countertops and sleep in the store at night. Nearby a fur warehouse was stocked with stinking buffalo hides, elk-, deerskins, and the pelts of smaller animals. Products of the wilderness were readily traded for flour and kerosene, for sugar and whiskey.

Caroline moved about the store and wondered if in anyplace else on earth there was such a store, so many boxes, barrels and sacks. For a time she kept close to Mrs. Brenton, who busily examined thread and embroidered tape to match the cloth she had chosen. This proved too tedious for Caroline, who turned to watch a tall, young clerk who cranked the wheel of a giant iron coffee mill. Without slackening the speed of the grinder, he glanced at her and smiled.

"Hello," he said. "What's your name?"

"Caroline," she answered. "Caroline Ainsley." She stared at the steadily running machine. "Do you turn that all day?"

"No, but sometimes it seems like I do, when some outfit wants fifty pounds ground up." He let the grinder come to a stop. "What could I do for you?"

"I'm just waiting—for Mrs. Brenton."

He grinned widely. "Knowing the captain's wife, I'm afraid it may be quite a wait if she's at the dry-goods counter. Why don't we just look around the store, and get acquainted? My name's Fenimore . . . Chatterton."

Caroline appraised him, noting his smile and the twinkle deep in his eyes. "I'd like to, Mr. Chatterton."

They came to a many-tiered glass case that rotated on an iron base and caught the sun's glow from the largest of the store's front windows. At sight of it, Caroline stopped, gasped, and caught her breath in wonder. "What is that?"

"I thought you'd like this," Chatterton replied. "It's a special showcase filled with ore samples from many parts of the country. Gold . . . silver . . . copper . . . zinc. Lots of minerals and semiprecious stones."

Caroline stood tiptoed at the glass with sheer rapture in her eyes. "They're lovely. Are they yours, Mr. Chatterton?"

"No, but I wish they were. They're Bob Herndon's. He's a lieutenant at the fort. He studied geology in college back

East. His hobby's collecting and studying ore samples." Chatterton rotated the case a half turn. "See this one. It's copper from up around Battle Lake. This is silver from Montana. And here—this one—is leaf gold from Leadville."

Caroline looked up and down the case. "Are there any from Aspen, Colorado, where we're going?"

"I don't think so," Chatterton replied. "Why don't you ask Bob Herndon? He has lots of others. You're bound to meet him. Fact is, I'm expecting him in here in a few minutes."

For a long time she peered into the showcase, moving it so that sunlight fell on the specimens and gems to reveal their rich, deep coloration. Chatterton left her side to wait upon others who had come into the store. Minutes later, Mrs. Brenton joined her, peering over an armload of wrapped bundles. "Caroline, dear, I'm sorry I took so long. But just wait, wait until you see. . . ." Her words trailed off as Fenimore Chatterton, accompanied by a blue-uniformed stranger, approached them.

"I'm glad you're still here," Chatterton said. "I told the young lady about Lieutenant Herndon. Now she can meet him and ask all those questions about minerals that I can't answer."

"Good morning, Bob," Mrs. Brenton said in greeting the young officer, and then added, "Caroline, this is Lieutenant Robert Herndon. Bob, this pretty girl is Caroline Ainsley. She and her father are our guests. They arrived yesterday."

Caroline looked quickly at the stranger. In that moment a politely phrased greeting fled from her. Instead, she gaped silently into the face of the man bowing to her. He had lifted his hat and was holding it at his side, revealing curly sunburn-hued hair. His blue eyes were the liveliest she had ever seen. He was a scant six inches taller than she.

Her gaze raked over him again. "Why . . . why . . . you're not much older than I am," she said bluntly.

Chatterton's roar of laughter echoed through the store. "Bob," he remarked, "I wish a compliment like that had

70

come my way. Think of it, my *young* friend. And both of us born in '60."

The lieutenant threw Chatterton a withering glance. "That's because I lead a purer life, Chat," he said tauntingly. Turning quickly to Caroline, he said, "Thank you, Miss Ainsley, for a nice compliment, but it happens I'll be twenty-one in a few days."

Confused scarlet touched Caroline's cheeks. "I'm sorry I said that. I didn't mean you were a little boy."

"He's a good man," Mrs. Brenton interceded. "Bob, are you coming to the dance Saturday?"

"Surely I am, unless I'm out on patrol."

Mrs. Brenton laid a gloved hand on Fenimore Chatterton's arm. "See he doesn't forget."

Lieutenant Bob Herndon studied his hat for a moment and said daringly, "Mrs. Brenton, I'd like the honor of showing Caroline about the post."

"She would enjoy it with you as a guide. You'll have to ask Mr. Ainsley, of course."

"I already have," he answered teasingly. "He visited me for a couple of hours last night inquiring about the minerals of the Aspen area. I couldn't tell him much, but he borrowed a couple of my books."

Mrs. Brenton smiled kindly as she turned to Caroline. "Would you like to tour the fort?"

Caroline glanced quickly at the lieutenant. An inner emotion brought sudden gladness that she had spent so long a time brushing and plaiting her hair, glad that her dress was clean and pretty and starched, and very glad that she would explore this new and different world with Lieutenant Robert Herndon at her side. Her eyes held glowing eagerness.

"Can we do it now?" she asked.

An hour later after they had made a great circle of the fort and were crossing the parade ground toward Brenton's quarters a train whistle sounded, and a smoke-belching engine and half-a-dozen wooden passenger cars eased cautiously across the bridge and drew to a stop at the fort station. Caroline watched and listened.

"Let's walk over there and look at the train and the people," she suggested.

Wariness came into Bob Herndon's face. "I don't think we'd better."

"Why? Trains are fun."

He shook his head. "Some are. This one is different; it's an immigrant train."

"What does that mean?"

"Let me explain it this way, Caroline. Do you know anything of the Mormons?"

She nodded thoughtfully. "They're the strange, religious people who were driven out of Illinois and followed Brigham Young to the Salt Lake in covered wagons."

Herndon had squatted beside her, scanned her face, and said, "Some of them did, the first ones. The people on this train are Mormons, too. They've been converted in the European countries and are on their way to Utah."

"I'd like to walk through the train and see them," she persisted.

"Caroline, believe me you wouldn't like it. Most of these people have been on the road for weeks or months. They're forced to travel like animals because there aren't enough facilities for preparing food, or for washing their clothing, or for bathing. Many of them are desperately poor with little or no money for food. About all they have is faith."

Caroline reached out, seizing his arm. "I want to see them. Please take me through the train."

"If you insist. Remember I warned you."

She was quiet and serious-faced as they approached the train. Then she said, "I traveled out to Colorado with people like that. Religious people—sent out to start a new town. Only we had wagons and plenty of money and food."

"You were lucky," he answered grimly.

At the steps of the rear coach they were met by a hard-faced conductor who would have barred them from entering had not Bob Herndon stiffened, executed a military salute, and with calm authority said, "I'm Lieutenant Herndon, escorting this young lady through. How much time do we have?"

The conductor scowled. "You can hear, can't you? We'll sound all-aboard before pulling out."

They climbed the steps of the car, stood for a moment in the narrow vestibule, then pushed through a doorway. Instantly they were assailed by a stench that caused Caroline to throw her hand across her mouth and nose. It was the foul odor of a scantily ventilated and overcrowded space in which the smell of unbathed human beings combined with that of stale and spoiled food and of unwashed diapers hung upon strings to dry.

Beds had been formed of unaired quilts and blankets on the narrow wooden seats. The floor was littered with torn papers and overcrowded baggage.

As her eyes adjusted to the lesser light, Caroline glanced at Bob Herndon. He stood only inches inside the car and held the door ajar. His face was white and sickened. "Have you seen enough?" he asked hopefully and reached out intending to draw her back toward the door.

Her eyes were wide with dismay and unbelief. Her face was pale with the small scar on her cheek standing out vividly. Her teeth had clamped on her lip as she swallowed quickly. "I'm not going to leave," she said. "Not yet. I am going to walk through every car and see these people."

Herndon shrugged in hopeless acquiescence. "I'll go with you; you can't be left alone."

They moved down the aisle, stepping through debris and rubbish, and bent to avoid the lines of stiff and drying clothing. Most of the people in the car were asleep, sprawled on makeshift beds or leaning back against the wooden seats in weary postures. Their faces and clothing were different from any Caroline had seen. She surmised they had come from several faraway countries. The scant waking few stared at her and her companion with dull and exhausted expressions, and then spoke among themselves in low voices and unknown languages. Unwrapped food lay about. Flies hovered and crawled over dark bread, slabs of cheese, and pieces of heat-curled meat.

Caroline and Herndon finally came to the car's end and to another vestibule. There was suddenly a new sound: the fretful wailing of babies and of small children in the car ahead.

"Let's get off now," Herndon urged her. "You know what it's like."

73

"Not until I've seen the little ones ... the babies." Caroline threw her head erect. With stiffened shoulders she pushed open the door leading forward. The odor penetrated more intensely. Few men were in this car. It seemed given over to younger women and perhaps a score of babies and young children.

Only the children seemed able to sleep here. They were gaunt and undernourished. As her gaze moved about, searching the haggard faces of the women and the squirming or apathetic children, Caroline Ainsley's lips quivered. Tears rolled down her cheeks.

She seized Herndon's arm. "What have they done to these people? Who would let them travel like this?" she demanded.

His answer was low, and it damned. "They're victims of hellish circumstances, Caroline."

The stark horror in his voice caused her to clutch his arm more tightly as they stumbled along the aisle.

They had come almost the length of the second car when she stopped abruptly. In a seat beside her was a young woman with long, matted yellow hair and with eyes that were blue as a lake. In a distant place and another time she had been beautiful. As she leaned forward and cradled a young and blond-haired baby, she seemed a trapped and vacantly staring ghost. Her long, thin fingers held a piece of rag to the child's lips. The rag was removed, then dipped into a cup of sugar, and into another cup filled with water.

Anger flamed in Caroline's face. Her gray eyes narrowed and flashed about quickly. She jerked Bob Herndon around and looked swiftly into his face. "I know what that cloth is—why she has to do that. They've no milk here and the baby is starving. The baby will die!"

She beat her fist against her cheek as she glanced out of the dingy and fly-specked window. Then she ran toward the car door. Herndon reached out, but she evaded his grasp and jumped to the station platform.

"Stay here," she cried out. "Make them hold the train until I get back." Then she flew down the platform, around the rear coach, and off toward the Hugus's store. She burst through the door and sought out John Hugus.

74

"Mr. Hugus," she panted, "if I buy something, can I pay you later—after I see my father?"

He looked up at her curiously. "Of course, Caroline. What do you need?"

"Milk. All the fresh milk you've got."

Hugus shook his head. "I'm sorry. We don't have any."

Caroline looked desperately about and sought the rows of canned goods. "How much canned milk do you have?"

"Probably a dozen cases." Hugus rose to his feet and studied her agitated face. "I'll get you a can or so."

"No," she said quickly. "I want three cases."

"But why, Caroline? Mrs. Brenton wouldn't use that much in——"

She was already struggling to lift one of the wooden cases into her arms. "It's for the train . . . not Mrs. Brenton. Babies are starving on that train. I saw them."

John Hugus glanced from the window toward the smoking engine and the string of dust- and grime-coated cars. "My God," he said in stunned wonder. "How did you get in there?" Without waiting for her answer, he picked up the cases and followed her toward the station.

After the milk had been carried aboard the train, and Caroline had seen gratitude and some resurgence of hope in the faces of many of the strangely clad women, Bob Herndon walked with her to the doorway of Brenton's home. Before leaving her, he lifted her chin and looked for long moments into her serious, contented face. "You're a strange girl, Caroline, but a specially wonderful one." He paused, grinning wryly, then added, "You were right. I'm not much older. In many ways I'll never be so grown up, or as understanding." He turned about, waved, and walked toward post headquarters.

Caroline mounted the stairs to her room. She had washed soot and tear stains from her face and was busy with her hair, when Jim Daley found her. He stood in her doorway. "Gal," he said, chuckling, "I've been hearing things about you. The way you get around, I reckon you need more than shank's horses. I'm heading out with the crew for Elk Mountain. About that black mare . . . she's spoiled, plumb worthless for a cowman's remuda. So . . . so you're stuck with her. She's yours, Caroline."

She bounced up. Her arms encircled his neck and she pressed her cheek to his. "Uncle Jim, you mean——?"

For a moment his arms crushed her tightly. He held her from him and nodded. "Yes, I mean you'd better take good care of the mare. It's a long way to Aspen."

"But the dance," she exclaimed in sudden anxiety. "Won't you be here?"

"With any luck on the mountain we'll make it back in time. Don't worry." He paused. "You can do something for me, Caroline. The dance is Saturday. On Friday pick up a package that'll be at Hugus's store for me; save it till I get back."

"I will . . . I will, Uncle Jim. Is Papa going with you?"

"Nope. He's buried in books on geology and metallurgy." Daley was walking down the hallway without giving a backward look or an answer to the kiss she blew lightly after him.

The days that followed were too busy and exciting for Caroline to become bored or to have much time for thought and reflection. There were hours with Mrs. Brenton as the pale-green organdy took form under the scissors and needles of expert hands. Once, when Caroline was standing on a soapbox, draped for a fitting of the dress, Mrs. Brenton stood back appraisingly and smiled. "It'll be the prettiest dress at the dance. You'll create a sensation. And will some of the women talk! I know every word they'll say. *Imagine a twelve-year-old girl being allowed at an officers' dance. And that dress . . . so sophisticated for a child.* Yes, they'll say that. Then your father will bow them onto the floor and they'll forget—until they get together somewhere again."

A day passed. And another. Caroline spent long hours riding about the fort and the nearby river. Boundaries had been drawn beyond which she must not go. Often she would stop and scan the fold of encircling hills, the sun-drenched bluff, and the distant snowy upthrust of Elk Mountain.

Suddenly it was Saturday with officers' row busy prepar-

ing for the dance. Jim Daley and his men had not returned. As the hours wore on, Caroline went often to her
room and looked out, hoping for sight of riders moving in
from the east.

An hour before sunset they arrived. Caroline heard the
cowman come trudging up the stairs with weary steps and
go at once into Lance Ainsley's room. She removed a
bulky cardboard box from her closet and would have
taken it to Daley at once, but muted voices coming into
the hallway stopped and held her outside her father's door.

"Sure we got horses," Daley was saying in flat cold
tones. "But we buried two men on the mountain. We
bought twenty head of mixed geldings and mares. Damned
good ones. When we got into scrub timber about a dozen
miles south of the railroad we were jumped by maybe a
half-dozen hombres who rode in and tried to chase the
herd up a side canyon. Hell broke loose. We kept the
horses, but they picked off two of my men with rifles."

"Which two?" Lance asked.

"Brady and Nielson."

"How about your others and the horses?"

"They're at Medicine Bow. Mad as sin and hoping the
rustlers will make another play. I came on in alone."

"Would you recognize any of them if you'd see them
again?"

"Maybe—maybe a couple. I got a pretty good look at
three of the riders. We won't have to worry about one of
them. The coyotes can finish what's left."

"What are your plans, Jim?" Lance inquired.

Daley lowered himself wearily onto a bed. "Right now
I'm going to sleep a while, and then I'll clean up for the
dance. Tomorrow I'll look around a bit in Rawlins. That
rat hole is as good a place to start as any."

"Maybe the best place," Lance commented. "I'll ride
into Rawlins with you."

Tensely, slowly, Caroline moved toward Jim Daley's
room. She opened the door and laid the package on his
bed. Then she quietly went downstairs.

Mrs. Brenton was in the kitchen spooning white frosting
over a many-tiered cake. Caroline moved to her side.

"Uncle Jim is back. Two of his men got killed I ... I knew both of them. They were good to me."

Mrs. Brenton paused and faced her. "Yes, I know. There's always trouble. Too many men ride out, and their horses come back with empty saddles. I pray, then die a little, every time a patrol is ordered out. Then what—except to pick up broken pieces, comfort wives and children, and go on living." She was silent a time, then went on, yearningly, "Perhaps someday it will end and people will live safely because we've been here."

Moments later she smiled again. "Come along, Caroline. It's getting dark. We've got to dress for the dance."

An hour later Lance Ainsley came downstairs. Clad in a dark suit, he looked young and gay and carrying the debonair air of the days and nights on the *River Queen*. Caroline had little time for a proud and appraising inspection of him, however, because Jim Daley burst into her view. A surprised cry broke from her. Jim Daley could never look like this! Gone were the plaid shirt, the leather vest, and the dusty worn trousers thrust into scuffed boots. Jim Daley wore formal dinner attire. The width of his white shirt seemed enormous. His shoes were black patent leather.

As she flew to the two men, Caroline knew what had been in the box she had placed on Daley's bed. "Stand still," she commanded breathlessly. "Both of you. You're beautiful."

"Yep," Daley said dryly. "Just like a white show mule in black harness, and a darned sight less comfortable."

Lance Ainsley stared silently at his daughter. "Kitten," he said softly, "stand over there ... close to that lamp. Jim, am I really lucky enough to have a daughter like this?"

It was Captain Brenton, coming into the room with his wife, who answered, *"She walks in beauty like the night."*

Caroline stood erect. Her head was tilted teasingly, and the velvety darkness of her loosened hair fell in a cascade across her shoulders. The green organdy seemed to float about her and lend gossamer radiance. It was the dress of a young girl, but with a subtle beauty that caught and held the spirit that was Caroline Ainsley.

Jim Daley approached with outthrust elbow. "Lance, may I escort your daughter to the dance?"

Lance shook his head. "No, Jim. Not tonight. You'll have to trudge over with me, and pray that some widow, fat and forty, got invited. Caroline has a prior commitment."

"Hell," Daley retorted. "I know. That rock hound—that kid lieutenant!"

Caroline was gazing wide-eyed into her father's face. "Papa, you ... you didn't. I never went with a boy. I couldn't."

Suddenly Mrs. Brenton was shooing all three men from the room. "Don't mind them, honey We'll all be walking over to the dance together." She paused and listened for a moment. "But you'd better answer the door this time. We can't keep Lieutenant Bob Herndon waiting."

In the soft warmth of early summer evening, Fort Fred Steele was definitely on parade. A portion of the headquarters building had been cleared and decorated for the dance, and a four-piece orchestra had been brought in from Cheyenne. Enlisted men of the garrison were busily attending to the tasks that would aid in making the occasion successful.

Caroline was to remember it as the night when she danced until her feet seemed dead and then danced on and on, with her father, with Uncle Jim, with Captain Brenton, with Bob Herndon, and then with a waiting line of smartly uniformed men. There were waltzes. Schottisches. Polkas. Quadrilles. Many women were present who did not live at the fort. Caroline wondered across how many miles of frontier land they had traveled for this night of gaiety.

Eventually the most reserved and courteous of her partners stank of whiskey. She gave this little heed, remembering that men had drunk on the *River Queen*, and that only a few had become loud or annoying. They had quickly disappeared and were led or carried from the ballroom.

Arrangements had been made for a midnight lunch for the dance would continue into the small hours Caroline knew she would not be allowed to stay so long. Suddenly she was unbearably hungry. When Bob Herndon pushed through, asking for the next dance, she moved onto the floor with him, and said, "I hope it's the supper dance."

"It is," he said. "I'm to bring you to a table they've set up for Captain Brenton's party."

The waltz ended with a cornet's flourish, and they walked to an adjoining room. There was a buzz of conversation from couples and parties seated about. Caroline stood quietly waiting beside Bob Herndon.

Abruptly, she became alert and rigid. The voice of a heavy-jowled and portly officer had cut through to her. "You mean that's the kid who went messing around the immigrant train?"

He was answered by the murmured and indistinct words of a woman.

"Just the same," his voice sounded argumentatively, "there's better things for a nosy kid to do than run loose through those slimy cattle cars."

Caroline stared across the assembled and chattering crowd. Then she walked swiftly and firmly toward the table from which the conversation had come. Looking squarely into the officer's face, she said, "They aren't cattle cars. Those people aren't cattle. They're human beings—just like you and me."

He stared blandly at her, then laughed. "Well, you're a feisty kid. If you were mine, I'd——"

Caroline's clenched fists lay white upon his table. "Maybe you've never seen a baby starving to death," she said.

He flushed uneasily. "That's no fault of ours; none of us asked them to follow Mormon proselyters to America."

Caroline's eyes darkened. She was unaware of the lull across the room, or of Bob Herndon standing flushed and uneasy at her side. The look she raked across the seated officer was one of boundless contempt.

"Yes," she said finally. "I'm just a kid—a twelve-year-old kid—with no business on that train. Perhaps you should have been there. Perhaps you should have got some of the stink and the dirt on your pretty, polished uniform." Her voice gathered in a lashing storm. "Those children needed milk. But you wouldn't understand that.

All that matters to you is feeding yourself, your own pot gut. I'm ... I'm glad most officers aren't like you. What a hell of a mess we'd be in."

She drew away from him, whirled, and walked rapidly toward the unbelieving faces of Lance Ainsley, of the Brentons, and of Jim Daley, who had suddenly thrust into his mouth a half plug of chewing tobacco.

She waited silently as Bob Herndon placed a chair for her. Brenton's words broke the silence. "Well, that's that. He's a pompous ass and we'd all liked a crack at him one time or another. A child had the courage to do it."

Sunday morning was a quiet interlude, a languorous easing of one week's work and tension before another began at the fort. Only those whose duties demanded they be up and about could be seen around the buildings; even their movements and voices carried a lesser and unhurried tempo. This was another warm, pleasant, sun-drenched morning. Overhead, in a vast blue sky, a few white cumulus clouds drifted indolently eastward. From some far southwest place, a breeze wafted in with scarcely enough force to sway the spires of grama grass.

Toward mid-morning, Caroline awakened. For a time she snuggled contentedly beneath the blankets and relived moment by moment the events, the color, and the music of the dance. Her thoughts came finally to her father. She stretched sleepily, then listened for sounds to tell her that Lance was out of bed, that perhaps he and Uncle Jim——

She quickly sat upright. This was Sunday morning. This was the tomorrow they planned to ride into Rawlins. A small, but undeniable thrust of fear passed through her. She could again hear the deadly cold tone with which Jim Daley determined upon this effort to pick up a trace of the men who had killed and who might kill again.

Minutes later she was dressed and downstairs. Mrs. Brenton was clad in a blue robe and her hair was secured in tight rag-bound curls. She sat alone at the kitchen table, sipping coffee from a fragile cup. Caroline guessed that the captain had already departed for some duty about the fort.

"Good morning, Caroline," Mrs. Brenton said cheerily.

"You look wide awake and rested. Did you like the dance?"

Caroline slid into a chair across the table. "It was a wonderful dance—the nicest ever." She cupped her chin in open hands and smiled warmly across the table.

"I just remembered, Mrs. Brenton—I never thanked you for the dress. You must have worked most of every night to finish it. It's the most beautiful thing I ever had. May I keep it—always?"

"Of course you'll keep it. It's yours. No one else could look half so lovely in a green organdy." The captain's wife paused. With lurking satisfaction she said, "You proved quite a sensation. Right now I'd like to be hearing comment along officers' row."

Caroline grew thoughtful. "I was pretty nasty ... what Papa calls a brat. That fat man made me mad."

Mrs. Brenton laid a reassuring hand over Caroline's fingers. "Just forget that part of it. What can we think of now to keep you occupied today?"

Caroline rose and clutched the curved back of her chair. "How long ago did Papa leave ... and Uncle Jim?"

Mrs. Brenton stirred uneasily. "A long time ago. Probably two hours."

"Is Rawlins far from here?"

"Not so far on horseback. About sixteen miles. Why?"

Caroline's lips tightened. A small frown gathered across her forehead. "I wish I could have gone; I wish they had taken me to Rawlins."

Mrs. Brenton shook her head firmly. "No siree, Caroline. It's no place for you, that rowdy, brawling, infested town. Just wait here; they'll be back."

Slow-crawling hours passed. Caroline paced restlessly through the house and out upon the deserted parade ground. Often she gazed westward where the wagon trail and the railroad wound upward through a barren gully and was lost to view. The miles to Rawlins would be a short and speedy trip for her black mare. Her teeth clamped in frustration over tightened lips. Stern orders already forbade her riding beyond sight and sound of the fort. She had promised to obey them.

Mid-afternoon found her in the Hugus store, one of the

few places with Sunday activity. The telegraph operator dashed hurriedly over from the station, found her and pushed a yellow paper into her hands. "This telegram came for your dad. I ain't got time to look him up. Give it to him soon as you can. It seems important."

Oblivious to the curious men who gathered about her, Caroline scanned the short, ink-smudged page.

LANCE AINSLEY
c/o POST HEADQUARTERS
FORT FRED STEELE, WYOMING TERRITORY
NEW DEVELOPMENTS AFOOT. NEED YOU AT
ASPEN SOON AS POSSIBLE. WIRE ME IMME-
DIATELY. HELLO CAROLINE.

H. A. W. TABOR

As she read the final words, Caroline listened to a distant sound: a growing rumble, punctuated by the staccato blast of a whistle. A train approached, westbound and slowing for the Platte River Bridge and its stop at Fort Steele station.

Moments later she smiled firmly, but was deceptively quiet. With a great and indifferent yawn, she folded the telegram and thrust it beneath the neckline of her dress. Then she approached Fenimore Chatterton, who cranked the coffee mill. "Mr. Chatterton, do you have five dollars?" she asked.

He gave the crank a whirling spin and let go of it. "Sure, Caroline. I just happen to have that much. Why?"

"Can I borrow it—just until tomorrow morning?"

He put a gold piece in her hand. "Here's ten dollars. Invest it wisely."

"Thank you. I intend to." She smiled airily toward him and walked slowly from the store.

The train eased over the bridge. She gazed speculatively toward it. This was no immigrant train, nor would it linger at the fort. Slowly, she walked to the railroad station. A ticket would be demanded, but the gold piece would have to do if she were to avoid those in the station and on the platform. She edged close to the steps of an open vestibule and waited. The train was moving, gathering speed.

She clutched an iron railing and swung quickly onto the platform. A moment later, pressed against the car door, she made herself small, and hoped to be unnoticed.

Because she stood quietly and silently, she failed to notice a blue-clad figure who stopped in his tracks and yelled loudly at her. Nor did she see Lieutenant Bob Herndon break into a galloping run alongside the rear coach, grab the rear guardrail, drag his boots noisily in the dust of the station platform, and hoist himself aboard.

The train gathered speed; dust from the unballasted roadbed rose in a swirling, gray cloud. The last buildings of Fort Steele fell behind. They were in open and desolate country, except for the green tracery of the river bend off to the north. Caroline peered about and wiped dust from her face. She opened the car door and stepped inside. Compared to the immigrant cars, this one was spotless and luxurious. There were the same wooden benches, but these were painted and well padded. Overhead in ornamented and lacquered fixtures lamps were spaced evenly down the car.

The car was occupied, but not crowded. She quickly sought out a vacant bench and sat warily down, watching the approach of a trainman down the aisle. She clutched the gold piece. Momentary fear swept over her. She thought she might not have enough to pay her fare, and that the train might be stopped and she would be put off here in the desert.

Shortly there was the sound of a slamming door. She felt the pressure of a firm hand on her shoulder and turned with startled quickness. The angry face of Bob Herndon towered over her. His hat was battered and his uniform in grimed disarray. Sweat beads broke into small trickles that he wiped from his eyes, leaving gray and muddy streaks.

Suddenly Caroline laughed. "You look just like a muddy scarecrow."

Herndon dropped to the seat beside her, pushing her closer to the window. "Why is it," he demanded, "I always have to be around when you pull a crazy stunt?"

The smile faded from Caroline's face as she realized the fullness of his anger and bewilderment. She edged farther from him. "You don't have to follow me. I can take care of myself."

"The devil you can! In less than one week you've riled up the whole garrison. Now what are you up to?"

"I'm going into Rawlins with a telegram for my father."

"Oh, you are, are you? Just like that. I suppose the Brentons know all about this."

Her answer was uneasy. "No . . . no, they don't. I didn't have time to tell them."

Herndon slapped his hat onto his knees and ran puzzled fingers through his hair. "And how about me, leaving the post without a pass? Maybe they'll court-martial me for it. Just sixty days or so in the guardhouse because I saw a kid running away and like a damned fool followed her." He broke off as he saw the trainman coming and said, "How'll I explain this to the conductor? Me, caught without a ticket or a dime?"

Caroline glanced furtively toward him and slid the gold piece into his hand. "Here, take this," she said. "Will it pay for both of us? Maybe you could tell him I'm your little daughter and not old enough to need a ticket."

Herndon stared at the coin. "This'll do it—with plenty left. It'll get us right back on the next train." He sprawled in the seat, sighed deeply, and closed his eyes. "I'll say this for you," he remarked in whipped tones, "whenever you get into a hell-bent mess, you seem to have the answers." After a time his arm moved across the back of the seat and rested lightly on her shoulder. "Maybe it'll be worth a stay in the brig just to see what you do next."

Shadows of the surrounding hills lengthened as the train slowed to a grinding, bumping halt in the small and primitively built settlement that was Rawlins. A row of unpainted and false-fronted buildings faced the railroad tracks. Beyond lay a sprinkling of widely scattered houses, shacks, and tents that abruptly gave way to brown-and-gray slopes of brush land.

"It's such a small place," Caroline said as they dropped to the station platform. "We'll have no trouble finding Papa and Uncle Jim."

"Maybe yes—and maybe no," the lieutenant replied. "First off we're going to send a wire back to the fort, to

Captain Brenton. It'll keep him and his wife from going crazy over where you are. After that, you're to stay right here in the depot until I can look up your father."

"I'm going with you," she insisted.

Herndon stopped short on the platform and placed his hands solidly on her shoulders. "Caroline, I know you well enough to know you don't break promises. Now I'm asking you for a promise that you will stay here until I can get back. This is a rough and rowdy town. At night, when fellows get liquored up, it can be dangerous, even for men."

She warmed to the grave concern in his manner. "Isn't there some other place I could wait? I'm hungry."

He stood for a time, thinking. "There's a trading post—a store—that might be even better, safer. I'll take you there after we send the telegram. I know the people who run it; they'll take care of you and feed you. This may take a long time."

At a dingy counter, Bob Herndon wrote the telegram and asked that it be sent to Fort Steele with army priority and urgency. When he had finished, he dropped half-a-dozen coins into Caroline's hand, and said, "Here's your change, let's go."

At this hour the town was quieter than usual, with only a few men lounging before an endless row of bars and dance halls, eating joints and gambling houses. The sound of a player piano and of shrill laughter came to Caroline's ears. She paid scant attention, for these were the remembered sounds of Evans and the Prairie Star, to which she had become accustomed.

They turned a corner and came onto a short and narrow street leading northward past a harness shop, a Chinese restaurant, a stone-fronted bank, and a vacant lot strewn with broken scraps of lumber. Toward the rear of the lot was a makeshift sawmill. Half-a-dozen men gathered about a mule-drawn wagon from which they hoisted logs to an insecure and rickety skidway. Three tall and heavy poles had been set upright with their tops bolted together to form a tripod from which a block and tackle had been strung to aid in maneuvering the logs.

Bob Herndon hurried the curious Caroline on. At the

trading post, a sprawling, clapboard building, there was merchandise and supplies of every kind stacked about.

It was quiet. Near a front window three men played cards with a worn and greasy deck. The oldest, a lean-faced man of about sixty, turned to peer at them. Then he came to his feet, ran a smoothing arm over a heavy apron that had once been white, and held out his hand to Herndon.

"Howdy, Lieutenant. Been a long time since I've seen you in Rawlins. Don't tell me there's something you need that Hugus don't carry."

Herndon grinned. "I'll think of something, provided my name in the book is good until pay day."

"For anything except my pipe or my wife," the storekeeper answered. He stared curiously at Caroline. "And who is this young lady?"

Herndon looked ruefully into Caroline's alert, interested face. "Sorry I forgot to introduce you. Caroline, meet Mr. Jorgenson. And Jorg, if you've got patience, endurance, and steady nerves, meet Caroline Ainsley. She's hungry. Can you fix her something? I've got to get out of here and look for her father. She'll need to stay here—hogtied if necessary—until I can get back or her father shows up."

"Well, flag your hind end out the door then, Lieutenant," Jorgenson growled, as he gave Herndon a friendly shove. "The lass is welcome and safe here. Besides, Herndon, you've been mighty disrespectful to a harmless and pretty little girl."

"I'll be back as soon as I can," Herndon said over his shoulder, "but, my friend, you've got a lot to learn about *harmless* little girls."

An hour later, in the mellow glow of a kerosene lamp, Caroline pushed herself up from the scrubbed boards of a kitchen table from which she had eaten an enormous and different sort of supper.

"My woman cooks good," Jorgenson said, pointing his pipe toward his white-haired, beaming wife. "She remembers how it was in Sweden. You should come here when she is baking bread and cakes."

"It was a fine supper," Caroline breathed contentedly.

"Maybe I can help now, by washing dishes or turning a coffee mill, like Mr. Chatterton does at Fort Steele."

Mrs. Jorgenson smiled, shook her head, and pressed a jelly filled tart toward Caroline. She spoke strangely broken words.

"My wife don't speak English good ... just Swedish," Jorgenson explained. "She has only been in America a year; I sent for her when I bought the store." He puffed clouds of smoke about the kitchen and asked, "Do you live at the fort?"

"No. We're visiting there with the Brentons. We're going to Aspen, Colorado, over on the Western Slope."

"That's good," Jorgenson said, nodding. "Already word is about it will be a fine city—a rich one—someday. You have brothers? Sisters?"

At his words, Caroline's face turned blank and distant and guarded. "I'm traveling with my father," she said, and the words carried warning finality.

Jorgenson studied her. His gaze was penetrating and thoughtful as he watched her move to a window, draw back the curtain, and stand looking into outer darkness.

"The lieutenant will probably be here soon with your father. I have chores up front in the store. Want to help me?"

She dropped the curtain and turned about. "I would like that," she said simply.

They were alone in the store, and Caroline was putting cans of tomatoes on a shelf, when footsteps thumped on the porch and two men entered. She turned quickly and expectantly, hoping for familiar faces, but they were strangers, and she continued her task. She noted, though, that another man had been with them, that he had stopped to stand silently outside in the nearly deserted street.

The two moved quickly toward a plank counter, beneath which were open bins of dried fruit. Jorgenson moved behind the counter and leaned forward. "Can I help you gents?" he asked.

"That depends," the older of the two said shortly. "We need two weeks' supplies for six men. You know what it takes. Speed it up—or we'll help ourselves."

Caroline wheeled about as a black and wicked revolver was thrust across the counter and into Jorgenson's belly. The other stranger whirled to face the open door and a sound of voices mounted in the street. She paled, standing stiff and strained. One voice had cut through to her, that of Jim Daley.

From somewhere in the outer night, there was the barking sound of a shot. The stranger who had stayed at the door started to fling himself inside. Then as a second shot sounded, he stumbled, fell to his knees, and slid forward face down on the floor. His fingers jerked in momentary spasms, then fell away from his clutched gun.

Men spilled through the open door. The younger of the strangers at the counter clawed swiftly at his holster and fired. With the gun's roar, Caroline saw Bob Herndon spin about and crash into the wall. For a moment he weaved unevenly, then seemed to throw himself onto a dozen sacks of flour piled on the floor. The mustached old stranger snatched his weapon from Jorgenson's midsection to send a quick shot toward Jim Daley, who crouched inside the door. The hurried shot missed Daley by inches and tore pine splinters from the door casing.

Instantly there were two flashes, followed by a deafening roar across the room. Crouched, Daley sent a heavy slug through the mustached gunman's chest, smashing him backward to sprawl across the counter. In that moment the robber's body had been cut through by lead from a shotgun Jorgenson had jerked from beneath the counter and fired four feet from him.

Through choking smoke, the other stranger ran swiftly toward the rear of the store, dodging behind the shelter of counters and stocked goods. He was almost to the rear door, leading into the living quarters, when he wheeled and fired again. The bullet caught Jorgenson in the face. The storekeeper jerked erect, stiffened, and then jackknifed abruptly to the floor.

Jim Daley was sending another—and another—shot toward the shadowy darkness, but the smoke-hazed room was a protecting screen about the escaping man. There was the sound of an opening door, momentary silence, then the banging of another door.

Throughout it all, Caroline stood spellbound and wordless. Seared in her mind and memory was the face above the red bandana. It was narrow and long-chinned, dark and cruel. She remembered his black-browed and squinted eyes as a swirling blackness rocked about her, and she slumped and fainted.

Her father hovered over her as she came again to awareness. She gasped and threw herself into his arm.

"Papa. Papa, they killed everyone," she moaned.

"Stop it, kitten. Stop it," Lance said sternly.

She clutched him with wild, searching arms. "I told you they were all killed. Lieutenant Herndon. The storekeeper. Maybe Uncle Jim." Her eyes were stunned pools in a drawn face.

"No, Caroline. No. Your Uncle Jim wasn't hurt. Right now he's helping tie up the lieutenant's busted leg."

Her eyes roved the store. "But they killed Mr. Jorgenson."

"Yes," he said softly. "They did."

The room was full of people now. There was a din of excited voices. Close by, a stockily built man with a sheriff's star on his vest had begun questioning Jim Daley.

"You say one of the bastards got away?"

"He wouldn't if I'd had five seconds more," Daley said grimly.

"Did you get a good look at him?"

"Not too good this time. Things got hot too suddenly. I had a better look a couple of days ago. This fellow and his outfit killed two of my men on Elk Mountain. Me and a friend spotted them here in town maybe a half hour ago. Followed them here. This one was slim and sort of young, fast on his feet."

Voices lulled to an awkward silence across the room. Men were coming from the living quarters, leading a white-haired woman who moved in trancelike blindness and silence.

Caroline glanced toward her, then buried her face against her father's neck. "That's her," she whispered. "That's Mrs. Jorgenson. She fixed supper for me, and ... and ..."

Lance stroked her hair. "Come, kitten, let's get out of here."

She was silent a time, then straightened. Sudden and total anger swept her. "No. I want to stay here. I want to see Uncle Jim and Lieutenant Herndon. Wasn't Captain Brenton over there?"

"Yes, came into town and looked me up. He was worried about you."

Caroline walked toward the man from whose vest the star gleamed in the lamp's yellow glow. "I want to talk to the sheriff. I saw the man's face—the man who ran away. I'll never forget it."

In the following minutes, Caroline dug from her mind the details of a young and arrogantly cruel face for the lawman to scribble onto paper. Before she had finished, fury-ridden words sifted through the store from men gathered in a knot at the front of the room. There seemed to be a dozen voices sounding in loud and determined anger.

"Damn the murdering thieves. Jorgenson was a square, honest man. I'll ride a month with a posse. This town's had a belly full——"

One high pitched and panting voice cut above the din. "They've rounded up another of the sons-a-bitches. Down past the stockyards guarding their horses."

"Where is he?" someone shouted.

"Over at the jail. They're locking him up."

"I say let's string the rat up!"

The words brought a roar of approval. The lawman listened, then turned from Caroline and strode toward the swelling group.

"I'll handle this," he said sharply.

A blond middle-aged man was pulling fresh rope from a coil against the store wall. "Just flag out after the one that rode off, Sheriff," he said coolly. "Leave this to us."

The sheriff moved in a quick effort to block the door. "We're not going to have no lynching," he protested. Even as the words sounded he was seized by the hands of men outside on the porch.

"Just try and stop us," a low, savage voice said.

The store was emptying as men rushed out and were

91

joined by others crowding the street. Jim Daley and Lance came quickly to Caroline's side. "We'd best stay here until it's over," Daley advised. "It'll be no sight for the little gal to see."

Caroline lifted her face grimly. "I don't care what they do to those men. They killed Mr. Jorgenson. I don't care if they hang the . . . the whole mess of them."

She would have said more in rising fury, but Bob Herndon's pain-ridden voice brought her to kneel at his side as he lay on the flour sacks.

"Cool off, little Miss Mischief." He laughed weakly. "Seems I've followed you about as far as I can. You just sit here and hold my hand until they figure how to get both of us back to the fort."

Because she was crouched by his side, she failed to see men enter, lift the bodies of the redheaded stranger and of Jorgenson, and carry them through the rear door.

Minutes later, the angry sound of many loud voices brought Lance Ainsley to his feet. "Good God," he said uneasily. "They're not going to bring that one here to hang him!"

"I sure don't know," Captain Brenton said as he stepped quickly to the door and peered out. "They're headed up this street."

Jim Daley shoved Lance and Caroline toward the door. "Get her out of here. Get going. You too, Captain."

Brenton shook his head. "Not me. I'll stay with my lieutenant. You three go. Fast."

Even as they reached the store porch, Lance knew that it was too late to get clear of the scene. A thickening crowd surged up the street toward the store. In the opposite direction an even larger crowd gathered. It seemed that all of Rawlins had spilled into this street, pressed together, and blocked any chance of their getting through. He threw his arm about Caroline, starting to guide her back into the store. Already the light from a score of roughly made torches was flickering on the outer wall.

Caroline stopped suddenly. She turned about, and looked into the sawmill lot where the crowd had begun moving. Momentarily she caught sight of a bareheaded figure that was being led and pushed and shoved by a dozen men of the mob.

"Get inside," Lance said harshly.

"No. I'm not going in," she said. "I saw one of them kill old Mr. Jorgenson. Shoot him in the face. I'm going to watch . . . watch this one pay . . . watch him hang."

The work of the mob, revealed in the smoky glow of weaving torches, was fast and ruthless. They moved to the pole tripod and halted. A rope was flung upwards and over the bolted top of the poles, with one end to fall and dangle beside the block and tackle. The other rope end, fashioned in a noose, was quickly slipped over the bare-headed man's head, looping his neck. He had been lifted to the flat bed of the logging wagon and stood now in full view.

A score of hands reached out to grasp the loose end of the rope. Speedily it was snubbed about a half-dozen logs. A shot sounded. The wagon was jerked swiftly forward and from under the snared man. For a time he struggled, as the rope swayed back and forth beneath his weight. Then he hung limp and quiet; his head fell slightly forward. Silence came over the crowd as they stared toward him. One by one they moved away.

Caroline looked steadily at the scene for a long time. Finally she turned, as though to put it from her mind and her memory. "Someday," she said in low, but resolute, tone, "I'll see the other one die—the one who shot Mr. Jorgenson."

Despite the ordeal of the night, and the long, jolting ride back to Fort Steele in a horse-drawn ambulance, Lance Ainsley was destined for scant rest. Morning sunlight had become only a newborn red band atop the river bluff when he was awakened by Jim Daley.

"Wake up, Ainsley. Get dressed. We're wanted over at post headquarters."

Captain Brenton rose as they entered a small and almost barren room in which the glow of lamps battled grudgingly with the light of the new day. His face was tired and unshaven, and the open and wrinkled V of his shirt front spoke of a sleepless night. An enameled pot of coffee simmered atop a stove. He poured tin cups full and handed them to Lance and Daley.

"I hated to roust you out. The major's aide did it to me about thirty minutes after I got to bed."

Lance's thoughts turned to Bob Herndon and the lieutenant's rough trip from Rawlins. "What's up?" he asked. "Is Herndon worse?"

Brenton shook his head. "No. And thank God for that. It's bad enough for him, though. They dug the lead out of him over at sick bay. He's got a shattered kneecap."

"It'll be rough going," Jim Daley said. "Probably be weeks before he gets about."

"Likely he's through with the cavalry," Brenton answered. "He'll be mustered out after a while."

"How about his being off the post without leave or a pass?" asked Lance.

Brenton grinned. "Don't worry. He had sense enough to wire me. I had a pass written and signed before the command even knew he wasn't about." He paused, yawned deeply, then said, "Now about my getting you over here. There's a column, company strength, to leave here at midday and move over to Colorado, to the forks of the Grand. It's short notice, Lance. I hate to see you go after so short a visit, but it may be your best and safest chance to get close to Aspen."

For a time there was silence in the room. Then Lance drew from his pocket the crumpled telegram that Caroline had remembered and given him only after they had come halfway back to the fort.

"Thanks, Captain, for letting me know. It'll work out about right." He shoved the wire across the table to Brenton. "I couldn't have dallied here, much as I and Caroline would have liked to. We've got nearly five hours before the column rides. We'll be ready."

Brenton rose, walked to the window, and peered out before he answered. "Damned if I don't wish I were going with you up into that high mountain country. It would be good for me and the wife. Well, forget it. Here we are, and here we're tied for many a month."

"We will look for you up there someday," Lance answered.

Brenton smiled wistfully. "Daley, I hope you won't leave so soon. It will be dull here with all of you gone."

"I was hoping you'd offer that," Daley said, and lifted a booted foot onto his knee. "Likely I can squeeze in a couple more days before those men of mine get too impatient over at Medicine Bow. I'd like to get better acquainted with that rock-polishing lieutenant—see how he comes along."

An hour later Lance and Daley were hunkered down in the sunlight warmth beside a shed. Men of the garrison had been freely assigned to load Lance's buckboard, so there was little work for either of them.

"I'll miss you," Daley said studiedly. "But the truth is, Lance, I'm apt to miss your little gal even more. My ranch needs someone like her." He broke off, picked up a stick, and scratched concentric circles in the dust at his feet.

"I know," Lance nodded, then added, "Jim, remember that time, back in Evans, when she mentioned ranch land on the Western Slope? It was a kid's idea, but——"

"Kid or no kid," Daley cut in firmly, "it was a smart idea. There's something I want you to do about it."

"Just name it, Jim."

The rancher's gaze fixed and held to Lance's face. "First off, get this straight: lots of ways, your girl is smarter than either of us. She knows already there's something big and worth having ahead. She'll go after it. Right now, if she told me I'd better sell off my steers and heifers and then stock the range with baboons, I'm damn sure I'd do it. There'd be a good, logical reason."

"Whoa, Jim, hold up," Lance said, laughing. "Caroline isn't thirteen years old yet."

"Maybe not in your eyes, or by the calendar. Well, Ainsley, remember this—I asked her to look for good ranch land over Aspen way. If she finds it—if she comes to you—do exactly what she asks. Buy it. Draw a draft first on my Denver bank account. You can write explanations after the deal's tied up."

Lance Ainsley's face tightened in surprise and seriousness. "If you say so, Jim, but what amount, what limit?"

Daley came to his feet and glared impatiently. "Who the hell said anything about a limit?"

The post was astir with urgent preparation, shortly before noon when Caroline finished her packing, tarried for a time over a late breakfast, and then walked swiftly to the post hospital. A few compelling words and a smiling toss of her head cut through cavalry red tape and gained quick entry into the cot-filled ward where Lieutenant Bob Herndon lay.

His wan, pain-twisted face turned slowly toward her and watched her sit stiffly on a nearby stool.

"Hello," he said with a momentary smile.

"Good morning," she answered quietly, and then was silent, as though what she had meant to say, or wanted to say, had escaped her.

"I hear you're leaving today," he said at last. "I wouldn't be much of an escort this time. Maybe someone else——" His words trailed off as he struggled to rise onto an unsteady arm, and to reach out to place his hand on hers. For suddenly Caroline Ainsley was crying, her head in her hands and her shoulders heaving in the torment of her tears.

"Why did I do it—get you into all that trouble, and hurt?"

His fingers clutched and pressed hers. "Listen, Caroline. I wouldn't have had it different. For all my complaining, all my ranting, I'm the luckiest man on the post. Believe me, Caroline, I am."

"But your leg," she whispered.

"It'll heal. After all, it could have been my head."

Caroline stood up and wiped a trembling palm over her cheek. "Thank you ... thank you again for being patient and ... and so kind."

"Good-bye, Caroline—you tormenting rascal," he breathed.

She straightened suddenly, her gray eyes steady, yet distant. "I won't say *good-bye*," she said firmly.

He gazed at her in wonder. "Why?"

Suddenly she leaned close; her fingers touched the flame glint of his hair. "Because," she whispered, "because someday ... I'm going to marry you." She whirled from him and ran toward the door.

For a long time Lieutenant Bob Herndon lay staring at the doorway through which she had gone. He still peered toward it—and far beyond—when a briskly sounding bugle told him that the column was moving outward from the fort, moving toward Colorado, the River Grande, and the unfathomable years ahead.

Chapter 5

Lance and Caroline Ainsley rested their horses on a grassed knoll close to the place where the waters of the broad and fast-moving Grande River were deepened by their meeting with the Roaring Fork, a cold, clear stream rushing noisily in from a southeastwardly direction. It was June 20, 1881. Within a few years a town would spring up here; the river's name would be the Colorado; the rails of the Denver and Rio Grande Western Railroad would pass this way, thrusting toward the Great Salt Lake and an ever-expanding Mormon empire.

Their rest beneath a huge spreading cottonwood tree was a welcome respite from long hours astride their horses. The buckboard was now but a memory, for they had been forced to abandon it on the second day out of Fort Steele. The trail had narrowed to impassability for wheeled vehicles. Their belongings had been sorted and then packed atop an army mule and the gentler of Lance's bays. The other bay, tough and spirited, had objected to a saddle. Even now she resented his strange and heavy weight and occasionally made her opinion known when she bucked him to the ground.

Throughout the days of their incredible journey, Caroline rode her black mare. The column of troopers proved good and helpful companions, but military orders dictated that no time be lost, and they pressed relentlessly forward.

By the alchemy of long and saddle-weary days, they left Wyoming, came at last to the Yampa Valley, and then to the White River country and into the settlement to which Nathan Meeker had given his name and his life. They camped overnight, secured scanty supplies and then rode on toward the Grande.

It seemed to Caroline that the country was too big and too lonely a wilderness ever to be subdued and settled. They moved through the river valleys and by way of slopes leading up and down natural passes. About them nearby and in purple-hazed distances were countless ranges of towering and snow-crested peaks. Often valleys widened toward grassy, sage-strewn infinity or gave way to forests climbing to vast, unknown horizons.

Fresh meat was no problem for even before they had skirted Rawlins there were herds of antelope and deer. Within the forests, they constantly sighted elk, moose, deer, bear, and mountain sheep. Game birds could be flushed out. When they camped beside a stream, fighting trout swam in abundance.

Two days earlier they lost the companionship of the troopers. A wide and gently descending valley had brought them to a cluster of log cabins close to the banks of the Grande. The troopers planned to move downstream and seek their destination at Grand Junction. Their own route, roughly sketched by Captain Brenton, and confirmed by occasional settlers and trappers, led up the Grande some thirty miles, and diverged onto the Roaring Fork and a rough and grueling trail toward the high country and Aspen.

At the log hamlet of Rifle, Lance managed to find and buy three mules, and transferred their travel-frayed gear to these animals. At Rifle they joined company with another pack train, belonging to half-a-dozen miners who were headed for the silver camp of Aspen. The cavalry column held for an hour while its cautious commander talked with the miners and satisfied himself that the Ainsleys had the protection of added numbers and would come to no harm at the hands of these travelers.

Lance sat in the shade, his back against the rough-barked cottonwood, and the sleeping Caroline, who had stretched on the grass beside him, as one of the miners walked rapidly to his side.

"Mister, you know what?" the man said, grinning.

Lance looked up and studied the stranger's face. About all he could see were excited eyes above long, bushy whiskers and under a black hat too large for this wizened old man.

"All I know," Lance replied, "is that I'm tired as tarnation. And that they say there's a beastly rough trail ahead."

"Which is about the truth of it," the old man agreed, nodding. "I've been up the Roaring Fork trail, clean to Aspen. Forty miles and more. We'd do well to pitch camp, rest a time, then get a fresh start in the morning."

Lance glanced at a westering sun. "It makes sense to me, if the others agree."

The stranger plopped down on the grass and gathered his knees into locked arms. "I'll see they agree, mister. I'm guiding them. Now shut up and let me finish what I started to say." He waved briskly to the east, and continued. "Up that way a short piece there's hot springs, and as fine a swimming hole as you'll find this side of Tennessee. Maybe you and the little girl. . . ."

Lance studied his sweated, dusty arms. "You've made a point, old-timer. Lead the way."

They were still splashing about in the warm and acridly scented pool when darkness came on and the campfires were a reflected and restless pattern on the water. Later, a scrubbed and refreshed Caroline sought out her blankets and watched the men with sleepily contented eyes.

"This pool," she asked, stifling a yawn, "what do they call it?"

The old miner squatted beside the fire; its glow cast a pink and flickering light over the white length of his beard.

"I don't know rightly as it has a name. Maybe so . . . once I did hear a fellow talking about it—called it Glenwood Springs."

Presently Lance threw a heavy log on the fire. Sparks

showered upward in the darkness. He noticed that Caroline's eyes had closed and that her breathing had deepened to the rhythm of sleep. She had endured the long journey well. The healthy radiance of her face was reassuring. He judged that she had gained ten pounds and grown a couple of inches since those winter days at Maude Selby's place in Evans. She's growing up, he thought. What sort of life can I provide for her in a raw mining camp? She'll need a woman's hand ... a woman's understanding.

He soon turned about to the old man, who was rubbing his hands in the warmth above the fire.

"You say you've been to Aspen. What sort of place is it?"

The old miner plucked a long grass stem and laid it crosswise of his lips. "It's changed since I was up there last year. Just a few log shacks then. Fellows were too busy claim staking and digging potholes to put up real houses. But there's ore there. Mostly silver. Richer than Leadville or Central City. I hear tell there's five hundred people at the camp now; more're pouring in every day. If they had a smelter, things would really be humming."

"The smelter will come; so will a railroad and a great deal more—if the ore's good and there's enough of it," Lance said.

"Just wait till you see what they're bringing out of them mountains," the old-timer said firmly. His wrinkle-rimmed eyes swept the length of Lance Ainsley as he asked, "What might you be aiming to do in Aspen? You don't fit the picture for a mining man."

Lance drew cigars from his pocket and handed one across the fire. He was remembering how H. A. W. Tabor had cautioned against letting his Aspen business be generally known. "I'm just looking around. There's people up there. Where there are people—and money—I'll find those that want to spend it."

"A gambling man. I thought so," the old miner said nodding.

"How about the trail up that way, and the country?" Lance shyed from more intimate questions.

"It's a rough trail, but passable. Mostly it follows the Roaring Fork. Sometimes you're right down where you

100

can dip your hat into it. Again you're two three hundred feet above it."

"The valley?" Lance asked. "It must be a big one to spawn a stream like that."

The old-timer's eyes gleamed with excitement. "You're doggoned right it's big! And it's beautiful, all the way. High, wide, and lonesome. Mister, God made a special valley up that way, between special mountains."

Lance was tugging off his boots. "I'll get some sleep then," he said, "or I'll be too bleary-eyed to see it."

They made breakfast next morning in the cool and quiet of daybreak. When the sun broke clear of the mountain heights, they were already two miles from Glenwood Springs. The miners would have pushed steadily ahead had not Lance and his daughter paused more and more often to gaze about and gasp in awed delight. Here was a clear and shining river that must be born among the snowfields of the highest-pinnacled peaks. Through eons of time it had carved and smothered a valley lovelier than any other they had traveled. At times the mountains converged to deep narrow chasms through which the river poured with a white-foamed and spray-flung roar. Then the valley widened and the waters flowed broadly and smoothly as the river made gently sweeping curves through immense meadow lands.

Always there were the tall and symmetrical pines and fir and spruce of the forest. Virgin timber stands reached down from vastly remote mountain ranges to thin and become emerald-studded parks beyond the meadows.

Toward noon they plodded around the base of a mountain ridge and came onto a brush-tangled summit. Caroline looked ahead and cried out in delighted surprise. Miles above them, its snow-mantled crest peeking above a cloud bank, was the solitary and majestically rugged peak that had beckoned them ever since their arrival in Glenwood Springs. Now in late morning sunlight, it stood radiant and clear.

The smiling old-timer turned toward her. "What do you think of this one? It's Mount Sopris."

101

No member of the party complained of wasted time and dallying.

"God, what a mountain," one of them said in quiet and unbelieving tone.

"Look at the size of it," another commented. "If that hunk of mountain is mineralized, the whole damned world can eat off silver platters."

They rested for a time, dug into their packs for the makings of a scant and hasty meal, and allowed the horses to graze about them. Then, as their journey resumed, they passed through country which became more incredible and more beautiful with each passing hour. The mountain, shadow-dappled and enchanting, was always ahead of them.

As the sun dropped toward mountains already behind them, they moved down a wooded slope toward a level meadow.

The old guide reined his horse and waited for Lance. "We're nigh onto halfway to Aspen. That valley off south is Wilderness Creek coming in to join the river."

Lance swung down from his saddle, stretched tiredly, and studied the direction of the old man's gesture. "Wilderness Creek, eh? Must be quite a valley in itself. Seems these meadows are three miles wide."

"Could be. I never calculated it. We'll ford the river and make camp on the Wilderness. I know a fellow who's got a little cattle spread and a cabin maybe two miles up the creek. I'd like to see how he's getting on."

On a clearing, midway between heavy timber and the creek bank, the old-timer halted and turned to the miners plodding behind him.

"You boys wait here; it'll make a prime camping place. Don't light any fires till I have time to let them up in the cabin know who we are." He motioned Caroline and Lance ahead. "You folks come with me. Likely there'll be a couple of spare bunks up at the cabin."

As they neared the house, a dog's warning bark heightened to an anxious frenzy, and a door was flung abruptly open, spilling lamp light. A man's figure stood silhouetted. A rifle lay across his arm.

The old guide cupped his hands about his mouth and

hurled loud words through the darkness. "Call off that damned dog, Bentley. It's just me—Hardrock Corlett. Remember me? Got a couple of friends with me needing shelter for the night."

"Hardrock Corlett," Caroline repeated softly, and realized this was the first time she had known the old-timer's name.

The man in the doorway motioned them closer, then, when they were near the cabin, ran appraising eyes over them and lowered the rifle. He seized the old-timer's hand and pumped it. "A whiff of silver sure brings queer characters out of hiding. Hardrock—how are you?"

"Steak hungry and whiskey dry!"

"Well, come on in. Bring your friends. There's plenty of grub, but not a drop of hard liquor. Ran out about a week ago and too busy to get to town."

Even as Caroline bowed in introduction to the cabin's owner, her gaze moved into the open doorway and swept the room's disarray. She realized that only men lived here, and that no woman would put up with the disordered and piled ranch gear strewn across the floor and the few pieces of homemade furniture.

She noted the slow and pain-ridden limp with which the stranger moved about the cabin. Silently she watched him lower the rifle beside the door and then fall heavily into a chair of small aspen logs and stretched cowhide. His face was gaunt and white, and he spoke with labored breathing.

Hardrock Corlett was also staring. "Bentley, what in hell has happened to you?"

The reply came through clenched teeth. "It's this leg. Last winter a horse started bucking and broke the saddle cinch. Threw me onto a rock up-creek half a mile. I was alone and had to crawl down here to the shack. I made it just ahead of a blizzard and it was three days before my hired man could get me up to Aspen and have a doc work it over. It's been hell ever since. Now they want to take it off."

Lance Ainsley moved quickly to the rancher's side. "Let

103

me take a look at it." He knelt down and cautiously rolled up Bentley's pants leg. Moments later he stood up, turning to Hardrock Corlett. "Bring in the pack from my bay horse. There's some pain pills and a bottle of rye whiskey. Your friend here needs both."

The old-timer moved quickly to the door. "I'll do that, then corral and feed the horses. Maybe I'd better let the miners know whether it's okay for them to pitch camp downstream." He turned to Bentley, explaining, "We left some fellows down below a quarter mile. I'm guiding miners to Aspen. They're on your land. Care if they stay there all night?"

"I couldn't care less," Bentley answered.

Later, when the whiskey had eased the tautness of Bentley's face, and he was stretched on a blanket-covered bunk, he motioned Caroline to his side. "What's your name, girl? I didn't catch it."

"Caroline. Caroline Ainsley."

"Caroline, eh? I had a little girl once. She's married now . . . living back East, in Illinois."

"Do you live here all alone?" Caroline asked.

"Now I do. Both hired hands left about green-grass time, so anxious to get to the diggin's up at Aspen they nearly busted a gut heading out."

She unfolded a coarse blanket and drew it over him. Then she straightened, to stand beside him with anxious face. "You'd better rest, Mr. Bentley. I'll fix you some supper."

"Fix plenty for everybody," he said. "There's supplies in the back room, and a half beef in the ice cellar. Hardrock can get it for you."

As Caroline turned to a battered cookstove, Lance had taken off his coat and was rolling his sleeves. "Kitten," he said, "I used to be pretty fair with a skillet myself; let's give it a try."

After the meal was finished, and the cookstove was pushing welcome heat against the encroaching chill of the night, Lance Ainsley left his daughter and Hardrock Corlett busy doing dishes and sat down at Bentley's side.

"How have you managed to keep going alone here and with a leg in such condition?"

"It wasn't so bad until the last few days. Since then I've just did things that I couldn't let slide."

Lance's face was grave and thoughtful. "I'm not a doctor—and you need one."

"I know it," Bentley said tiredly. "I've an idea either I lose this leg or I'm a goner. Wouldn't be so bad if I had help here. This cow outfit is all I've got. And I'd damn sure like to see my daughter."

Lance rose and moved thoughtfully about the room. "This meadow?" he asked finally. "How far up the creek does it go?"

"About ten miles, in and out ... along the Wilderness."

"Any other ranches?"

Bentley shook his head. "Not now. Couple of fellows staked claims, but gave them up."

"You've got homestead rights?"

"Just to a half section. Rest is open land."

Busy with a dishcloth, Caroline paused, and then walked across the room. "How do you get homestead rights?" she asked.

"It ain't hard," Bentley answered. "Pick out your ground. Stake it, then file with the land office in Aspen. Takes time and some improvement work. Then you get a patent to the land. I'll show you mine."

"How many head of stock can you run here?" Lance queried.

"Could run a hell of a lot. But I ain't got them, or help to handle them. I've got maybe eighty head, provided the panthers and coyotes ain't cut some of them down."

Lance bit the end of a cigar, then seeing the hunger in Bentley's eyes thrust it toward him. "How much," he asked slowly, "would you take—cash money—for this ranch?"

Bentley lay quietly and let blue smoke drift up from his lips. Then he slowly said, "I'm not in much shape to bargain, but hanged if I'd take less than seven thousand dollars."

Lance Ainsley's gaze moved toward Caroline, his eyebrows raised and his face questioning. "Kitten," he asked, "how do you suppose that would set with Jim Daley?"

Before she answered, Hardrock Corlett lifted the bottle of rye, took a healthy pull of it, and wiped his knuckles across his mouth. "I'm no cowman, but it seems a fair figure to me."

Caroline was sitting stiffly upright in the cowhide chair. "Can anyone stake out a claim to a ranch?" she asked.

"Sure. If they're citizens and twenty-one years old," Bentley assured her.

"How many homesteads could you water from the creek?"

"I don't know." Bentley laughed. "One hell of a lot of them. There would be more neighbors than I'd want."

"When you have a homestead," Caroline persisted, "do you own the water for it?"

Bentley leaned forward, studying her intently. "You've a sharp girl here," he told Lance. "Fact is, I never gave the water much thought. It was here. Plenty of it."

Suddenly Lance knew that in Caroline's mind was a memory of Greeley and of how the waters of the Cache la Poudre River were portioned out through canals and laterals. Into his own mind came a remembrance of legal papers he had seen and read at Swope's bank. Documents of water decree and adjudication.

"You can file on water rights," he said. "Just like you can on land. Only difference is that the state of Colorado issues the ownership rights—the decrees—to water."

An intensely interested glow swept Caroline's face. She rose, walked to Bentley's bed, and sat down gently. "We'll buy your ranch—tomorrow, Mr. Bentley. But I'll have to write a letter for the money."

Lance shook his head. "No, Caroline, you won't have to write or wait. Jim Daley talked to me. We can draw a draft on his bank in Denver. It can be handled from Aspen."

She clasped her hands excitedly. "Then, Papa, it's settled. Mr. Bentley can go to Aspen with us and see a doctor. After that he can visit his daughter."

"Whoa up, Caroline," Lance warned. "Who's going to take care of your ranch?"

"You are," she said with finality in her voice. "Until Uncle Jim can get some real cowboys over here." A minute passed, and she gazed at the log wall and beyond. "In the morning," she asked finally, "can we get the miners up here before they get away for Aspen?"

Hardrock Corlett scratched his beard and looked questioningly at her. "I reckon we could," he said. "Why?"

"Because," she answered quickly, "tomorrow every one of them is going to stake a claim to homestead land."

Lance watched her in silent and stunned wonder.

Her lips pursed thoughtfully. "Now, Papa, about filing on the water. Do you know how to write out papers claiming water?"

"I—I think so," he managed.

"Do it tonight. Will you, Papa? Write out papers claiming the water for—let's see——" Her fingers grasped in a slow and methodical count, and her lips moved in silent rhythm. Then her voice sounded firmly through the room. "Write out a claim for water enough for all the land in eight homesteads. Ask that they, they—" She paused, searching for a word. "Yes, ask that they *adjudicate* that much water to a ranch owned by Daley and Ainsley, on Wilderness Creek, Colorado."

The chillness of the mountain night crept into the cabin, to be baffled by a huge wood-stocked fire, as Lance Ainsley quietly wrote. Caroline watched the movement of his pen. Bentley lay on the bed and tossed restlessly between short snatches of sleep. Hardrock Corlett had propped his feet on the stove and puffed on a black, evil-smelling pipe.

Lance eventually laid the pen aside and glanced toward his daughter. "This should take care of our filing on the water. Now, Miss Rancher, just how do you propose to hold those miners—hell-bent for Aspen—and get them to file or stake homesteads?"

"You'll pay them to do it, Papa," she said confidently.

Lance sprang upward from his chair. "*I'll* pay them? The devil I will! I've got just four hundred dollars with me; we'll need that to get located in Aspen."

Caroline smiled broadly. "Four hundred dollars will do

107

it nicely. If we pay each of them fifty dollars, and counting Mr. Corlett, you'll have a hundred dollars left."

Consternation grew on Lance's face. "So I should pay each of those men fifty dollars to file a homestead claim in his own name. Caroline, you're crazy!"

She slowly rose to her feet and leaned across the table toward him. "Papa, we aren't going to pay them for staking their homesteads. Don't you see? We'll pay them to sign a paper that says when they want to sell their homesteads that the Daley and Ainsley ranch is to have the first chance to buy them out. You write it down on a paper for each of them to sign."

Hardrock Corlett's sudden laughter rang loudly through the cabin. "Ainsley," he said, "damn if it won't work. Them miners are so broke they'd sign a hangman's order to get a fifty-dollar grubstake."

"Maybe," Lance replied. "How about you? Would you do it?"

Corlett's eyes rested for a time on Caroline's anxious face. "I'll stake a homestead, and you can forget the fifty dollars—provided one thing."

"What? What thing, Mr. Corlett?" Caroline asked quickly.

"Just make my paper say you'll pay me one dollar for my claim. That'll make it legal. Then you folks write out permission for me to prospect on any of your land. You can go up to Aspen and about your business. Take Bentley up there to a doctor. I'll stick around here and look after the cattle until you can get regular ranch help to take over."

A rueful, yet satisfied, smile played about Lance's mouth. "So I arrive in Aspen damned near broke. Good Lord! I've been euchred—cleaned out—a lot of times. Never this quick—and by my own daughter."

Hardrock Corlett pointed the chewed stem of his pipe toward the pages Lance had written. "I'd like to hear what you wrote down there, provided there's still a drink or so in that rye bottle to make the listening pleasant."

When the whiskey was but a glowing memory, Lance began to read aloud:

To The Honorable Secretary of State
State of Colorado
Colorado State Capitol
Denver, Colorado

Honorable Sir:

It is respectfully requested that as of this date, June 21, 1881, a decree of adjudication be entered and issued of the waters of Wilderness Creek, Pitkin County, Colorado, said creek being a tributary of the Roaring Fork River, which is in turn a tributary of the Grande River, as follows:

Establishing the priority of the undersigned to one-half (½) of the total flow of such waters of Wilderness Creek, in perpetuity, for use upon land belonging to the undersigned, for purposes of irrigation, domestic use, and such other purposes as may be deemed right and proper.

It is specifically requested that no other or subsequent decree or adjudication be made at any time that will jeopardize or infringe upon the rights and ownership established by said decree of adjudication as long as these waters are properly, wisely, and lawfully used. It is the intent of the undersigned that full use of such waters will be made as quickly as land can be properly prepared.

/Signed/_____
      James Daley

/Signed/_____
      Lance Ainsley, Parent and
      guardian of Caroline Ainsley,
      a minor.

"It sure sounds legal as hell," Corlett commented.

"Maybe it is, and maybe it ain't," Lance said quietly. "It's the best I know how to do. We'll send it to Jim Daley, and ask him to sign it and fire it off to H. A. W. Tabor. If I know Tabor, he'll put seventeen smart lawyers to work on it for us before handing it on up to the Statehouse." He paused, yawning broadly, then added, "I'll write something for the miners to sign. Then I'm going to bed. You'd better crawl into the blankets right now, kitten, before you come up with some other idea that keeps me smearing ink all night."

She came around the table, plopped onto his lap, and ran excited fingers through his hair. "Good night, Papa." She had kissed him and was halfway across the room when she turned. "How long can we live on a hundred dollars in Aspen?"

Lance glared at her and lifted a boot as though to plant it firmly on her behind. "You would think of that—now. Well, if you live on beans maybe it'll last long enough for me to come up with a royal flush somewhere ... somehow."

The next day the trail led them farther and farther up the virgin and beautiful valley of the Roaring Fork. They rested at noon where the Frying Pan River poured its cold rapid waters into the Roaring Fork. There were creeks to ford, tangled thickets to push through, and endless steep ridges to be crossed. On either side the mountains rose swiftly to white-crested peaks.

The breath-taking vistas of the Snow Mass country behind them, they moved tiredly toward the deep chasm of Castle Creek. Then Caroline caught her first glimpse of Aspen. Aspen—the silver camp of the Roaring Fork! Mid-afternoon sunlight fell across a broad and timbered meadow and lent a soft and mystic haze to this remote area. The sprawling, unplanned town site seemed close as it nestled between the winding course of the river and the precipitous slopes of Aspen Mountain off to the south. Northward was Red Mountain. Beyond the settlement, and higher still, the valley narrowed and swept endlessly toward the jagged spires of great encircling peaks.

A warm and enchanting stillness lay in the air. Few words were spoken.

As they approached the town an hour later, Caroline could see the raw scars of shafts and prospect holes pitting the northern and southern mountain slopes. A cluster of buildings broke into view. Caroline saw log buildings, slab-sided buildings, and an array of tents. There were sounds: voices of men, the sound of hammers and saws, of work teams busy in the town and the surrounding timber.

The camp's main thoroughfare was fronted by rude and makeshift stores and varied businesses. Dust swirled about them, but there were frequent and ominous mud holes left by summer rains.

Lance Ainsley surmised that already there were five hundred or more people in the settlement. He had an idea, too, that living quarters or shelter of any kind might be hard to come by. But H.A.W. Tabor had assured him that arrangements would be made. Somewhere in this new and busy and lusty town there would be a roof to shelter him and Caroline.

In the middle of the town, they halted before a sprawling log cabin fronted by a smoke-blackened tent and a scrawled sign declaring that meals were served inside. Lance turned to Bentley. "I'm glad we're finally here, Bentley. First thing is to try and find a doctor for that leg of yours."

"I wasn't sure I could make it," Bentley said hoarsely. "It's been rougher than a cob. I know where to find a pretty good doc . . . if he's sober. I'll get a couple of the miners to tag along with me. You get set to take care of your little girl. Look me up if you need help finding a place to roost." He thrust out an unsteady hand to Lance, then laid it wistfully on Caroline's black curls. "I'll see you before I leave town. Likely the doc will keep me here a spell."

When Bentley had ridden off, and the miners scattered, Caroline stood watching the activity of the cook-tent restaurant. A high chimney had been fashioned from half-a-dozen lengths of stovepipe, and from it blue smoke lifted lazily into the air. Toward the front of the tent were two tables of rough-hewn planks, with benches running their length. The odor of roasting meat reached her, and she realized that she was hungry. She turned to Lance. "That smells good," she said. "Why don't we eat here, then find a place to stay?"

He tied their horses to a hitching post a few yards away

and walked to her side. "It sounds like a winner. Maybe we've got money enough left for one or two square meals—after what your homesteading ideas did to my wallet."

The meal set before them on the scrubbed table proved that their choice of an eating place had been a lucky one. It was served on tin plates by a lean and black-whiskered man. The food was plentiful, well cooked, and more varied than they had anticipated. Only the hovering, darting flies were a problem. These were kept somewhat controlled and baffled by a small boy who swung a heavily leafed cottonwood branch incessantly above the table.

They had finished eating when a young man, clad in high boots, black pants, and a plaid woolen shirt entered and sat down. He studied them for a few moments, then spoke to Lance in a guarded and appraising tone.

"Is your name Ainsley?"

"Yes."

"I heard you were in town. I'm Matt Shaner. A friend of yours in Denver wrote me to be on the lookout for you."

They shook hands. Lance had no need to ask from whom such word had been received. Already Tabor had been at work arranging for their arrival. Lance laid his arm about Caroline's shoulder. "I'm glad to know you, Mr. Shaner. Glad we're expected. I want you to meet Caroline, my daughter."

He gave Caroline a short and disinterested nod as she curtsied.

"Hope you won't mind my being in a hurry," Shaner said. "I'm a busy man ... lots of things to do. When you're ready, come down to the office; it's the fifth shack north, on the right. There's mail for you. Someone can show you to the quarters we've got set up."

"We can go with you now," Lance said.

"As you wish," Shaner replied. "Lead your horses. I'll have someone unpack and corral them." Noting the doubt on Caroline's face, he added, "Don't worry. The horses will be safe. So will your gear." His words were impatient and irritated.

Shaner's office proved to be a log cabin, larger and

more solidly built than most of those of the settlement. Caroline chose to wait outside, for her reaction to Matt Shaner was not enthusiastic.

"I won't be long, kitten," Lance promised. "I want to talk with Mr. Shaner a few minutes and pick up the mail."

There was a log bench at the front of the building, and Caroline wearily lowered herself upon it. Minutes passed, and her gaze moved about the settlement. There were more men on the street now, as the miners and workmen moved toward the houses, the tents, the wagons, and the few eating places. She was aware of the increasing glow of lighted windows and camp fires. Darkness seemed a swiftly descending mantle.

Abruptly she remembered how darkness of the previous evening had found them riding along Wilderness Creek toward the beckoning light of Bentley's ranch. Now, just one day later, it no longer belonged to Bentley. Bentley was here in Aspen where a doctor could care for him. And those broad and wonderful acres of meadow land, those forested slopes above Wilderness Creek, belonged to Jim Daley—and to her!

She peered about through the darkness, sensing the vibrant and restless energy of this town. It will grow, she thought. It will grow fast . . . and big. Someday Aspen will be a rich and beautiful city. People will want and need a lot of things. Things that grow on a ranch. My ranch will grow, too. A momentary feeling of guilt encompassed her for thinking of Wilderness Creek as *her* ranch. Of course, Jim Daley was putting up the money. But Jim Daley was far away, far off beyond countless ranges of peaks and vast expanses of prairie. She—Caroline Ainsley—was here, here in Aspen, and only a day's ride from the ranch. Maybe, she reasoned, Uncle Jim wouldn't mind me *just thinking* it's my ranch.

Her head dropped back against the log wall. Her eyes closed.

She was sound asleep when Lance Ainsley came out of the cabin, lifted her into his arms, and followed a lantern-carrying guide toward the large and log-sided tent that would be their first home in Aspen on the Roaring Fork.

113

She awakened to the sheen of late-morning sunlight on the sloping canvas roof above her bed. For a while she looked about, quietly wondering where she was and how she had come to be here. The sight of familiar belongings, unpacked and carefully placed about the tent, reassured her. She listened to sounds drifting in from out of doors. She distinguished the rumbling passage of a freight wagon, and the incessant rhythm of hammers and saws. At times there were voices, too distant and muted to be understood.

Later the sound of children playing and laughing brought her out of bed. She peered cautiously from the canvas draped doorway. There were a dozen boys and girls, all younger than she, moving about a swing under a giant tree across the street. Caroline smiled as she watched. Where there were young children there would be older ones and their mothers. So Aspen wasn't just a camp of men. She moved about the tent to locate a small mirror and prop it on a table. Then she began combing her hair. She was still working with the long and unruly locks when her father came to the tent, looked quietly in, then entered.

He placed a box of groceries on the table and cast a wary glance at the small wood-burning stove.

"Good morning, kitten," he said. "I thought perhaps you'd sleep all day."

"It is a good morning, Papa," she answered gaily. "I feel wonderful." She studied the grocery box. "I'm starved. Are we going to cook our breakfast?"

"You're going to cook breakfast," he answered firmly. "And most of our other meals until I can have more money sent here. You blew three hundred dollars on homesteads. Remember?"

She dashed water from a tin basin onto her face. "Maybe I can cook better than you think."

"I hope so, kitten. I truly hope so. While you're proving it, I'll get over to the courthouse and file the ranch papers. Then we'll mail a letter to Jim Daley with the water application. I wrote to him last night."

Caroline turned and studied a stack of papers on the bed in which Lance had slept. Her lips pursed into a puzzled, questioning line. "Papa, Mr. Shaner must have given

114

you those papers. You've never told me why Mr. Tabor hired you to come to Aspen. What are you going to do? What is your job?"

Lance lighted a cigar and blew smoke thoughtfully toward the ridge pole of the tent. "Kitten, you can be mighty tight-lipped, so I'll tell you. Tabor and his friend Elkins are the power and money behind several things getting started here. It's not so much what I'm to do, as to find out what and how well other men are doing their jobs."

Caroline sat down beside him, her hands firmly on her hips and intenseness in her gray eyes. "You mean," she asked, "you're a *spy?*"

The cigar jerked upward between Lance's suddenly clenched teeth. "Good god, no! What an idea, Caroline. I'm to watch that things go right and to make sure they do."

Her head tilted in a doubting gesture. "Just the same, Papa, it sounds like snooping to me."

Lance's hands spread in a gesture of patient explanation. "In my book, kitten, it isn't snooping or spying to make sure that a man's money ... a friend's money ... is spent wisely, the way he would have it spent if he were here. This summer we're going to build a sawmill and a planing mill. It'll take several thousand dollars. A lot of it could go down a rat hole if someone isn't here to keep a tight rein on things."

Caroline's face grew pensive. "Some men aren't going to like having you buzzing around and cracking a whip." She paused. "Is Matt Shaner one of Mr. Tabor's men?"

Lance searched her face, while his own grew thoughtful. "Yes. Up to now Shaner has been top man. He is capable. Knows how to keep men about him and busy."

Caroline filled a granite teakettle, then sat down to face him again. "You'll have to be gone a lot, Papa. Maybe I can meet some of the women, so I can visit them."

"I've thought about that, kitten. Our three-room cabin will be ready in a couple of weeks. Perhaps we can arrange for one of the women to stay with you when I have to be away, and to help with the housework."

"We won't have to do that, Papa. Do you remember

115

Mrs. Jorgenson—in Rawlins? She's awfully nice ... and she can cook. You ought to taste things the way she cooks. Her house was clean, too. Papa, will we have enough money? Can we send for her? She'll need a place to stay now that Mr. Jorgenson ..." Her voice lowered to a whisper and trailed off. Memory of that night and its terror was a swiftly resurgent thing upon her.

Lance rose, lifted her erect, and picked up two letters from the table. "Let's find out if mail is going out today. We'll send for Mrs. Jorgenson right now. Come along, kitten. You can burn the salt pork and potatoes when we get back."

There was no regularly scheduled stage route to Aspen because the high mountains were jealous guardians of this remote valley of the Roaring Fork. Despite this inaccessibility and the hardship of travel, men and women poured into the settlement in increasing numbers. Word was out, proclaiming the rich promise of the silver lodes, and of the opportunities opening for miners and craftsmen and businesses.

The mountains over which men struggled to reach the valley were sheltering abutments against winter storms and the gale-force winds that plagued many other mining camps of the West. The soil was fertile. Water from summer rains and clear-running streams was plentiful. The growing season was not prolonged at an elevation of 8,600 feet, but crops of hay and potatoes and grain came safely to autumn ripening. Flowers and gardens attained a profuse and riotous growth under long days of summer sunlight. Livestock flourished on the valley meadows, surprisingly free of the diseases common to lowland areas.

Chapter 6

It was entirely by chance that Lance Ainsley and his daughter happened to be standing in front of the warehouse station of the Leadville freight line early on a sun-drenched and lazy afternoon in mid-August. They had ridden up Hunter Creek in order to exercise the bay team and Caroline's black mare, and had just unsaddled the horses and turned them into a small rail-fenced pasture.

A sudden burst of excited voices and the barking of a dog drew their attention to a caravan of mounted riders and a half-dozen freight wagons coming into view beyond the building that served as a temporary courthouse.

Lance said, "That's a sizable trail outfit, kitten. I'll bet they had the devil's own time getting over the pass to Independence."

A surprised cry broke from Caroline. He turned just in time to see her dash from his side and run swiftly into the street. Her words were flung over a shoulder. "Papa! Up there—in front. It's ... It's. Jim Daley—Uncle Jim."

The riders were nearing now, and Lance hurried in the footsteps of his daughter. Moments later he realized that this was no ordinary freighting outfit. There were two more men. H. A. W. Tabor rode into town, seated on a large and slow-moving wagon. Beside him on the spring seat was a younger man, a man clad in cavalry blue— Lieutenant Robert Herndon!

In a frenzied, delighted burst of speed, Caroline came alongside Jim Daley's horse.

"Well, I'll be double damned if it ain't my partner!" the rancher roared. "Caroline, how are you?" He leaned sideways, and with a single sweep of his arm encircled her and pulled her into the saddle with him. Her hands

117

grabbed his neck and she thrust dark curls against his shoulder. She started to speak, but her words were stifled in small and happy sobs.

Softness came into Jim Daley's face, and when his hat slid from his head and into the dusty roadway he was heedless of losing it.

"Here ... here, little gal," he said. "That's no way for my ranch partner to act. I've got some surprises for you. Wipe them eyes and take a look back."

She straightened, eased into a less perilous seating, and peered over his shoulder, just in time to see Lance Ainsley climb to a freight wagon's seat and crowd between the two men already there.

"Why ... why it's Mr. Tabor—and Lieutenant Bob!"

Her waving arm blotted out Daley's vision as it swung back and forth across his eyes. "If you'll ease down, gal—and provided I ain't got blind staggers—there's another surprise waiting."

He swung his horse about and drew close to the three men perched on the freight wagon. Caroline shouted elated greetings. She would have slid to the ground had not Daley's grasp been tight upon her. "Not yet," he said to Tabor and Bob Herndon. "Pretty soon you can have her." He urged his horse into a swinging gallop that carried them back along the other wagons. When he reached the tailgate of the last canopied wagon, he reached out to draw the dusty canvas aside. He lifted Caroline quickly from the saddle—into the wagon and practically onto the lap of an elderly, white-haired woman seated on a roped feather bed. "Here, Mrs. Jorgenson," he said. "Here's the little gal you've been so anxious to see."

In that moment Caroline Ainsley's happiness bubbled over. As the wagons jolted down Aspen's sprawled and growing streets, she lay across the feather bed, her head on Mrs. Jorgenson's knees. Her eyes closed in utter contentment.

The arrival of the wagons meant many things to Caroline. Heavily loaded with equipment, they would bring a burst of activity as workmen hurried to ready the mill in order to meet the demands of the town for mine timbers, house siding and flooring, and the milled lumber for stores and saloons and other budding enterprises. They had brought items of hardware, surveying instruments, medical supplies, and clothing for Lance and for her. She wondered how someone in faraway Denver had known so well what would be needed. Only a woman could have chosen many of the articles, and she guessed that Mrs. Jorgenson's stopover in Denver had been a busy one.

Toward sunset when her father had gone with Tabor to Matt Shaner's office and Jim Daley had led others of the crew toward a tent saloon, Caroline came outside and gave the wagon's guard a flashing smile. She peered under the canvas covering of the load. There were only wooden boxes and crates inside, and no telltale evidence of what they might contain.

A movement of the canvas caused her to jerk abruptly about, and stare into the grinning face of Bob Herndon.

"You were told to lie down and rest your leg," she said accusingly.

"Sure I was. But knowing how you get about, I had a hunch I'd better come out before you had my assay equipment set up and opened up business on your own."

They stepped back from the wagon; the beams of a shafted sunset fell across his red hair and enlivened his eyes as he glanced upward toward the surrounding mountains.

"Lord, but this is beautiful country," he said softly.

"Just wait until you see Wilderness Creek—and my ranch," Caroline replied. She sat down on the wagon tongue and watched the caution with which he swung a stiffened knee as he walked to her and lowered himself at her side.

"Jim Daley told me how you've already engineered a land deal for him and yourself. Caroline, who could keep up with you? Not me—that's for sure."

She watched the dying flare of day on the snow fields. "Somehow, Lieutenant Bob," she said, "I've a funny feeling about Wilderness Creek, and the ranch, and Aspen. It's as though I'd been away a long time and come home, home to stay, and never, never leave."

"I imagine anyone could feel that way about so lovely and peaceful a place, Caroline. But how about school?"

She folded her hands tightly behind her head. "They'll have a school here. There's a lot of kids." She sat quietly for a minute, then said with finality, "Besides school can wait. I've got to take care of father and the ranch."

He shifted to ease his leg and to look studiedly into her face. "It can't wait, Caroline. Furthermore, the sort of a school they can have here isn't what you need, what you must have."

She scrutinized him levelly and openly. "You've had a lot of school work, haven't you?"

"I wish I'd had more. Mine was prep school, two years at Princeton, then West Point."

Caroline glanced toward the rigid outthrust of his leg. "That knee still bothers you a lot," she said.

"Some. I suppose it will for a time. There will be quite a catch in my get-along. Maybe it won't matter too much for a tenderfoot geologist or an assayer to carry a limp."

She smiled brightly and threaded her fingers into his. "You'll be the best assayer in Aspen."

"I hope so. Are there many others?"

A perplexed frown gathered on her forehead. "Why ... why ... none that I know of."

Bob Herndon laughed aloud. "Then I'm apt to be the best, until someone gets wise to me. Tomorrow you can help me find some sort of building I can get set up in. Maybe the gear I've got in the wagon will impress a few prospectors. Especially that mineral case from Hugus and Chatterton's store in Fort Steele."

"How is Mr. Chatterton?" Caroline asked quickly.

"Fine. He said tell you he's still whirling the old coffee grinder." Bob Herndon reached for the wagon and pulled himself erect. "Oh, by the way," he added, "Chat's got an added duty at Fort Steele. He's chairman of the Caroline Ainsley Milk Fund."

"The what?" she asked in perplexed voice.

"Your milk fund. The troopers took up what you started. Now they make sure that milk is loaded onto every immigrant train for the kids."

Caroline's gray eyes glowed softly as he stood beside

120

her. "What a nice thing for them to do. I wish I could see them—all of them, especially Captain and Mrs. Brenton."

Bob Herndon sniffed the air. Aware of tantalizing odors drifting through the cabin doorway he said, "Let's go inside and find out what Mrs. Jorgenson is baking. Maybe we can talk her out of a slice of whatever it is." He walked toward the cabin and paused for a final survey of the twilight-shrouded valley.

"Don't worry about the Brentons," he commented. "They're already talking of a trip up here. It was the last thing they mentioned when I left."

Caroline stood for a moment in the doorway, listening to the evening sounds of the settlement. "Lieutenant Bob," she asked, "why did you come to Aspen?"

He glanced into her upturned face. "An assayer has to be where there are minerals."

"But there's lots of mines in Wyoming."

His hand moved across her shoulder, flicking the long braids forward to fall before her. "Let's just say," he said, grinning evasively, "that a couple of inky pigtails got in my way."

A week later Jim Daley got his first sight of the ranch on Wilderness Creek. He would have shoved off for that spot the morning after his arrival in Aspen, taking his young and black-tressed partner with him, had not H. A. W. Tabor laid down a few firm words. "You'll not take a step down that way, my friend, until I can get away to go with you. Before I left Denver I promised myself two things for this trip: to see the Wilderness Creek country, and to polish off two gents, Daley and Ainsley, in a poker game that never got started back in Evans."

"We'll wait and you can tag along to the Wilderness ranch," Daley agreed with a grin. "When we get back for the game you can sweeten the pot with a sawmill."

"When I'm through with you, Daley, you'll have to manhandle logs for a grubstake," Tabor answered coolly.

When finally the hard trek down the Roaring Fork was behind them, and they came onto the level meadows of Wilderness Creek, Jim Daley veered his horse abruptly from them. "Go ahead up to the house; I'll join you later."

Caroline watched his retreating figure with a troubled face. She turned to Tabor. "He didn't say a word about the land, or the grass, or the water. Maybe he doesn't think it's very good. Maybe I've wasted his money."

"Take it easy, Caroline," Tabor said in unconcerned tones. "I know Jim Daley well. He'll look, then look some more, before he talks."

It was two hours before Daley showed up at the ranch cabin. Hardrock Corlett was nowhere to be found. Caroline noticed at once the well-ordered appearance of the rooms, and the many small mending and patching jobs that spruced up the barns and corrals.

She paced restlessly about until H. A. W. Tabor drew her into conversation and insisted that she recount every detail of their trip to Fort Steele and to Aspen. She told him very slowly and carefully of the deal that had been made with Bentley for the ranch, and the method by which the miners had been prompted to file homestead claims and to sign purchase options. He took a small black book from his vest pocket and jotted quick notes when Caroline paused, saying suddenly, "My father wrote that paper about the water. That, that. . . ."

"Request for adjudication," Tabor supplied. "I imagined he did. It was a first-rate job. My lawyers added some legal wording. Then I made a small change when they were through. It has been sent up to the Statehouse in Denver. Likely, Caroline, you'll get the water. I'm not so sure about those homestead options. The miners will have to *prove up* before they get title and can sell."

Concern swept Caroline's reply. "Then maybe I've talked Papa into wasting his money—same as I did Uncle Jim's."

H. A. W. Tabor strode to the open door. He stood with his hands behind his back and stared out over the valley.

"Perhaps not, Caroline," he said finally. "I seem to have an idea rattling around. Daley is riding in now. Let me think about it a bit and talk to him."

Caroline flew out of the door. Anxiety seethed within

122

her, but her face was calm and her eyes quietly intense. "Did you have a nice ride?" she asked lightly.

Daley swung down from the saddle. "Tolerably good, partner. I met your man Hardrock Corlett up the valley looking after some yearlings. He'll be along shortly."

He strode to a nearby post, looped his bridle reins around it, and walked into the cabin. Caroline's impulse was to run after him, to cry out anxious questions and draw from him the decision that she both longed for and dreaded. Instead, she steeled herself to wait outside. Wilderness Creek ran a tumbling and chattering course a scant ten rods away. She moved to it and dropped her sweaty palms into the cold water. After she dried them on a tall grass clump, she turned and went into the cabin, where Jim Daley was sprawled in the cowhide chair. "That's about it," he told Tabor. "It's a cowman's heaven. Likely I couldn't have found anything as good if I'd spent a year looking. With this ranch and Caroline's homestead claims we'll build an empire—and the damndest biggest and best herd . . ."

H. A. W. Tabor cast Caroline a flashing smile as he cut in. "Sure, Jim. I knew it when we first topped the ridge and saw these flats. But about those homestead claims. I'm not sure paying fifty bucks apiece to those miners will solve anything."

"I have thought about that," Daley said nodding. "What's to make them take time off from jobs and prospecting sashays to spend the time required here to do improvement work?"

"Suppose," Tabor said slowly, "they were to owe money, quite a bit of money, that they had agreed to pay off by doing the improvement work down here. Say they were to accidentally get into a little poker game and——"

"Hell," Daley snorted. "Come right out and say it, Tabor. You want me and Ainsley and you to finagle them into playing cards."

Tabor laughed. "I know their breed. They've got a lot of respect for a gambling debt."

Jim Daley slid from the leather chair and hunkered down on the floor. He drew a knife from his pocket and scratched small concentric circles on the bare boards. "H.

123

A. W." he said after a time, "I for damn sure hope it'll work. Just the same, I suspect you're promoting this to get away from that showdown game with Lance and me."

Tabor propped his boots onto the kitchen table and reared his chair onto two legs. "You think so? Well, here's a bit of news, old friend. One of these days we'll play that game—to your eternal sorrow."

Caroline had listened in wordless wonder, staring first at one and then the other of them. Now her gaze fastened on the knife Daley moved restlessly over the floor. She dropped to her knees. "Uncle Jim," she said, "let me have that knife a minute."

He passed it to her. "When did you take up whittling?" he asked.

With swift strokes she scratched out a huge "D" on the floor. "We'll need a cattle brand for the ranch," she explained. "How would that do?"

"Not so good. It could be blotted from hell to breakfast. Gimme that knife." He moved the knife suddenly about. "Maybe something like this: ⊃D It's a lazy CD Bar. That would mean the Caroline-Daley Outfit."

"Lazy CD," Caroline repeated softly. Suddenly she laughed. "Let's use that, Uncle Jim. CD Bar. Lazy CD. We can call it the L-a-z-y S-e-e-d-y Ranch!"

"Christ Almighty," Jim Daley snorted as he reared to his feet. "I'm stuck with that, eh?"

They remained at Wilderness Creek another day because Jim Daley was making careful plans for men and equipment to be moved from his Platte Valley ranch. Agreement was reached with Hardrock Corlett to continue working. This phase wasn't hard to arrange, for the old miner discussed it with an avid and eager glint of eye and toss of white whiskers. "There ain't," he said, "any decent outcroppings down here on the flats. But maybe I've stumbled onto something tolerably interesting up-creek about ten miles."

"Go to it," Daley agreed. "Just keep a good eye on the ranch and stock, and report to my partner once a week. Besides, up that far there's canyons that wouldn't be worth a shuck for grazing. And anyway it's hell and gone off our property."

Tabor listened silently, then said, "If you do hit something worthwhile, I'll be open to deal."

Darkness closed in before they caught sight of Aspen's lights when they journeyed back two days later. They rode as a silent group along the main streets, between the lights of the stores and the saloons and the merrymaking spots that sprang up with dizzying rapidity that summer.

They turned onto a side street to short-cut their way to a livery stable and Caroline realized that this was the one small segment of Aspen that Lance Ainsley had insisted that she never visit. She curiously glanced about. Sounds beat into the street from two rambling buildings with well-lighted porches. The sounds of lively music, of men's voices, and the occasional high-pitched tones of a woman's laughter. A few people lounged on the porches. A heavyset girl with a scantily cut dress and paint-touched face stood in a doorway.

Suddenly Jim Daley seized her bridle reins and wheeled her horse about. "Good Lord, Tabor," he said shortly. "Let's get her out of here."

In that instant Caroline Ainsley's face froze as she sat rigidly in her saddle. She was staring toward the porch of the second building. Two people came from inside and were revealed in yellow lamp light. For a single moment she looked straight into the face of Lieutenant Bob Herndon—and across the form of a blonde girl about whom his arm was encircled.

She looked back blankly as both men flailed her black mare into a sudden gallop.

The next morning Caroline toyed quietly with her breakfast and gave short and disinterested replies to Lance's questions about Wilderness Creek. Jim Daley ate beside her, and after a time he put an understanding and merciful end to the conversation. With a warning jerk of his head toward the door, he said to Lance, "My partner's pretty tired this morning. She'll talk about things later. Let's go outside. I'll tell you my ideas for the Wilderness Creek ranch."

Before they went outside, Caroline looked squarely at her father. "Papa, I'd like to go through some of the stores today. I haven't been in them very much. It may take quite a while."

"Of course, kitten," he agreed. "Take your time. And you should go by and see Bob Herndon's assay office. It's quite a little humdinger."

Her answer was a silent stare that went beyond him, beyond the walls, and beyond the mountains.

Her vigil began within the hour as she stood outside the door of the largest store in Aspen. She still stood there, watching the street and all who passed by, when noon came. She was tired and thirsty, and small, cutting pains flashed through her legs. She eased into a half-sitting posture on a narrow windowsill and searched the street with alert eyes. By early afternoon people were glancing curiously toward her.

The storekeeper came outside and spoke. "Is something wrong, girl? You've been standing there for hours."

She smiled broadly, but her eyes continued sweeping across the street and those who came onto it. "I'm perfectly all right, thank you," she said. "I'm waiting for a lady. Maybe she'll be quite late."

"Okay," he said. "But let me bring you a drink of water."

She had half-finshed the tin cup of water when she jerked erect, her eyes narrowing into greater watchfulness. A blonde girl came onto the street and moved along with small and mincing steps that accented the sway of her hips. Caroline set the cup upon the window ledge and walked unconcernedly across the street. There was a harness shop, and she waited before it when the older girl came by.

Caroline stepped forward and almost blocked the other's path. "Hello," she said. Her voice was politely sweet and friendly. "I haven't met you."

The yellow-haired girl moved as though to sweep by her. "I'll say you ain't met me, kid," she said haughtily.

Caroline fell into step beside her. "Do you mind if I

walk along with you? There's so few pretty young ladies in Aspen. I get lonesome to talk to someone."

"Have it your own way, kid. It's a free world, as I always say."

Caroline glanced at her companion's tightly bodiced and laced lavender dress, and the small, tasseled umbrella she carried. "You dress beautifully. I like nice clothes. Are you a dressmaker?"

The girl laughed, a short and mirthless laugh. "Don't gas me, youngun. You know where I work. You're the one on a black horse who gaped at me last night."

For a moment Caroline was silent, taken aback. "I thought you were a beautiful lady; that's why I wanted to meet you."

The words were rewarded with a smile from the girl's heavily rouged face. "I'm glad someone in this lousy town knows class. You've gotta dress well to do well, I always say."

"What is your name?" Caroline asked innocently.

"Ellen's the name. Ellen Bradley."

"Miss Ellen, may I go shopping with you?"

"Why?"

"Maybe you could show me the right material for a dress. A party dress."

"Oh, I guess so. Always glad to help. If there's anything Ellen Bradley knows its how to pick duds—and wear 'em."

"I know that," Caroline affirmed hastily.

An hour later they came onto the street again. Caroline faced her companion. "Thank you for picking out the yellow material. I think I will buy it tomorrow. Will you help me with the sewing?"

"Sure, kid," Ellen agreed. "Come around anytime."

"I'm afraid I can't," Caroline said blandly. "I'm not allowed on *that* street."

"What the hell," Ellen Bradley said loftily. "I don't live there. I just work there. I'm a dancer—not one of them upstairs girls."

"But where do you live, Miss Ellen?"

"I've got a shack ... cabin, I mean, a couple of blocks south. I'm not one of the all-night girls."

Caroline continued walking beside her. "Well, then, I guess it will be all right for me to walk home with you."

Ellen Bradley stared at her, then offered a brittle grin. "You're a funny kid. Come along up to my place. But you can't stay too long. I'm expecting a gentleman friend."

Within minutes they reached a small and secluded cabin. Ellen pushed open the door and stood aside for Caroline to enter.

Her first glance about the interior brought Caroline to the verge of a hasty retreat. The room was small and cluttered and permeated with a faint but strangely nauseating odor. There was an unmade bed and a table littered with bits of food. The floor had long since relinquished hope of being scrubbed.

Only Ellen Bradshaw's clothing was in order. Her well-pressed garments hung neatly from a wooden bar in one corner of the room.

"Find a place and sit down, youngun. Place is sort of a mess. Maybe I'll clean it out tomorrow."

Caroline lowered herself gingerly on a dusty chair. "Miss Ellen," she said in feigned excitement, "tell me about the place where you work."

"Nothing doing, kid. It's a lousy honky-tonk. But anything to get started—that's what I always say."

"Maybe some day I can sing or dance in a place like that."

"Maybe so—if you ain't got brains. You look more like you ought to be in school."

"I don't like school," Caroline said carefully. "What good would it do a dancer?"

Ellen Bradley had plopped onto the bed, which sagged beneath her weight. At that moment Caroline identified the strange smell about the room. Beneath the bed was a white and covered utensil. A chamber pot. She knew absolutely that it had not been emptied this day, or yesterday, or perhaps the day before.

She quickly smiled, hoping to stifle the disgust that must not show on her face. "About my dress, Miss Ellen. Could you take a piece of paper and scissors and help me cut a pattern?"

"I guess so. "I'm a swell seamstress. Ma taught me back

in Ohio. Learning to sew made sense to me. None of that learning crap they tried to cram down my throat at school. I wasn't buying none of that stuff."

A discomforting but urgent uneasiness built within Caroline Ainsley. *Will I be like this? In a few years will I be like Ellen Bradley if I stay in Aspen? If I don't go away to school?*

Ellen got up from the bed, found scissors, and began laying out a pattern. Her fingers moved with swift nimbleness. Concentration stamped itself on the hardness of her face. Minutes stretched into an hour.

When she later glanced at a clock, she quickly folded the pattern and thrust it onto a shelf. "Kid, you'll have to leave—right away. My friend will be here any minute."

Caroline rose, stepping unconcernedly toward the bed. "I'm sorry we didn't finish the pattern." She was glancing out the window. "I'll go right away. I see your friend, your friend the army lieutenant with the limp—Mr. Herndon."

Ellen Bradley whirled to face Caroline. The hardness of her face twisted to an ugly snarl. "So that's it. That's why you buttered me into letting you get into my cabin. You know him, don't you—you two-faced little brat?"

"Yes, I know him. He was a friend of mine."

Ellen Bradley's hand lifted to start a slapping gesture, but she pulled it back. "Get out of here, you sly little skunk!" She pointed angrily toward the door. "Beat it—before I bash your silly head."

Caroline cast another hurried glance through the window. She judged Bob Herndon's nearness to the cabin and the time left to her.

"I'm sorry I made you mad, Miss Ellen. Thank you for the pattern. May I have it?"

Ellen turned to snatch the pattern from the shelf. Caroline pushed her foot hard against the object beneath the bed. The white chamber pot slid into view. She stooped quickly to pick it up. When Ellen Bradley turned to face her, Caroline put the pot gingerly into Ellen's hands. "Maybe," she said sweetly, "you'd better empty this before he gets here."

Ellen turned and searched in sudden frenzy for a place

129

to hide the white porcelain utensil. "Damn you," she hissed. I'm going to tear every hair—"

The words ended in a scream. Caroline Ainsley had thrust out her foot and tripped her companion, who sprawled across the room. The pot flew from her hands. Its amber-hued contents cascaded down across her face and her hair and her dress.

Caroline sped to the door, opened it as Ellen Bradley struggled wildly to her feet and wiped her face with blind and desperate strokes. "You filthy slut," she howled. "You goddamned bitch. I'll cut your guts to shreds."

Caroline side-stepped a wild grab. In the next moment Ellen Bradley looked into the shocked face of Robert Herndon.

Caroline never knew what words, if any, passed between them. She had slipped through the door and sped down the street toward home. After a time her pace slackened . . . to a trot . . . to a slow walk. There was a pine stump near, and she threw herself down beside it. Her face was buried in her arms as great and tormented sobs racked her body.

She had been there many minutes when a hand fell on her shoulder in effort to turn her face upward from the ground.

"Caroline. Listen, Caroline. I've got to talk to you." There was desperate and humble pleading in Bob Herndon's words.

She shoved his hand from her. "Go away. Leave me alone."

"No, Caroline. I have something to say, something I've got to tell you."

"I, I won't listen."

"Then I'll be quiet—for now. But I've got to tell you—later."

"You can't tell me later," she said through her sobs.

"Why?" Bob Herndon asked softly.

"Because I won't be here. I'm going to leave Aspen. I'm going away when Mr. Tabor goes. I'm going to Denver—to school."

PART TWO

1888–1890

Chapter 7

The window faced toward the sunset and the mountains in the west. It would be an hour before Eric Duane would come to escort her to the Windsor Hotel. She drew aside a brocaded drapery and stood for a time in quiet and studied reverie as the pattern of Denver's lights gained added brilliance and the last crimson patch of day was engulfed somewhere beyond distant and unseen peaks. Through the years, this hour of deepening twilight, when day was ending and night not yet upon the city, had been a time of comtemplation, an interlude when memories would gather about her, and when the enigma of the future would become an urgent and demanding reality.

In the mellow and shaded lamp glow, her figure was no longer that of the child who so long ago had been silhouetted on the kitchen wall of Swope's mansion. In the maturity of her nineteen years was the same erect and eager bearing, the graceful and swift ease of movement, and an intense awareness of life and its every moment.

Tonight she had chosen a simply designed gown of deep lilac saved from plainness by a strand of pearls and a thin bracelet. She was not conscious of having chosen for this farewell party attire that would accentuate the soft radiance of her black hair and the calm depths of her gray eyes.

She glanced pensively toward the western sky, but the last red ember of sunset had disappeared. She wondered if it were still aglow above the valley of the Roaring Fork or marking the horizon beyond Wilderness Creek.

She knew that the darkness of this October night would mantle a vastly changed and larger and different Aspen than the small, turbulent settlement she had left with H.

A. W. Tabor and Jim Daley seven years earlier. A city had sprung from the richness of the tunnels, the shafts, and the stopes that now honeycombed Aspen Mountain. Each year, when summer vacation had led her back to the city of the Roaring Fork, she had marveled at the swiftness of its growth. A dozen streets were lined with business buildings of brick and stone. Beyond were rows of homes about which trees and shrubs and flowers lent an air of stability and permanence.

The smelters had come, as Lance Ainsley had predicted. The rails of the Denver and Rio Grande Western Railroad coursed up the valley from Glenwood Springs in a path paralleling the trail along which Hardrock Corlett had led them under the spell of Mount Sopris, to Bentley's ranch, and by which they had come at last to Aspen. The Midland Railroad would soon link Aspen with Leadville and Denver, competing with the D&RGW for the never-ceasing inward haul of materials, supplies, and people. On their outward run they would carry incredibly valuable cargoes of silver bullion, the varied mail of the community, and often the families of miners who had died in some underground labyrinth or under the crushing whiteness of cascading snow.

Caroline listened to the sound of shuffled objects in an adjoining room and smiled as she sensed the alacrity with which Mrs. Jorgenson was stripping and packing the furnishings of the small Capitol Hill apartment in preparation for their departure. She glanced at the small watch pinned to the bosom of her dress. Within minutes it would mark the hour of seven; there was still time to wait.

Caroline moved quickly toward the kitchen. The time could be spent in aiding the older woman with small, seemingly endless tasks. Abruptly she laughed aloud, causing Mrs. Jorgenson to pause, holding half-a-dozen teacups aloft, as she studied the girl's face.

"And what is so funny?" Mrs. Jorgenson demanded. She had changed little with the passing years. Only the added whiteness of her piled and pinned hair, and the maze of small wrinkles framing her eyes, marked the difference from the busily scrubbing and baking wife toward which

134

Jorgenson had once pointed his pipe and stated that she cooked well and spoke English badly.

"I was remembering," Caroline answered. "Remembering what you said the night I told you I was coming to Denver to school, and asked you to come with me and take care of me."

"Time I hadn't had to straighten your Papa's house. Or the clothes to wash."

"You were scrubbing the porch when I asked you. Remember? You looked at me as though I had stolen all your pies ... or been nipping from Papa's bottle of rye. "Yah," you said. "I go with you. But God help me. Over that mountain I have to walk again, so soon."

Mrs. Jorgenson smiled as she lifted more cups from the pantry shelf. "Yah, my feet they ache yet, as you tell of it. But now, tomorrow we go home to the big mountains. On a train." Her lids closed for a time over misty eyes, but the smile lingered about her lips. Caroline wondered how many times this small and busy woman had herself stood at the window and searched the sweep of mountains beyond which lay the magic of Aspen.

Moments later, Caroline was shooed firmly from the kitchen. "For an hour I work to make you ready for the party," Mrs. Jorgenson said testily. "Now the dust you want to get on your dress and on your face. I need you not at all."

Caroline walked restlessly back to the window. Once more the city's lights shone a jeweled pattern outside. She could mark the brighter glow of Sixteenth Street, leading up the hill from the railroad yards to its crossing of Broadway.

The slash of Broadway across the city led her gaze northward to where the street dwindled to open and dark countryside. From long habit, she turned quickly and looked elsewhere. Yet, in some deep and locked place within her, was knowledge that a road and a railroad led beyond Broadway, led through the wide valley of the South Platte toward Evans, toward the Colony, toward Greeley.

Throughout the busy years of her schooling in Denver, she had never gone a dozen blocks north on Broadway. A

135

veiling and yet impenetrable blockade, born of those nights of agony in Maude Selby's house, kept her thoughts from Swope's mansion and those who lived there.

Once the barrier had been shattered. The memory of a single devastating hour closed vividly about her now and blotted from her mind and senses the room and the light-studded panorama beyond. With startling clearness, she remembered a late and snowy afternoon, almost two years earlier, when she had gone alone to downtown Denver and entered Daniels and Fisher's store in search of a particularly styled coat that Lance Ainsley had requested.

She located the garment easily. A slight alteration required half an hour. Caroline relaxed and drank a hot chocolate with piled cream topping. Then she began an unhurried tour of the sprawling, busy store. It was the din, the color, and the crowded magic of the toy department that drew and held her. She had never seen toys like these. There were large and lifelike dolls, animals that could be wound into jerking movement, and endless tables of books and games.

She tarried long beyond the time when her father's coat could be picked up. Entranced by this cleverly designed and stocked fairyland, she was held as evening arrived and more lights glowed through the store. A table was piled with gaily painted trains. Caroline had reached out to touch the smokestack of a model of the Denver and Rio Grande's latest model freight when she became aware of someone standing near her, and of a boy's hand outthrust close to her own.

She glanced down, catching sight only of the serge cap topping his head and of his heavy matching coat, as he bent forward and stared at the train.

"Excuse me," she said, and moved aside. "I didn't mean to crowd you." There was no reply as she walked a dozen steps from him, and paused before another counter.

Within seconds he was at her side again. His hand moved to lie lightly on her sleeve, and tightened. He crowded closer, and lifted his face to gaze at her with puzzled, questioning eyes.

It seemed she ceased to breathe. Her temples pounded wildly; her jaw dropped in full and shocked realization.

136

With trembling fingers, she reached swiftly out to touch his head and his cheek, and then to lift his chin in order to keep his face clearly in sight as the haze of welling tears threatened to blind her.

"Why . . . why did you follow me?" she asked.

"I don't know," he answered slowly. "I just like you. You're a pretty lady."

Her arm stole about his shoulder, bringing his head against her side. "How old are you?"

"I'm eight, but going on nine." There was boyish pride in his words.

"Do you live here in Denver?" Caroline was striving to keep calmness in her words.

"No." He shook his head. "We got here this morning." I rode on a train. A big passenger train."

It came then in blurting, demanding desperation, the question to which she already knew the answer.

"What is your name?"

"Shawn, Shawn Ainsley." As he voiced the words, he again stared into her face. His hazel eyes were deep and solemn and questioning pools. His arm encircled her waist, as though to regain and hold steadfast something he sensed he had once known and lost.

Oblivious to the crowded room, to the melee of nearby children, and to the curious glances of older people, Caroline Ainsley dropped to her knees. Her arms drew him close in a fiercely possessive embrace; her lips laid tender kisses on his cheek as he nestled long moments with his face crushed to her neck.

When she rose at last to her feet, he still clutched her. His smiling face was determined. "Stay here with me," he pleaded. "Stay here. We'll play with the toys until Grandma comes to get me."

His words caused Caroline to stiffen. Her frantic eyes swept the room and the open doorways. Even as she took him again into her arms, short and panicky words broke from her. "I can't stay to play. It's getting late and dark."

She plucked his fingers reluctantly from her arm. "No, I'll . . . I'll have to go. But I love you—love you so very much, Shawn Ainsley."

She stood in utter silence as her fingers pushed back his

cap and moved trancelike through his hair. Abruptly and blindly she turned from him, rushing to escape the room and the store. It wasn't until the next day she remembered her father's coat was still at Daniels and Fisher's.

She stood beside the window, searching these Denver years, when the muffled chime of the doorbell told her that Eric Duane had arrived. She glanced appraisingly toward a wall mirror and crossed the room to open the door.

The man standing in the subdued light of the hallway was tall with the lithe and muscled grace of an athlete. The dark shade of the evening clothes he was wearing contrasted sharply with his shock of sandy-hued hair, his alert blue eyes, and the bridge of freckles across his cheeks and aquiline nose.

"Come in, Eric," Caroline said, smiling easily. "You'll find the apartment quite a mess. We've been packing."

He dropped a fur-collared coat and a bowler hat onto a chair and turned to her. "I'm going to miss you, Caroline."

She sat on a sofa, reached out her hand, and drew him to the seat beside her. "I'll miss you too, Eric. Do you remember, five years ago, when I first came to school here—a little girl, and frightened by the city?"

Eric Duane grinned teasingly. "I remember sitting behind you in school, and getting angry because most of the time your infernal black braids were swishing across everything I tried to read or write."

"Not for long, Eric. Not after you pasted them to a geography book with that white and gummy paste. It took Mrs. Jorgenson an entire evening to wash and comb my pigtails."

He glanced toward the soft sheen of her hair. His face became serious. "Perhaps, Caroline, I had an unheeded premonition of how lovely you would become, of how I would dread this time when school days would be over, and you'd leave Denver."

Caroline laid her hand firmly into his. "We've had some wonderful times together, Eric. More than anybody, you've made these years swift-moving and pleasant."

Eric Duane rose restlessly to his feet and looked toward

her. "There could be more years, Caroline, for us—together."

She stood up, faced him, and placed her hands gently on his shoulders. "I know, Eric. But I have to go home to Aspen. Don't ask me why. I'm not sure that I know myself, except that whenever I think of any other future, my thoughts and plans are blotted away, shoved aside by quiet meadowlands, by the hammering of stamping mills, and all those endless peaks jutting toward the sun."

He smiled slowly, and said, "All that is something hard for me to compete with. I'm just a man, short of six feet tall, equipped with a college fraternity pin, a shaky education in business, and an even shakier family grocery firm that may or may not need me." He paused for a second, his voice dropped, and he added, "Just that and love of a black-tressed, gray-eyed mountain princess."

"Don't, Eric," she whispered. "The world won't end when I step on the train."

He picked up his coat. "I'm not so sure, Caroline. Not sure at all." He glanced at a clock. "We should be hurrying along. There will be half a hundred people at your good-bye party. We can't keep them waiting."

When they were seated behind sleek black horses trotting down Sixteenth Street, he turned to her with a troubled, but determined face.

"Caroline, perhaps I have no right to ask—but I must. Who is the other man?"

Her open, level gaze held to his face. "Eric, I'm not sure there is another. Maybe I have to go home to find out for myself."

He slapped the reins to quicken the horses' pace. "Write to me Caroline when you're sure. I don't forget, or give up, easily."

Despite the belabored snorting and smoke belches of two engines, the train from Glenwood Springs seemed to Caroline to crawl inch by inch up the Roaring Fork Valley. It was a mixed train. Three passenger coaches followed a long-linked series of boxcars, coal cars, and a few manure-stained ones which from time to time and with bruising jolts were detached and onto a spur to be filled

139

with cattle and picked up on the return trip. This was a narrow-gauge line, snaking a tortuous way through raw cuts and over high and uncertain fills and bridges.

Caroline Ainsley sat in silence most of the time. Occasionally she peered out in effort to recognize places she might recall from the past, from the time she had ridden a black mare up this valley in company with Aspen-bound miners.

When a long, sweeping curve brought them at last in view of Mount Sopris, she awakened Mrs. Jorgenson who was napping on the uncomfortable seat beside her.

"I thought you'd want to see this," she said, pointing quietly at the mountain.

Mrs. Jorgenson stared for a long time at the distant and vastly molded peak. "Is wonderful, Caroline. Is maybe the father of mountains."

"I thought so when I first saw it. Look. The wind is blowing hard on the summit. See how the snow trails away, almost like smoke. It is called a snow plume."

The older woman nodded. "I've seen it often in Sweden. Up there, on the top, is always winter. Beautiful. Cold."

"I've always liked snow plumes," Caroline answered thoughtfully. "Liked them, yet somehow dreaded them. It is something like life, isn't it? Something like a person from whom the winds of life and fate whip the cloak of strength. Yet another year brings more snow to the mountain. To a person it brings replenished courage and determination, to lie quiet and protecting and shining during the calm and serene days. Then trouble comes, and ordeals, that whip strength away in a swirling plume of adversity. But beneath it all, most people have the enduring rock of understanding and strength and compassion."

Mrs. Jorgenson peered intently into Caroline's face as the words came to a slow-spoken close. "My little girl has grown up. She's a woman now," she said. "A beautiful and headstrong woman that sees too much, too clearly."

The miles slid by. Caroline dropped into light sleep. The banging of a car door brought her awake. An instant later the conductor's voice filled her ears.

"Caroline," he said sharply.

She turned her head. "Yes?" she answered.

He seemed unaware of her reply. "CAROLINE," he said again.

She half-rose from her seat. "Yes, I'm Caroline," she said aloud and firmly.

He glanced curiously toward her. "CAROLINE!" he barked with loud authority in his voice.

She stepped into the narrow aisle. "Yes!" she answered, and her clear tone echoed throughout the car. "Yes, Conductor? What?"

He glared at her. "For Christ sake, lady," he roared. "Will you sit down, shut up, and let me announce that we're pulling into Caroline station?"

She sank back into the seat, knowing that a crimson glow surged through her neck and her face.

Across the aisle, a gray-headed stranger lifted the broad-rimmed hat from his face, blinked, then grinned at her.

"It appears you're new in these parts, ma'am. There's a small station just up the line. Place opposite the mouth of Wilderness Creek. There's a helluva big ranch there, ramrodded by old Jim Daley. The D&RG put in a station for the ranch. Wanted to name it Haller, for some high railroad mucky-muck. Daley tore into them. Told them either to name the station *Caroline,* or shove it up———! Pardon me, ma'am, to shove it down their boots."

Caroline had spent her vacation months in Aspen the previous year, but she marveled at the city's growth as the train crawled across the High Castle Creek Bridge and entered a sprawling and freight-choked railroad yard. New buildings clustered about the Smuggler, the Molly Gibson, and other older, larger mines perched on the steep slopes of Aspen and Red Mountains. New mines, mills, and dumps seemed to have sprouted in every direction. Block after block the residential districts stretched out with finished homes, half-completed and unpainted ones, and the rawness of new excavation and foundations.

The business district was no longer a scattering of log- and false-fronted buildings. Most of these had given way to solid brick-and-stone structures. Aspen was growing, and already boasted of five thousand people. There was

141

shack town and quality row, hotels and flophouses, alley hovels and an opera house. There were churches, schools, a red-light district, and the Ladies Aid society.

The train bumped to a clanging halt alongside a station platform on which it seemed to Caroline that half of the people of Aspen had gathered. She searched the throng for familiar faces. Her face pressed closely and eagerly against a smoke-streaked window. Finally she spotted Jim Daley and her father working their way through the crowd. The car cleared as she moved quickly through the doorway, down the vestibule steps, and into the arms of Lance Ainsley.

Her weight and the pressure of her arms about him caused him to take a staggered step backward. He held her at arm's length and measured her height. "Lordy day, kitten. You've grown up," he said in awed voice.

Jim Daley shoved his way to their side. "Howdy, partner," he said. "Welcome home."

"Yes, home at last," she sighed contentedly. Even as her arms snuggled over a shoulder of each, her gaze swept the platform for another face that had not appeared. Deliberate and studied gaiety marked her words as she walked toward Lance's buggy and the bay team.

"I'm glad you drove your bays to bring me home, Papa."

"Of course," Lance answered. "They're privileged characters now. Fat and lazy. Pensioned except for special occasions. They're getting old, kitten."

"My black mare," Caroline asked anxiously, "is she still . . . ?"

"Sure," Jim Daley answered. "She's got it pretty soft down at the ranch. That one should live forever."

"How are things on the Wilderness, Uncle Jim? I heard on the train that it's a helluva big cow outfit ramrodded by old Daley. And thanks for *Caroline Station*," she added, laughing.

"It's time people know I've got a partner," Daley replied. "Not much of a working partner, just one arriving fresh from Denver and the bright lights."

Caroline turned a puckered face toward him. "As Mr. Tabor would say, I've got news for you, my friend. We're going to really start building that ranch. Tomorrow. I've got ideas."

"I've got a better one for right now," Lance interrupted. "Our dinner will just about be ready over at the Clarendon. We may be lucky enough not to be served tough steaks from a Lazy Seedy steer."

The trotting bays caused dust plumes to rise from the surrey wheels. Caroline sat beside Lance and scanned the blocks for new buildings and for familiar faces. On Galena Street she caught sight of the small and unpainted building with an outthrust sign that read: ROBERT HERNDON, METALLURGIST-ASSAYER. For a moment, in their passing, she stared through the meager window, but the shop seemed dark and deserted. Her lips were a firm line as she spoke to her father. "It does seem Bob Herndon would at least wash the windows ... clean up his office. It's shabbier now than last summer."

Troubled, Lance turned. "Kitten, you're riled because he didn't meet you at the train. He skipped it on purpose. He wanted to keep his troubles and—and his failure from rubbing off or embarrassing you."

"He shouldn't have failed in Aspen," Caroline answered heatedly. "There's plenty of work here for a good assayer."

"Not as much as you'd think—nowadays. The big outfits hire their own assayers. Others, the small miners and prospectors, are either slow pay or never pay."

"They wouldn't get me to do their work without paying," she commented coldly.

"No. I'm sure they wouldn't, kitten. With Bob Herndon it's different. Long on ability—short on business sense. Too many people get their work done free or on credit. He never seems to collect much of it. I wonder sometimes how he manages to eat."

"It isn't right that way. It's not fair."

Lance shook his head ruefully. "No, it's not. But you were a little unfair yourself, one time. You never gave him a chance to talk a certain affair over with you or let him explain. Why don't you look him up tomorrow, kitten? He could sure stand encouragement."

"Maybe I will, sometime later," she replied uneasily.

143

"Now, tell me what you've been doing, Papa, how things are going."

Jim Daley interrupted his conversation with Mrs. Jorgenson and leaned forward from the rear seat to thrust his head between them. "Take it from me, partner, your pa's doing all right. Got his fingers in everything from a brewery to opera. What beats hell out of me is where he ratholes the money. Don't let him keep you living in that cramped log house any longer. Make him shell out, gal. Build you a house with elegant gingerbread and lawn enough to pasture——"

Lance was grinning quietly. "How about taking your own advice, Jim? I haven't seen any castle sprouting down on Wilderness Creek."

Daley's arm encircled Caroline. "Of course you ain't; I've got a partner to be consulted first."

"Fancy buildings can wait," Caroline said firmly. "How do we stand on getting land?"

"Real good," Daley nodded. "Your cussed Lazy Seedy is one solid hunk—about two thousand acres. Last of the miners proved up on his homestead and sold last winter. Needed money for a sure system he'd figured out to bust a faro bank."

Caroline was destined for little sleep that night. Dinner at the Clarendon Hotel lasted for a long time. There were many people to meet. Awareness grew upon her of how well Lance Ainsley had become entrenched in Aspen during the years of her schooling. Here in this hotel, with its plush furnishings, its gleaming linens and crystal, and its heavy carpets, she could sense the wealth and the growing maturity of the town.

Later at home and in bed, her thoughts whirled kaleidoscopically. There was the wistful and lonely face of Eric Duane as he had stood on the station platform in Denver when her train drew away; there was a memory of the tiny depot and rambling stockyards at Caroline station; but clearer still was her picture of an unpainted shack and a wind-blown sign that seemed a swaying end of the bold dream with which Bob Herndon had come to the silver city on the Roaring Fork.

She tossed restlessly and was up in the brisk coolness of

sunrise. She helped Mrs. Jorgenson with their unpacking and with household chores, but she knew these were delaying moments, small things to consume time and allow her uneasiness to wear off.

She knew what must be done. Her movements became brisk and purposeful as she changed into a knitted, rose-hued dress and carefully combed her hair. She walked swiftly up the street, circled a tangle of weeds, and entered Herndon's assay office.

The front room was strewn with sacks and boxes. She paused to look about and listen. The multi-tiered mineral case, which so long ago had roused her ecstasy in Hugus's trading post at Fort Steele, was unkempt and dusty at the rear of the room. She reached out and turned it slowly around. Sunlight played across the rainbow of specimens it still held.

The sound of a hammer upon breaking ore led her slowly through an open door and into the inner room. She stood silently. Her gaze fell upon the bent and fiery-haired form of Bob Herndon working at a cluttered bench.

"If you have time," she said finally, "I'd like you to guide me on a tour." She was aware that her words were tense and uncertain in the hollowness of the room.

He swung about to stare at her and his mouth opened in unbelieving wonder. The old boyish grin fought its way across his face and sparked his blue eyes. "Good god, no, Caroline. You'd head for the railroad and an immigrant train."

Her laugh swept tension from the room. "Perhaps not, Lieutenant Bob; I'm a bigger brat now. We might find something even worse." She walked toward him as he laid both hands on the bench and maneuvered the stiffened leg to allow him to stand up. "Bob, it's good to see you. I missed you, I missed you at the train and at the hotel last night."

His eyes, kindled into urgent, baffled hunger, and swept over her. "Stand still, Caroline. Right where you are. Let me look at you. Grown up. Beautiful."

"That's pure flattery," she answered lightly. "And I like it." She tilted her head and peered at him. "With a shave, a haircut, and more sun tan, you would pass an acid test

145

yourself. Now out with the truth. Why didn't you come running to welcome me home?"

His lips curved into momentary bitterness. "You couldn't have lacked a welcome. Half of Aspen, the upper half, made it a point to be in the hotel and get a glimpse of Lance Ainsley's daughter. And the Clarendon dining room is hardly the place for a broken-down . . ."

"Stop it," she flared suddenly. "Stop it right now. There's nothing in this town you couldn't have."

"Except money," he said wearily. "But if you want a grand tour——"

Caroline moved closer, lifted his hands into her own, then sat firmly down on the cluttered table. "Of course I want you to show me the town, and the mines, later."

"Later?"

"Yes, later. Today you and I have work to do. We're going to clean this office. Scrub it. Paint it. Then you're going to turn your records over to a bookkeeper—me!"

"It's no use," he answered bleakly. "I couldn't pay."

"How many people owe you for assay work?" she demanded.

"Lots of them. Maybe they'll pay me someday."

"They'll pay all right," Caroline said firmly. "Just as soon as I can get letters written and get a list of them nailed outside the office door."

Bob Herndon's eyes widened as he scratched thoughtfully at his temple. "I never could keep up with you, Caroline." He lowered himself to the bench beside her and reached out to clasp her arms and turn her toward him. "Why did you come, Caroline? I've fumbled away half-a-dozen years."

"I wanted to be here with you," she said. "I knew that even before I left Denver."

"The pigtails are gone. You're taller, older, and so lively I wish you'd never come back."

Her black curls lay against the roughness of his cheek. Then she moved from him and laughed. "Just wait till you see me with a bandana bonnet and a scrub pail this afternoon."

Lance Ainsley walked home for lunch at noon. His pace quickened as he thought of having a leisurely meal with

146

tasty dishes prepared by Mrs. Jorgenson and of having ample time to talk of many things with Caroline. He turned off Cooper Avenue onto Galena Street. In the middle of the block he stopped, his eyes widened and his chin dropped in astonishment. The weatherbeaten sign of Herndon's assay office lay propped upside-down in the yard. Bob Herndon stood midway to the street taking vicious swings at weeds with a sythe. Caroline, with sleeves rolled above her elbows, was atop an overturned powder box and busily washing windows.

Lance strode near the fence and laid his elbows on a gatepost. "When you two are through and have open house," he called out, "I'll wear a swallowtail coat. Now how about my lunch?"

Herndon flailed a thistle twenty feet into the air, then dropped the scythe beside the walk. "Take her with you," he pleaded. "She's got eyes behind her ears; she sees a weed just breaking ground if I miss it. Look at this blister." He shoved out a grimy hand for Lance's inspection.

Lance tipped his hat to a rakish angle and grinned. "Come along with me," he offered. "Mrs. Jorgenson will have something cooked that'll make you forget——"

Caroline had turned and was grinning impishly at her father as she interrupted. "Papa, you can take Bob downtown to eat. Mrs. Jorgenson is inside helping us."

"Eat downtown!" Lance shouted. "Darned if I will. Caroline, I've eaten downtown for over a year. My pants have dusted every restaurant chair in Aspen. Kitten, have a heart. Let's eat at home."

She shook her head and leaned down to swish the cleaning rag in a bucket. "Tonight we'll get supper at home, Papa, if we're through here."

Lance was silent. Finally, he said, "If you had two men here right away, how soon could you be through?"

She straightened, peering speculatively toward him. "If you'll have the two men here right away and arrange for a painter, we'll quit in time to cook a good supper at home!"

Lance pulled thoughtfully at his ear and shoved the sagging gate aside as he came into the yard. "Damn it, Bob, give me that scythe. Get over to the Clarendon Hotel. I just

147

saw Jim Daley heading that way. Tell him I said to get over here and get busy if he wants to freeload any more meals from Mrs. Jorgenson. Then look up a painter. Hell, get three painters."

On Monday morning Caroline sat down at the table in the outer room of the assay office. There were paper-filled boxes at her elbow. She knew she must work tediously and carefully if the records of Bob Herndon's business for the past years were to be put in shape. The pungent odor of acids, and a soft humming that drifted from the adjoining room, brought a smile to her face. Early as she was, Bob Herndon had gotten there before her and was already at work. She appraised the cleanliness and the newly painted glow of the room. Through an enlarged and spotless window, she studied the border of newly planted flowers.

She thought with satisfaction of other new things outside the office, a larger, gold-leafed sign; a small, glass-fronted building that had been built beside the gate. In this building they had set the mineral case in a strategic way that would catch the attention of those passing by. Near the showcase, in the little building, was a long, white paper on which already were written the names of a score of men owing Bob Herndon for work performed. After each name she had carefully printed the amount overdue, and the date upon which the work had been completed. From the boxes beside her, she would add to the list. Names would be scratched from it only when payment was received.

By ten o'clock a small but growing crowd had gathered about the white gate and were staring at the ore samples and the printed name list. Caroline surmised that word was spreading through the streets of Aspen. From a box she lifted a handful of dusty papers, studied them, and began writing a column of figures. The crowd outside grew larger. Muffled voices reached her. She bent over the table. She worked and waited.

Ten minutes later the sound of heavy footfalls mounting the steps caused her to glance up. The door swung open, and a small, elegantly dressed and dapper man entered. His face was set in a furious scowl. She recognized him as

148

a man she had met on the evening of her arrival at the Clarendon.

"Good morning, Mr. Barton," she said cheerfully.

"Yes, yes—good morning," he said impatiently. "Where's Herndon?"

Absolute quiet from the back room told Caroline that Bob Herndon had ceased work and was listening. "Do you have an appointment?" she asked quietly.

Barton stepped close to the table and squinted into her face. "I know you. You're Ainsley's daughter."

"Yes," she affirmed, "I'm Caroline Ainsley. Did you enjoy your evening at the Clarendon?"

"Of course. Nice to have you in Aspen." His answer was short and indifferently polite.

"Now about your appointment?" Caroline persisted.

Barton drew back angrily from the table. "Since when do I need an appointment to see an assayer. Young lady, I own the Apex mine."

Caroline's eyes came levelly to his face. "I know, Mr. Barton. Let's see. The Apex owes us six hundred and twenty dollars. Do you want to settle by cash or check?"

"All I want," he rasped, "is my name taken from that—that blackmail list this minute!"

"We can arrange it," she agreed. "I'll write a receipt while you make out your check for six hundred and twenty dollars."

Barton strode toward the door leading to the inner room. "I'll talk to Herndon about this. I'll nail his ears to the wall for making me a public laughingstock."

"That's your privilege," Caroline said calmly. "While you are pinning ears, I'll have time to add your name to this list to be published in *The Aspen Times*. Or perhaps you'll take time enough about it that I can run over to the courthouse and ask the sheriff to serve papers."

He wheeled about to face her. For a time his face pictured baffled rage. Then a slow and rueful grin broke across it. He dug in a vest pocket and pulled out a checkbook. "Here," he said, thrusting it toward her. "Make the damned thing out. I'll sign it." He listened silently to the scratching of her pen.

"I'll go right out and strike your name from the list,

149

Mr. Barton," she offered. "And thank you. Thank you very much. If you need more assay work done . . ."

Barton took short, determined steps toward the outside. At the door he turned. "What ever Herndon pays you," he said, "I'll double it if you want to work for the Apex."

She smiled warmly. "Thank you again, Mr. Barton. I'll keep it in mind."

Throughout the day an intermittent but growing stream of men made their way up the path. Some faced her with angry defiance or arrogance, and some wheedled slyly. Most of them, however, stated honestly that they had forgotten to pay, or that they had never received notice of the amount due, or that they believed that they had already paid. Caroline became aware that many of those entering the office were men whose names were not yet on the posted list. They had heard what was happening and wished to forestall the placing of their names for public scrutiny.

Toward evening she called Bob Herndon to her side and laid a box of checks, currency, and gold pieces in his hands.

"Count it, Bob. There's nearly three thousand dollars there. Within a week we should have things pretty well cleared up."

He glanced in wonder at the box and laid it back on the table. "You've already counted it, Caroline. You handle it. You're the banker and the business brains. I'm darned if I know how you do it." He paused, thrust a hand into his pocket, and stared down at an ore fragment scarcely an inch across.

"Take a look at this," he said.

She turned it over and over, peering at its mottled staining. "It's silver," she said slowly. "But I am no judge. Is it good?"

"Good enough to go eight hundred dollars to the ton, or better."

"I suppose," she said laughing, "it's from the Apex, the Molly Gibson, or the Smuggler."

Herndon shook his head. "Not this one. Remember that lanky chap who came in a couple of hours ago?"

"You mean Jed Curry?"

"He's the one. He brought some samples in from a claim up on Castle Creek. Wants me to run an assay on all of them."

Caroline juggled the piece of ore impatiently. "I suppose he offered to pay cash for all your work."

Herndon avoided her gaze and turned sheepishly toward the window. "Jed Curry hasn't got two bits in cash. Just the same, I'm going to run the samples. They look interesting.

"You mean," she said, "you'll spend hours, maybe days, on work for someone who can't pay?"

"Maybe someday he'll have a good mine and pay plenty."

"Sure," Caroline answered angrily. "And maybe someday the Roaring Fork will flow Scotch whiskey."

"I have to gamble on a lot of men."

When she failed to answer, he turned curiously toward her. Caroline had grabbed a sheet of paper. She wrote furiously. It was minutes before she finished, looked grimly up, and shoved the paper into his hand.

"All right then, gamble," she said. "Gamble big. But let these prospectors sweeten the pot. From now on you work on a percentage, Bob Herndon. It's all there. In writing. You do their assay work—after they sign the paper. It gives you ten percent interest in every darned claim. Maybe it's worthwhile if all the good claims haven't already been developed."

He stared at her in dismay. "They wouldn't do such a thing. Wouldn't consider it."

"Let's see," Caroline answered firmly. "They all have to get through this room, past this table, to reach your shop and see you. I'll be here every day. Just two things will get them through that door. Cash or ten percent."

Bob's response carried mingled consternation and awe. "You'd make them sign, Caroline. Surer'n hell you'd make them do it."

She rose to her feet, linking her arm through his. "Come along, my easygoing lieutenant. Tonight there's a band concert you're taking me to."

151

In the autumn of 1888 Aspen was approaching the status of a mature city. With the steady and astoundingly rich outpourings of the mines, wealth and manpower were at hand for new businesses, for expensive homes, and for a variety of civic enterprises ranging from a gaily uniformed volunteer fire department to an association dedicated to luring eminent stars of the stage and the operatic world.

It was pleasant to walk the broad and busy streets, pausing before store windows stacked with vast arrays of new and intriguing items of furniture and clothing and food. Few years had passed since it had been difficult or even impossible to buy the necessities of life.

To the north and west, a dozen streets were lengthening into well-kept and quiet residential sections, along which elaborate Victorian dwellings were secluded by fenced lawns and screening trees. These were homes designed and built for gracious living and ambitious entertaining. Silver had built them—the silver of the mines, the smelters, the railroad, the breweries, the lumber mills, and a host of booming businesses.

The magic veneer of wealth did not extend throughout Aspen. Along high, raw-slashed riverbanks bordering the mine dumps were dingy tarpaper and slab shanties where the mine laborers and their families eked out a day-to-day life of smothering poverty, and from which the gray pallor of bitterness and resentment mingled with the smoke from ugly tin chimneys. After grueling hours in a dark underground world, the miners would return here for food and rest and the scant moments of rough relaxation that would make another day's work endurable.

The town was born of adventure, founded by men with a hope and a dream that could be satisfied only by reaching for the mystic, luring promise that lay beyond distant peaks, beyond the next hill. Aspen thrived on action and excitement. The arrival of a prospector with promising "color" could start half a hundred men toward a far off mountain slope. A public event or holiday would see the streets—Main, Hyman, Durant, Dean, Hunter, Galena, Monarch—crowded with throngs spilling from the sidewalks into the dusty thoroughfares. Often three or more brass bands trekked about. Instruments caught the glow of the street lamps, and their lively melodies mingled with the murmur of the crowds.

Such was the evening on which Lance Ainsley insisted that Bob Herndon and Caroline drive his bay team to the concert being held in a grove near Hallam's Lake.

"It isn't that far," Herndon argued. "We can walk."

"Sure you can walk and be shoved smack off the sidewalk by half the town, milling down Main Street. Take the bays. They're lazy and need exercise. Just treat them with due respect."

Caroline was drawing on a pair of elbow-length gray gloves. "Of course we'll drive your bay team," she agreed and added, "Come along with us tonight, Papa. After the concert you can splurge and take us to the Clarendon for dinner."

As she spoke, she pondered the tireless, driving force that had marked her father's years in Aspen. Success had come to him. She knew that he had become a trusted and extremely well-paid associate of Tabor and Elkins. Throughout her school years money had been available for her every need. But beyond this she had no clue as to the use he had made of his income. Rumor had reached her of studied and expert gambling sessions from which he seldom emerged loser. Yet he still insisted on living in a comfortable, but unpretentious house, with no outward signs of affluence.

"Come along, Papa," she urged. "I don't want people saying, someday, that Lance Ainsley's silver all went back into the mountain in his grave. Use it now; build yourself a mansion."

Lance thrust his fists into his pockets and walked to the window. "I'll have a mansion—someday. Swope's mansion."

Even as the words escaped him, he whirled uneasily and studied his daughter's face. Her gaze remained serene and calm.

"You wouldn't live there if you had it, Papa," she said.

"I'm sorry I said that, kitten. After all these years I blab out something like that." Lance paused, toying with the sash cord. "Caroline, while you were away in Denver

153

in school, did you ever see them? Your mother? Little Shawn?"

When she answered, her voice dropped to a whisper, and the soft wistfulness of her gray eyes accentuated her smile. "I saw Shawn—once. It was in a toy shop, and I talked to him. He didn't know me." Caroline's words trailed off, unable to voice the anguish and terror with which she had left her brother before Florence Swope appeared.

"How was he? What was he like?" Lance urged quickly.

"Tall, and quite serious. With a mop of brown hair. Hair like . . ."

Lance nodded, then reached quickly for her hand and held it. "Like your mother's," he supplied.

"Yes, like hers. Papa, she has remarried. A man named Gartrell, a minister. There was an account of it in *The Rocky Mountain News.*"

"I know," Lance nodded. "Tabor sent me a clipping of it."

Caroline's arms encircled him to draw him close for a lingering kiss. "Now," she said firmly. "Are you going to the concert?"

"I can't, kitten. I've an appointment. Made it this afternoon with . . ." He paused, reading the thought behind her smile. "Damn it, no, kitten! It isn't a card game. I tell you what—why don't I meet you and Bob at the Clarendon Hotel after the concert. We'll live it up tonight. How's that?"

"I can hardly wait," she said, laughingly.

The concert, performed by a visiting Leadville band, was lively and well received. Most of the way back to town, Caroline hummed and sang the music she had heard. Bob sat quietly beside her for a time, letting the bay horses plod along. Then he, too, broke into song.

> "When I was a student at West Point,
> I played on my Spanish guitar.
> I was always a friend of the ladies,
> And I think of them now from afar."

154

Caroline listened to his words, voiced in a pleasant but off-key tenor. Presently she glanced slyly at him.

"Which one of all those ladies are you thinking of right now?" A teasing smile played about her lips. "There have been so many, in college, at Fort Steele, here in Aspen."

His answer came after he turned the team into the sheltering darkness of a cottonwood cluster and reined them to a halt. His outstretched arms pulled her to him. Then his lips were upon hers in a first, urgent kiss. Response awakened in her, and her hands tightened to draw him closer, and to prolong the ecstasy of the moment.

He tilted her chin, letting a stray gleam of moonlight play upon her face as her lips moved again toward his. "Lord, but you are beautiful," he said hungrily.

"You never told me that years ago on the train," she teased.

"I've always been slow-witted, Caroline. Besides, you were twelve years old and had pigtails. Remember?"

"I was a brat."

"Sure you were," he said. "I've an idea you still are and always will be. Now, now I'm hopelessly in love with a beautiful, mystifying, and very ambitious brat."

"But about all those others?" she asked laughing. "Those ladies you think of from afar?"

Bob Herndon reluctantly picked up the reins and urged the team ahead. "Most of those ladies are already spoken for," he said, smiling, "but perhaps tonight, down at the Clarendon Hotel, there'll be some bright-haired girl, not too discerning, that I can talk to while Caroline Ainsley mingles with Aspen's elite."

"There will be," Caroline agreed. "Tonight ... and tomorrow. I'll have to make a specialty of fending off bright-haired women." Her words were light but carried conviction as they ended. She snuggled close to him, her face eager and radiant as they drove into town.

A blaze of light marked the door of the Clarendon and the waiting figure of Lance Ainsley as they drew abreast and stopped. They walked toward him, hand in hand.

"It must have been a good concert," he said.

"It has been a wonderful evening," Caroline answered.

The glow of the lighted doorway caught the tenderness of her face.

Lance's arm moved tightly about her. "I know how it is, kitten, when you're young, and know that you've suddenly reached out to touch a star."

As they moved toward the dining room, Bob glanced self-consciously at the elaborate furnishings and the attire of people moving about. "This isn't exactly what I've been accustomed to lately." He grinned sheepishly.

Already Caroline had linked a reassuring arm through his. "It's where you belong, Mr. Herndon. You had better get used to the Clarendon. Just think of how many of the people here owe you money."

"Besides that," Lance said encouragingly, "there probably aren't half-a-dozen fellows here who didn't start out with red-flannel drawers, muddy boots, and a grubstake of flapjacks and——" His words gave way to a short, startled whistle. "I'll be a well-digger's behind," he whispered. "Look over there at the corner table. Remember him, kitten?"

Her gaze roamed the direction of his quick nod. Then she was standing still, looking toward a small and white-whiskered man seated alone and busy tucking the corner of an enormous white-linen napkin between a flowing black tie and a seamed and leathery neck.

"Why—why," she gasped, "it's Mr. Corlett—Hardrock Corlett!"

"How right you are," Lance agreed, chuckling. "I forgot to tell you. Last spring Hardrock went back up Wilderness Creek to some claims he staked before Jim Daley got moved onto your Lazy Seedy ranch. Smack along the creek he dug into a respectable vein of gold. He's not in town very often—he's no millionaire. But the old goat is sure on his way." His final words were spoken to Caroline's back, for already she was halfway across the dining room with an eager smile on her face.

"Hello, Mr. Hardrock Corlett," she said happily, and thrust her hand toward him. "Remember me?"

He was biting into a sandwich fashioned of a dozen olives between two crackers, when his bright, wrinkle-wrapped eyes peered upward to study her.

156

He shook his head. "An old man's a blasted fool to deny knowing a pretty girl. But I'm durned if——"

"Of course you know me." She laughed. "I am Caroline Ainsley. Remember? We met at Bentley's ranch. There was a bottle of rye."

Hardrock Corlett clambered to his feet, heedless of the sandwich dropping from his fingers and of olives spilled and rolling on the floor. "You mean," he asked excitedly, "you're that little pigtailed gal who thunked up them fifty-dollar homestead options?" He seized both her hands and held them in a tight grasp.

"I'm afraid I am," Caroline answered. "It's good to see you again."

"You're darned tootin' it's good." He beamed. "Sit down. Let's talk. Let's celebrate. And say, that batch of homesteads—have you seen them? The sweetest cow ranch this side——"

"I heard it's a helluva big ranch," Caroline said, laughing.

"Which ain't no lie. Sit down, gal." Hardrock was waving mightily toward a waiter.

She shook her head. "Thank you, Hardrock, but my father and a friend are with me. We have a table reserved. Why don't you join us? We can talk over old times."

"It's a good idea," he said, "except that I'm waiting ... waiting for my wife."

Lance stepped to the table and grasped Hardrock's hand. At the old man's words, his jaw dropped in surprise. "Why you old cuss," he said. "Did you say *wife?*"

Hardrock's eyes twinkled. "That's exactly what I said. My wife, she'll be here in a minute or so." He was momentarily silent, studying Herndon.

"Ain't you that assayer chap?"

"Sure, Mr. Corlett. I'm Bob Herndon."

The old man pumped Bob's hand and glanced quizzically toward him. "If my name's on that scandal list I hear you've nailed up——"

"It isn't," Caroline assured him quickly.

"Well, it should be. This youngster ran everything from calcite to fool's gold for me back in '81 and '82. Send me a bill, Herndon."

Muffled footsteps and a soft rustle came suddenly to Caroline's ears. She glanced up in time to see Bob stiffen. His face became strained and pale in the subdued light. She swung slightly about to look squarely at the blonde, beautifully clad woman who had approached and was standing in frozen silence at her elbow. Above the neckline of an exquisite blue dress was a face that caused Caroline's eyes to widen. The last time she saw the face it was twisted by snarling anger and drenched with amber filth—the face of Ellen Bradley!

Hardrock Corlett's arm swept out to encircle the girl's waist. "Folks," he said proudly, "I want all of you to meet my wife, Ellen."

Lance recovered first and executed a sweeping bow. "Wonderful ... wonderful," he breathed. "Congratulations. Hardrock, you lucky duffer, when did this happen?"

"Yesterday. Just yesterday," Hardrock Corlett roared happily.

In that awkwardly tense moment, Caroline heard Bob's mumbled acknowledgment. His face reddened and his gaze darted about the room seeking means of escape. She was sure that only her restraining hand upon his arm held him from blindly confused retreat.

Hardrock's unsuspecting words gave Caroline precious seconds in which to gather her wits.

"Imagine all us old-timers together," he was saying. "We're some of the first blasted idiots to catch Aspen fever. Pull up them chairs and get comfortable. I reckon we've got a lot to gab about."

Caroline's gaze moved quickly up from Ellen's button shoes of light-blue, dressed kid to a flawless dress of dark-blue serge in basque style with pointed back and front. She noted it was trimmed with light-blue bone buttons and piping of the same hue. An exquisite full gathered shirt with a small train was looped up with a light-blue cord. Ellen's hair, worn in bangs, was cut straight and smooth, gathered in a French roll at the back of her head. Upon it sat a jaunty, blue pancake hat covered with pastel-shaded flowers. At this moment, everything about this blonde girl—except her face—was lovely.

Her lips accented a cold and unrelenting face and were

twisted into scorn and anger. Her eyes narrowed as she slid possessively into a chair beside her husband.

Caroline managed to appear calm and increasingly serene as she said, "Ellen, I wish I could sew as beautifully as you do. That is about the loveliest dress I've ever seen."

Ellen's reply was a momentary and venomous stare that ended with a dismissing shrug as she turned to Hardrock.

"Tell these people to get the hell out of here," she demanded furiously.

Hardrock Corlett's whiskers bristled to a white and out-thrust plume as his head snapped backwards. "What?" he roared. "Are you daffy, Ellen? They're friends—all of them." His baffled eyes swept from face to face. "What's this about?" he pleaded. "What is wrong?"

Lance reached across the table and grasped the old prospector's hand. "Just a little mix up ... a misunderstanding, Hardrock. But we really must move along. Nice to see both of you."

Hardrock held fast to Lance's hand. "This ain't right, Mr. Ainsley. I wanted to tell you about my diggings up on Wilderness."

"I've heard they are good. I'm glad, Hardrock."

"Durned tootin' they're good. I'm taking me a partner, Matt Shaner. Watch things hum."

At his words, a quick frown gathered on Lance's forehead. "Have you signed any papers with Matt Shaner?" he asked.

Hardrock's answer was drowned in an abrupt torrent of angry words voiced by Ellen, who propped her elbows on the table and waved a hand to display a flashing ruby. "It ain't none of your business what my husband does. Like I always say, people with class sure get fawned up to. Mr. Shaner is different. He's a real gentleman with real money."

Bob Herndon had turned from the group, edged a dozen steps away to study a potted geranium.

Lance listened in silence to the woman's tirade, then ignored her as he spoke with finality to Hardrock. "There's a few things you should know about Shaner. Look me up, Hardrock." He bowed and walked away from the table.

Caroline stood quietly, listening. Now, as she turned,

her gloved hand laid for a moment on Hardrock Corlett's shoulder. "The best of everything, old friend," she murmured, then added, as her eyes moved to Ellen with slow and bland scrutiny. "My dear, I do believe your hair should be dampened quite often."

As she moved to rejoin Lance and Bob, she heard Hardrock's puzzled and incredulous words.

"What in tarnation did the little gal mean by that?"

Ellen's hate-ridden reply came also to her ears. "Little gal my ass—the dirty slut."

When the seclusion of their own table and the excellence of the pale sherry had dulled the vividness of the encounter, Caroline turned a serious and studied face to Lance.

"Papa, you mentioned Matt Shaner. You almost warned Hardrock against him. Wasn't he the man who met us at the tent restaurant and took you to the office that first night here in Aspen?"

"The same fellow." Lance nodded. He was silent as his fingers searched the thin crystal of his glass. Finally, he said, "Matt Shaner represented H. A. W. Tabor and his partner Elkins before they sent me here. I had to fire Shaner that first year."

"I didn't like him the first night," Caroline confessed.

"I knew that, kitten. You don't let a capable man go just because your daughter doesn't like him, or because he rubs you the wrong way. Matt Shaner is efficient. He can work the devil out of men and make them like it. He's got a personality that attracts people to him, even though it's mostly the wrong kind of people. It took me months to find out Shaner had about the smoothest operating crew of high-graders and claim-jumpers west of Denver. But his brother's the one who bears watching."

Bob Herndon leaned forward. Interest kindled across his face. "I've heard of Len Shaner, but I've never met him."

Lance spoke in a low and guarded voice. "You're not apt to meet him. He makes it a point to keep out of Aspen. Matt fronts things here. Likely I wouldn't have know either, except that Doc Holliday——"

Caroline sat bolt upright. Her face was curious and questioning. "You mean *the* Doc Holliday. You've met that . . . that——"

Lance grinned wryly. "I've sure been rattling off. Keep what I have said under your hat. The Doc is a gambler; I've known him a long while. Once in a while he and Wyatt Earp drift into town for a few days or a few weeks. Len Shaner used to have some deals working down around Tombstone, Arizona. Holliday and Earp were there." Lance became silent. His manner warned them he would say no more.

Each seemed immersed in private thoughts born of the evening's events. The dinner might have ended in silence had not Caroline seen someone and spoken with sudden excitement.

"Uncle Jim Daley just came in. I saw him. He's got on a black-wool shirt and muddy boots."

Lance rose. "I'll bring him in." He surveyed the table. "Not much left here to eat. Order a rare steak; that's what he'll want. He'll have time to wash up while they fix it." He walked swiftly toward the lobby. His head was carefully turned from the table occupied by Hardrock Corlett and his bride.

Bob's fingers sought out and laced Caroline's. "Now I can say it," he whispered. "I love Caroline Ainsley."

Her answering smile was tender, and touched with memory of the homeward ride. "I'm glad, my shy lieutenant. It took you an awfully long time to tell me."

He glanced furtively toward Ellen Corlett, paused to grasp for words, then said, "Caroline, about that . . . that day at Ellen's cabin. I've never been able to tell you . . ."

"I never want you to," she interrupted with soft firmness. "I was a little girl, dreadfully jealous and hateful. You were already a grown man in a town where there were very few women. There are such women, such houses, such streets in every town. Perhaps for lonesome men life wouldn't be endurable otherwise." She smiled, then finished with brightening words. "It's all of a dim past, Bob. We've today and tomorrow to think of. Please, let's never mention it again."

He gazed at her for a moment of awed wonder, then

blew a subtle kiss across the table. "I'll never be as wise, Caroline."

Minutes later Jim Daley's voice boomed across the dining room and caused her to glance up, smile, and call out, "Howdy partner." She noted that Hardrock Corlett reluctantly was getting up from his table at the urging of his bride. Ellen's gestures attempted to be disdainfully haughty. Her steps toward the outer door, as she clutched Hardrock's arm, were the same short and hip-swaying ones with which Caroline had once watched her walk down a plank sidewalk of pioneer Aspen.

Before they disappeared, Hardrock Corlett turned. His glimpse toward Caroline and those gathered about her was troubled and wistful.

Jim Daley slid into a chair that Lance held for him. The manner of his squatting brought resurgent memories to Caroline. For an instant she wondered if the old cowman might ignore the seat and hunker down on the luxurious carpet to begin tracing endless circles.

"Looks like I'm late for a celebration," Daley said.

Caroline laughed aloud. "Just when did you ever miss a celebration, Uncle Jim? Remember those trips you used to make to Evans? Business. Just business, you told me. Ha!"

Daley squinted at her. A slow grin worked along the leathery seams of his face. "It's one hell of a note, having a snoopy partner to check up on me." He covered her hand with a darkened fist, then added, "But it sure is business this time."

"Is something wrong at the Lazy Seedy, Uncle Jim?"

"Nope—and yes. I'm taking you back with me this trip. Maybe you can round up and lasso figures and records for the last five or six years. Me, I've always counted critters and asked the bank how I stand come freeze-up. It won't work on the Wilderness spread. The ranch is getting too big. We need a pencil pusher to make sense out of it. You're elected so pack your gear."

Caroline read the dismay in Herndon's face. "Whoa up, Uncle Jim. I'm helping Bob with records and figures at his assay office. I could do yours there, too."

Jim Daley scratched fork-formed circles on the snowy

162

damask of the tablecloth. He avoided her gaze, but she knew that an expectant hope was leaving his face.

Finally he said, "So I'll just tell your old black mare you ain't coming."

She reached out and took the restlessly moving fork from his hand; the ᴜD she drew on the linen would bring a scowl from the waiter. "Sure I'm going to the ranch, Jim Daley. It's the Lazy Seedy. We're partners. It's time I do my share. I'll come down on the train Tuesday and stay a week at the ranch. I'll spend alternate weeks here and there all winter."

Daley was suddenly eager and confident. "Damn it all, Lance," he growled. "Why ain't H. A. W. Tabor in town? Right now I could win me his Matchless mine up at Leadville."

Chapter 8

The mellow sunshine of late October lay across Wilderness Valley when the train arrived at Caroline Station three days later. Caroline had guessed in what way Jim Daley would meet her. She put on clothing that allowed her to swing astride a horse. As she stepped to the gravel in front of the tiny depot, Daley was afoot and waiting. His rangy, piebald roan was frightened. He danced alongside a black mare that belied her age with wary and trembling snorts. Caroline seized the reins and quickly led her horse away from the noise and dust. Then her arms encircled the old mare's neck, and her cheek pressed to the soft sheen of the animal's withers.

Jim Daley waited a long time before joining her. Caroline Ainsley was crying softly, happily.

She could only guess how many miles they rode that day through hay-stacked meadows, groves of golden-tinted

163

aspen trees, and through the darker corridors of the high forest. They ate lunch in a peak-encircled park. Half-a-dozen men had gathered an uneasy, bawling herd of cattle and were preparing to drive them to the meadows of Wilderness Creek.

"We summer up here in the forest," Daley explained. "It's time now to get all cattle down into the valley. Snows are due; they come hip-high to a tall Indian up here, and then keep coming."

They returned to the ranch house as night and a biting chill came quickly. The low, rambling log cabin was a man's domain. Stone fireplaces threw a warm glow across the rooms. Furnishings were scanty and entirely practical. Bits of ranch gear, racked rifles, and rugs fashioned from the pelts of mountain animals were strewn about.

In the long living room that faced the Roaring Fork Valley, Caroline spotted a chair and sank contentedly into it. "I remember this chair, Uncle Jim. The cowhide, the aspen legs. I cuddled in it the first night I ever saw Wilderness Creek."

She was quiet for a long while. Jim Daley had backed up to the fireplace, and was rubbing his hands briskly behind him.

"Uncle Jim," she said suddenly. "Get married. You need a wife."

He glanced quickly toward her. "Can't do it, Caroline. I'm too old for you."

"Good Lord," she gasped. "I ... I wasn't proposing." She blushed, then laughed gaily. "Just the same, this room, this house, and this ranch needs a woman's hands. So do you."

"I'll give it some thought," he said, grinning. "Right now the cook should have some supper ready. Let's find out."

The remainder of the week Caroline divided her time between exploring and studying the vastness of the ranch. Many hours were needed to unravel and sum up the facts and figures born of its growth and its yearly routine.

On the last afternoon Caroline sat in the cowhide chair. A table was pulled in front of her. Papers were scattered about. Storm clouds rode the valley, and an occasional gust of wind threw snowflakes against the window. She piled another log on the fire as Jim Daley tramped into the room and threw off a sheepskin coat. "We're lucky to have the herd down out of the forest; there may be a heavy storm moving in."

Caroline peered from the window. She was satisfied with her count of fenced hay stacks. "You won't have to worry about winter feed like you used to do over on the Platte."

Daley smiled. "We've probably got plenty. Likely this snow will melt off and the herd can graze the bottom land and the meadows for weeks. Spring thaw's a long time off." He turned a chair toward her, sprawled, and said, "How are the figures coming? Getting anywhere?"

She pulled a record book toward her. "Far enough to know that the management of this ranch has been a helluva lot better than the bookkeeping." She handed the book to him. "There's lots of details to work out, but this is how it looks year by year since you moved here."

Daley studied the book with a satisfied grin. "Now, partner," he said finally, "how much profit do you calculate we show to date?"

The figure she named brought a quick nod. "Not too far from what I figured, pocket to pocket. Half of it's yours, Caroline. I'll write you a check."

"You'll do nothing of the kind, Uncle Jim. You put up all the money, furnished the stock, did the work. I was away at school. Thank you, but no!"

His chin jutted stubbornly as he rose and pawed a table drawer. "We made a deal—remember? We're fifty-fifty partners on a ranch you connived to put together for us. Now where in tarnation is a pen?"

Caroline slammed the book firmly. "Now you listen to me, Jim Daley. I'm your partner. I have a say-so coming. This ranch needs quite a few things. Maybe you didn't notice, but the profit isn't as good now as it was a couple of years ago. I think I know why."

He hunkered to the old familiar squat. "I noticed it at shipping time. Didn't need a book for that. What's your idea about it?"

"I'll need to prove what I suspect by going through a lot of figures," she replied. An increasing pattern of snow flashed past the window. A distracting and tantalizing thought had flashed through her mind. It was far removed from ranches and cattle and bank balances. *I'll be back in Aspen tomorrow, at the assay office. Bob will be close by. His arms. His kiss.*

She bit into a pencil and forced her thoughts to the reality of the moment.

"Uncle Jim, we need better cattle. Better breeding stock. There's farm-animal competition now when you ship to Denver or, even here, in the valley. We need some good beef-type herd bulls."

Daley studied her approvingly. "Find out the best we can buy for this part of the country. Where we can get them. How soon."

She rose and pulled him to the window. "These meadows can produce endless tons of better beef. Right now I want my share of what we've made plowed back into the ranch into building the best herd on the Western Slope."

"Caroline," he said slowly, "it beats hell out of me, the way you look ahead and figure. Maybe I ought to marry you—or adopt you."

The winter of 1888 and 1889 sped swiftly by for Caroline. The work of both the ranch and the assay office had to be done. She discovered, too, the pitiful need of many of the shack-housed families along the river bluff. For them, the storms and cold meant a time of added misery and sickness. Her visits to shacktown became almost a daily occurrence when she was not away at the ranch.

She acquired great respect for the miners and their families. Friendships were forged slowly. These were people with little but scorn for do-gooders and for those who offered aid in the unconcerned manner of professional charity. She sensed quickly that hours spent with an ailing child, helping parents to work out a household need, or just sitting and talking often filled a greater need than could be supplied by baskets of groceries and clothing. Often she would return home with an embroidered scarf or a

166

hand-carved animal on which countless hours had been spent in wordless gratitude.

Her good-natured, hopeful attitude proved contagious. She became adroit in learning the pressing problems of the families and then finding means by which they could iron out their troubles.

Most of these people were fun-loving and eager to gather for a few minutes or an evening of music and food and laughter. That winter, among miners from a dozen European backgrounds, Caroline tasted more liquors than she had dreamed the human mind and homemade stills could concoct.

It was not hard for her to appear happy that winter. She was eagerly and utterly in love with Bob Herndon. By unfathomable instinct, the women of shacktown knew this even before full realization was upon Caroline herself. They acknowledged their awareness only with soft smiles when she was among them, but they gathered and talked of it with excited expectation when a door closed behind her.

In late April, when the Roaring Fork surged with weary resentment at its icy sheathing and crocuses lifted timid sprouts sunward, Caroline walked swiftly from a dry-goods store and headed for the assay office. She carried a bundle of yard goods and accessories for two spring dresses. For a moment she wished there was some way she could have Ellen Corlett make these for her, but she gave up the idea in a hurry. Ellen had become the mistress of a two-story, dormered house, gave lavish parties, and bought clothes only in Denver.

Caroline burst through the door of the office and hurried to tell Bob of a tweed suit he should buy. Inside, she stopped short, the eagerness of her face giving way to a masking and impersonal smile as she looked toward the tall and lanky man who was seated on her desk. A mud-stained boot lay across her most prized ledger.

Bob Herndon was sitting in a chair tilted against the wall, and was saying, "I'd like to take you up on the deal, Jed. Could be it's the best chance either of us ever had. But the money angle lets me out. It would take——"

Caroline's eyes flashed angrily. "It'll take just one min-

167

ute for me to bounce both of you out of here if those dirty boots ruin my book."

She slammed her package down on the desk and eyed Jed Curry as she said, "It's too much, I suppose, to hope you are here to pay part of your bill."

Bob's face flushed as he straightened his chair. "That's part of what we were talking about, Caroline," he said uneasily. "Jed has been telling me—darn it, Jed, maybe you better explain."

Curry thrust a folded paper toward her. His words came in a slow, unhurried drawl. "That paper is Bob's analysis of another batch of samples from my claims up Castle Creek. Look for yourself what it shows."

As Caroline studied the report, her eyes widened. A minute later she turned to Bob. "Are you sure these values are correct? It's, it's astounding."

"Sure they're correct," Bob affirmed. "I checked and then rechecked all samples. They are consistently high."

She handed the paper back to Jed Curry. "You surely are to be congratulated, Jed," she said, then added firmly, "It won't take much production of that grade ore to pay Bob what you owe him."

"That's the hitch in it," Curry said dolefully. "Production up there will mean putting up a heavy investment. There'll be one god-awful water problem to contend with. I ain't got the kind of money it will take to get underway."

"How much money?" Caroline asked. She sat down and began drawing aimless pencil marks on her wrapped package.

Bob Herndon drew his chair close to the desk. When he spoke, there was certainty and authority in his voice that caught and held her attention. "I figured all this out for Jed. Pumps will be the big expense. They have good used ones in Denver that can be picked up. I checked with Mine and Smelter Supply, then figured every angle. Seventy-five thousand dollars will put his mine in production."

Caroline wrote rapid figures. "A couple of good shipments would pay that much off. Jed, with clear title to the claims, and with these assay reports, you shouldn't have trouble raising that much money."

Curry shook his head. "Not without signing away better than half interest. The money lenders want control."

There was a long silence. Bob Herndon uttered words of bitter frustration. "Jed has offered me a fifty-fifty partnership if I can come up with the money. Fat chance I've got of doing it." He rose and stared out the window. "Me and my fumbled years. The brilliant rock hound who was going to have Aspen at his feet. Damn it! Double damn it!" He was white-faced as he turned and shuffled stiff-legged past them and out to the street.

Jed Curry rose, grinned ruefully, and started to leave. Caroline waved him back to his chair. "Jed, how long has Bob been working on this?"

"Nigh onto a year."

"It means a lot to him, doesn't it?"

"Sure." Curry nodded. "To both of us. It's the only real break either of us have had, or likely will have."

Caroline's hands tightened on the desk. As she spoke, her words seemed strange to her, laden with reckless audacity.

"Jed, if I raise the money ... the full seventy-five thousand dollars ... will you give Bob twenty-five percent—and me twenty-six percent?"

Curry scratched thoughtfully at his chin. His eyes grew dark, level, and sharply appraising. "I'd be signing away control," he answered.

She nodded, then asked calmly, "Hasn't Bob always played square with you?"

"Sure, and all-fired patient about the money I owe him." Curry rose and paced about the room. "Herndon's the best friend I've got."

She studied him closely, then said, "But you don't know about me."

He faced her, waited a bit, then stretched and grinned. "Nothing except you are Lance Ainsley's daughter, that you're prettier than a clump of columbine, and that Bob is head over heels in love with you."

"Thank you, Jed." She smiled, then said, persisting, "You know my father. Have you had cause to doubt an Ainsley's word—or honesty?"

"Hell, no!" Curry sat abruptly down on the corner of

169

her desk and folded his arms. "Sorry about shoving my muddy boots onto your book, Miss Ainsley. If you want the twenty-five and twenty-six percent—it's a deal."

Caroline laid her hand in the one he had thrust out. "Jed, come back a week from today, around noon. Be sure and bring all of your papers. And . . . and one other thing, Jed. Look Bob up right away and send him back here. Don't tell him. Let me."

"Sure thing, partner."

When the sound of his footsteps had faded, she sat very straight and very silent. *What have I done? Seventy-five thousand dollars. Is there that much money in the world?* But even with these unspoken thoughts, she knew, deep within her, the course she must follow.

Her pencil had not ceased its idle tracings when Bob came slowly through the door, and she looked into the abandoned hopelessness of his face.

"Come here," she said softly, and reached out to grasp his sleeve and pull him to the desk beside her. Suddenly her arms were about his head and her fingers moved gently through his curly, flaming hair. Her lips touched his ear. "I love you so much, you big lug. Listen. Go down to Bowles's store. Right this minute. There's a tweed suit there, just right for you. Buy it. Then get back here so I can show you the goods I picked out for my new spring dresses. We'll be all dressed up next week—when we sign the papers as Jed Curry's partners and start our mine."

Two days later she sat in the cowhide chair in the living room at Lazy Seedy ranch. In glorious warm sunshine she had dropped from the morning train at Caroline Station and walked the path along Wilderness Creek to the ranch house. For once, she had tried not to see these mountain meadows where young calves were wobbling uncertainly about. Nor had she wanted to hear the merry chatter of the ice-free creek.

Jim Daley stood before her and studied her pale but determined face.

"What's wrong, gal?" he asked worriedly. "I didn't expect you down this week."

She clutched a wilted and sweat-stained handkerchief in her palms.

"Uncle Jim," she said quickly, "how much is our Lazy Seedy ranch worth?"

He shot her a penetrating stare. "Why, Caroline?" he demanded.

Her eyes were tear-dimmed, but level upon him. "I need seventy-five thousand dollars—this week. Is my part worth anything near that?"

A startled whistle escaped him. Then he strode to her side, drawing her against him with an encircling arm. "Sure it's worth that ... maybe a lot more."

She pressed the handkerchief against trembling lips. "Uncle Jim, would you buy me out, pay me that much?"

He shook his head. "Of course not, little gal. We've been partners since '81. Partners we stay. If you need the money, likely I can raise it and loan it to you. Or we could borrow against the ranch."

She drew his rough hand upward and rubbed it against her cheek. "Thank you, Uncle Jim. But I won't borrow from you or let you mortgage the ranch. I want to sell. Buy me out."

He hunkered slowly to the rug and studied the bleakness of her face. "Can't you tell me why you need all this money?"

She dropped to her knees beside him. "Of course I'll tell you. It's to open a mine, a wonderful one, for Bob Herndon and myself."

Daley smoothed her black hair, then turned her face toward him and studied it gravely. "You must love him very, very much, Caroline."

For the first time, she smiled, a gentle, mystifying smile. "I do, Uncle Jim, I do. And he's worked so hard on this mining proposition. Just now it is about his life, his whole future."

The cowman used a forefinger to trace circles on the rug. "I don't know much about mines or ores or even rocks. A rock's just something to grab up and fling at a cantankerous steer or a porcupine. Caroline, have you talked this over with your dad? Lance knows the mining game upside-down."

"No," she answered. "This is something we want to do on our own. We'll tell him when we're sure it's going to pan out."

Jim Daley looked deeply into the eagerness dawning in her eyes. "Of course it'll work out. You have a way of making things work out. Now forget this foolishness about selling out. I'll loan you the money, or . . . or damn it, give it to you as a wedding present."

Caroline rose to her feet. "What a wonderful thing you've said." Her chin jutted stubbornly as seconds ticked by. "I'll take the money only if you accept a bill of sale for my interest in the ranch. You must agree to keep it. Maybe someday I'll want it back."

"I've an idea you will," he answered slowly. "All right. Make out the bill of sale. Then fix up some drafts on my Denver bank for me to sign. Right now I'm gonna pour us a shot of whiskey to drink to the best doggoned mine in Colorado. What are you naming the diggings?"

"I don't know yet." She smiled. "Why don't you name it—for luck?"

He stared across the meadow awhile, then turned to her. "Call it the Buccaneer, Caroline. There's a bit of pirate in every mining man I ever met up with."

It was mid-summer of 1889 before Caroline saw the Buccaneer mine. Once before she had been up the narrow and swiftly ascending valley of Castle Creek. She knew that this way led into an almost impenetrable peak-guarded solitude, and that somewhere high on Castle Creek was the small but busy mining camp of Ashcroft. Beyond this lay a high-thrust never-summer land from which the waters of the Gunnison river flowed southward.

There had been a thousand details to keep her desk-bound and busy. Equipment and supplies flowed from Aspen and Denver suppliers. She had never seen Bob as busy or as happy. Despite long hours at the mine site, endless trips by horseback and freight wagon to and from Aspen, and night hours given to blueprints and details of paper work, there was a jauntiness and a determined capability about him that caused her to smile proudly. Even his off-key whistling carried assurance these days. Bob Herndon had become a man who knew exactly what was to be done and how to do it.

She saw little of Jed Curry during those weeks. He, too, was busy. She knew that a shaft dropped inch by inch toward the vein of silver-bearing ore from an outcropping of which had come the samples that their activity and their hopes were founded upon.

In the quiet of a morning of early August, she walked to the assay office while the sun had scarcely lifted above Independence Pass. She noted with surprise that two saddled horses were tied close beside the gate and the little white building housing the mineral specimens.

In the office, Bob greeted her with secretive smile. "You can go right back home and change your clothes," he said.

She glanced quickly down at the neatly pressed, orange-tinted dress she was wearing. "Why?" she demanded. "Mrs. Jorgenson spent half an hour getting this dress ready for me."

His gaze swept her with a hint of pent-up hunger. "It's lovely, Caroline, but hardly suitable for a long ride up Castle Creek."

"You mean—today we're——" She caught her breath in excitement.

"Today it is," he nodded. "The construction phase is over and the Buccaneer starts breaking ore. You'll have to be there to officiate and maybe to break a bottle of snow juice on the portal."

She clasped her hands behind his neck and noted the healthy and confident glow of his face.

"I'm proud of you, Bob. You have worked wonders, getting the mine open in so short a time. And saving money too; we still have several thousand——"

"We'll need it. Opening day isn't payday. There will be expenses."

She placed an unabashed kiss on his lips. "Of course we will, and we'll meet them."

Bob grasped her shoulders and held her at arm's length as a quizzical smile marked his face. "Caroline, I've never asked before, but how did you manage to pry all that money out of your father to get our Buccaneer set up? Lance Ainsley sure isn't noted for shelling out cash."

Her gray eyes were steady but veiled for moments of silence. *He mustn't know where it came from. Not yet. Not until we make good.* She forced a lurking, knowing smile to her lips. She was aware that it must block her thoughts of a sold and relinquished Lazy Seedy, of broad meadowlands and grazing herds now owned only by Jim Daley. "Perhaps someday I'll tell you, my dear. My father is a remarkable man, you know."

He pulled her to him again. "He's got a remarkably adorable daughter. Now skeedadle and get into a riding outfit. We've quite a trip ahead."

Caroline paused beside clear pools where trout lazed with snouts thrust upstream and where beaver slapped indignant tails at her intrusion. There were waterfalls, formed by small creeks plunging white and misty to join Castle Creek. The hum of crickets mingled with the songs of birds and the excited chattering of squirrels.

An hour later they turned suddenly into a small box canyon, edging through a narrow rock gateway by means of a wagon trail blasted out a hundred yards toward the Buccaneer.

She was disappointed. There was only a large, slab-sided shanty, a steep-sloped mine dump topped by narrow-spaced rails and a few battered ore cars, and the blackly yawning portal of a horizontal tunnel that was scarcely high enough for a man to enter erect. Only a column of black smoke, lifting from the shack, spoke of habitation.

They tied their horses to a tree, and she looked about with a worried frown. "There surely isn't much going on," she said.

"Oh, isn't there?" Bob beamed happily. "Wait until we get inside. You don't find ore under a blue sky or alongside a trout pool. Come with me."

Inside the shack, already marked by the odor of muddy and sweated clothing, he helped her put on a protective cap and lighted the carbide lamp it held. "You'll need this inside," he explained. "Likely we'll find Jed waiting at the hoist room or tending the pumps."

"I thought the pumps would be out here."

"Only the boiler. The pumps are operated by steam. We

174

pipe the steam in and the water out—a devil of a lot of water."

He led her through the portal, cautioning her to walk carefully along the small ties and rails leading into utter darkness.

"If you hear a clatter, flatten against the wall," he warned. "It will be someone pushing a muck car out to the dump."

It seemed that she had walked and stumbled a mile, though reason told her it was probably less than a hundred steps, when they came into a room carved smoothly from black rock. It was dimly lighted, and she could look about. Here, the din and whine of steam pumps was a deafening thing. She leaned close to Bob as he shouted to her.

"Watch your step. Hang onto me. The hoist is right ahead ... set over a shaft that drops eighty feet."

"Exactly eighty-one and a half feet." The words were spoken by Jed Curry, as he loomed from behind a pump. "Welcome to the Buccaneer, Miss Ainsley. Want to go down? You'll have to ride a bucket."

Caroline shook her head reluctantly. "I want to. But I know better. Most miners consider a woman bad luck where they're working."

Curry nodded. "It's sort of silly, but true."

"Just show me the pumps and how they work," Caroline said. "They fascinate me. Do they run all the time?"

"Every minute. Night and day." Curry pointed to a large pipe leading toward the portal. "This is the discharge line—a two-inch one. We may have to go to a four- or six-inch one. The better the ore promises below, the more water we fight. Sometimes I think Castle Creek starts along our stope."

Bob Herndon pulled a nickel-plated watch from his pocket. "Jed, have the men come up at noon. I brought up a case of beer and two bottles of brandy. Caroline can meet the crew and christen the shebang out by the portal."

"I'll set down a tub to salvage the brandy," Curry said.

The westering sun dropped beyond mountain crests as they began their homeward ride. The narrow valley was bathed in a mellow and golden afterglow through which

175

small sounds came with startling clearness. Even the splash of a feeding trout or the evening call of a thrush seemed deceivingly near. They were content to ride slowly, their horses side by side, and their fingers entwined with unspoken happiness.

In gathering twilight they passed through a narrow gorge when Bob veered his horse abruptly aside toward the screening laurel thicket. "Come along," he said. "Follow me. There's something I want you to see. Bend over, so those branches won't lash your face."

Seconds later they had penetrated the brush then broken into the open along a small tributary stream whose waters had slowed to form a large, placid, and incredibly clear pool. At their feet was a semicircle of level and heavily grassed ground leading to a narrow, sanded shore.

Bob grinned and pointed across the tiny stream to a high vermilion cliff from which a small waterfall cascaded to the pool.

"Like it?" he asked.

Caroline slid from her horse and knelt in the white sand. "It's the loveliest spot I've ever seen. So quiet. So peaceful."

"It's the best swimming hole, too. I stop here often. There must be a hot spring underground that keeps this pool warm. The main flow of Castle Creek is too cold even to risk dabbling a big toe. It's different here ... makes me always feel like plunging in, swimming, then just soaking and resting."

Caroline turned a mischievous smile toward him. "Are you daring me to do it—to go swimming?" she asked.

His face reddened, but his eyes held calmly on her. "I hadn't thought of that. But you would love it. There's a couple of sacks in my saddlebag that'll pass for towels. I'll wait beyond the thicket, where you can call to me. Just don't be too long. Night comes on fast up here." He knotted the bridle reins, then disappeared into the green foliage.

Caroline removed her clothing, folded the garments, and laid them upon the sand. She stood for a few moments, erect and eager, letting the last glow of evening play over her lithe, bronzed body. Already a slight chill

176

rode the air, and made the water seem warm and welcome. She waded in, threw herself forward, and splashed toward the opposite shore of the pool.

Minutes passed. Reluctantly she crawled onto the clean sand, rubbed down with the coarse muslin, and dressed. She was attempting to bring damp orderliness to her long, unruly hair when she called aloud, and Bob came to her side. Throughout her was a tingling and refreshed excitement that shone in her face and enlivened her eyes.

"Your pool is wonderful. Thank you, Bob."

He lowered himself to the little beach beside her, watching the deftness of her fingers as she bound her hair. "I'm glad you like it, Caroline. It's my favorite spot." He paused, then added with a slow smile, "I didn't peek—not even once."

She paused, cupping her chin in her palm. "I knew you wouldn't. But would it have mattered? All of us have bodies. Is there anything so indecent or immoral about them that they should be seen only when clothed?"

He grasped her hand and laid a softly lingering kiss on her wrist. "You have so much honesty, Caroline. Vast, clean-minded honesty. I've nothing to offer. But I love you, love you beyond words—and need you. Perhaps ... perhaps someday——"

She leaned forward, encircling him with one arm, then laying a silencing finger on his lips. "Someday isn't soon enough, my dearest. A long time ago, at Fort Steele, I vowed to marry you someday. Ask me ... ask me now, Bob." Her words broke off breathlessly as he drew her hard against him and his lips found her cheek, her forehead, and the eagerness of her mouth.

Moments later he reached out and broke the thin stem of a wildflower. Quickly he fashioned it into a small, tightly woven circle. Then he slipped it onto her finger and lifted it to his cheek. "It's not much, but maybe it will last until we can get into town—to a jeweler. It says one thing: Caroline Ainsley belongs to me. My god, how lucky can one man be?"

If there was an answer to his question, it was written across a softly darkening sky by the one star that was reflected in the pool, unnoticed as they came again to each

177

other's arms and the enchanting promise of days to come.

After a time, Bob gazed wistfully at her. "We can be married in the fall. By then the Buccaneer should——"

"It's a long time to wait, dearest."

"I know. But my two-room assay office wouldn't make the kind of home I want for you. It's old and small and dilapidated. Maybe that rotten threshold would cave in as I carried you across it."

"I'm not marrying a house," Caroline answered calmly.

Herndon looked proudly at her. "Let's set the date now, Caroline. How about one week after our first ore shipment. I'll work like the devil . . . night and day."

They rose, and her fingers were gentle upon his face as he aided her to the saddle. "I've got work ahead, too. I'm not fast at sewing. Not like——" She bit her tongue suddenly, and was glad that mention of Ellen Corlett's magic with a needle had not escaped her lips.

They rode slowly through the night, heedless of time or of the lights of Aspen that finally twinkled before them.

It was late when she turned from a final embrace and walked onto the porch of her home. A light still burned inside, and she noted it with anxiety. The shiver of expectant fear disappeared as she entered and saw Lance seated alone.

"Why up so late?" she asked, and bent to kiss his cheek. "It's an hour past your bedtime."

He pulled her onto his knee, then sniffed the dampness of her hair. "You fell in the creek, eh?"

"I went swimming—in a glorious pool up Castle Creek. You won't believe it, Papa, but the water was warm and grand."

"I know the place," he said, nodding, then added, "I suppose you've been sightseeing up at your Buccaneer mine?"

Caroline dropped to her knees, and rested her folded arms on his knees. "They're getting into good ore already." She paused and turned a glowing face upward. "Papa, Bob and I are going to be married when we ship the first ore." She lifted her hand, showing the woven stem around the third finger of her tightly clutched hand. "See." She laughed. "I've got a ring—an engagement ring."

178

Lance lifted her hand and studied the circle of flower stem. Then he tilted her chin and stroked the halo of her hair. "It's a jim-dandy ring, kitten. I've an idea it will always mean more than any gold one that replaces it. Take care of it. Always."

There was a long quiet in the room, broken only by the ticking of a clock. Lance Ainsley seemed strangely unsure of himself, as though choosing and discarding words. Finally, he said, "I waited up to tell you a couple of things. First, you have a visitor . . . came in on the evening train. Eric Duane—from Denver. He's over at the hotel." Lance searched her face anxiously. "You will see him, won't you, kitten?"

"Of course I'll see Eric. He's a good friend."

"And in love with you, kitten."

"I know." She nodded. "Papa, I'll be honest with him . . . tell him that Bob and me are going to be married."

"Of course you will. Be gentle about it, honey. I like Duane. He and I seem to hit it off together." Lance kissed her forehead, then went on quickly. "But damn it, kitten, I like Bob Herndon, too. If I just had two daughters——"

"You would never have managed it," she teased, laughing. "Not with two brats like me. Now. What else kept you up, waiting to tell me?"

A searching perplexity grew in Lance's eyes, deepened by the lines furrowing his forehead. "Kitten, I wish you had come to me—you and Bob—before getting tied into Jed Curry's claims, before you put one hell of a lot of money into the Buccaneer."

Caroline's eyes widened. "Why, Papa? We wanted to do it on our own and surprise you. What's wrong?"

"I hope nothing is wrong. But there's likely trouble ahead. Kitten, I want to talk to you and Bob. Yes, and Jed Curry too. Tomorrow. Title to claims in that section along Castle Creek is mixed up by early day filings and claim swapping. Nothing can be really tied down and established yet. You've got thousands of dollars skating on thin and melting ice."

"But Jed had clear and valid title," Caroline protested.

"That's what he thought he had . . . honestly thought so," Lance said slowly. "Making such title stand up in

179

court can be something entirely different." He stood and drew her to her feet. "Don't let it spoil your day or your sleep. But make sure Bob and Jed come with you when we talk it over."

Lance moved across the room, then turned. "Take care of that ring. A coat of shellac and a velvet case should do it. Good night, kitten."

When morning came, Caroline dressed quietly and walked from the house. Sleep had not come soon or with ease. Events and problems pressed closely about her.

Within minutes she had passed Hallam's Lake, crossed the railroad tracks and the Roaring Fork, and sought out the early morning serenity of Hunter Creek. She noted its mid-summer languor, so different from its snowy floods of springtime. It had narrowed to a clear and unhurried course, moving through deep pools and along rocky, brush-guarded stretches.

She sat for a long time on a smooth rock and watched the movement of the water as it defied obstructions and went its own way. Life moves like that, she thought, pulling us on whether or not we wish to go. The streams deepen and widen as they drop seaward. Our lives gain force and our horizons widen as the rivulets of experience trickle or gush in.

She studied the eddy of water about a fallen tree. The tree ... the barrier ... only delays it. Within seconds or minutes, hours or days, a pent-up force must carry the water ahead. There is no ceasing, no complete rest, un-til——

She came abruptly to her feet, knowing this morning walk for what it was—a frail and futile dam, a delaying action.

At home she changed to a simple blue dress and walked thoughtfully to the assay office. Bob was busy with a Bunsen burner, test tubes, and acids. She called him to her side.

He kissed her, then glanced at her fingers. She shook her head. "I left your ring at home; it's too fragile and too precious to risk losing."

"Caroline, you sentimental sweetheart, it was only a

flower stem," he protested. "Today we'll look for a real engagement ring."

She shook her head. "Not today. We've other things to do. Besides, Bob, I'd rather have you choose it and surprise me."

He glanced anxiously toward her. She ignored his unspoken concern as she looked steadily into his face, and said, "Papa wants you to get Jed Curry into town as soon as you can. He wants to talk to all of us about the mine. He thinks we may be headed toward serious trouble."

"What sort?"

"Something having to do with making our title to the claims stand up in court. He hinted maybe we've put our money down a rat hole."

He paced thoughtfully about the room. "All of us studied Jed's title to the Buccaneer claims. I don't know how they could be clearer or stronger. Just the same, I'll have Jed get here before night. Your dad is no fool. If he wants to talk to us . . . the sooner the better."

"Good," Caroline answered. "I'm glad you see it that way." She paused, searching for words, then said, swiftly and tensely, "Bob, dearest, there is a man in town I have to see and talk with today. A man from Denver who is in love with me. I must make him understand and I've got to send him away. God knows I want to do it without hurting him too deeply."

Bob stood still, his face gravely questioning. He rubbed an acid stain on his hand and waited for her to continue.

"His name is Eric Duane. We were friends in school. I didn't know, until the last few weeks there, that he cared so much."

"Does he know about us, Caroline?"

He reached out and drew him to her, as she answered, "He knew when I left that there was someone here." She smiled, wanting to ease the tightness of his face, and added, "Besides, I didn't have my ring then."

For a time Bob silently watched smoke rise from a distant mill. "Ask him to come here before he leaves," he said finally. "I would like to meet him."

"I will. Of course I will," she answered. "You'll have to spare me from the office today. But let me know when

181

Jed gets here and we can arrange to meet with Lance." She rose and planted a resolute kiss on his mouth. "I adore you——Mr. Bucaneer." She wheeled about and walked from the office.

She sat at a white-linen-covered table in the Clarendon Hotel dining room, and was waiting there when Eric Duane came to her side. The gladness of his blue eyes gave instant warning that what she must do would not be easy.

Eric reached for her hands. "Don't say a word. Not yet, Caroline. Just let me look at you . . . so much lovelier than I dared remember."

Her hands were still firm within his as he lowered to the seat facing her.

"Eric, it's nice to have you here. Welcome to Aspen." Her gaze moved across him, noting his dark, conservative suit, the maturing aspect of his face, and the well-remembered shock of sandy hair. "How do you manage to look so healthy, so athletic, and so ambitious this early in the morning?" she asked.

"How does a mountain princess maintain an eternal spell?" he countered.

She laughed and withdrew her hands. "Flattery won't save you from having to feed me, Eric. I'm famished."

When a stiffly polite waiter had disappeared kitchenward, she fingered a tall crystal vase that held one dew-studded rose. "How long can you stay, Eric? There's so much I want you to see, so many people you must meet."

"A day . . . or a month, Caroline. As long as it takes you to show all of it to me." He leaned toward her. His face was open, honest, eager. "I'll stay as long as it takes to win you, Princess."

So suddenly the moment had come. There must be no delay, no futile blocking of the inevitable. Her eyes were tear-threatened but looked calmly upon him as she answered, "Eric, why do I have to hurt you? I'm engaged to Bob Herndon. We're to be married this fall." She became silent, knowing the determined steadiness with which he took the thrust of her words.

"Do you love him, Caroline?"

"Yes," she answered simply, and was suddenly remem-

182

bering the magic of a mountain pool, a flower stem ring, and Bob's urgent arms about her.

"I sensed it. Yet I had to hear you say it. Tell me about him."

"How do I start?" she asked hesitantly. "I met Bob when I was only twelve. He was a cavalry officer in Wyoming. He has a stiff knee, an assay office . . . and—darn it—he's just Bob. He wants to meet you."

"Of course we'll meet. He must be quite a man, Caroline, for you to love him so much. The luckiest——" His words trailed off. She knew that there must be rancor which he strived to hide and that only time could quiet.

"Thank you, Eric. Thank you for so much. Would I be asking too much—wanting you to come to Aspen again for my wedding?"

He leaned far across the table and kissed her. "You couldn't keep me away, Caroline. You'll never keep me away if you should need me."

She managed an uncertain smile, as she said, "I'd hate to play havoc with that grocery firm of yours."

Eric glanced toward their approaching waiter. "I'll tell you as we eat. I'm out of the grocery business. Nowadays that's my older brother's headache. I wasn't the type. I've landed in the investment end of a bank, and I like it."

"Then there are men here in Aspen you should know, men needing investment advice." She was glad for his understanding turn of words to practical matters, for this opportunity to recover a little from the shattering moments they had endured. But his reply brought vivid realization of hidden tumult.

"Some other time, Princess. Not this trip. I'm . . . I'm returning to Denver. Tonight. Now, let's eat, then spend a day seeing your high empire."

Later, after the crowded tour of the town, the brief and restrained meeting of Eric Duane and Bob Herndon, and a quickly arranged dinner party that was timed to the departure of the Denver train, Caroline walked tiredly to the assay office. Lance accompanied her. He was quiet and thoughtful.

He sat down inside, to face Herndon and Curry, and he

183

quickly came to the point of the meeting. "All of you know why I asked you to come here. It's been a hectic day, so I won't keep you long."

Jed Curry nodded, his face puzzled. "Bob sent word for me to hightail it into town. We've been talking this thing over. I understand you're worried about my claim titles and the Buccaneer. What's up?"

Lance lit a cigar. "Don't get riled up, Jed. I came here to help—if I can. All of you are into the venture hip-deep now. It's a question of foreseeing rough possibilities and being ready to cope with them." He blew a smoke ring ceilingward, then asked, "Jed, do you understand how an adverse claim works?"

"Sure. It's an opposition claim that contests ownership."

"That's right. A lot of legal contests and lawsuits have come about because of the ruckus between the apexers and the sideliners. In such cases it boils down to whether claim to the apex of a lode gives the owners the right to mine along the entire length of the veins leading to the apex. The sideliners say HELL NO! They believe a claim three hundred by fifteen hundred feet is enough mining ground for anyone. They say that for sure no one who holds the outcrop of a contact lode should have the right to take the whole adjoining country."

Relief showed on Bob's face. "How does all that concern us, Lance? We won't have any apex ruckus up on Castle Creek."

"I'm aware of that," Lance agreed. "I'm just pointing out how tricky—how downright nasty—adverse claims can be. There are other kinds. Your mine is smack in an area where titles can be questioned because of early day claim filings, some claim-jumping, and damn scanty records of those early day shenanigans. Don't get the idea I'm a prophet of gloom. But I've got some advice—if you want to take it."

"You bet we want it," Curry answered quickly.

"All right," Lance continued. "First off, nobody is interested in fighting for all or a part of nothing. It'll be after you've put up the money, done the work, and brought in proven production that the shysters, the crooks, and the fast-dollar boys will try to cut themselves in."

"We're due to cut into some interesting ore within a month," Herndon said worriedly.

"Fine." Lance smiled. "Now play it smart. Don't let word leak out how the silver and lead content is assaying. Treat your men decent. Pay them top wages, double wages if necessary, so they'll be on your side and keep their mouths shut. Send in a load or so of low-grade stuff to the smelter, then act downright worried about it. Sort the high grade and store it in one of the stopes. Be sure none of it gets onto the dump where a snooper can get to it. Keep strangers out of the Buccaneer."

"You make it sound like a mystery . . . an intrigue," Caroline interrupted.

"Call it what you want," Lance answered, "but it's serious business. Wait until you have every possible ton stored. Then bring it all in at one time for rail shipment to a smelter. I'll get with Jim Daley and we will help you round up enough wagons. We'll have to guard the move closely."

"But after that?" Curry asked. "After the news gets out?"

Lance looked thoughtfully toward him. "Maybe nothing will happen. But if it does, you'll have money behind you to carry on—or for legal maneuvering."

Herndon offered him his hand. "Thanks for coming, Lance. For tipping us off." He turned toward Curry. "Jed, I've an idea we better do as he says."

"We'll do it exactly as he says," Curry agreed with finality.

As he was leaving, Lance turned. "One other thing. Bob, back in '81 and '82, did you know a couple of prospectors named Gagnon and Lorentz? Run any samples for them?"

Bob shook his head thoughtfully. "Not that I remember. Could be though. I knew a lot of the old-timers better by first name or by face."

"Try and look it up in your records," Lance said quietly. "If you find anything, let me know. Just don't mention the names to anyone else."

Chapter 9

With the sudden coming of Indian summer, the days became even busier for Caroline. She had enlisted the nimble fingers of Mrs. Jorgenson in preparing a trousseau for the unscheduled wedding day. This was evening work, sometimes stretching far into the night as yards of cloth and lace and thread followed the dictates of 1889 fashion.

Sometimes Caroline paused and smiled tenderly toward this woman who had become a part of her life. She had never known or asked her companion's age, but the snowiness of her bun-pinned hair and the deepening lines of her face spoke freely of the march of years. Recently she had been persuaded to wear glasses. She regarded them as a nuisance, and often put them aside, pulling her work within inches of her eyes and continuing her swift and delicate stitching.

Once, when the tedious needle work of a white chemise was complete, and the older woman handed it proudly over for inspection, Caroline spoke with delight.

"It's lovely work. These hidden seams ... I'll bet Ellen Bradley Corlett hasn't that much magic in her sewing."

Mischief lurked deep in Mrs. Jorgenson's eyes, as she laughed softly and answered, "Other magic she must have with men. Else why the pee pot did you douse her with?"

A startled gasp escaped Caroline. "You've known about that all these years and never mentioned it. How? Who told you?"

Suddenly Mrs. Jorgenson was intent upon threading a needle. Her mouth was pursed and stubborn. "A bird it was told me, Caroline. Ja, a gossip bird."

"Maybe an old bird named Lance," Caroline guessed. "Whatever happens in Aspen, he'll find out."

Abruptly she spilled cloth from her lap, knelt on the carpet, and laid her head contentedly on her companion's knees. "Jorgie, God was smiling the day you VALKED over the big mountains and came to Aspen and to me."

"For me, too, he smiled. And gave me you—a daughter." For a moment the old lady's hands pressed Caroline's cheeks, then she added firmly, "A daughter who never will be married unless we stitch the dry goods more."

Minutes passed in silence as they pinned a complex pattern to the tablecloth, unwound shimmering voile, and began the studied cutting.

"Your Buccaneer mine," Mrs. Jorgenson said. "I hear the ore is low grade, not good."

Caroline looked intently toward her. "You heard that in town?"

"Ja."

Caroline glanced about the room. Her reply was voiced as an instinctive whisper. "It's wonderful that people are saying that. It's what we want them to believe. We're storing the good ore. Some of it assays terribly rich, up to twelve hundred dollars a ton. Jorgie, don't breathe a word of it to anyone."

"So rich as that? For you and your Bob I am happy. My mouth, shut it will stay."

Caroline smiled toward her and knew it would be so.

Mrs. Jorgenson's flying fingers stopped and she straightened with excited abruptness. "Old I am and forgetting things, Caroline. A man was here today. A man with a telegram for you. I'll get it."

The few words, written in bold script across the paper, caused an excited howl to break from Caroline. "It's ... it's from Jim Daley. He's married!"

Mrs. Jorgenson's scissors leaped upward and snipped thin air. "You mean a wife that cow herder has? Read it, kitten."

Even as she began reading aloud, Caroline was realizing that it was the first time Mrs. Jorgenson had ever called her kitten, the pet name Lance had used throughout her lifetime.

MISS BUCCANEER: ASK YOUR DAD TO HAVE
HIS BAY NAGS AT THE DEPOT FRIDAY MORN-
ING. ARRANGE CLARENDON SUITE FOR JIM
DALEY AND WIFE. CAN YOU SEND SOMEONE
TO DUNG OUT LAZY SEEDY. MRS. DALEY
SENDS LOVE. ME TOO. A HELLUVA LOT OF IT.
                                    JIM DALEY

Caroline sprawled in a chair, heedless that she was
crushing folded yards of voile, and stared in limp disbelief
at the telegram. The door opened and Lance entered.
Without uttering a word, she handed him the message.

His eyes skimmed it quickly. "Godamighty," he
breathed, "He's done it. Gone and got himself a mailorder
woman."

"Maybe I'm to blame," Caroline said haltingly. "I told
him he needed a wife. He said he'd think it over."

Lance grinned widely. "The old coot's done some traveling along with his thinking. This wire was sent from
Reno—Reno, Nevada."

Mrs. Jorgenson began unpinning the pattern. She said,
"To that cow chaser's house I'll go, in the morning. Make
it clean and ready.

"If you do," Lance answered, "some hefty girls are
going along to help you." He paused, then added, "Friday.
They'll be on the Friday morning train. Good Lord—just
two days. This is Wednesday."

Caroline plucked the telegram from his hand and reread
it. "So Mrs. Daley sends love. That's laying it on a little
thick—from a stranger." Her voice was tart.

Lance fingered a vest-pocketed cigar, oblivious that an
unlighted one was already in his mouth and shot a quick
glance at his daughter. "Kitten, what in—are you
jealous?"

"Jealous! How silly. But he could have told me."

"Don't you mean asked you?"

For once Caroline had no reply. Lance smiled, as he
said, "He didn't tell me either. Jim Daley isn't in the habit
of seeking advice or talking a lot. I'm glad he's getting
back. We're about to need him."

"For what?" Caroline asked quietly.

"To get rigs lined up for your ore haul. I've been with Bob and Jed Curry most of the evening. They can't store much more ore without hampering production."

Eager excitement lit Caroline's face. "How soon, Papa? When will we make the haul?"

"Next week; payday's about here."

Caroline laughed. "At least we'll have a few days to recover from Friday after greeting Mrs. Uncle Jim Daley."

"Take comfort, kitten," Lance retorted. "He didn't hitch to Ellen Bradley."

She retreated to her bedroom door, turned and thumbed her nose. "Goodnight, Papa."

By an infrequent feat of railroading, the Denver and Rio Grande passenger train came into Aspen station Friday morning at scheduled time. For fifteen minutes Caroline had paced about the platform, ignoring amused smiles from Lance and Bob. The coaches halted, and a trainman stepped down, when she felt the pressure of her father's grasp on her elbow.

"Simmer down, kitten," he said easily. "You're here to welcome the bride, not for a duel."

She ignored the remark and walked to the car vestibule. Already luggage-bearing people were passing her. She searched every face. Moments passed. Then she stared at a grinning Jim Daley as he came through the car door, but she was unaware when he spotted her and hollered out a greeting.

Already she looked intensely at the woman with him. The rankling within Caroline died as her gaze met and held that of the hazel, green-flecked eyes of Jim Daley's middle-aged bride. A strange perplexity swept Caroline. Suddenly she searched far back through the years, probing with quick thoughts for something she must remember.

She heard the excited gasp of her father, but it seemed unreal and far off, far from the place that memory had swept her on urgent wings. This woman's face had once looked softly and anxiously into her own. This woman's arms had held her close, and drawn her slowly upward from torment.

Caroline did not know that she had paled, nor that her breath was a quick and broken thing, as she ran forward, jolted a trainman aside, held Jim Daley's wife in her arms.

"Maude," she whispered. "Oh, Maude ... Maude ... I'm so glad it's you. Welcome home."

Maude Selby Daley's smile was serene and utterly happy. "I could hardly wait to see you, Caroline," she said. "Jim told me you were grown up and beautiful. Every mile I tried to picture you."

Maude turned to Lance Ainsley as his arm swept about her, and he said, "Aspen is complete now, Maude. What a party we'll throw tonight."

"Lance," she laughed happily, "you're still a good-looking devil—when you're shaved." She squeezed Jim Daley's arm.

Caroline glanced up and caught the bewilderment in Bob Herndon's face. She quickly drew him forward. "Maude, may I present my fiancé Robert Herndon."

"Who surely thinks we've all gone wacky," Maude said, and laid her hands on Bob's shoulders.

He gave her a long, appraising glance. "I'm proud to meet you, Mrs. Daley." He quietly added, "Leave it to Jim Daley to bring home the prize—cattle or a bride." His face reddened at the boldness of his own words.

Caroline said, "Why can't you say something as romantic as that to me?" She turned to Maude. "I have trouble with him and his roving eye."

"Then you're lucky, Caroline," Maude answered. "Any man worth having comes equipped with roving eyes."

Jim Daley had stood in silence. Now he grinned at her words. "I'll remember that, honey. I'll work like hell at being worthy."

"My dear," Maude retorted, "you've worked at it twenty years and I've news for you, you're retiring!"

They sat in the surrey and moved leisurely toward the Clarendon Hotel. Caroline asked the question pressing upon her. "Maude, where have you been? How did Uncle Jim manage to find you?"

"I went to San Francisco and bought a house." Maude

190

paused, then looked squarely into Caroline's face. "No, not *that* kind of a house. Just a small one to live in. Before I even got settled, I sold it to a man who wanted the whole block. Next thing, I'd bought a couple of houses and was dabbling in real-estate rentals—'Selby Rents.' "

"Nowadays," Jim Daley cut in proudly, "Selby rents a fair slice of San Francisco. That's how I tracked her down. Some of H. A. W. Tabor's men gave me a hand. Them and a couple of letters Maude and me had exchanged."

As they stopped before the Clarendon, Lance pointed with his tasseled whip. "Maude, this ain't San Francisco, but you folks will likely find it comfortable."

She quietly studied the town, the valley, and the encroaching mountains. "This is home now," she said finally. "Wonderful and peaceful home." Her hand squeezed Caroline's. "I'll try to take good care of your Big Lazy Seedy ranch, but you've got to help out."

Three days after their arrival in Aspen, Jim Daley took his bride home to Wilderness Creek. She was firm in her insistence that Caroline go with them and be the first to show her about the broad acres of the Lazy Seedy. It was well that she did, for already Lance had broached the subject of the impending ore haul to Daley and they quietly prepared to assemble the teams and wagons and men needed to bring the stored ore of the Buccaneer down the narrow wagon trail of Castle Creek for shipment. Railroad officials were contacted. They made certain that ore cars would be sided and waiting, and that after loading they would be switched to an outbound train without delay.

October 20, 1889, was the day chosen for the haul. Throughout the preceding day ore wagons left Aspen one by one and headed up Castle Creek. Their departure had been well planned and spaced to avoid a mass movement that would arouse curiosity. Caroline noted no excitement. She attributed this to the skill with which Lance and Daley had planned their move.

She was in bed early that night, awaiting the long and hectic tomorrow. Minutes later she was up again, pacing restlessly about the house. She picked up a half-finished blouse and tried to sew. It was no use. Tonight there was no concentration of mind and fingers. Reading was also futile. An hour passed. She raided the pantry as Mrs. Jorgenson came quietly to her side.

"Is not good you worry so much, Caroline. Tomorrow they will bring the ore here, your Papa and that cow driver, Daley. In bed you should be, and asleep."

Caroline studied the old woman's slight figure, draped in a long woolen nightgown. "How come you're not sleeping, Jorgie?"

"Sleep I could not, with you about the house like a caged animal." Mrs. Jorgenson squinted appraisingly into Caroline's face and said, "Come. I read something to you. Then we sleep."

She guided Caroline to a chair, disappeared for a moment into her bedroom, then came out and opened a worn Bible.

"See, child . . . it is here."

She began reading slowly, and Caroline knew the effort with which she formed English words from a Swedish text.

"It is from Isaiah, and God to Jacob is speaking: Behold I will do a new thing; now it shall spring forth; shall ye not know it? I will make a way in the wilderness, and rivers in the desert. . . . Put me in remembrance: let us plead together: declare thou, that thou mayest be justified."

For minutes her voice continued its halting but confident softness in the room. Then it faded as the tenseness of Caroline's face merged into drowsiness.

When Mrs. Jorgenson closed the Bible and darkened the room, Caroline Ainsley was sound asleep.

In late afternoon the heavily loaded wagons appeared from Castle Creek Canyon. Lance had arranged for his bay team to be at Caroline's disposal, and she had driven far beyond the edge of town. Mrs. Jorgenson was with her. Caroline sensed that with the coming of this moment her companion's expectant tenseness matched her own. They drove into a small clearing that would get them off the road and allow the wagons to pass.

192

As the first wagon went its noisy and dusty way past them, Caroline admired the precision with which the haul was being accomplished. A scant wagon length separated the sweaty and plodding teams. Before the last one had passed, Caroline counted eighteen. They were escorted by mounted and armed men; she recognized several of them as riders from the Lazy Seedy. At intervals she waved a greeting to Bob, to her father, and to Jim Daley. The tiredness of their faces told of a night and day which had no wasted moments.

The wagons had passed, and she had turned the bays about to follow, when Bob Herndon slid from a wagon and stood waiting until her team drew alongside.

She thrust out a hand toward his grimy one and helped him to the seat beside her and Mrs. Jorgenson. She eyed him closely. "You're a sight," she said. "A dirty . . . tired . . . wonderful sight. You've made it, Bob, our ore haul is done."

He drew a sweaty wrist across reddened, tired eyes. "Not yet, honey. All of this has to be gotten to the freight yards, up a ramp, and into the railroad cars. I hope to God the cars are there."

"They are," she assured him. "Waiting and ready. I drove by the siding and checked as I left town. How long will the unloading take?"

"A good part of the night," he answered. "But we've got enough help."

"Where's Jed Curry?" Caroline asked anxiously. "I didn't see him."

"Still at the mine. His part's over. His men will be at work in the morning. There's more good ore—and so incredibly much water——"

"This ore," she interrupted. "Bob, is it good . . . really good."

Excitement broke the fatigued lines of his face. "We'll get the smelter report and their check in a few days. You'd better brace yourself for it if big figures make you dizzy."

She nestled a spotless white glove in his hand, heedless that both lay in Mrs. Jorgenson's lap. "I want to be dizzy, Lieutenant, hopelessly and wonderfully dizzy."

It seemed to Caroline, during the two weeks that followed, that the railroad cars bearing their ore and their hopes had rumbled out of Aspen only to be engulfed in some faraway and unknown silence. With each mail arrival, she waited at the post office hopeful of a letter from the smelter at Leadville. Each day she walked slowly back to the assay office, trying to mask her impatient disappointment. She managed to keep busy, but during these days there was little zest and enjoyment and she wasted precious time in staring at the wall or out across the mountains. She knew that Bob was equally impatient and tension-ridden; wisely he had chosen to spend his time at the mine, where more ore was constantly being lifted from the water-plagued depths and stored for another shipment.

At home, her mood led alternately to exhausting bursts of sewing and hours of pensive yet restless silence.

"Hang it all, kitten," Lance would counsel, "these things take time. You'll get your check if you haven't driven yourself crazy first. Slow down. Take it easy."

The smelter's response was entirely different in manner from what Caroline had expected or pictured. She was alone in the office shortly before noon of a chilly, wintry day and was thumbing a fashion magazine, when the outer door banged, and Lance came in, accompanied by a well-dressed stranger with quickly appraising eyes.

"Caroline, this is Henry Girard, vice-president of the Leadville Smelter. I imagine you're pretty glad to see him."

Caroline wondered if her breathing and the pounding of her heart were loud in the room as she acknowledged the introduction. Henry Girard sat down in the chair Lance drew close to the desk.

"I didn't anticipate the pleasure," he said, "of doing business with anyone so young and pretty, Miss Ainsley." He drew a packet of papers from his pocket, then said cautiously, "You are a major stockholder of the Buccaneer Mining Company?"

Caroline smiled and nodded. "I own exactly twenty-six percent of the company stock. I'm also secretary and treasurer. If you care to see our organizational papers, I have them here."

"I'll need to see them later. Can you arrange for an immediate meeting with your other principals? In view of the business I'm here to transact, we should all get together."

Lance stood near the window, his fists thrust in his pockets. He turned and grinned at his daughter. "I had an idea something like this was in the wind. I've already sent a man up to the mine with word for Bob and Jed Curry to heist themselves in here."

Caroline's eyes fixed in tense expectancy on the papers still folded in Girard's hand. Her question came scarcely more than a whisper. "Can you tell me about our shipment, Mr. Girard? The silver content? Its net to us?"

Surprise marked Girard's face as he peered quickly toward her. "Good Lord, young lady, didn't you realize what you were shipping?" He glanced toward Lance and smiled. "No use keeping a major stockholder in suspense. We can go over the smelter sheets when your associates meet with us. Meanwhile—take a look at this." He slipped a check from the folded papers and laid it on the desk before her.

As her eyes focused on the figures, Caroline Ainsley reared upward from the desk, stumbled against her father, and threw her arms about him. "Look at it, Papa," she gasped. "Read it; then pinch me. God in heaven ... it ... it says one hundred and sixty-eight thousand dollars." The words ended in a muffled sob as she moistened Lance's shirt front with happy tears.

When a measure of composure had returned, she wanted to ask many questions. Lance forestalled them. "Mr. Girard has traveled all night. I've an idea he's tired and hungry. Let's take him home with us and treat him to one of Mrs. Jorgenson's dinners. When Bob and Jed ride in, you can have half the night for questions and business." He turned to Girard. "We have a Swedish housekeeper. You won't forget her meals. Come along."

"I'm going to like Aspen," Girard said laughing.

The lights burned late at Lance Ainsley's home. Bob Herndon and Jed Curry rode in at dusk. With the aid of a neighbor woman, Mrs. Jorgenson had prepared a meal that Lance swore surpassed any she had ever served. Every room was the scene of gaiety, laughter, and excitement.

They later gathered about the dining-room table as Henry Girard untied the sheaf of papers. He laid them momentarily aside and studied the organizational documents of the Buccaneer mine. His scrutiny was brief but thorough. He checked the ownership percentages, then smiled. "Just three owners, eh? Caroline Ainsley twenty-six percent, Robert Herndon twenty-five percent, Jedidiah Curry forty-nine percent. Closely held, closely held indeed. I like being able to meet all owners."

Caroline listened with polite interest. Half-a-dozen times before and during dinner Bob and Jed had sought to find out from her the result of the shipment. She evaded answering, wanting this moment to come as a triumphant climax of the day. She drew a steadying breath as Girard handed the check to Jed Curry. Curry glanced at it for a time, then thrust it into Bob Herndon's hand. "Look at that, Herndon," Curry yelled and rose to tower excitedly above the table. "We've hit it, boy—a fortune—a whopping fortune!"

Triumph swept Bob Herndon's face and blazed in his blue eyes. "Caroline," he murmured, "read this figure out loud. Read it again . . . again. We've paid for the Buccaneer with one shipment. There'll be another ready in sixty days or less. A richer one." His arm swept about her, pulling her head to his shoulder. "Can I tell them now—about us?"

Caroline gazed happily at Henry Girard. "I think Mr. Girard has the smelter tallys ready for us."

"Reports can wait," Bob roared. "Folks, I've simply got to say it." He came to his feet and faced those about him. "Caroline and I are going to be married on December fourth. We agreed it would be soon after the first ore check arrived." He moved to Caroline's chair, drew her to her feet, and placed a resounding kiss on her lips.

Jed Curry's response was a howling "hurrah" as he thrust out his hand. "Happy day," he said, then eyed Lance, who moved around the table to throw an arm about each of the excited couple. "Make that hug big and fast, Lance," Curry ordered chuckling. "This calls for drinks from your private stock. Make it a double-double for Mr. Girard, the best gol-durned messenger since Paul Revere."

When Henry Girard lifted his glass, he asked, "May I propose a triple toast? To a long happy marriage, to continued success of the Buccaneer, and to Mrs. Jorgenson's wonderful dinner?" The old housekeeper moved to Caroline's side, and cradled the girl's head on her shoulder. She was silent a moment, then lifted her own glass in trembling fingers. "That God should be so good to us," she said firmly. "To my child . . . to my family."

It was an hour before the semblance of a business meeting could be regained. Girard ran quickly through the smelter report. "I won't go into detail," he said. "You can study all of this later. Sufficient for now to say you apparently have one of the better discoveries of the district. We of the Leadville Smelter would naturally like to continue processing the ore. That's my reason for being here. I'd like to add that it has been a momentous occasion." He paused, then continued in a brisk tone. "We prepared milling contracts before I left Leadville. I have them here for your consideration. We believe them to be as reasonable and as fair as any competitor could legitimately offer." He laid bound papers in Caroline's hands. "Don't read them tonight. We can all meet tomorrow and discuss them."

Girard cast a quizzical smile toward Caroline and then said to Bob Herndon: "There's a time for a crowd to gather, and a time for it to disperse. Mr. Ainsley, would you and Mr. Curry care to join me for a nightcap at the hotel bar?"

Caroline, knowing the eagerness of Bob's arms about her, murmured an appreciative "Good night."

Dream castles were built and the promise of a shining future explored as the loving pair sat far into the night watching a blazing log fall to embers in the fireplace.

"Can you be ready in so short a time?" Bob asked anxiously. "Seven days isn't much time to prepare for a wedding."

"A week is plenty of time," Caroline assured him. "Jorgie and I have been sewing like crazy for two months."

"I can arrange for the church, or do you want to be married here at home?"

Caroline was pensively quiet for a time. "I've thought a lot about that. Bob, would you mind if we were married at the Lazy Seedy on Wilderness Creek? Somehow I feel that it is meant for us to start our lives together there."

"I think it's a grand idea. Of course we can be married at your ranch."

There was no revelation and no regret in Caroline's eyes, as she said, "It's Maude Daley's home, but I'm sure she will want us there. So will Uncle Jim. I expect them in town late tomorrow afternoon. I'll ask them."

"What about our honeymoon trip, sweetheart?"

"Does there have to be a trip just now?" she asked. We've so much to do here. Later we can take a long trip."

"Wait a minute," Bob exclaimed excitedly. "How about the bridal suite of the new Jerome Hotel? The Jerome will be open next week—just in time."

"Bob, you dear, that's perfect. Simply perfect. Can Jed manage things alone at the mine for a few days?"

"He'd better be able to. For at least a week I'll be the unavailable assayer." Bob kicked off his shoes, and slid his head contentedly onto her lap. "Just think," he muttered, "a peach of a bride and a hundred and seventy thousand dollars—all in one week."

"One hundred sixty-eight thousand," she corrected him teasingly.

"A mere accounting detail, Caroline. Know what? I've been sizing up that corner lot out on Bleeker Street. We could build a two-story house with an acre to spare."

"Perhaps. . . . someday, my thoughtful lieutenant. We've heavy mine expenses to think of now."

"I know," he said, sobering. "And I want us to pay back the money your dad loaned you to start the Buccaneer."

"Of course," she answered swiftly. "That must be paid." She smiled gently down into his face, but in the secret recesses of her mind a plan had already taken shape. *The Lazy Seedy belongs to Jim and to Maude and to their children should there be any. I've no right to ask them to let me buy back what I have sold. I can put the money away. This will be a backlog for Bob and for me. For a*

198

*moment she was recalling her father's caution of trouble
ahead for the Buccaneer. Bob must never know. Nor Jed
Curry. If we must fight, this will be my means of sustaining
them, or hanging on until we win.*

The hearth log became a charred and smouldering thing
as their dreams and plans again carried them beyond the
horizon of a month . . . a year . . . a. . . .

Long after midnight, Lance's treading on the porch and
his purposeful slamming of the door drew them back
again to reality.

Chapter 10

They were married the mid-afternoon of December 4,
1889. It was a chilly, but sun-mellowed day on which the
vast and serene Lazy Seedy ranch seemed in tune with
their own eager happiness. From Denver greenhouses had
come flowers with which Maude Daley had transformed
the long, heavily beamed living room, and had banked the
stone fireplace before which they stood as the minister of
Aspen's Presbyterian church joined their lives together.

The morning train from Aspen brought more than fifty
guests. Others arrived from Denver. As Lance led her
down the aisle, it seemed that those seated about her were
the closest, most beloved friends of her lifetime. She was
aware of H. A. W. Tabor's beaming face, and of the pale,
restrained gaze of Eric Duane seated beside him. She gar-
nered a bold wink from Jim Daley. She knew that from
the bedroom where she had dressed two women would
soon enter and take their places for the ceremony. Mrs.
Jorgenson would be here. Dear old Jorgie. How could she
have possibly done so much, taken care of so many details! And with Jorgie would be a friend and a face from
so many years ago . . . Mrs. Brenton, who had sewn the

magic party dress at Fort Steele. Captain and Mrs. Brenton now stationed at Ford D. A. Russell near Cheyenne had arrived the previous evening.

Momentarily she gazed at another guest. He was slight of figure with white and bushy whiskers. I'm glad, she thought. So awfully glad Hardrock Corlett came to my wedding. She knew that Ellen would not be beside him or in the room, and she wondered for an instant what device the old-timer had used to thwart Ellen's dominance for even a day.

A parlor organ sounded the soft notes of a wedding march as she continued toward the fireplace and the small table where Bob Herndon awaited her. She had asked but one person to stand with her. Now Caroline thrilled to the warmth of Maude Selby Daley's smile and the youthful and radiant happiness that marked her friend since Jim Daley had sought her out and brought her to Aspen and to Wilderness Creek.

Her father touched her hand as he turned to leave her beside the man who would soon be her husband. He moved to the empty seat beside Jim Daley and H. A. W. Tabor. Suddenly he was intensely aware of the quietness of the room, of the scent of roses, and of sunlight falling through the windows upon Caroline and Bob and the minister, who had begun reading in slow and measured voice.

He studied his child's tall and graceful figure covered by the French Chantilly lace of her gown. He knew the hours Jorgie had spent to create this white and beautiful gown with its high, rounded neckline, exquisite long-tapered sleeves, and the full, many-tiered skirt.

His gaze rose to her veil, held in place by an old but beautifully matching tiara that he knew Mrs. Brenton had brought for her.

He saw only her profile, but he knew that her gray eyes were softly gentle and unafraid.

What does a girl, a child, see as she searches the future, he wondered. The years ahead are so long and inscrutable, and the moments so short before words and the ring make her a wife.

A sudden anguish was upon Lance Ainsley. If only her mother, if only Emily could see her now. His letter asking

Emily to come to Aspen for the wedding had brought only silence. His teeth bit a quivering lip, and he stared harder toward Caroline as she knelt beside Bob. The minister's hands hovered above them.

Kitten, thank God for your good sense and honesty and courage. This marriage will last, it'll last because you have strength, enough of it for both if need be. You'll need that strength someday. God knows how soon. Deep within him in that moment a warning bell was sounding. *She didn't tell me, but she sold her ranch for love of this man. Her hopes and dreams are in a mine called Buccaneer. She'll fight for it. What a dirty and disastrous mess it may become. I'm alone now. Just a house and an aging housekeeper. I've a son somewhere. Please, God, take care of him.*

The sudden pressure of H. A. W. Tabor's hand on his knee roused Lance to realization that the ceremony had ended, that he must rise and be first at Caroline's side. The hoarsely whispered words of Jim Daley came to his ears. "My partner's the prettiest gal ever lassoed herself a man. Ain't she a beauty?"

"Hell," Tabor scoffed. "You just waking to the fact? I told Horace Greeley's whole blasted colony how lovely she was back in '81."

The reception was neither formal nor lengthy. Caroline had wanted to spend the precious moments with her friends. As quickly as possible, she sought out Hardrock Corlett and gathered his hands into hers. "This is only the third time we've met here on Wilderness Creek. I think of you as part of this ranch and this valley. I'm so glad you came to my wedding. Hardrock, believe me when I say I wish Ellen had also come."

A grateful smile broke the tired graveness of his face. "She's busy with painters sprucin' up our upstairs. Third time since we bought that drafty old castle." He paused. "I wish our place was simple and cozy like this. I wish I had that old cowhide chair of Bentley's. There's a lot of memories here."

"Indeed there are," she agreed nodding. "You should come here more often. Uncle Jim and Maude would like that."

Hardrock's face sagged again to anxiety. "I don't get around much now. Ellen handles most everything. Maybe ... maybe it'd been different if I'd talked to your dad about things before I took Matt Shaner as a partner."

"Papa's here. Why not talk to him today?" Caroline squeezed his arm with comforting assurance.

"No. It's no use now—too late." He pulled her quickly to him, touching his lips to her cheeks. "You're going to be happy, you and that assayer chap. Hang onto your happiness; there's so all-fired little of it." He clamped a bowler hat to his white hair and walked slowly to the door.

Moments later she turned at the sound of a voice that still brought resurgent memories of the past. "Happy years," chanted Captain Brenton. "Say! I almost forgot. Be sure and open the blue box with a red ribbon first when you come to your gifts. A special friend sent it."

"Who? What is it?"

"Don't go prying." He laughed. "But it's something special."

"Having you and Mrs. Brenton here is special too. You had so far to come from Cheyenne. It's hard to think of Fort Steele as abandoned ... deserted."

"We'll be farther away soon," he said sadly. "I'm being transferred to the Presidio in San Francisco next month."

"Oh no!" Caroline protested. "Doesn't the army ever let you stay in one place?"

"Likely they will now. I asked for Presidio duty until retirement."

After H. A. W. Tabor and Jim Daley had teased her for a time with remarks that brought a blushing glow to her cheeks, she insisted that Bob join them at the punch bowl. She moved across the room to face Eric Duane.

"Eric," she said uncertainly, "your being here makes this day more wonderful. Wish me well, Eric."

For a moment she was certain he would kiss her, but a resolute self-denial steadied his eyes. "You know I want every day to be golden for you, Caroline." There was a long and potent silence before he added, "Just the same, I'll come if ever you ask me to—in happy times—or—God forbid—in unhappy ones."

"You're not rushing back to Denver tonight?" she asked.

"No. I'll be in Aspen a day or so. Your father has some things he wants to talk over and then have me handle in Denver."

"Eric," she said firmly, "come and visit Bob and me when you can. We've been friends so long."

He lifted glasses from a nearby tray and handed one to her. "Caroline," he said in a low voice, "let's drink just this one to yesteryears."

A minute later Bob was again at her side, and they were swept by the guests into a room where presents were stacked and waiting.

"Look at all this," Bob marveled. "Do we open all of them?"

"Every one," she assured him. "And I know just where to begin." Already her gaze had searched out a blue box with a gaily crossed ribbon festooned with an army epaulet.

Her fingers swiftly removed the wrapping and lifted the lid. There was a small card, flowing script, and a name that caused her to cry out in amazement.

FENIMORE C. CHATTERTON

Her eyes swept the words above the name. *"I'm relinquishing my rights, Caroline. You take it from here. Be good. Be happy. Be your wonderful self."*

She lifted folded tissue paper, paper that crinkled aside to reveal an ebony and silver coffee mill, the prettiest and daintiest she had ever seen. Along its side was a pair of miniature fly wheels and a small but practical crank.

"From Mr. Chatterton ..." she gasped. "Bob, it's just like the one he used to whirl at the Hugus store." She hugged it to her, then handed it to Mrs. Jorgenson. "Take care of it, Jorgie. I want to keep it always."

Finally they were away from the guests, the well-wishers, the friends, and the family. An evening train brought them back from Wilderness Creek.

Other friends awaited them at the depot and in the sparkling new lobby of the Hotel Jerome. Even as they ascended the wide stairs to the bridal suite friends were about them.

Abruptly they were alone and acutely conscious that they were a man and a woman and they were married.

Caroline moved to the heavily curtained window and looked out over the wide streets that had sprung from a single dusty trail.

"Every time I come into Aspen," she said softly, "I remember how it was the first time. Just a cluster of tents and shacks. Even the restaurant was a tent. Now it's a beautiful city with twelve thousand people." She waited, then added impulsively, "Bob, my own, I'm so, so glad we're here in Aspen tonight. I'm home, home, Bob."

"This Jerome is a pretty classy hotel. Beats the Clarendon all hollow." He took her into his arms, and added, "But it's not half as beautiful as my wife. Caroline, can you realize how much I love you."

"Tell me this way," she said, and her lips searched his cheek.

"I can only tell you the beginning in one night," Bob whispered.

"Make it a continued story, Mr. Herndon."

Caroline howled with laughter as she lifted a lacy garment from the suitcase.

"Look at this. Look at this nightgown. The bottom of it is sewn shut. Those stitches. They're not Jorgie's or mine." She stared at the inner folds of the hemline. "I know who did this. It's Maude Daley's work and Mrs. Brenton's. It explains some sly winks I was wondering about."

Caroline threw the gown onto the bed. "It'll take tiny scissors and an hour to get all those stitches out so I can wear it."

Bob studied the sealed garment, then his eyes lifted to hers with the beginning of a happy grin. "Why waste time on the damned thing—just to have it on for a few minutes?"

She looked steadily into his face, her breath quickening. "Why indeed!" She laughed. "This is exactly the way those two busybodies planned it." Her hand moved out to dim the light. Soon the soft glow of moonlight was about her as she moved slender, graceful, naked to the bedside.

204

And so she came to him, fulfilling the promise that a pigtailed child had whispered to a wounded cavalry officer in those time-hazed days of Fort Steele.

The holiday season soon was upon them. The first heavy snow had fallen, followed by low and icy temperatures that curtailed much of Aspen's activity. Christmas drew near. The tempo of merriment and expectancy quickened with a rash of parties and events that drew Mr. and Mrs. Robert Herndon away from the ecstasy of hours spent only with each other.

On an afternoon when lowering clouds obscured the peaks, and occasional snowflakes dampened her face, Caroline walked hastily toward the Jerome Hotel with brightly wrapped bundles stacked chin-high. She entered their suite and dropped the packages and her coat on the bed. She plumped down on Bob's lap as he lounged in a mohair chair. Her happiness at his being here mingled with lurking excitement. He had gone that morning to the Buccaneer mine, his first trip since their wedding. She doubted he would return this early.

Her head snuggled contentedly on his shoulder. "I missed you so darned much, Bob. Imagine it. You were gone almost seven hours."

He stroked her hair and gazed speculatively from the window. "I made a fast ride both ways. Wasn't taking a chance of getting caught in a storm. More snow up that way could have meant being stranded seven days at the mine instead of hours."

"How are things up there?" she asked. "I worry during storms. So many mines have been trapped in snow slides with men buried for weeks and months."

"Our Buccaneer is safe from that. There's no dangerous slope above. The men are snug and busy. Plenty of supplies; Jed saw to that."

"I'm glad. I want Christmas to be perfect for everyone." Caroline was relieved. "When can we have another ore haul?"

"Jed thinks we should do it next week. Right after Christmas. Not take a chance on getting snowbound." Proud excitement brightened his eyes. "This will be a rich haul, sweetheart. Not as many tons, but the ore gets better every day."

Her arms tightened about his neck. "We're so lucky ... so blessed." She tilted his chin and asked suddenly, "Honey, do you remember Mr. Barton from the Apex mine?"

"I ought to," he said, grinning, "after the way you shanghaied him into forking over six hundred dollars to clean up his assay bill."

"I met him in a hardware store today. He owns a cute little brick house a block west of Papa's house. He's just had it redecorated. He offered it to us. Bob, we can rent it or buy it."

A frown creased Bob's forehead. "Aren't you comfortable here?"

"Of course, silly." She laughed. "But we can't live in a hotel all the time. It'd cost a fortune. Besides, I like that brick place. A home of our own."

"It's not the best part of town," Bob persisted.

"It's the part where I've always lived," Caroline replied firmly. "We can fix it up adorably."

"If you want it," he agreed, "we'll rent it tomorrow." He gathered her into his arms and whirled her gaily about. She noted in his face and words the reluctance of his consent. He worded it as he eased her to her feet. "It'll do for now, Caroline, but you belong in a mansion, a big, rambling mansion with a servant in every room."

She eyed him in a tender beguiling way. "Aren't you glad right now there isn't a butler or maid to get rid of?"

"You gorgeous, enticing hussy," he said. "Come here!"

What would have inevitably taken place in the following minutes was forestalled by a light rapping at the hallway door. Caroline dashed quickly to a mirrored bureau and swept quickly buttoning fingers down her blouse, as Bob strode to the door, and swung it open.

"Maude!" he called out in surprise. "Come in. Where's Jim? Isn't he with you?"

"Hello, Mr. Lucky Bob," Maude Daley responded. "Jim stayed at the ranch this time." She glanced toward Caroline's abashed face, reflected in the mirror. "I'd better come back later," she said slyly. "Say in an hour."

206

Caroline turned and sped toward her. "You'll stay right here. Take her wraps, Bob. Maude we're going to have our own home tomorrow. Can you stay and help me have it ready by Christmas?"

Maude sank into a chair, unbuttoned her shoes, and kicked them off with a relieved sigh. "Of course I'll help if I can, honey. It'll give me days enough in town to find a present for a cantankerous cowman that swears he's got everything he wants."

"We'll work fast," Caroline said.

"We can have a Christmas-Eve housewarming. That'll bring Uncle Jim to town."

"Eating his own cooking for a spell will do that," Maude said, laughing.

Caroline glanced at her husband. "Bob, why don't you go downstairs and reserve a room for Maude? We'll join you later. Maude and I have plans to talk over."

He turned at the door. "I wouldn't plan too much for that little brick place. It's temporary, you know, until we build on Bleeker Street."

Within moments Caroline drew a table close to Maude Daley's chair. As she searched for pencil and paper, she realized that the room was darkening, that outside the snowfall was heavy and steady. She turned on a gas light, sat down, and began rapidly sketching. "The little house has a kitchen here ... a pantry ... a ..."

She wakened late the following morning, drowsily aware of someone pounding at the hallway door. For a moment she lay quietly, staring at the tousled curls and relaxed, peaceful face of the man lying belly-down beside her with his arms about a bunched pillow. Imagine my husband, she thought suddenly, looking like a tired little boy.

A more insistent knocking brought her to her feet. "Just a minute," she called. "Who is it?"

"It's me—your dad," Lance's voice cut through. "Hurry up, kitten."

She grabbed a robe, threw it about her, and opened the door. The seriousness of her father's face tore the last

207

remnant of sleep from her. "What is it, Papa? What's wrong?"

"We'd better wake Bob. Right away. There's been one hell of an avalanche, a snow slide. Two men were caught in it coming down from Ashcroft. Killed both of them. The Castle Creek road is locked for a quarter of a mile."

His words brought Bob Herndon stiffly upright and wide-eyed in bed. "Our ore haul," he said dazedly. "How long do you think the road'll be blocked?"

"God knows," Lance answered. "Until April at least."

"But Jed, and the men, will they be all right," Caroline asked weakly.

"Sure, kitten. We can pack grub in after the storm breaks. Or they can snowshoe into town."

"April." The word escaped Bob Herndon as a curse. "And we have ore for a big haul. Planned it for next week."

"It'll still be there come spring," Lance said. "That's for damn sure."

In later years, Caroline Herndon was never able to remember whether those first winter-swept months of the year 1890 drug out interminably, or whether they sped so swiftly she wanted only to catch and hold the happiness of every hour.

The demands on her time were endless. The little brick house echoed her laughter and songs as she busied herself to make it comfortable.

Bob was at home a lot during these days. His moods were swiftly and unpredictably changing. He cared little for the house. Often Caroline would return from her desk at the assay office to find him pacing the room or scowling from a window toward the snow-piled mountain slopes blotted from view by storm clouds gathered about them. At other times he would be in the kitchen, intent in study of plans and blueprints piled in disorder on the table. "This infernal weather," he raged. "These storms. The damnable snow. Won't it ever end?"

She came eagerly to him. From her calmness and her love and her body, he would draw reassurance and temporary patience.

"Live for today," she would urge him. "Every minute offers us so much. Be glad it isn't spring yet, when you'll be away at the mine. When both of us will be too busy for such hours as these."

Only through deftly gentle persuasion could she keep him at the assay office more than an hour or so each day. At moodier intervals her insistence would fan smouldering resentment within him.

"Stop nagging about the assay office," he flared on a dismal February morning. "That rat hole has served its purpose; we've all the Buccaneer papers here at home."

His tone brought her stiffly erect, her gray eyes chilled. "Bob, you've plenty of unfinished work at the *rat hole*. Responsibility to a lot of people. You can earn money there."

"Yeah . . . dabs and trickles of money."

"When did small sums become unimportant?" she retorted. "Just now there isn't even a trickle from the Buccaneer."

"We have plenty to get by," he insisted. "Don't worry."

Caroline had put on her coat and was buttoning it. "I don't intend to worry. I intend to work—at the assay office. You'll find plenty for lunch in the pantry. I want to stop by and see Mrs. Jorgenson at noon. She hasn't been well; I'm worried about her."

Bob stared at her firmly composed face. The old winsome grin lifted his lips. "Hold up, beautiful. Wait. I'm going with you. Maybe some acid stinks will flush you out of that office."

"They won't today. I'm working on something special?"
"What?"

"Some of those ten percent deals we made with prospectors. We've neglected them ever since the Buccaneer."

"Those deals," he said, with a depreciating wave. "You can have them—lock, stock, and worthless barrel."

Outside, she linked her arm cozily in his as they leaned into a bitter wind.

Shortly before noon, when she had become engrossed in paper work, and contentedly aware of the old familiar odors and sounds of his work, the activity of the inner room ceased. Moments later Bob was at her side, buttoning his coat and pulling a cap over his ears. "I ran enough samples," he said hurriedly. "The rest can wait. There's a fellow I have an appointment to see up town."

Caroline straightened his collar and flicked an imaginary strand from it. "See there—a long yellow hair. Already. Are you sure it's a fellow, my dear? Remember? Fairhaired women?"

He drew her swiftly from her chair and planted a resounding whack on her bottom. "I still prefer home cooking—brat!"

"Just see you're home before supper gets cold," she said blushing, then pushed him toward the door.

Caroline turned back to her desk, but the zest of work had fled. She wrote a dozen figures, scratched them out, and left the office.

Minutes later she sat in Lance's living room. Her gaze was unsmiling and concerned as she studied the face of Mrs. Jorgenson, who sat in a rocking chair swathed in a woolen shawl. The old housekeeper struggled to control and hide a deeply clutching cough. Caroline came to her feet, moved closer, and laid firmly comforting hands on the older woman's shoulders. "Jorgie, you've been house cleaning and baking again," she accused softly. "You should be in bed."

"In the bed! No. How could I your papa's house have clean? His meals ready?"

"Papa can eat with Bob and me, or downtown. Jorgie, have you seen a doctor?"

"Ja, twice he come. Your papa called him. Some pills he left—and this." She held up a small bottle, her face contemptuous.

"Have you been taking it? Regularly?"

Jorgie's gaze wavered and fell. "Like, like rotten bugs it smells."

Caroline walked to a bedroom, then returned with a blanket which she held before the heater. "To bed you go after you take the medicine. I'll cover you with this."

Another series of coughs left Mrs. Jorgenson white and gasping. As it ended, Caroline lifted and carried her toward the bedroom. She was frightened at the limp lightness of her burden.

When Lance came in a short time later, Caroline's greeting was abrupt and serious. "I've put Jorgie to bed. That cough scares me."

"Me, too," he agreed. "It got worse this morning. I've asked Doc Miller to stop by again. He's sending a woman to stay and help out." He leaned over the heater's warmth. "If only we'd get a break, a warm up of the weather."

"We all need that," Caroline yearned. "Papa, if this keeps up, can they get the road cleared by April for another ore haul from our mine?"

"Guess with me, kitten. I don't know. Say, speaking of your mine, did Bob ever find any records pertaining to those two men Gagnon and Lorentz? I asked him to look it up."

"No." she shook her head. "Bob searched the office. So did I."

"There's got to be something there." Lance's face drew to a puzzled frown. "Unless——"

"Unless what, Papa?"

"Unless it's been burned or destroyed."

Caroline eased thoughtfully into a chair. "Who were those men—Gagnon and Lorentz? You never said."

Lance studied the wall for a time. "They were two early day prospectors, partners. They prospected the area where your Buccaneer is. Filed some claims. As I recall, Lorentz was killed. Then Gagnon left town. Somehow I've a persisting idea Bob did assay work for them."

"The claims wouldn't be valid without assessment work."

"That's the hell of it, kitten. Some work was done."

"You mean——" Caroline's eyes were frightened.

"Now don't jump to conclusions. Likely nothing'll come of it." He paused, then added, uncertainly, "Unless Gagnon were to show up again. Take another good look through Bob's records."

"I'll start tomorrow," Caroline answered. "This afternoon, I'm going to stay with Jorgie. Make sure she takes medicine."

"She'll argue that a goose grease and onion poultice is better," Lance said grinning.

"And perhaps she's right. I vaguely remember that I stank of onions for a month after that time in Maude's place at Evans."

The firm clamp of winter wavered toward the seduction of fickle March weather before Mrs. Jorgenson was up and about. The tearing cough was gone, but also absent was much of the old housekeeper's energy and vitality. She had lost weight; her face remained white. Her illness, though, had taken none of her stern demands that Lance Ainsley's home be spotless, that his meals be superbly prepared. She demanded perfection geared to her own ways and beliefs. Lance, who constantly sought a woman to replace the one Jorgenson had dismissed, swore blazingly as he related his plight to his daughter. "She's a tyrant, kitten. No girl could work for her. I've damned near run out of places to look for someone to help her."

"So I've noticed, Papa. Know what's wrong? I do."

"It's high time you told me."

"She's lonesome. I'm not there for her to fuss over. She's getting quite old, Papa. And she has been away from her own people so long. I've an idea if you'll hire a young Swedish girl to help, things will straighten out."

He glanced at her oddly. "So I should have a young girl in my home and half the tongues in Aspen gossiping."

"Then hire a married one, who can be home nights."

"So simple as that," Lance jeered. "Swedish people aren't flea-thick in town."

"I know a family in shacktown."

"Why waste time telling me? Get the hell over there and hire the woman; hire the whole blasted family if you have to."

No one who lived in the dingy shacks of the bluff above the Roaring Fork was surprised to see Caroline Herndon trudging their way toward sunset. Despite her mine and her marriage she regularly visited these people among whom she counted so many friends. At the neatly raked yard of a tarpaper dwelling, she was greeted by towheaded children of stair-stepping ages. When their mother appeared, beckoning her in, she asked, "Where is your oldest daughter, the married one?"

The woman shook her head. "Today she is helping Mrs. Edmonds."

"Mrs. Edmonds." Caroline's words and face were blank.

"The woman who is new in town and works for Dr. Miller. She lives across the street. One block down. A gray house with a leanto."

"Would your daughter want a steady job? Working at my father's house, and helping Mrs. Jorgenson?"

"Mrs. Jorgenson . . . the Swedish lady?"

"Yes," Caroline answered, and added silently, Definitely a Swede.

"That my Olga would like."

Caroline moved away. She was aware of their reluctance to see her go. "I'll be back soon to visit with you. Now I must hurry."

She found Olga at the gray house, and was relieved by the alacrity with which her offer of a job at Lance's house was accepted. She turned to leave, when the door opened, and a middle-aged woman entered, holding the hand of a delicate, solemn-faced little girl that she surmised to be eight or nine years old.

"This is Mrs. Edmonds," Olga introduced, "and her daughter, Kathleen. Mrs. Edmonds helps Dr. Miller."

Caroline held out her hand. "It's nice to meet you, Mrs. Edmonds, and you too Kathleen. I am Mrs. Herndon, Caroline Herndon."

The woman nodded. "I've heard of you. You've many friends here."

"Indeed, I have. Some of my best——" Caroline's words trailed off under the peculiar and searching stare that Mrs. Edmonds had fastened upon her.

"From somewhere I know you," Mrs. Edmonds said studiedly. "From someplace, some time, long ago."

Caroline's gaze moved from the woman to the child. "I'd like to think so. But you must be mistaken."

"No. I'm not mistaken. We've met. It will come to me."

"May I come again and visit with you and Kathleen?" Caroline smiled. "You may not wish me to. I've offered Olga steady work."

Mrs. Edmonds' eyes were still intently puzzled. "Do

213

come again. I'm glad you could hire Olga. I can pay her so little. Just an hour or so a week she helps me."

Caroline was silent a moment, aware of the meager furnishings of the house and of the child's wide gaze. "Olga will still help you. We'll make sure of that."

On sudden impulse, Caroline knelt and hugged the girl. "We're going to be friends, Kathleen," she said.

As she walked rapidly homeward, the child's face was vividly imprinted in her mind. Mrs. Edmonds is right, she thought suddenly. Somewhere we have met. But when ... where?

Caroline always had been fascinated by the growth of Aspen. The sight of a new building, a mine warehouse, a stone fronted business block, or the unpainted freshness of a new dwelling would bring a quickening of her pulse and infinite pride in the mountain city.

It was in this mood that she left home early on a mid-March morning, trudged up Monarch Street, then veered onto Center to view Hallam's Lake and its expanse of ice. Later, she moved along Smuggler, then turned past Frances and Hallam Streets. She was on Bleeker, and returning toward home, when she stopped abruptly to stare at two and a half stories of house that neared completion. It was Victorian in style, elaborately ginger-breaded and scrolled, and faced Bleeker from the depths of a lot that was at least an acre in size.

Someone, she thought, is going to have a house bigger and more expensive than the one Hardrock Corlett built. Ellen will be knotted up with jealousy. It's a monstrosity. Just curtaining it will cost a pretty penny. She walked on, her mind sharply contrasting the unfinished house with the cramped and meager dwellings of shacktown. She grew thoughtful. Why must it always be so unfair, even here in rich and beautiful Aspen? Hundreds of men breaking their backs, their health, their spirits at underground work that pays enough for a meager existence, while a few fortunate ones reap millions and waste so much on mansions and castles?

Her mood was questioning and somber as she passed

214

through the gate and mounted the steps of her own small and cheery house.

Bob had been asleep when she started her walk. Now he was in the kitchen. The welcome scent of coffee drifted to her.

"You should have gone walking with me," she said in greeting him. "The air is clear. Wonderful. I believe we're about to have a big thaw."

He kissed her in a perfunctory way. "I hope to Christ it's a big enough thaw to clear the road up Castle Creek. Jed's got ore running out of his ears. It'll be a big haul this time."

"I'm sure it won't be long to wait now," she studied his face, and knew his mood would call for all her patience. "I came down Bleeker Street, honey. They're working on a huge house out beyond the school. I wonder who owns it."

He poured coffee and handed the cup to her. Sudden defiance firmed his face. "We do," he said crisply.

She stepped backward, splashing coffee onto the floor. "Bob," she gasped, "what do you mean?"

"Just what I said, Caroline. We own that big beauty. I'm having it built."

Caroline leaned across the table, grasping its edge to steady her. "Why didn't you tell me?" she asked.

He attempted a grin that faded beneath the disbelief, the concern, and the growing anger of her tone. "I had several reasons for not telling you yet. I wanted it as a surprise. No one but the contractor knows. Besides, this winter I've needed something to keep me busy, to look forward to." Bob's words gathered speed and anger. "You may like this cramped-up little cubbyhole. I don't. I hate it. Hate seeing you messing around here when you should have a lovely and spacious home. One where we can entertain. One we can be proud of. The Buccaneer will pay for it."

Caroline sat weakly down. "Bob, if I'd only known in time, could have asked you to wait. Sure we have a mine, but it isn't Aladdin's lamp. We've had just one ore shipment. The money——" Sudden panic slackened her face.

215

"Bob, you, you didn't tie up mine funds, corporation money?"

He paced the room angrily. "Sure. Where else would I——?"

"But it has to be released as dividends. Jed Curry will get almost half of it."

"Don't fly off the handle. I asked Jed. He went along with the idea." Suddenly he wheeled about and slumped to a chair opposite her. The defiance and arrogance was gone from his face. At that moment she saw him as a small and troubled boy. "I wanted it for you, Caroline. Maybe to prove I could provide one decent, worthwhile thing. I, I failed so often."

For half a minute his wife's gaze silently probed him. Her decision was a solid thing before she spoke. "It's a wonderful house, dearest. I'll love every minute in it." She kept her words tender, steady, as she added, "Of course we should have a better place. The next ore shipment will put us in shape to handle it. Come along. Let's go plan how we're going to furnish it."

There was no ore shipment in April. A grim, white-faced Jed Curry rode in and knocked at the door of the little brick home. "The mine is closed," he muttered dazedly. "The sheriff came out about noon, posted a notice, then locked everything tight. Left one of his men to tend the pumps."

"Why? Oh, why?" Caroline cried out.

"Suit's been filed, claiming our title is void and worthless. It'll come up in court. God knows when."

"Who the hell did it? Filed the suit?" Bob raged.

"Someone name of Gagnon." Jed slumped to a chair; his hands trembled as he covered his face.

"Good-bye Bleeker Street," Bob Herndon said slowly. "I might have known I'd fail again. We'll sell the big house. Caroline, I'm sorry."

His words brought her erect. Her eyes flashed. "Listen to me. Both of you listen. We're not whipped. That mine and that ore belong to us. We're going to fight. Fight clean or fight dirty. Fight in court and out of court!"

She paused; her voice was lower. "I haven't told you,

Bob. I wanted to be sure. You and I will have a child in October. He's going to be born in that house, our house on Bleeker Street."

Jed Curry first caught the impact of her words. His face changed and gathered the spirit and the challenge she radiated. "Surer'n hell the youngster will be born on Bleeker Street if my share of the Buccaneer means helping arrange it."

Bob Herndon took Caroline in his arms. "I succeeded in one thing, didn't I, brat? It'll be a boy. It'll have to be a boy. A son. Caroline, I hope he's like you. Strong and wise and enduring."

An hour later Caroline coordinated the catastrophe with her father's words. "Jed, you say a man named Gagnon has brought suit. That's the name Papa has had us turning the assay office upside-down looking for." She turned purposefully to Bob. "Now we've got to find some record. Something about Gagnon and Lorentz."

As the greening promise of spring gave way to summer, and summer yielded to autumn, the enigma of Gagnon and Lorentz remained. An inch-by-inch search of the assay office and workshop produced no clue regarding the phantom prospectors who once had staked claims and delved into a rocky slope in the wilderness of Castle Creek. Through power and persuasion, Lance Ainsley and H. A. W. Tabor achieved postponement time after time in Pitkin County Court of the case of Gagnon vs. the Buccaneer Corporation.

Caroline was glad she had acquiesced to her husband's arrangements to build and to live in the pretentious home on Bleeker Street. She speedily learned that the political adroitness and behind-the-scenes maneuvering of Lance Ainsley offered a far better, far more effective preparation for the forthcoming legal battle for control of the Buccaneer than either she or Bob or Jed Curry could muster. Theirs would have been a bluntly impatient approach, serving only to irritate and probably alienate the very people on whom they must rely to achieve the all-important delays. Time was surely the essence of the situation. They needed time to seek out the identity of their true opposi-

217

tion, and time to continue searching for the elusive and seemingly nonexistent records of the past.

She realized their cause could be impeded, and perhaps put in jeopardy, by either secret panic or outward indications of financial worry or instability. Their lives must go as nearly as possible a normal, routine way. Friends must be kept; new ones made. Social activities and their contacts must never be neglected. Smile. Laugh. Joke. Never for a single moment discard the outward façade that all was well and the future secure.

"This is a time to look at our hold card," she advised Bob. "We've several hidden aces. Such things as the assay office and its income, bank accounts, the mine equipment. Maybe our best assets are intangible. Those ten percent contracts for one. The very fact we came here when the town was a collection of hovels, then stuck here and built. Papa's position is solid as a rock. It all adds up."

"You're forgetting one of the whopping big ones," Bob reminded her. "That you half-own a ranch any cowman would give ten years of his life to own."

Caroline's answer was immediate and unwavering. "Of course. People have a lot of respect for Jim Daley and the Lazy Seedy."

There was a long silence between them then. Then Bob kicked savagely at the rug. "Caroline, who are we fooling except ourselves with all this talk? Sweetness and light. Telling ourselves everything is just fine? Let's be honest. We're in a stinking mess. We need that ore stashed away at the mine. It's ours. With some teams and gunslingers——"

"Oh, shut up," she cut him off angrily. "You know that's no solution. No smelter would touch it; if they did the proceeds would be impounded. Try that sort of move and we'll be in lawsuits up to our—— Maybe in jail. A fat chance we'd have of winning anything. Even Papa, or Uncle Jim, or Mr. Tabor couldn't help."

"So what am I supposed to do? Start a hurrah society? Sit around and pick my nose?"

"You've got a big house to help me get furnished and to move into. That'll take plenty of work and time. You've got an assay office. Work at it more. Make it pay. Pay enough to cover some parties I'm going to give. If you've

218

any time left over, and I doubt you will have, try meeting people. Making more friends. We're going to need every friend we can get."

He took the stinging rebuke in silence and stalked off to bed. When she joined him, they slept tightly curled and there was adoration in the hand that cradled her breast.

The housewarming party drew a full column in the local press, and was echoed by Denver's *Rocky Mountain News*. The roster of those who came to dinner spoke of success, position, prestige.

Chapter 11

The sorcery of high-country autumn had touched the valley of the Roaring Fork on an October evening when Caroline felt the first and strangely new pain. Within hours her child would be born. Relief and the impatience of anticipation mingled with her quick review of the preparations that had been so carefully made.

Mrs. Jorgenson and Maude Daley had been with her for several days. Their presence was comforting, but her mood of the past half hour had led her to the solitude of a small, dormered room upstairs. It adjoined her bedroom. From its eastward-facing window, she gained a panoramic view of the jutted never-summer peaks guarding Independence Pass. Up there, from vast snow fields, the creeks tumbled down and formed the headwaters of the Roaring Fork.

After another seizure her impulse was to go downstairs or to call out to the women waiting below. She moved to a small, brightly padded windowseat and lowered herself awkwardly upon it. A westering, horizon-seeking sun sifted its lessening light upon the town. Upriver, in the narrower canyons, dusk was already deeply shadowing. The peaks seemed close and strong. Their snowfields took on a flame-tinted hue. She recalled that Spanish explorers, seeing such a sunset glow, had spoken of its crimson as the blood of Christ, and had named a distant snowy range the *Sangre de Christos*.

She rarely meditated or looked back to assess past events. The present and the future were what counted. She realized that this attitude was an outcome of the completeness with which she had divested her memory and her thought of the Union Colony, of Swope's mansion, of her mother Emily and even of Baby Shawn, the brother she had known so short a time.

Her lips tightened at the thought of Emily Ainsley. What would it be like, what greater comfort would there be, if her mother were downstairs right now? She leaned her head forward to the coolness of the windowpane. Her eyes closed. The memory of her mother's face clung about her. "God," she said, "it has been so long, so many years."

Darkness enfolded the room. She jerked upward when a warning pain caused her to gasp. She moved to the hallway, then to the post marking the top of a broad stairway. "Jorgie ... Maude," she called. "Call Dr. Miller now."

Her son was born at dawn October 16, 1890. There was no quibbling over his name. Months before, Bob Herndon had settled it. "If it's a boy, Caroline, I wish we could name him *Fred*. That was my father's name." She had conceived the child in love of her Lieutenant Bob. Her son would be christened Frederick Charles Herndon. Her first, drowsy words, as they laid him in her arms, were "Hi, Freddy."

A week had passed, and a degree of normality had returned to the house, when Lance chose a time to broach an important development to his son-in-law.

"You'll need someone to help at the shop now that the baby is here. Caroline won't be available much for a while."

Bob shrugged indifferently. His face lighted at the resounding and spunky new wail floating down the stairway. "The little devil's got a temper. And a set of lungs."

"Tempers are hereditary, I've heard." Lance said proudly, "About the shop. There's some well-paying work I can toss your way."

"How come? You opening a mine?" Bob's face was curious.

"No, but I know some people in the San Juan country who need plenty of work done. They'd ship it to you. Maybe you've overlooked a good bet by not taking on work from outside Aspen."

"There are plenty of assayers around the state," Bob answered.

"Sure there are. But business is where you find it. Dig it up. How about me lining this San Juan deal up for you? You'll find expenses higher with a growing family."

Bob filled glasses from a decanter and extended one to Lance. "Thanks. But not now. We've money to get along all right until we reopen the Buccaneer. Comes a tight spot we can use Caroline's income from that ranch down on Wilderness Creek."

Lance drained his glass and set it firmly down. The clipped coolness of his words swung Herndon about to face him. This was a Lance Ainsley, a father-in-law, he had never run up against. He stood wide-eyed and silently listening as Lance said, "Bob, I've always liked you. Not just because you're Caroline's husband, but because you're intelligent and know your business. But it's high time you learn a few of the facts. You'll need this new income. If you turn it down, you're apt to wish to hell you hadn't. The Buccaneer won't open before spring. The case has been set for the spring term of court. Sure I arranged it. If the case was tried right now you'd lose it so fast your belly would flop. There's heavy odds you'll lose when court convenes in the spring. You can't count on that mine for a single dollar—now or ever."

Bob Herndon's face was shocked and white.

"Another thing," Lance said, "Caroline never told you, but I'm going to. She doesn't have any ranch income. She doesn't have any ranch. She sold her half to Jim Daley for money to develop your Buccaneer.

An agonized groan broke from Bob's lips. He was marked by utter disbelief, with near incomprehension of what he had heard. "She sold her ranch? My wife sold her Lazy Seedy?"

"You're damned right she did. Willingly! Gladly! Bob, she loved you. She still loves you. With her, love is an all out. It's a sacrificing thing."

"But, but you're wrong, Lance. You must be wrong. She said. . . . I thought she got the money, the seventy-five thousand dollars, from you!"

"How could she have gotten it from me," Lance growled. "I didn't even know about the damned venture until machinery began coming into town for it. Besides, I've never had that sort of money that wasn't invested."

Bob rose unsteadily and walked toward a window. "My wife did that. How can I face her now? How can I ever face her?"

The old winning smile played across Lance's face as he dropped a hand to his son-in-law's shoulder. "Why not start by telling her you've a devil of a lot of new assay work coming in? That your shop'll be busy as get out all winter?" The words dropped to a confidential whisper. "You can tell her pretty quick. She'll be looking for you upstairs in a few minutes. One other thing, Son. If things get really rough, I'm always around."

Lance picked up his hat and his walking stick. Then he left the house.

PART THREE

1891

Chapter 12

Lance Ainsley fidgeted. The five cards dealt in this stud poker game were decent enough, but his hand dropped repeatedly to pluck at his trouser leg and pull it gingerly away from his thigh. Amused speculation marked the faces of the men ringed about the table in the quiet room of the affluent Roaring Fork Club.

In the memory of those gathered here, men whose wealth enabled them to belong to the club and to sit in on high-stake games, Ainsley had never acted like this. Usually his cool, professional mode of play and the inscrutable calm of his face called for wariness and studied calculation on the part of those challenging and opposing his play.

An irritated scowl swept his face as he again clutched his pants.

"What in tarnation ails you, Lance?" The question was voiced by a coal dealer who annually swore that the output of the best shift of his mine at Carbondale was donated across this table.

"Don't you know?" another player said grinning. "He's trying out a new spot to slip an ace."

"When I hide an ace, my friend," Lance retorted, "your eyes'll hook into a permanent cross trying to figure whether it went to my collar or my boot."

"Then what's making you prance?"

"Maybe," an onlooker observed slyly, "he's been on Durant Street visiting the girls once too often and got himself dosed."

Lance snapped a card to the table, then stood up. "Truth is," he said sheepishly, "I'm diaper-rashed." They were laughing loudly as he went on. "I just came from my daughter's house and a session of bouncing her baby on Grandpa's knee. The kid let me have it good, soaked me hip to knee. It's dried now, but it itches."

"Why didn't you change pants?" the coalman demanded. "Maybe it wasn't the baby. Maybe your bladder is gettin'———"

"Go to hell," Lance thrust back. "I was going home for a bath and fresh outfit. Met up with you, heading this way and so anxious to lose a bundle you drug me along."

Another player sized up Lance's trim waistline. "I've a spare suit in my locker down in the gent's room." He threw a key onto the table. "Locker eight. Wash up. Change and come on back."

"Thanks," Lance replied. "That's the one sensible thing that's been said. Deal me out for a few hands."

His tread was silenced by the luxurious pile of the carpet as he descended the stairs. Nearing the last step, he was aware of clean, cool air moving about him. He breathed deeply, welcoming this respite from the smoky haze of the card room. Far off was the rushing sound of the Roaring Fork. In early May the river was at a noisy and turgid flood stage.

He stopped abruptly, listening to another and lesser sound. He identified it at once. The soft rattle of a key being tried in a locked door. He leaned quietly over the banister and his eyes swept the dimness of the lower hallway.

The rear hallway window was open, the sash was slid upward, and the breeze billowed heavy draperies. Midway in the hall, at the locked door of the club office, a man was crouched. He nervously fumbled at the lock. In the subdued light, Lance knew that the man was a stranger, a shabbily dressed prowler.

It took but seconds for Lance to step cautiously down, slide round the newel post, and with leaping steps rush upon the intruder. His hands flashed out to seize the other's wrists and wrench them into a painful lock.

"You sneaking bastard!" Lance snapped. "What do you think you're up to?"

The stranger jerked to a stiffening erectness. His head swung wildly about in a terrified scanning of Lance's face.

226

His breath, coming in a panicked hiss, was sour and nauseating.

"You old wino." Lance said, and turned from him in revulsion.

The man's stare came from bleared, bloodshot eyes. There was a quivering whine in his voice. "Please Mr. Ainsley, don't call anyone. For Christ sake don't call anyone. Don't turn me in."

"How'd you get in here?"

The man nodded an unbarbered, matted head toward the window. "I jimmied it, Mr. Ainsley. I'm broke. Hungry."

"You wanted a bottle. Isn't that the truth of it? Thought you could find a little cash in the office till. The men upstairs can deal with you." Lance dragged him toward the stairway.

A graying terror swept the prowler's face. "Don't call them. Don't, Mr. Ainsley."

Lance eyed him curiously. "How come you know who I am?"

"I know you all right, Mr. Ainsley. You're Bob Herndon's daddy-in-law." Craftiness edged some of the fear from the man's eyes. "I could help you, Mr. Ainsley, if you'd let me go. And not tell anyone I was here."

"It's a good try, old man. But no dice." Lance's head lifted to call out to those in the room above when his prisoner uttered a frenzied whisper. "Jesus! Don't holler up there. I'll tell you about Gagnon!"

Lance's gaze jerked about. "Say that again," he demanded.

The old man's voice was strained and scarcely audible. "I know where Gagnon is. What they're up to."

"You'll go with me? Talk? Spill the details?" Lance queried sharply.

"Sure, sure, Mr. Ainsley."

Lance's decision was swift. "Stand back then. Be quiet while I call up and make an excuse for leaving." His hand dropped threateningly toward a pocket. "Stand still or I'll shoot your head off." Then he called up the stairs. "The pants don't fit, Henry. I'm going home to change."

When an acknowledging voice drifted down, Lance

fumbled for his pass key to the street door. "Come along now."

The old man recoiled. "Not that way. Not out there. Maybe they'd see us together."

"Who?" Lance asked.

"This way, Mr. Ainsley. Out the window and through the alley where it's dark."

Lance followed; his grip was tight on the man's shirt. "You'd better know something," he said savagely.

The alley was gloomily shadowed. Despite this, there was caution and fear in the way this stranger peered about with every step. "Where can we go?" he quavered. "Where they won't see me with you?"

Lance's mind worked nimbly. "You'd be roughed up, eh, if they saw me and you together?"

"Worser'n that. Maybe have my throat cut."

Lance thought of several places—his own office or home, the sawmill, the assay office, Caroline's house, or carriage house. All too risky if this man was really being watched or shadowed. A dozen steps later he knew the solution. At the building's end there was an outside stairway, boarded in and leading to a small landing. A fortuneteller had occupied the rooms above, utilizing the stairway for those of her clients wanting to shun public gaze. She had abandoned the rooms and now they were vacant.

Lance twisted his prisoner toward the steps. "Up there. Quietly. We'll have all the privacy we need."

They sat down side by side on the dusty landing, their feet planted on a lower step. "Now talk," Lance whispered. "I want the full details, everything you know. It'd better be all, and be the truth."

It was half an hour before they came down the steps. "Wait here while I crawl back through the window into the club," Lance cautioned. "Then get out of here." He thrust a gold piece into the old man's hand. "Take this. Maybe I'll want to see you again."

He moved to the window and slid inside the club. After he had found the switch that cut the hallway into darkness, he returned to the open window and peered out. The old prowler edged from alley blackness toward the glow of a street lamp. The slow and cautious manner of his steps confirmed his fear-stricken words. This man was indeed afraid that someone might have seen him in company with Lance Ainsley.

Lance was at his office at the usual time the next morning. Outwardly, he gave no indication of worry or agitation, but he shunted aside his routine work and spent the hours of that day alone in deep thought.

During the noon hour he saw Jed Curry and asked him to be at the Herndons' home that evening.

They gathered in the privacy of the upstairs parlor. "There's been a break in your Buccaneer affair," Lance told them. He related the events that had brought about his talk with the frightened old prowler. "At least we know now where our man Gagnon is. Before I tell you, get this straight: you're up against as tough and deadly an outfit as the Colorado silver camps ever spawned. You're up against the Shaner brothers. Matt Shaner fronts things here in Aspen. And worse yet his brother, Len, masterminds things from God knows where."

A grimly shocked silence held Caroline and Bob and Jed as Lance went on. "This bunch has already wrestled control of Hardrock Corlett's claims away from him!"

"Oh, no!" Caroline cried out. "How could they do that?"

"Through playing up to his wife, Ellen. Her social ambitions, I suppose. They finagled it, somehow, after Hardrock took Matt Shaner as a partner."

Caroline's thoughts ran back to her wedding day, to an agitated and dispirited old Hardrock and his saying that it was too late to talk with Lance.

Bob shook his head sadly. "They've swiped a valuable property if they've got Corlett's setup."

"It won't satisfy them for long. This old man I collared last night worked for them up on Wilderness Creek. The Shaners are getting ready to placer-mine. Gouge out and rape those creek banks in a hurry. What they're really after is something else, your Buccaneer. They're working through Gagnon to get it."

"It's peculiar about Gagnon being up on Wilderness

229

Creek," Jed Curry said. "No one remembers his being in these parts for years."

"Gagnon isn't there." Lance answered. "He's likely holed up wherever Len Shaner is."

"But he filed the suit," Bob argued. "The suit that shut us down."

"Wrong again," Lance explained. "He signed the suit papers. They were filed by a Denver law firm."

Jed Curry strode throughtfully about the room. "This mess is beyond me. How come they could bring suit anyhow? Shut us down? Get the mine sealed up—locked? My title to the claims was clean as a whistle. They issued 'em right here at the land office."

"Sure they did," Lance agreed. "In the Pitkin County land office. But if Gagnon can prove he has valid prior deed, as he claims he has, it will supersede your title. Back ten years ago when Gagnon and Lorentz were working claims up Castle Creek, Pitkin County hadn't been established. This was part of Gunnison County. Papers would have been filed, and titles issued, from Gunnison, or maybe Leadville. Records of those days are slim. Hazy. A lot of them have been lost through fires and carelessness. Some cases show land records stolen."

"Where does that leave us?" Caroline asked.

"Out on a thin and shaky limb," Lance replied. "Unless——"

"Unless what, Papa?"

Lance slowly voiced the thoughts and the possibilities that had threaded his mind throughout the day. "Unless perhaps our boy Gagnon isn't Gagnon at all. Not the real McCoy. Possibly someone the Shaners have dug up to play the part. Len Shaner might try that or a forged deed." Lance paused. "Somehow, Gagnon's partner enters into this puzzle." He stared silently at Bob Herndon. "Bob, I'm darned if I know why. Can't pinpoint a reason yet. But every time I think of Lorentz I tie him in with your assay office. It'll come to me, sometime."

"You're barking up a wrong tree," Herndon said. "We've fine-toothed the office, the shop, the whole building. I even searched my sleeping quarters there. Nothing. No scrap of paper. No Lorentz."

230

"Try again," Lance urged thoughtfully. "This thing comes up in court in almost thirty days."

"Maybe I'd better get over to Gunnison and Leadville," Curry said. "See if I can find record of a deed to Gagnon or Lorentz."

"You won't," Lance replied. "I've already had records checked at both places. Just the same, if Gagnon produces an authentic deed we're sunk."

"What can we do?" Caroline's query was tired and strained.

"Wait for them to show their hand in court. The burden of proof is on Gagnon or Shaner. Meanwhile turn that dratted assay office upside-down. Something's there; it's got to be."

"I'll finger every paper . . . old and new, Papa."

"One other thing," Lance added. "Don't talk about my seeing that old prowler down at the club. Keep mum and nonconcerned. If you do find anything at the office, be damned careful that nobody knows. I've an idea we're being watched. Every day. Every place."

The following Tuesday Caroline was grim and weary from reopening bundles of old records. Jim Daley's heavy step pounded the porch of the assay office. He came inside and flung the door shut with a viciously angry slam.

Startled, Caroline wheeled toward him. Then she stood shock still, staring at his grimly set face, his smouldering eyes. "Uncle Jim," she whispered "What on earth?"

"Where's Lance?" he demanded. "Where's your dad?"

"I don't know? Did you try his office?"

"Just came from there. They said he left an hour ago."

Caroline shoved a chair toward him. "Sit down. Papa'll show up here. It's close to lunchtime."

Jim Daley was moving to open the door. "Tell him to wait. I'll be back. This'll give me time to buy enough Winchester slugs to wipe out the whole damned——"

She flew to him, grabbing the arm of his leather jacket. She yanked him backward, slid around him, and planted herself firmly against the door. "You're not going anyplace. Not like this, like a crazy man. Tell me. What's wrong?"

He stared silently at her for a moment, then leaned

231

across the paper-strewn desk. In unconscious gesture, his fingers traced tight concentric circles. "It's that god-damned crew up in the canyon on Wilderness. Them bastards up at Hardrock Corlett's diggin's. They're placering into the creek. It's running mud and filth. Part of our upper meadow is covered with an inch of the slimy muck." He reared upward. "Lemme out of here, Caroline. I've got men waitin' for the word. We'll blast them to hell'n gone."

She was shaken by his words and by his face. "How awful. How sickeningly awful. How can they? We've got prior rights, a decree, to the water." In her agitation she was unaware that she spoke of the water and the ranch as her own.

They were staring at each other, wordless and sickened, when Lance Ainsley came up the walk. Caroline slid from the door to let him through. His eyes swept her and then fastened on Daley's face. "What the devil's going on?" he asked.

It was Caroline who uttered swift, revealing words. "Shaner is placering Wilderness Creek, ruining the meadows, the hay fields, the stock water."

Jim Daley's flint-chipped eyes bored at Lance. "You want to ride with me and my men? We're gonna hang every last one of them."

Lance was shocked. "Why didn't I foresee this?" He threw an arm about Daley's shoulder. "Whoa down, now Jim. Take it easy. We'll see my lawyer, then get over to the courthouse and get an injunction served today."

"Let 'em serve it on corpses, that's all there'll be left of that crew when I. . . . You riding with me or not, Ainsley?"

Lance eyed the cowman appraisingly. "You're loony as a turd-bird, Jim. Think of Maude. Where would it leave her if you go gunslinging and end up on the gallows at Canyon City?"

Daley answered slowly and growled, "We'll try it your way for now. Providing by tomorrow they've stopped using the creek as a sewer. If they ain't, I'll ride at 'em. I'll surer'n hell ride at 'em!"

The speed with which Lance Ainsley and Jim Daley were able to achieve the issuance of a temporary restraining order involved both persuasion and a degree of subtle pressure. It was issued by County Judge Wallace Langford, who studied them through heavily lensed glasses as he prepared to sign the document. "You must realize, gentlemen, that this is merely a temporary injunction, instructing the defendants to cease and desist from their placer operations on Wilderness Creek until a proper hearing can be held in this court. It is to become effective upon service by the sheriff. Limit is ten days."

Lance nodded. "Thank you, Judge Langford. I'm sure that Mr. Daley's attorneys will have his case ready for presentation by that time."

Doubt mingled with anxiety and lingering anger in Daley's face, as he said, "I ain't so sure that placering outfit, Matt Shaner and the others, will pay any attention to a piece of paper."

Judge Langford looked at the old cowman unsmilingly. "Mr. Daley, that *piece of paper* carries the authority of this court, of Pitkin County, and of the State of Colorado."

"How many men'll go up there with the sheriff to hand it to Shaner?" Daley persisted.

"That is a matter for the sheriff to decide. Usually he sends one deputy."

" 'T ain't enough," Daley growled. "I'll send half a dozen of my——"

Mr. Daley," the judge retorted sharply. "I insist that you leave this matter in the hands of duly appointed officers." He glared briefly at Jim Daley, then smiled wryly. "Hang it all, Jim. I know how you feel. Don't prejudice your case by a passel of fool tricks."

"Right now," Lance said firmly, "the only trick he's going to pull is lift a bracer over at the Jerome bar."

Jim Daley shrugged, then studied the judge. "Supposin' you happen by the Jerome after a while, I'd buy you a snifter." He swung about to Lance. "Leggo my arm." Lance was already yanking him from the room. Safely outside the door Lance added, "You confounded idiot, Jim. Judge Langford could have thrown the book at you. Buy him a drink. Lord Almighty! Contempt of court. Coercion. Bribery."

In the distance, there was the sound of Judge Wallace

Langford clearing his throat. A sound that deepened to roaring laughter.

As Lance surmised, the restraining order was promptly complied with by the placer mining crew. Work came to an abrupt halt. The waters of Wilderness Creek laboriously cleansed themselves of the sludgy tailings. Two days later the creek again ran clear, unsullied, cold.

They knew that it was only the lull before an impending and stormy court session. Matt Shaner had made a gesture of civil obedience that would strengthen his cause. Lance studied every aspect of the case and complained to Caroline, "Maybe I should have studied law instead of poker dealing. Looks like we'll be in court a month or more with your Buccaneer case docketed to come up smack after Daley's fracas."

They faced Judge Langford again at ten o'clock of a warm spring morning. This was no private hearing. Already the courtroom was filled and curious people moved about in the adjoining hallway.

Aspen had known many lawsuits and court battles. The riches yielded by Aspen and Smuggler Mountains, and the rich silver districts about them, had provided both the means and the incentives for court action. Fortunes were often at stake, and the mining barons had not been loath to use every legal maneuver in furthering their individual bids for money, for financial power, and for fame.

The case now at hand, that of James Daley vs. Hardrock Corlett, Ellen Corlett, Matt Shaner, *et al.*, to determine whether a ranch owner could by legal means force operators of a placer mining operation to cease operations provided a new question. Word had been widespread of this impending battle. Spectators came long distances. The solid force of a growing ranch and farm economy was being felt on Colorado's Western Slope. Someday it would have to be reckoned with, and the supremacy of the mining industry would be challenged, and, perhaps, surpassed.

This had been carefully considered by Clay Withrow, the young, but experienced and shrewd, attorney in whose hands Jim Daley had placed his case. "We could," Withrow had remarked, "ask for a change of venue, ask

234

that this case be heard in a community not so closely tied to mining and those interested in nothing except mines."

Lance Ainsley studied the possibility of a venue change for several minutes and said, "It seems to me, Clay, that one of Jim Daley's strongest points is the fact that he has lived in this county a long time, that he has built friendships and a fine reputation while he was putting together and developing his ranch. People here consider him a darned good neighbor. Besides, wouldn't such a request, one that the case be moved to another court, have a connotation of weakness or fear of local justice—of uncertainty?"

"Bring it into court right here in Aspen," Jim Daley said flatly. "Judge Langford will give me as fair a shake as anyone."

"I'm glad you see it that way." Withrow nodded. "Now, Jim, your decrees establish beyond question your right in perpetuity to one half of the water of Wilderness Creek. Any court would sustain that. The outcome of this case, as I see it, will hinge on the question of the damage to your land and your ranch because of sedimentary tailings washing downstream onto your property."

"That crap would damage——" Jim Daley began.

"Agreed," Clay Withrow interrupted. "We could base this case entirely on damages. Enter damage claims so great that payment of them would be prohibitive and leave Shaner's placer workings without any hope of profit."

Jim Daley had banged his fist onto the desk. "Nothing doing, Withrow. I don't want damages. I want to be rid of slush and mud and corruption. I want clean, clear water. I want green meadows, not slimy mudholes. Damn it, I want what's mine. All the blasted gold and silver in Colorado can't stack up agin' a new-dropped calf or a Morgan mare trotting about."

"I see your point," the young attorney answered. "At best, damage procedures would take a long time, months, maybe years. A board would have to be appointed to arrive at damage amounts."

"And with precious little experience to base damage amounts on," Lance offered. "Who can say what Jim's ranch is worth, now or potentially?"

"We'll go all out then," Withrow said firmly. "We'll demand a permanent injunction to put Shaner's placer mining to a halt. I hope one of you gentlemen has a rabbit's foot in his pocket."

Jim and Maude Daley, accompained by Lance and Caroline and Bob, entered the courtroom and caused a craning of necks and many murmurs. Caroline peered about, quickly studying the faces of many people. A large number had assembled out of curiosity. She sensed that others had a more personal reason for attending. From this hearing they hoped to garner some realization of what the future might portend as the interest of the mines would become increasingly interwoven or at odds with ranching and farming interests.

Another stirring of those about her told that the opposition group was entering the courtroom. They passed close alongside, and she studied each one.

The first three men who passed her were strangers, roughly clad and booted miners whom she had never met or known. They were followed by a well, but quietly, dressed man that she sensed instantly as Shaner's attorney. He moved toward the tables at the front of the room when Caroline sighted Matt Shaner. She had seen Shaner only a few times since the night on which she had first come to Aspen, and this man had talked to Lance and to her in the tent restaurant. Now, he looked her squarely in the face with a wide, disarming smile. This was an older, heavier face than the one she had distrusted so many years before. That smile, Caroline thought quickly, it's from his lips, his teeth. Not from his eyes. His eyes are bleak, cold, calculating. Before she could analyze Matt Shaner further, he passed her.

The presence of another person drew Caroline's eyes upward. Ellen Bradley Corlett was coming toward her, clad in a light-tan suit so beautifully faultless that Caroline gasped in admiration.

At Caroline's elbow, Ellen Corlett paused. Then she bent quickly down, and spoke words that carried shrilly in the room. "Hello Mrs. Herndon. How about your high and mighty ranch now? Worm turns, I always say. It's

236

someone else's turn to throw piss today. Took a long time to get even, to watch you squirm an' crawl."

Before Caroline could voice an answer, Ellen Corlett had swept down the aisle, her steps timed to the amused but uncertain laughter her words had called forth.

A hand dropped gently for an instant on Caroline's shoulder. Even as she looked about, she knew that the touch was that of Hardrock Corlett, but his face was turned from her as he plodded ahead and followed his wife.

Within minutes, the voice of the court bailiff brought silence to the courtroom. Judge Wallace Langford entered and took his place. He came quickly to the point of business.

"This is a preliminary hearing," he said, "in the matter of James Daley vs. Hardrock and Ellen Corlett, Matt Shaner, and others. The plaintiff, James Daley, has been granted a temporary injunction which prohibits the defendants from continuing certain placer-mining operations on Wilderness Creek in this county. The defendant alleges that such operations create a hazard to his ranching operations through the pollution of the waters of Wilderness Creek. The defendant seeks a permanent injunction. If counsel is ready, we will proceed. Mr. Withrow?"

Clay Withrow rose from his seat beside Jim Daley. "Your Honor, I have here copies of the decrees issued by the State of Colorado, on July 18, 1881, adjudicating in perpetuity one half of the waters of Wilderness Creek, Gunnison County, to James Daley and to Lance Ainsley, parent and guardian of Caroline Ainsley, a minor. The decree spells out that such water shall be used for a ranch owned by said Daley and Ainsley for proper and lawful purposes." Withrow handed the papers to the bench. "I ask, Your Honor, that these decrees be marked as plaintiff's Exhibit 'A.' "

Judge Langford turned toward the attorney seated beside Matt Shaner. "Objection?"

"No objection." Shaner's attorney waved a deprecating hand.

"They shall be so entered. Continue, Mr. Withrow."

"We shall prove," Clay Withrow began quietly, "that the

237

placer-mining operations recently undertaken by the defendant on Wilderness Creek constitute an unlawful——"

"Objection!" The words cracked sharply from Matt Shaner's attorney. "Your Honor," he said, "Mr. Withrow's choice of words is unfortunate. If it pleases the court, considerable time can be saved here. Mr. Shaner does not challenge the validity of the decrees submitted as Exhibit 'A' by the plaintiff. No indeed. Mr. Daley's title to his land and to his portion of the waters of Wilderness Creek are incontestable. He is getting the water. He shall continue to get it. There is no cause for my esteemed opponent's allegation of unlawfulness."

"Sure. Sure I get water." Jim Daley's voice sounded in the room. "Along with tons of filthy, slimy s——!"

"Mr. Daley," the judge's words cracked. "Contain yourself or I'll hold you in contempt." His gaze flickered back to the defense attorney. "Mr. Jackson, you are well aware that the bench cannot entertain an objection at this time. Counsel for the plaintiff is merely making a preliminary statement. Continue, Mr. Withrow."

Lance whispered to Caroline, "So that's Shaner's trick. Clever. Darned clever. Admit Jim Daley owns the water. Press the fact that he isn't getting any less water. Insist that the matter of silting it is one for damages only. Then drag it out. Drag it out."

"What then?" Caroline whispered anxiously. "If this becomes merely a damage suit, can Matt Shaner continue placering?"

"I'm afraid so, kitten."

As voices droned on, Caroline studied her folded hands. The words eventually lost meaning and context. She silently searched back through the years, reliving that night in Bentley's cabin when her father, by yellow lamp light, had written the request for water. Slowly, almost painfully, she sought to recall each written word. Later, she strived to recreate H. A. W. Tabor's words, spoken on the day he had first visited the Lazy Seedy, the day when he had comforted her as she awaited Jim Daley's appraisal of the raw homestead on which she had gotten options.

Toward noon she jerked back in her seat and clutched

Lance's arm. "Uncle Jim is apt to lose this case—isn't he?"

"It's not going well," Lance answered. "That lawyer of Shaner's is smooth. Knows what he's about."

Caroline drew him closer, her lips close to his ear. "Try and get a delay, Papa. Talk to Uncle Jim and Mr. Withrow. Do everything you can. But get the decision held up. Three days." She rose to her feet. "I'll be back in three days. Sure."

"Where," Lance gasped, "are you headed?"

"To Denver, Papa, on the first train."

She had scarcely cleared the courtroom door when her husband and Maude Daley fell into step beside her. "Lance says you decided all at once to rush off for Denver. What on earth for, Caroline?" The words poured from Bob in an irritated, tumbling way.

"I don't know why, myself. Not yet. I've got an idea shaping up. This showdown isn't going well for Uncle Jim. He needs help. I'm going to try."

"It sounds crazy to me," Bob argued. "I can't possibly get away to go with you. How about little Freddy?"

"I'll take him, of course. I'll manage somehow." Caroline's words carried finality.

Maude Daley glanced searchingly into Caroline's face. "I'm going with you. Jim can get by."

"It sounds half-cocked and crazy to me," Bob persisted. "Maybe Judge Langford will have the case wrapped up, decided before you can even get to Denver."

"I don't think he will," Caroline said thoughtfully. "Papa and Uncle Jim are going to ask for a three-day recess. Besides, we will know before my train leaves."

"We all want to help Jim and Maude," Bob answered. "But if you have an idea, why not tell us."

"If your wife has an idea, she's the only one of us who has." Maude threw her arm about Bob Herndon in a persuasive gesture. "I'll take care of her, Bob. And the baby, too. Don't forget it was one of her ideas that established the Lazy Seedy Ranch."

An hour later Lance entered the Bleeker Street home with news that their request for a three-day delay of proceedings had been granted. Four hours later Caroline and her son, shepherded by Maude Daley, boarded the Denver-bound train.

Ordinarily Caroline would have been excited by her arrival in Denver and by the spaciously comfortable rooms assigned them at the Windsor Hotel. Now, only one thing filled her mind. She must accomplish her mission before the sweeping hands of the clock marked off so many hours that she could not return to Judge Wallace Langford's courtroom for the critical session ahead.

The porter had hardly dropped their luggage and left the room when she turned to her companion. "Maude, I'm going to ask a man to come here this evening and ask him to help me tomorrow."

Maude shook her head worriedly. "If it's H. A. W. Tabor, child, you're facing a blank wall. I found out at the desk that he's in Washington."

"I know. No, Maude, it isn't Mr. Tabor." Caroline's eyes were calm and her voice level as she added, "It is Eric Duane. I hope you understand. Eric can help me. Help us." She was conscious that her face was reddening under Maude Daley's scrutiny. "You'll have to believe in my motive. Believe me and then say nothing of this to Bob. Bob is wonderful, but, Maude, neither of us could make him understand my seeing Eric, my spending a day with him."

Maude turned swiftly from a window that revealed the city in the mellow sunlight of late afternoon. Her arms went around the girl.

"Caroline Ainsley Herndon," she said in a reproachfully quiet voice, "don't you know it would mean nothing to me if you were to go out with a dozen men? I knew you as a child. I know you as a wife and mother. I hope to God I never become one of those women who sniff for scandal in motives as clear and clean as yours."

"Thank you, Maude," Caroline whispered. "Now," she added energetically, "I'll need to get to old records up at the Capitol Building. Need to get to them fast, then have certified or notarized copies made. Eric can see to that detail as we search them out." Caroline frowned at the marching hands of a mantel clock. "We've got just until four o'clock tomorrow. Less than twenty-four hours."

Maude started to answer, then stopped, listening to a sudden impatient howl from young Freddy who had awakened. "Just so you can dodge back here to the hotel about every four hours to nurse young Freddy. That's something I can't handle yet."

Caroline's jaw dropped as she ran quickly appraising eyes over her companion. "Oh, Maude!" she gasped. "You mean——?"

"Maybe. Just maybe." Maude Selby Daley smiled. "Now get on with all that important work. No more questions, mind you."

The following morning she was seated in a well-furnished reception room and impatiently scanning a wall plaque bearing the seal of Colorado's secretary of state. She turned, seconds later, to Eric Duane who was seated beside her. The confidence of his quiet smile brought a relieved sigh from her.

"Everything is arranged," Eric assured her. "I got in touch with Secretary Morris late last night. Routed him out of bed. Pretty grumpy at first. Then he thawed when I told him the urgency for your seeing the records of water decrees issued in 1881." He paused, his hand moving with uncertain timidity to clasp her fingers. "Just what do you hope to find, Caroline? You or Jim Daley already have copies of the decrees."

She was mindful of the unspoken adoration of his grasp as she said, "Eric, in a hazy way I recall Mr. Tabor saying something of changes he made in Papa's letter asking for the adjudication of water. Perhaps it means nothing. But again——"

With the aid of a clerk assigned to them, it took only a few minutes to find the Record of Decree in a large and yellowing book. Caroline's face fell as she studied it. "Eric, it's just the same. The same as the copy Uncle Jim has in Aspen." She started to close the book, hesitated, and swiftly flipped the pages again. "Wait!" she said. There was a number stamped in the corner of that copy of the decree. Caroline turned to the clerk. "What would a number like that mean? What would it indicate?"

The clerk bent forward and peered above her pointing finger. "That's a filing number, ma'am," he answered. "In those days they filed the letters, the applications, on which decrees were issued."

Caroline was trembling as she asked, "Would you still have that letter? Would it be in your file?"

"Oh, assuredly, ma'am. Would you like to see it? Might take a little time to search it out."

"Please find it," she breathed. "And hurry."

The clerk's curiosity changed to a hurried scamper as Eric Duane thrust a gold piece in his hand.

A half hour later he returned, dust-smudged and bearing a cardboard file. He laid it before her. "It's there all right. I've marked it with a piece of cardboard."

Caroline read and scanned the paper on which Lance Ainsley long before had written carefully studied and chosen words by lamp light in Bentley's cabin while Wilderness Creek chattered outside and Hardrock Corlett smacked appreciative lips above a bottle of rye whiskey.

"Eric, look there!" Her startled cry brought both men to stare over her shoulders.

As Eric Duane's eyes encompassed the page, he whistled an astonished and happy whistle. "That could do it, Caroline. That could win your case, save the ranch." His arm swept about her in a happy hug.

"How long will it take to get absolutely legal copies made of this letter, Eric? Can we do it in time?"

Eric turned to the clerk. "Bring this file and the decree record book to Secretary Morris's office. Yes, Caroline, you'll have your copies in time, plenty of time."

If Secretary of State Morris had lunch that day, it was long delayed. The copying and certification of the letter was routine to his office, but there was nothing routine or common about the sharply penetrating questions Caroline Herndon put to him, nor about her insistence that Colorado's attorney general be asked to join them and provide explicit answers to several of her questions.

When it was over, Secretary Morris grasped her hand.

"I've heard rumors," he said, "of a child who put together a ranch over on the Slope—a big ranch."

"A helluva big ranch is the term," Caroline answered with a relieved and warm smile.

"Yes, a helluva big ranch," the secretary agreed, laughing. "And a helluva smart girl did it. Mrs. Herndon, it has been a rare experience and honor to meet you."

They left Denver on the evening train. "Well, that was a short stay," Maude Daley said. "I washed cinders out of my ears, changed Junior's diapers a dozen times, and, whammo, we're off and running. Me, I was going to D and F and buy three hats, a corset, and a nightie."

There was the inevitable moment at trainside when Eric Duane held Caroline's hands, reluctant of the moment she would be gone from his sight.

"You were wonderful, Eric," she said softly. "I couldn't have succeeded without you."

"You would always succeed, Caroline, if I had my way. It was fun. A mountain princess came to Denver and brightened it for a time."

She was aware of the trainman's warning bark as she looked thoughtfully into Eric's troubled face. What she would have said was lost in the swift kiss he gave her in the moment before he turned and fled.

Throughout much of the night the train labored westward along steep grades and sharp mountain curves. Caroline tossed about restlessly. Her mind pinpointed one by one the events and spoken words of her brief stay in Denver. At Leadville there was an agonizing delay. When the train again moved forward, she listened to the wheels clicking off rail joints and miles. Dawn found her sitting up, reading again and again the documents that had not been out of her hand since she had left the gold-domed Capitol Building.

They waited for her at Aspen station. Bob. Lance. Jim Daley. Attorney Withrow.

Jim Daley's greeting was anxiously abrupt. "Did it pay off, partner? Find anything?"

"Wait and see," Caroline answered, but her smile was eagerly triumphant. "I'll have to hurry home and change clothes."

Lance shook his head. "Not enough time for that, kitten. We have to be in court in twenty minutes."

"But the baby? I can't take him into the courtroom."

Jim Daley glanced questioningly at his wife. Maude shook her head in set refusal. "Not this time. I'm going along. I wouldn't for the world miss what's coming up."

Lance reached out and gingerly lifted the blanketed boy into his arms. "Come along, sonny. Looks like it's grandpa's knee again. And hang that beagle-eyed bailiff! He's not ordering us out of court." Lance ran appraising fingers over the blanket. "Just don't get any funny, flooding ideas, youngster."

The courtroom was even more crowded than it had been during their previous appearance. An air of expectant silence, of tension, marked the crowd. Only those gathered about Matt Shaner were at ease, confident and smiling.

"Look at Shaner," Jim Daley whispered. "Looks like a panther that's stalked down a fawn and lickin' his chops for the kill."

The day's proceedings began with the banging of a gavel. The defense counsel ran a smoothing hand over bulky yellow papers, from which Caroline surmised he would begin a long, well-pointed and oratorical statement. He was forestalled by Clay Withrow who rose to face Judge Langford.

"Your Honor," he said briskly, "if it please the court, I request a somewhat radical departure from established procedure. I should like to introduce a witness."

By its suddenness the move caught Defense Attorney Jackson by surprise. A grim caution tore at the complacency of his face. "Objection," he said quickly.

The judge studied Clay Withrow intently. "Mr. Withrow, what is your purpose in seeking such a ruling from this court?"

The young lawyer's answer was swift and determined. "My purpose, Your Honor, is twofold: first, to introduce evidence so striking, so relevant to this case, that it may well preclude the necessity of this trial continuing beyond the morning. Second, the time of this court is limited and valuable. The funds of this county are also limited. I believe this case can be quickly terminated. I believe it should be."

For perhaps a minute Judge Langford sat back in his chair, studying the tips of his closely pressed fingers. "Objection overruled," he said finally. "Mr. Withrow, you may call your witness." He leaned forward and added, "But I warn you, this evidence must be highly relevant."

Clay Withrow bowed. "I call Caroline Ainsley Herndon to the stand."

As she moved toward the bailiff to be sworn in, Caroline knew every eye in the room was upon her. She repeated the oath in low but firm words, then sat down in the massive and uncomfortable witness chair.

Clay Withrow strode close to her, speaking in a clear and comforting way. "Please state your full name."

"Caroline Ainsley Herndon."

"You are a resident of this county, and of legal age?"

"I am."

"Mrs. Herndon, were you present at a Mr. Bentley's home, on the night of June 20, 1881, when your father, Mr. Lance Ainsley, wrote a letter to the Colorado secretary of state requesting a decree of adjudication of the waters of Wilderness Creek."

"Yes, sir, I was there."

A chair scraped noisily, and Attorney Jackson rose swiftly to his feet. "I object. This isn't relevant testimony. It is only a rehash of what all of us know and concede. The question of the validity of the adjudication of water has already been acknowledged by my client."

The judge lifted a questioning face toward Clay Withrow. The young attorney smiled blandly. "Sir, if the esteemed defense counsel will be patient, I'm sure he will find the testimony of this witness relevant."

"You may proceed, Mr. Withrow."

Withrow turned again to Caroline, his words short . . . brisk. "You were in Denver yesterday, Mrs. Herndon?"

"Yes." As she uttered the word, Caroline was aware of the more intent interest of those assembled, and of surprise mounting Matt Shaner's face.

"While you were in Denver, Mrs. Herndon, you secured

245

certain documents, sworn and attested documents, from the secretary of state?"

"I did."

With emphatic movement, Withrow laid in her hand a heavy sheet of paper. "This is one of the documents you secured?"

Caroline studied it. "Yes. This is a copy of the Decree of Adjudication."

Withrow turned to the bench. "Your Honor. We shall later enter this copy of the Decree as evidence, should the court so desire. However, it is an exact duplicate of those already submitted as Exhibit 'A' three days ago."

Withrow faced Caroline, smiled, and rubbed his neck. "Mrs. Herndon, please read the portion of the Decree that I have lightly underlined in pencil."

She drew a deep breath and began: "ADJUDICATION IS HEREBY MADE TO THE ABOVE DESCRIBED WATERS PURSUANT TO AND IN FULL COMPLIANCE WITH THE TERMS OF THE REQUEST MADE BY JAMES DALEY AND LANCE AINSLEY, FATHER AND GUARDIAN. ..."

"That will do, Mrs. Herndon. Thank you." Clay Withrow swung about to face those seated at Matt Shaner's table. "Please note gentlemen, the exact wording: 'IN FULL AND COMPLETE COMPLIANCE.' "

Attorney Jackson again reared to his feet. "Your Honor, what is relevant about such a rehash? I simply insist——"

"Sit down, Mr. Jackson." There was authority in the command from the bench.

"Now." Clay Withrow said quickly. "Mrs. Herndon, I hand you another document. Is this also an attested copy given you yesterday by the secretary of state?"

"Yes, it surely is. It is a sworn true copy of the letter written by my father requesting the adjudication of water. It is word for word as filed and on record at the state house."

"Please read the first five lines of the second paragraph of that letter. Read it aloud. Read it slowly—clearly." Clay Withrow moved back, and the dramatic nature of his stance brought absolute silence to the courtroom.

Caroline was reading: "Establishing the priority of the undersigned to one-half (½) of the total flow of such waters of Wilderness Creek, in perpetuity, in their pure, unadulterated, and natural state——"

Claw Withrow lifted the paper from her hand, stepped close to the bench, and laid it before Judge Langford. "Yes . . . Yes indeed. Mark those words, gentlemen. In their pure, unadulterated and natural state. Is the muddy slime . . . the filth of sedimentary tailings to be construed as pure, unadulterated, natural water? Is this obvious subversion of the will and intent of the Decree to be tolerated? Is placer mining, with its pollution of Wilderness Creek to be condoned? Never! Your Honor, I ask for an immediate and permanent injunction prohibiting the defendant from placer operations. A cease and desist order, Your Honor."

Defense Attorney Jackson stared for a moment at the white and ugly face of Matt Shaner, then approached the judge. "Your Honor, I request an adjournment of this court until two o'clock this afternoon." Even as Caroline heard his words, she knew that the afternoon session would be brief and routine. The permanent injunction would be issued. The creek through the Lazy Seedy in days and years to come would run clear and sparkling and clean. She bowed her head, hardly aware of the pandemonium that had overtaken the room. *Thank you, Mr. Tabor. Thank you for seeing, so long ago, that this question might someday arise. Thank you for inserting the words, "Pure and unadulterated and natural," before you had the papers filed.*

She glanced toward Lawyer Jackson who bent over a table. His hands were spread palms up in hopeless response to the low, savage words Matt Shaner was throwing at him. She saw Ellen Corlett rise and move toward her. She steeled herself for slashing words from Ellen, but the girl turned toward the door. Ellen's face in that moment held no anger. Instead there was but vacant and staring shock.

Caroline moved to her father's side. "I want my baby. I want to go home."

That night Jim Daley stooped on the creek bank and

listened for a long time to the merry chatter of Wilderness Creek. He touched his pocket, then smiled at the comfort of the permanent injunction he had folded and thrust there. He dipped both his callused hands in the stream and let the water sift through his fingers.

When he entered the ranch house Maude waited near the fireplace. He took her in his arms and brushed the sheen of her hair. A vast contentment was upon him. After a time he moved back, pulling a small and furry object from the pocket. "My rabbit's foot," he said, laughing. "Have we this to thank, or a guardian angel?"

"If we've an angel," Maude replied. "Her name is little gal, or brat, or kitten."

Jim glanced at his wife awkwardly. "Maude, I've never spouted much religion. Mine has been in pine boughs and sunsets. But, Maude, God does work in mysterious ways his miracles to perform."

She strode across the room, dropping her hands to the worn back of the cowhide chair. "Jim ... Jim darling, God is kinder than we know. I haven't told you. I wanted to be sure. Jim, we are going to have a child."

Minutes later, when he lifted her triumphantly into his arms, Jim Daley sang the quiet and plaintive words of a tune that on many nights had calmed the cattle bedded down on a Texas trail drive.

Chapter 13

Throughout the days of the Wilderness Creek showdown and its tumultuous climax, Bob Herndon was a silent, and somewhat bewildered, spectator. He viewed it in a detached way, ever mindful of Lance's revelation that Caroline had sold her interest in the ranch to Jim Daley. Her trip to Denver and her testimony brought victory, but victory that would benefit only Jim and Maude Daley. It could in no way affect the outcome of the imminent struggle for ownership and control of the Buccaneer mine. For Bob, the Shaner-Daley affair had taken on the aspects of a stage play to be witnessed while his mind struggled with the engulfing aspects of the far greater drama in which he, his wife, and Jed Curry were enmeshed. Would to God that Caroline, or any of us, could pull a second rabbit from the hat, he thought.

He had spent the days of Caroline's absence searching hour after hour for a trace or mention of either Gagnon or Lorentz, those phantoms of the past. When exhausted by hunting through papers he knew had already been combed again and again, he threw himself tiredly on a couch and forced his mind to relive day by day his years in Aspen. The events and the personalities of those time-hazed days of the early eighties seemed to fuse into a bewildering kaleidoscopic view of unnamed faces and of endless assay reports that he had written and attested. Soon he struggled up, wiped dust-darkened hands across his reddened eyes, and resumed the search. Then it seemed, through his tiredness, that he was pursuing a nebulous lamp-cast shadow that flickered momentarily and vanished.

His irritation, born of worry and exhaustion, flared through the quiet spaciousness of the Bleeker Street home toward midnight of the second day after Jim Daley had been given the permanent injunction. It found words as he paced the living room and listened to a rocking melody with which Caroline was attempting to soothe the baby. Little Freddy was cutting a tooth, and the painfully swollen upthrust of his gums made him sleepless and cross throughout the evening. "Won't the little tyke ever quiet down?" Bob demanded. "He's been howling for hours."

Caroline broke off the song. Despite her own tiredness, she managed a calm and reassuring smile. "He'll quiet down after a time. I've about rubbed the tooth through." She shifted the child in her arms and resumed rocking and singing.

Bob pressed his fingers to his forehead. "How can you be so cheerful, so, so unconcerned just now, Caroline?

249

Right now when everything is about to smash around us? You know we're going to lose the Buccaneer!"

She gazed steadily toward him. "I don't know anything of the kind. And if we do lose it, we have so much left— Your business, our home, our baby, each other."

"Oh, Caroline, stop the inventory," he groaned. "We'd have to turn to your dad. I'd be just what I was—a failure. But worse, I'd have squandered your ranch."

Caroline was quiet, absorbing the realization that at last, somehow, he knew of her selling the Lazy Seedy, of the means by which she had raised money to finance the mine.

"There are other ranches," she said guardedly, "other places ranches can be built. Someday perhaps we'll——"

Bob came quietly to her side, bent over the rocking chair, and kissed her forehead. "Sweetheart, forget what I've said. It is just that I'm nervous and on edge." He paused and let his fingers toy through her brushed, tumbling hair. "What would I do without you, brat? Your calmness. Your wisdom. Your endurance."

She pressed an endearing arm about his neck. "I love you. Love you so much, you big lug. Now go to bed and get some sleep. I'll be upstairs after the baby quiets."

He hesitated, then walked to the door. "I'm not a bit sleepy. I'm going down to the office for an hour. There's a shipment of samples in from the San Juan country. Maybe I'll run a few. Some of them are interesting. Bye, dear." His palm met his chin as he blew her three spaced and giant kisses.

Later he became absorbed in the San Juan specimens. A distant clock tolled the passing of midnight and he sat in concentrated study of a four-inch piece of amalgamate ore. He turned it over and over in his hand. Somewhere he had seen ore like this. Not recently. Not from the Aspen area. His brow gathered in deep concentration. Why of course, he thought, I should have remembered immediately. I got hold of this type of stuff in Wyoming. Made quite a study of it. It's in the old mineral display case out front.

He rose, dug a key from his worktable, and moved into outer darkness. At the front gate, he shoved the key into the lock of the mineral case. When it opened, he lit a match, peered within, and looked at specimen after specimen. The match glowed down to a finger-scorching end. He lit another. Then, after a time, he lifted a piece of ore and thrust it inside his shirt. He relocked the old specimen case and went back inside to his workbench.

He drew the piece of ore from his shirt front. A small piece of paper adhered to one side, colored paper that had been placed beneath the ore to embellish its luster in the display case. He pulled the paper from the specimen, laid it aside, and began comparison of this ore with the one from the San Juans.

Minutes stretched into an hour. Tomorrow, he could give the mine owners over in San Juan County an unusually complete rundown on this type of amalgamate.

He rose tiredly, ready now for home and for sleep. The faded and crumpled paper caught his attention. He started to throw it into a trash box, then unfolded it. There were words and figures, dim and discolored, but legible.

His hands shook. He moved closer to the lamp light and studied the old paper. His eyes widened. He muttered sharply broken words, words that at last became coherent.

"My God, here it is. Lance was right. Lorentz. Gagnon." With the paper grasped in his fist, he ran from the assay office, heedless that he had left a burning light and an unlocked door. He clattered noisily down the sidewalk. Within him was a consuming urgency to reach home, to thrust this paper into Caroline's hands.

He had gone only a block when the bullet tore through his side and smashed him backward. For a moment he regained his balance, weaving from side to side. Then he fell to his knees. Gray nothingness surged about him. As he fell forward to the plank sidewalk, his fingers opened in spasmodic jerking. The crumpled paper fell from his grasp, a wisp of wind ruffled it, and tossed it into the street. A stronger gust followed. The paper lifted from the ground, hung momentarily in midair, and floated into distance and darkness.

Frieda Edmonds caught the sound of rapid footsteps on the opposite side of the street. A man hurried past in the direction from which she had come. His footsteps quickened to a trot and receded to silence, when the sharp crack of a gun shot caused her to whirl about in fright. She stared backward. The hurrying stranger was only a vague and indistinct shadow, a shadow that staggered and then for a moment seemed to rear stiffly erect. The man sank to his knees, then fell forward, face down.

She and her daughter, Kathleen, were beside a darkened warehouse doorway. With instinctive and protective fright, Frieda Edmonds pushed her daughter into the blackness of the doorway. "Stand there. Stand still. Don't move, Kathleen." As she spoke she peered into the night with fear-swept eyes toward the fallen man. An instant gasp escaped her. Two other men, mere blots of shadowy movement, had broken from the darkness and stood above the slumped body on the board sidewalk. For a time they bent over him. Then they moved down the street toward her. She crushed backward, flattening herself and her child against the gloomy doorway. She bit her lip against the sound of her own breathing. Her hand pressed firmly over Kathleen's lips.

The two men were about fifty feet from her when they paused, seeming to search the street. With frustrated curses they moved away, and were lost in the darkness.

Frieda Edmonds stood for long minutes in rigid silence. Finally she grasped the child's arm. "Come along. Hurry. We must hurry."

As they came onto the sidewalk, Kathleen paused momentarily to bend down and pick up a scrap of paper. Her mother jerked abruptly at her shoulder. "Stop it, Kathleen. What a time to dawdle over trash. Kathleen, hurry."

The girl gazed upward with wide and solemn eyes. "But Mama I saw this blow away from——"

"Hush, child. Not a word."

They slipped quickly toward the darkness of shacktown. Within half an hour, Frieda Edmonds cautiously retraced her steps up the darkened street. With Kathleen safely in bed, the woman's fright gave way to her natural and long-instilled desire to aid the stricken. Perhaps the man sprawled in the street was alive and without aid.

But when she came to the darkened warehouse, and

even beyond, there was no silent form in the street. There was only the darkness, the silence, and the memory. She turned homeward.

The first light of day touched the sky above the peaks off eastward as Caroline knocked loudly at the door of her father's house. Lance blinked sleepily as he let her in. A moment later he was wide awake. The pallor of her face, the terror deep within her eyes, and the manner in which she held her blanketed baby caused him to throw a steady arm about her, as he gasped, "What on earth, kitten? What is it? What's wrong?"

"He's disappeared, Papa——Bob's disappeared. Oh, God, Papa. He's been hurt. I know he has."

"You mean," Lance said, "Bob isn't at home?" He had taken Freddy from her arms, and was helping to lower her into a chair.

"No," Caroline answered. "Last night he came down to the office. It must have been ten o'clock. Said he wasn't sleepy and wanted to work awhile. The baby is cutting a tooth. He's cross, wouldn't sleep. I stayed up for hours waiting. I haven't been to bed at all."

Lance's face grew grave, but he forced reassurance into his words. "Now whoa up, kitten. Take it easy. Perhaps he slept at the office."

"No, he didn't, Papa. I've been there. There's a light burning. The door wasn't locked. It was scarcely closed. Bob isn't there."

Lance laid the child back in her arms. "I'll get Mrs. Jorgenson up. Likely she's awake already. Then I'll go over to the office and have a look around."

"I'm going with you, Papa. I'll ask Jorgie to tend Freddy for a while. I've got to go with you."

They hurried side by side to the assay office in the growing dawn. The town was just awakening; an occasional vehicle moved through the lonely streets. Bob Herndon's workshop was deserted and quiet. A light still burned over his table; the odor of acids hung in the air.

For several minutes Lance studied broken pieces of ore that littered the table. "Bob got a lot of work done," he said finally. "Could be he stopped in a restaurant for cof-

253

fee or a snack before heading home." He paused, looking into Caroline's eyes. "I don't know, kitten. Don't know what to think."

"I'm going back over to our house," she answered tiredly. "Maybe he is home now. I've got to know."

He shook his head. "No, kitten. I'll walk over and find out. Go back and stay with Mrs. Jorgenson and your baby. I'll hurry."

Lance left the office. He took the quickest route to Bleeker Street.

Within two blocks he stopped short and recoiled. His eyes fixed on blood-stained boards. A sense of impending disaster swept over him. He stooped and studied the dark splotches. Someone or some animal had bled badly here, then crawled away. His gaze moved swiftly ahead, following the bloody traces of the crawl.

Within fifty feet Lance stood still again. He realized the bleeding crawler had paused for a time.

The darkened splotches brought him to the closed door of the office of Dr. Miller. He knew then that the trail was the agonized way of a badly wounded man. His face was grim, foreboding, and steeled as he opened the door, moved a dozen feet along a shadowed hallway, and into the doctor's office.

"God almighty!" he gasped, and stood momentarily in frozen stance as his face drained of color and his gray eyes dilated in horror.

The room was in utter shambles, with broken furniture and bottles, strewn papers, and blood-stained walls. The body of Bob Herndon lay sprawled, face up, on a black horsehide couch. He was dead. Lance knew that at least three heavy bullets shot in close range had torn through his son-in-law's body.

Lance Ainsley was hardly aware that suddenly he was calling time after time for Dr. Miller, or that his words echoed through the lonely doom of the office and the hallway, or that they were answered only by silence. Numbly he walked to the couch and stared down at boyish face and red hair. His fingers trembled as they picked up a blanket and drew it across Bob Herndon's body. "Bob," he whispered brokenly. "Bob, how am I going to tell her? Tell kitten? Your wife."

He moved slowly from the office and retraced his steps to the assay shop. Morning sunshine accentuated the blood stains on the wood sidewalk. Already Lance's mind sought the meaning and the causes of what he had found. The assassin must have shot him once in the street, returned, and followed him to Dr. Miller's office. But what brought about such a struggle? Bob couldn't have put up a battle? Who did? Where is Dr. Miller?

Caroline sat at the assay bench and gazed vacantly upon chunks of ore. She looked at Lance an instant and dropped her head to the bench. "You've found him; you've found Bob. He's dead, Papa, isn't he? Isn't he dead?"

"Yes." It was the only word he could speak. For a long time he stood beside her, bent to allow his cheek and his lips to touch the dark softness of her hair.

When she finally lifted her face, it was white and drawn and older than he had ever seen it. Her eyes were clear and steady upon him. "Tell me about it, Papa. Tell me now."

"He must have left here in a hurry, or been terribly excited. He was shot out there, then managed to get to Dr. Miller's office. Who ever did it followed him. I can't figure what happened, except there must have been an awful commotion. Dr. Miller's office is in shambles. Bob was shot again there. Dr. Miller isn't anywhere about. That's all, kitten; that's all I know."

Lance put arms tightly about her and drew her to her feet. "I'll take you home. Then I'll report this to the officers."

Halfway to the door Caroline stopped and turned. She walked again to the bench, reaching out to pick up two ore samples. "I want these, Papa," she said softly. "I want to take them with me. Perhaps they were the last he ever touched." She hesitated; her voice was a small, plaintive cry. "Papa, last night just before he left the house, he said I was calm . . . and wise . . . and enduring." She stumbled to Lance. Her face sought his shoulder. "Oh, god, Papa, if only now I can be what Bob thought I was."

Within a week Caroline Ainsley Herndon sat twice in warm afternoon sunlight in the wooded cemetery as friends gathered about, as final words were spoken, and as men with white gloves and solemn faces lowered part of her past ... her life ... herself to the enfolding earth of the Roaring Fork Valley. She buried Mrs. Jorgenson, her beloved Jorgie, only three days after Bob's funeral. The sudden shock of Bob Herndon's murder had caused Mrs. Jorgenson to collapse. In the quiet and lonely hours before dawn, her life flickered and ended.

Caroline neither noted nor cared that during those tense, shock-ridden days the greening promise of May gave way to a warm and sun-gladdened June. She knew only that suddenly the kindly press of friends was no longer about her, that the stream of police and reporters had subsided, and that the myriad, time-consuming details no longer filled her days. Now there was but the realization of a vast and unending loneliness.

Lance had been insistent that she leave to him the grim task of seeking out the man whose hand had held the gun, and those who had conspired to bring about its use.

She determined, within hours of her husband's death, to give up the sprawling house on Bleeker Street. With Mrs. Jorgenson's passing, she realized that her father would now need her as deeply as she would need him. But it would take time to dismantle and dispose of the Bleeker Street mansion. This was the first task to which she gave herself as she spent the days in the lonely, memory-ridden rooms, comforted in a quiet way by the sounds of Freddy. Lance suggested that Caroline go to Bleeker Street only by day and stay at home with him at night. He told her too that she should keep Olga with her.

During those hours of grief and of dull, unheeding bewilderment, she found sanctuary in the small upstairs room where she could see the upper river valley and the eternal guarding peaks of Independence Pass. It seemed to her, as she stared eastward, that she saw not only the reaches of mountain grandeur, but glimpses of her years on the Roaring Fork. It was then that Lieutenant Bob seemed near, his smile somewhere on the horizon, his voice in a passing breeze or the muffled sound of the Roaring Fork.

She sat close to the window one mid-morning when the sound of the doorbell drifted to her, to be followed shortly by Jim Daley's voice. "Partner," he called, "come take a look. Me and Maude have got something for you."

She quickly came down the stairs and into the comfort of their arms. There were few words spoken for a time, but Caroline clung to the rock of their love and compassion.

When she stepped back, it was with her first smile, her first eagerly formed words. "Now. What did you bring? The surprise?"

"We've each got one. Maude, can I tell her yours?" He glanced teasingly at his wife, then added in strangely boyish tone, "Partner, can't you guess? Maudie's in delicate condition. We're going to have a baby."

Caroline's smile widened; her arm encircled Maude Daley. "Uncle Jim, how wonderful. For both of you. For all of us." In her words were no hint that earlier in Denver, Maude had hinted of this.

Jim Daley grasped her arm. "Getting to what I have for you, come over by the window. Look outside."

Caroline's gaze swept the yard. A happy cry escaped her. "It's my mare. My fat old, black mare."

Jim Daley looked steadily into her face. "Sure it's your mare. Partner, you need her. She needs you. Now change your clothes, get the hell out of this house—and ride. Ride somewhere that there ain't smoke or noise or stink or people. Ride and keep riding, partner. We'll be here until tomorrow morning. Your dad wants to see me for something. Maudie can help your hired girl with the boy. Forget everything. Ride through it. Ride out of it."

Hours later the black horse's slowed but steady plodding had carried her far into the lovely and secluded narrows of Castle Creek. She reined to an abrupt halt near a tangled and screening alder thicket. She sensed another time when she had come this way.

Suddenly she knew. Beyond the thicket lay a sanded shore, arced with wildflowers. From a vermilion cliff a

257

waterfall tumbled into a pool. The pool was warm, inviting, and memory-haunted.

She slid from her horse, fastened the reins to a sapling, and crawled through the thicket. The pool lay before her, lovely and lonely. Surely no one had been here since the evening Bob proudly had shown her this spot.

She walked onto the sand and dropped to her knees. Wildflowers were about her. The wildflowers had stems the same as that from which he had so nimbly braided a ring to slip over her finger. *It's not much but it says one thing: it says Caroline Ainsley belongs to me. My God, how lucky can one man be?* The words echoed from the spruce bows and from the tiny ripples of the pool. She flung herself face down in the warm sand. Pent-up tears and anguished cries broke from her in a terrible and relentless surge. It was her moment of summing up, of final agony. She would rise from this spot tired, weakened, trembling. The torture of separation would remain here. Only courage and determination and tender memories would ride with her the outward way.

Caroline reached home when evening shadows dappled the town and a lull was upon the activity of the streets. She went at once to the stable, to rub down and feed her mare. She would have headed across town to her father's house had not Jim Daley sought her out.

"Hurry up and come in, gal, Supper's about ready. Maude has cooked up a storm. We're eating here tonight, then having a confab. Your dad and Jed Curry are here." As she walked with him across the lawn the old cowman was quiet, but his gaze held to her face. "How was your ride, partner?"

"It was what I needed, Uncle Jim," she answered steadily. "Thank you for knowing. I gave them up today—Bob and Jorgie. Gave them to the hills, the creek, the sky."

"I'm glad," he murmured. "A long time ago, back on the Platte, I rode most of a winter before I could give up a woman and a child."

Arm in arm, they mounted the porch steps.

Caroline stood in awed wonder at the work Maude Daley had performed during the day. Many boxes were packed, but there was no disarray. The rooms were spotless. In the time of packing and cleaning, a meal had been prepared. Caroline realized that for the first time in many days she was enormously hungry. She hurried to Maude with bright and teasing words. "You shouldn't have, Maude. Shouldn't have done all this. Your *delicate condition*, you know."

Maude planted flour-spattered hands firmly on her hips. "Delicate flub dub. A lot Jim Daley knows about having a baby!"

They lingered at the table a long time. The conversation drifted to many topics. Each of them knew that inconsequential subjects must inevitably end, and that the real purpose of the gathering must be reached.

Lance broached it abruptly. "Caroline, there are things you must know. I'm not going to try beating around the bush. You've taken some nasty things with your chin up. You'll do it again." He paused only to light a cigar and spiral smoke ceilingward. "The decision about your Buccaneer mine will be handed down tomorrow morning. It will be against you. You've lost the mine. Gagnon has it."

Caroline studied her tightly clasped hands. There was no change in her expression or in the steadiness of her words.

"I think I already knew it. It's just that now it doesn't seem important." Moments later she turned to Jed Curry. "I am sorry for your sake, for what this loss means to you, Jed."

He drawled softly, "Hell, Caroline, I'm lucky. I wasn't the tycoon type. My feet've been itching for a year to get up into the Montana country. They're still good feet, good for tramping and prospecting. All I'll regret is their taking me away from the best doggoned friends I'll likely ever have."

"Jed, thank you," she whispered.

Jim Daley broke the ensuing silence as he pointed a fork at Lance. "Well, go on, Ainsley. Ain't you going to tell her the rest?"

"I'm coming to it," Lance said, nodding. "Kitten, there's some of the most imponderable angles to all this that anyone could imagine.

"First, we know that Gagnon is tied in with Matt

259

Shaner and his brother, Len. He's the real Gagnon all right. That's been established. He predicated his case, and he has won it, on the validity of claims that were signed over to him by Jacob Lorentz before Lorentz was killed back in 1881. Oh, he's got papers. Papers signed by Lorentz, and dated——"

"Tell her about the ore," Daley interrupted.

Lance leaned quietly toward Caroline. "That morning when we went to the assay office when we knew Bob was gone. Remember, kitten? You picked up two pieces of ore and brought them to my place. I've studied them. They tell a lot. Good God, if they could only really talk. One of them must have been a sample sent in from the San Juan area for assay. It's a conglomerate ore different than any found hereabouts. The other one's almost exactly like it. It came from the mineral case out in front of the assay office. Bob must have wanted to compare them."

"But what does that prove?" Caroline's voice was puzzled.

"Several things. Bob went out and got it sometime that night. There's an empty spot in the case. But now—listen to this. That ore sample from the case might have stuck to a folded paper. Lots of the samples are on old papers. There are bits of paper adhering to the ore on which it laid all these years. Kitten, Bob found something so important he left the office and started home with it. He must have been excited, terribly excited, to have left the light on and the door unlocked."

Caroline's eyes widened. "You mean he found——?"

"I can only guess what he found. I do know this. I've looked at other papers under ore samples in that old case. Several of them are discarded tally sheets and memorandums Bob wrote in 1881."

"Then he might have been bringing home proof of some kind, Papa."

"I've an idea he found something."

"But we'll never know," she concluded tiredly. "Bob is gone. Dr. Miller hasn't been found. Alive or dead. Shaner, or whoever did it, has the paper, whatever it was."

"Yes," he said. "Yes. They got it. Murdered to get it."

Jim Daley shook his head sadly. "One thing for sure.

260

The sheriff hasn't come up with a clue worth a whoop or a holler."

Caroline laid her head tiredly in her hands. "I don't want to go into court to hear the decision tomorrow."

"If we just knew what Bob found," Jed Curry reflected.

"We don't. We never will," Lance answered. "I'll go to court and tend to any details. Wait. There's one other thing I know. Not that it's important now. You know how Lorentz's name has stuck in my mind—and Gagnon's—for months on end. Seeing that conglomerate ore brought it back to me. It happened my first year here in Aspen. Old Jacob Lorentz met me up on the mountain and asked where he could find a good assayer. I remember his broken English. I remember pretty vaguely suggesting he see Bob. He showed me some samples he had gotten around the state. One of them was that same San Juan conglomerate—amalgamate."

Jim Daley shoved back his chair and stood up. "Well, partner, that's the story. How about more coffee and making for home and bed? It's late. You're tired. Maude's tired. Doggoned if I ain't tired. We've got to be back at the ranch by noon. Cattle buyer coming."

Despite her decision to avoid the court session at which the fate of the Buccaneer mine would be made known, Caroline found her thoughts fixing again and again on the affair as the following morning wore by. She knew that her father's appraisal of the outcome would be confirmed, and that the mine would be wrested from her. But what would be the reaction of those attending? Of Matt Shaner? Of Hardrock and Ellen Corlett? Of her own friends? Of the townspeople?

She chose not to go to her own home today and face the silent rooms. Instead she stayed in the familiar and comforting surroundings of Lance's house. Olga was with her, and performed small tasks and kept an eye on the baby. Eventually, Caroline grew restless and moodily reflective. This was no good. Yesterday she had found solace and peace through horseback riding. Perhaps again today——

Olga eagerly agreed to care for the baby. Caroline walked swiftly to Bleeker Street, saddled her black mare, and rode eastward up the valley trail that skirted the Roaring Fork. Her travel was slow for she paused many times to look about at vistas that were familiar yet always new.

Shortly after noon she realized that she was not alone on the trail. Someone else was riding swiftly this way. She reined her horse into a small grassed clearing and waited for the hurrying rider to pass. Moments later, when he broke into view around a sharp curve, she stared at him curiously. The man flailed his rangy bay mule to a fast clip. He was a shabbily dressed stranger. As he neared, she saw his pasty white face and bloodshot eyes. She drew her mare farther from the trail, hoping he would pass without noticing her.

Instead, he came abreast, stared at her, and drew the mule to a jerked halt.

"So here you are." His voice was an unpleasant whine. "I thought I'd missed you. Sure thought it."

She stonily looked at him. "What do you want? I never saw you before?"

He spat tobacco into the dust. "I know you, Mrs. Herndon. You're Lance Ainsley's daughter. Ain't you?"

She nodded, edging away from him.

"Stay put. I ain't goin' to hurt you. Maybe I can help you?"

"No one can help me," Caroline said bitterly.

"I helped your dad. Enough that right now he's got word about Aspen for me to look him up again."

"Well, why didn't you?" Suspicion edged her tone.

The stranger looked nervously back along the trail, then said. "If I looked Ainsley up they'd get me like they got your husband, or maybe it'd be the river and rocks piled on me."

Comprehension brought a quick gasp from Caroline. "You—you're the man who told my father something about the Shaners. You must be one of their men from their crew."

"If I was," he said craftily, "would I have stolen this worthless jackass and be flagging out of town? I'm headed away, a long ways off."

262

"What can I do then?" Her words mingled curiosity and mistrust.

He spat tobacco juice. "I need money. Money to get away and stay away. "If you've got, say, five hundred dollars, I can tell you who planned the killin'—and who did it!"

"How would I get that kind of money up here on a mountain trail? How do I know you really can tell me the truth?"

He studied her for a moment. "When I tell you, Mrs. Herndon, you'll know it's the truth. About the money. Would you promise to send it to me—to a name I'll give you? Send it to Leadville?"

"You think I'd really send it," she answered in surprise.

"I know an Ainsley's word is good. You're an Ainsley. You want me to tell you or not? I ain't gonna hang around here long."

"Yes," Caroline decided. "Tell me. I'll mail the money today."

He sidled the mule closer to her, and his voice dropped to a strange hissing whisper. "Len Shaner—Matt's brother —planned it after you made monkeys of Matt in court over the Wilderness Creek water deal. He wants your mine powerful bad so he sneaked into town mighty quiet and set men watching to see if your husband stumbled onto anything. He didn't use the gun himself. He brought a hired killer. A fellow who's a stranger to me. A small peaked-faced guy."

"Go on," she insisted. "What else?"

"There ain't much else, except they're staying in about the swankiest rooms of the Jerome. Len Shaner doesn't stick his head out. Just sends Matt and the others. Tonight they're all gonna meet there planning how to reopen your mine and get the ore out."

Caroline had listened with stunned fascination. At last she asked, "How do you know all this when you're scared to death and running for your life?"

"I've got plenty on one of their men. He talks when I say talk." He was grinning slyly as he slashed bridle reins on the sweating mule. "Be sure the letter's in Leadville in two or three days."

"It will be," she said and watched with both amazement and revulsion as he rode off.

At that hour thirty miles away, Jim Daley stood beside a shrewd-faced cattle buyer on the porch of the Lazy Seedy ranch house. He listened quietly as his companion spoke of market and range conditions. His mind and his attention, usually keen and probing at such a time, were today far away from the business at hand. Presently he kicked thoughtfully at a pine cone, sending it in a spin toward the bank of Wilderness Creek.

"Jeff," he said abruptly. "Why don't you ride up creek a mile or so and look over the steers I'll be marketing in the fall? I'll join you after I talk to my wife and attend to something. It's downright important."

At the buyer's agreeing nod, Jim Daley swung about and entered the house. He went at once to the small room that Maude had refurnished as a ranch office. For a time he rummaged the pigeonholes of a desk. Then, following the direction of his wife's humming, he sought her out in the kitchen.

He thrust the paper into her hand. "Know what this is?" he asked.

"Yes," she answered after a glance. "It's the bill of sale Caroline gave you when you bought her half of the ranch."

"Sure. A bill of sale, Maude. A bill of sale to a ranch we would never have had except for my partner's finding it and putting it together when she was a wide-eyed kid with pigtails."

Maude Daley was rolling the paper absently in her hands, as she said, "And a ranch that would be nothing but filthy and slimy mudholes if the same girl hadn't saved it in court. Jim, why——?"

"Maude," he interrupted, "you're thinking of the same thing I am."

Her eyes were soft and unwavering as she stepped close. When she drew him tightly against her, he was aware of the slightly accented curve of her body, the promise of the child they would have, the child that would someday come to boyhood and to manhood on this mountain empire.

"Let's do it, Jim, darling. Get rid of that piece of paper.

Tear it up. Burn it up. Give back to Caroline the interest and the partnership she earned over and over. She has lost so much. She has so little."

Together they shredded the paper and lifted the lid of the kitchen stove. The paper turned from white to glowing brilliance to ashes.

As he moved from the kitchen, Jim Daley's steps were young and confident and proud. "Let's go back into Aspen, Maude, and tell her. Let's do it tomorrow morning."

"Of course we will. She's our partner."

Chapter 14

The somber uncertainty with which Caroline had ridden up the Roaring Fork that morning did not accompany her on the homeward ride. The words of a loathsome, mule-mounted stranger had swept it away. She was quietly and deadly angry now. For five hundred dollars she had bought ugly, damning facts.

At night in the pomp sanctuary of the Jerome Hotel men would gather. Gagnon, the prospector, Matt Shaner, the suave and deadly, Len Shaner, the sinister shadow from nowhere, their lackeys and their henchmen—yes, all of these and another. A peaked-faced hired killer whose shots had torn through Bob to leave her alone and her son fatherless. They all would be there together.

As her thoughts crystallized, Caroline's quick jerk of the bridle reins brought a resentful prance to her mare's gait. The two moved swiftly down the trail toward Aspen—an aged black mare and a woman who was stiffly erect in the saddle, and whose eyes were twin crystals of determined ice.

She stopped first at the bank and sought out her old

friend, the cashier. "I want to draw five hundred dollars from the Buccaneer mine account," she explained.

He glanced at her curiously. "Caroline, I can't let you. That account has been garnisheed—impounded."

"Impounded?" her voice was incredulous. "By whom?"

"By the new owners of the mine. Court action." He was studying the cold tenseness of her face. "I'm sorry about all this. It's, it's a rotten, stinking affair."

Caroline's lips pursed thoughtfully. "I must have the money. Can you loan it to me?"

He heaved a relieved sigh. "Of course. Will five hundred be enough?"

She hesitated. At that moment a strange compulsion was about her. She knew not why she said it. "I want fifteen hundred dollars in cash."

His glance searched her face. "Of course, Caroline. Sign this note while I count it out."

At the post office she dropped a Leadville-directed envelope in the letter slot. There was no return address upon it. Inside were five one-hundred-dollar bills.

At Lance's house she was greeted by a tearful Olga, who broke the news which Caroline already knew. The talk of the town that day and the headlines of the paper told of the passing of the Buccaneer mine into the hands of Gagnon and his associates. They would take possession at noon tomorrow.

"Has my father been home?" Caroline asked after the tide of the hired girl's tears and words had subsided.

"He was here, then left. Said tell you there's a note and some papers on your dresser. He'll be home tomorrow. He had to go up to Ashcroft. Something about a lumber deal."

"And my baby—has he been good?"

"A jewel," Olga beamed. "But the little tyke's hungry. Good thing you're home."

Caroline studied the girl thoughtfully. "Olga, I have to be gone tonight. Perhaps a short while or perhaps until quite late. Can you stay and care for Freddy?"

"Of course I can, Mrs. Herndon. I'll slip over home right now and let my husband know."

266

"Bring him back with you if you wish," Caroline offered. "And thank you, Olga. Thank you so much."

She waited until dark and changed into a plain dress, walking shoes, and a short, warm jacket.

She opened a dresser drawer, and was placing Lance's note and the copy of the court decision within it, when she thought of the package of currency she had carried home from the bank. She slipped it into the drawer under carefully folded blouses. Her forehead knotted in perplexity. Why did I do that? Why did I borrow so much money I don't need? Papa would say I'm crazy.

She was in deep study as she moved into Lance's room and stopped near a nightstand beside his bed. She knew that inside there was a stub-nosed and wickedly efficient pistol. For a long time she stared at the little wooden stand. But it remained unopened and the gun untouched as she walked from the room. She held her son briefly and left the house.

She entered the Jerome Hotel by the kitchen door and smiled at those working there. The lobby was almost deserted, and she was able to reach the main stairway without attracting the attention of those about the desk.

Caroline was glad at that moment that the first days of her marriage had been spent in this hotel. She knew its layout and its employee routine. She crept quickly up the carpeted stairs to the second floor. In the subdued light of a side hallway, she waited.

Half an hour passed before a uniformed porter came into view. She ascertained quickly that he was no one whom she knew or who would be likely to recognize her. She greeted him with a bland smile. "Hello. Could you help me, please? I'm looking for a friend, a lady from Denver, who has a suite. I've forgotten its number."

He succumbed to her smile. "Glad to help, ma'am. What's your friend's name?"

"Mrs. Evans. Mrs. Ada Evans. She's a dear old soul."

The porter's face grew blank. "Evans. We don't have any Evans staying here. Maybe she's over at the——"

"No," Caroline said quickly. "She must be here. I know! She's probably with someone else. They must be in Suite 'A' or 'B.' Mrs. Evans is wealthy and quite particular."

"Sorry, ma'am. There's some honeymooners in 'A.' Suite 'B' is unoccupied."

"But the third floor," Caroline persisted. "The suites up there?"

"There's only three, ma'am, on that floor. I'll ask at the desk about your friend."

"Please don't bother," she answered quickly. "I've only a few minutes. I'll go up and knock."

"Might be it's suite 'F,' the porter offered. "There's women in that one. 'E' ain't being used this year. And 'D'——" His words cut off sharply.

Caroline thrust a dollar into his hand. "Of course. The women in 'F'. I'm sure my friend is there. You're so helpful."

She turned quickly to the stairway. So they're in "D," the secluded one, she thought. The help has been warned not to give out information. Yes indeed, Mr. Shaner, et al. Suite "D."

She reached the third floor and paused again. Her gaze along the corridor was alert and cautious. She knew the location of the suite toward which she must move carefully and unseen. The side hallway, giving access to these rooms, was empty and quiet. The light from widely separated ceiling fixtures cast a yellow and subdued glow. Caroline sped with quick and quiet steps past the door labeled Suite "D" and glanced about. Within twenty feet there was an unmarked door that she knew must be a linen room. A quick twist of the knob told her this room was not locked, so she opened it quickly and stepped inside.

She pulled the door almost closed behind her, leaving only a narrow crack through which she could peer into the hallway. She was too far up the hall to sight the entrance to Suite "D," but she had a good view of the hallway.

Somehow she must gain entry to those rooms. Somehow she must face the men who no doubt gathered within. But how? At that moment her mind was clear and set and searching. She gave no thought to what she would do, or what she would say, when she had come among them. Nor did she think of what means would enable her to escape the suite. There was only the compulsion to stand be-

268

fore them and let the sight of their faces sear through her mind and her memory.

It was a long time before there was a sound in the hallway. When it came, she knew that the door of the suite had been opened, then closed. She heard voices, the low indistinct tones of a man followed by the higher-pitched and argumentative words of a woman. Caroline held her breath and listened.

"I don't see why I can't stay. You sure were glad enough to see me a while ago. Why all this secret stuff? And your old meeting, why can't it wait?"

The man's sharp answering words carried to Caroline's hearing. "The boss says no dice. Now go along. Have a drink. I'll see you later."

The woman protested, but her companion said, "I said get along, Sally. Now damn it, shut up and go!"

A moment later a door closed firmly.

Caroline spent several minutes in deep thought. Finally she nodded as a wryly amused smile twisting her lips. She stepped into the hallway and moved with phantom quietness to the door of Suite "D." Her thumb moved to her throat and her fingers pushed the corners of her mouth. Mimicry had never been easy for her, but there was no other way.

She knocked softly and insistently at the door. Her summons was followed by footfalls inside.

"Yes. Who is it?" It was a man's irritated voice.

"It's me, Sally," Caroline said, and her words were strangely similar to the voice of the woman who had been ordered away.

The voice reached her through the door as a flare of anger. "Ben, it's the bitch we told you to get rid of."

"I ain't going. You ain't going to get rid of me. Not until you give me some money for drinks." Caroline paused and let her voice come to tantrum pitch. "You hear me. I'm not going without some money. I'll stand here! I'll scream!"

The disgusted, angry voices within revolted Caroline. She waited as footsteps again approached the door. At the sound of a turning key, she flattened herself against the wall beside the door. It swung open, and a heavily

269

bearded man stepped into the hall. Momentarily the door was half-ajar behind him. In that instant she quickly slid through the door to Suite "D" and whirled to face those within.

"Christ," a voice barked. "That ain't Sally!" Caroline felt the breath of the man who had whirled in the doorway, and reached to grab her. She eluded him and sped across the room. About her, half-a-dozen men struggled to their feet. The room was hazed by tobacco smoke, but in seconds her eyes focused to the greater brilliance. She stopped beside a table and glanced from face to face.

"Who is this woman? What is she doing here?" The words, gruff, but quietly authoritative, caused Caroline to look quickly at the bulky form approaching from an adjoining room. Her gaze fastened on the face of a middle-aged man. He studied her with seemingly unperturbed interest. She noted that his eyes were blue, intelligent, and spaced closely above a wide, prominent nose. There was a resemblance in this face to the astonished one of Matt Shaner. She knew that part of her bold venture had already been accomplished. She had looked into the face of Len Shaner. It was indelibly stamped and catalogued within her.

Caroline stood defiantly erect. Her gaze was locked into that of Len Shaner. "Your brother knows who I am, but I'll answer for myself. I am Caroline Herndon. Caroline Ainsley Herndon."

Her words brought startled murmurs across the room. There was quick movement by a smaller, slightly built stranger at Caroline's side, but Len Shaner's head jerked in swift command and the stranger eased to a crouching halt.

"Matt," Len Shaner said. "Bring the lady a chair."

"Thank you, I'll stand," she said coldly.

"As you wish, Mrs. Herndon. You have an odd way of calling on us. What is it you want."

"I wanted to see your faces," Caroline answered in a low and steady voice. "I wanted to see the faces of men who could shoot down an unarmed, unsuspecting man at night on the street, then follow him when he crawled away for help and tear his body to pieces with bullets.

270

Men who would murder a kind and innocent old doctor. Men who were low and greedy enough to do this, just to steal a mine."

Again there was the quick movement of the man Len Shaner had waved back. He circled her now, and for the first time she caught a distinct view of his thin narrow face. Her eyes widened to a stare. The room was suddenly unreal. The walls and the faces, the furniture and the lights, seemed those of a distant and time-hazed place. The face before her seemed obscured by a red bandana tied about it. And this stranger was running, running swiftly and desperately, through the gun smoke of Jorgenson's store. He ran, then suddenly wheeled about and lifted a gun to send a bullet smashing into the face of a soft-spoken old storekeeper.

At the moment, Caroline Herndon was unaware of the menace that her searing words had brought about her. She knew she must not give outward hint of the recognition that had flashed upon her. She forced blankness into her eyes and her face and turned with utter contempt toward Len Shaner.

"I suppose," he was saying, "you have proof of all these wild accusations?" His words were quiet, but his eyes now were those of a swaying snake.

"Perhaps I have more proof than you think. Men such as these slimy ones will talk for money the same as they steal or kill for it."

Len Shaner's eyes swept those about him. She knew her words had thrust home. He could not now be sure that one of those in the room had not sold him out.

Matt Shaner spoke for the first time. "Len, if she knows too much she can raise hell with——"

"Shut up," Len Shaner hissed.

Deliberately Caroline walked toward the door. Again she let her eyes rest on the hatchet-faced gunman. There was no doubt within her. This was the man who had fled Rawlins and left a companion to the fury of a mob.

Caroline's hand was on the knob. With utter loathing she turned and swept every face with her gray eyes. "You've got the Buccaneer mine," she said. "It's yours. A mine that honest men put their hearts and their sweat and

271

money into. It'll make you rich. But every dollar will be like a maggot in your filthy bellies. You've won. I've lost. Lost a mine. Lost a ranch. Lost a husband. What a miserable, lousy, conniving, bunch of sons of bitches to lose to. Led by jackals feeding on carrion. Led by the Shaners. Take your mine, we'll meet again!"

"Grab the bitch." The mask of affability dropped from Len Shaner's red face under the fury of her words. "We'll fix her——"

Caroline's hand lashed out with a viciously stinging slap across the face of the first man to approach her. Her fury held them back as she spoke again. "If you touch me I'll get out one scream. One scream that will bring half the guests of this hotel up here." She turned the knob and pushed the door open. "And just in case you have ideas of following me, murdering me in a dark street like you did Bob Herndon, just listen. Listen to me. Two men are waiting outside this hotel. If I don't come out—alone—they'll come up here." She looked with utter chill into Len Shaner's face. "Want to know who those men are, Mr. Shaner? The men you'll be up against? The men you tried cheating once in Tombstone and ran from like a scared dog. Follow me and find out. Just follow me or send your killers. Mr. Shaner, outside both Wyatt Earp and Doc Holliday are waiting for me. Come meet them, you stinking cowardly murderer!"

She slipped through the door, slammed it, and walked down the hall.

As she pounded down the stairway into the coolness of the outer night, she realized what a foolish and hazardous thing she had done. And what had it accomplished, except to enable her to stand face to face with the men who had shattered her hopes and her life? Abruptly she thought that now she should be frightened. Instead she was swept by anger and hatred. It was not the flashing fury that had momentarily held those men in check and made possible her escape from the room. The wrath within her had changed, leveling to a cold and calculating passion for revenge.

Caroline walked swiftly toward home, glancing backward from time to time. Her mention of Wyatt Earp and

Doc Holliday had been a pure spur-of-the-moment lie, born of desperation and of her knowledge of Lance's friendship with the noted pair. Both men had drifted in and out of Aspen upon occasion, but she was unaware of their present whereabouts. Her bluff had worked, though.

When she entered the house Olga and her husband awaited her. They looked at her with apprehension as she spoke. The thing that she had already determined to do was pulling her face into cold, grimly unpleasant lines. "If I nurse my baby, can you stay here a while longer, perhaps until morning, and take care of him? There are things I still must do."

They spoke to each other briefly, and agreed to remain, but there was uneasy concern in Olga's face and the young husband said, in a worried voice, "Mrs. Herndon, you know we'll stay, be glad to. You shouldn't be out alone at night. Whatever is wrong, we want to help. Olga can stay. I'll go with you."

"No. I have to go alone. This is something I must do by myself."

The finality of Caroline's words silenced him. He stared at her, dropped to a chair, and studied his hands as though assessing their futility.

She walked into Lance's bedroom and stood before a mirrored dresser. The reflected face seemed that of a stranger, of someone to whom an appalling decision had brought a trancelike appearance and movements. Her hand dropped to the nightstand. Minutes later she left the house with the stubby pistol in her pocket.

In the dark and moonless night the sheen from endless stars lighted her way to the barn. Inside, she worked by sense of familiarity and touch as she placed bridle and saddle on the black mare that nuzzled her in recognition.

Within minutes she was at the assay office. Again she moved about in darkness, sought out the articles she needed, and remounted her horse. She chose the darker and lonelier streets as she rode westward out of town.

Later she veered onto the Castle Creek road and entered the canyon. About her was the sharp rise of mountain walls that towered to vast and gloomy heights before offering a sliced view of clear sky and a southward reach of stars.

For a long time she rode, oblivious of her exact location or of the passage of time. Tomorrow along this road would come the men chosen by the Shaners to claim and to open the Buccaneer mine. Down would come wagon after wagon laden with the silver-laced ore that had been Bob Herndon's hope and his destiny and his undoing. Caroline forced herself past the alder thicket guarding the pool that had become for her an enduring shrine. She rode farther. Farther.

The overhead swing of planets marked midnight before she came to the box canyon and narrow rock gateway controlling access to the Buccaneer. She stopped, studied the narrow opening, and dismounted. When her black mare was safely hidden in a laurel thicket, Caroline untied a sack from her saddle and walked silently afoot into the box canyon.

The mine dump came into view. Atop it, near the portal, a kerosene lamp cast feeble yellow rays from the boiler house. She strode ahead with added caution. Somewhere nearby a man was stationed. Throughout the months of the mine's inactivity, one individual had been on duty at all times in order that the pumps might be tended and the flow of water kept under control within the mine. A hundred yards up the canyon, beyond the mine and the dump and the building, was a small shack of hewn logs. As she had expected, a heavy hasp and lock barred entrance. The answer was in the sack she was carrying. Her steel bar would tear the lock and the hasp from the timbers of the door.

There was a loud snapping sound as the hasp gave way. Caroline dropped flat upon the ground as the sound echoed the rocky slopes. Minutes passed and she waited with hushed breath. When no voice or footsteps sounded, she rose and felt her way into the shack. She opened the gunny sack and worked quietly and hastily loading it.

Within minutes she reached a large and concealing slag heap midway between the boiler house and the portal. Now she must wait. Wait until she could determine and time the routine and the rounds of the man alternating his time between the boiler room and the pumps far within the mine tunnel.

After one o'clock, when she was cold and stiff from crouched waiting, she knew that the time had come. The guard made a second lantern-carrying trip into the mine, and reappeared. Now he was in the boiler house again. She would have no more than half an hour.

With the sack dragging her down, she drew close to the portal. It had been boarded up, and a door had been installed, but the lock hung unfastened in the hasp. Caroline voiced silent relief and thanks as she entered the tunnel and pulled the door shut behind her.

She had expected utter darkness, an inky blackness through the tunnel, along which she would have to stumble over the ties and rails upon which ore cars were pushed from the depths. Instead there was a far-off, dim light. She surmised that the guard had left a lantern burning above the shaft.

Step by step. Tie by tie. Her walk seemed endless, and the weight of the sack tore painfully at her arms and her shoulders.

Arriving at the pump room, she remembered a far-off and happier day. The drone of the pumps was steady and constant about her. She eased the sack to the slick rock floor.

Moments later she was at work. Seconds counted now. She had helped Bob lay sticks of giant powder and embed blasting caps and lead fuse within them. She had no idea whether it would take one or a hundred sticks of the explosive to accomplish her purpose. There were two pumps. She probably had fifty pounds of powder. Place it carefully. Place it beneath the pumps, equally divided, carefully fused. She went about the task with steady, swift-moving hands. Often she glanced backward toward the portal, but there blackness closed in swiftly beyond the lantern's flickering glow.

She finished the first pump, coiling a long lead fuse about the machinery. Would this be enough? Too much? Would she have time to stumble the length of the tunnel and gain safety and a place of hiding far beyond the door. Bob or Jed Curry or Lance would have known.

Suddenly, she knew that she was not alone in the dim hollowness of the room. As she jerked erect and turned, she saw him standing a scant six feet from her. A small and crouched man whose pinched, narrow face and merciless eyes were caught in the lantern's uncertain glare. The pistol was in her pocket. She knew that she could never reach it in time.

He studied her in an odd, piercing way, and spoke above the hiss of the pumps. "Somewhere I've seen you."

"You're, you're Shaner's gunman," she answered in terror. "You were there. In the room. At the hotel."

"Sure," he answered. "But that ain't the time I'm thinking about. Some other time. Somewhere else. Where was it? When?"

He edged closer. Caroline backed off from the pump, toward the menacing drop of the shaft.

"Talk," he yelled viciously. "Tell me, or I'll kill you."

"Of course you'll kill me." The words tore from her throat. "You killed my husband. Matt Shaner has ordered you to kill me."

"Hell with Shaner," he raged. "He's still swallowing that rot about Earp and Holliday. I didn't. I had a hunch you'd head here."

He now stood close; she could retreat no farther. Behind her was the framework of the shaft. In that instant her fingers touched and then closed with infinite caution about a cold and desperately assuring object.

"Yes," she said jerkily. "I'll tell you. I saw you in Rawlins. Rawlins, Wyoming. Years ago. I was a kid in a store. You killed Jorgenson the storekeeper. Shot him in the face."

The impact of her words caused him to jerk back. A startled oath broke from him. She knew his next movement would be for the holstered gun at his side. It would be deadly fast and accurate. Her fingers tightened. Her arm arced toward him. The yard-long piece of heavy drill steel caught him on the forehead and smashed him backward to the ground. His hand clawed toward the gun. She jumped forward to stand above him. The steel bar crashed down upon him again and again and again.

His head was misshapen and blood-soaked when she

276

turned from him. With numb, lifeless hands she coiled the fuse slowly about the second pump. A match flared and steadied in her hand. She moved slowly, no longer aware of time or of danger, as she touched it to the lead fuses and walked with unseeing eyes from the Buccaneer.

She was beyond the portal, halfway out of the box canyon, when the ground shook beneath her, spinning her headlong into the rock and dirt of the road. The crash and the rumble were muffled by the endless tons of rock torn asunder.

Caroline Ainsley Herndon, stumbling to her feet and groping her way from the canyon and toward her waiting mare, was not to know how well her task had been performed. Far underground, pent-up waters rose and gushed through the mine. A subterranean river formed. Never again could the Buccaneer mine be opened; never could men cope with the surging flow of water.

Throughout her homeward ride, and even as she entered her father's house, time and place had become strange and unreal. She knew that she was tired, very tired. The dragging weariness was a welcome thing. It held from her mind the vivid and unbearable details of what she had done. The man and woman she had left with her baby awaited her.

Caroline looked at them from vast and uncomprehending distance as she sought out a table and began writing with quick and urgent strokes.

Papa:
When you read this I will be gone—away from home, away from Aspen. Papa, I have killed a man. The man who shot Bob. I have dynamited the pumps of the Buccaneer. I could not bear to let them have it. It was my life as it was Bob's. Now it is over. Forever over.
Don't look for me. I shall take my baby who is all that is left, and be somewhere, anywhere, from this town where I have done so much harm to you and so many others.
I owe the bank fifteen hundred dollars. Sell our house on Bleeker Street and pay it.

Only God knows whether I shall ever see you again. Try only to remember the happier days, Papa. Those wonderful times that are only memory.

Papa, I love you. Love you beyond words, beyond distance, and beyond life itself.

Good-bye, beloved.
Caroline

She folded the note and placed it on the pillow of his bed. When she reentered the living room, she spoke to those watching her. "I killed a man tonight. Killed him and blasted the Buccaneer mine. You asked earlier to help me. Help me now. Help me to take my baby and hide. Help me to get out of Aspen tonight. By daylight it will be too late."

Olga and her husband wanted to take her to their own house, but Caroline's objection was swift and firm. "No," she said. "Shaner's men will comb the town. They'd find out you work for my father, then trace you down while looking for me. I've no right to risk your lives."

The man stopped. He pondered a moment, then answered in a hurried whisper. "She's right, Olga. They would find her. Surely find her." A moment later, he added, "Take her and the baby to Mrs. Edmonds's house." He suddenly pushed them ahead. "I'll be there in ten minutes. There are men here who would want to help, who can help. I'll bring them. Now go. Hurry."

At the door of the darkly silent house, Olga knocked cautiously. She waited and knocked again. A low, frightened voice sought their identity.

"It's me, Olga, Mrs. Edmonds. And Mrs. Herndon. Let us in. Please let us in."

A key grated, and the door swung open slowly. It was dark within, but even this gloom failed to hide agitation on Frieda Edmonds's face. After they entered, she relocked the door and said, breathlessly, "What is it? What has happened?"

Olga voiced the reply. "Mrs. Herndon needs help, Frieda. She must hide. Must get out of Aspen."

And Caroline said tonelessly, "I have killed a man. Blown up a mine."

"Eternal God," Frieda Edmonds gasped. "Will it never end?"

Even as the woman spoke, Caroline was conscious of the disarray and bareness of the dark room. Packed boxes were piled about.

Frieda Edmonds studied them through moments of silent decision-making. Her hand fastened on Caroline's arm. "You can go with us. We're leaving early in the morning. Kathleen and I are going across the pass into the San Luis Valley to Cascade. Perhaps you would be safe there. Perhaps all of us will."

A sudden, startling revelation was upon Caroline. "Mrs. Edmonds, you worked for Dr. Miller. Have Shaner's men followed you, threatened you? If so, I must leave and get out of your house now. It was a Shaner man I killed. I mustn't have you risk——"

The woman's hand tightened on her arm. "Stay here, but you must know something. Dr. Miller lives. He's alive and in this house in the next room. Two miners found him early the morning your husband was shot. They brought him here. I've cared for him. I thought he would die. He was terribly beaten. Now he will live, but his memory is gone. He remembers nothing. He's like a child. A helpless, slobbering child. With God's help, I will take him to Cascade."

Minutes passed. With Olga's aid, Frieda Edmonds drew a heavy blanket across the room's only window. Then she touched a match to a coal-oil lamp. Caroline's baby awakened and was fretful. She found a chair and sank onto it. She rocked him back and forth.

Mrs. Edmonds drew close. There was a folded and smudged paper in her hand. "My little girl found this. Perhaps you will know what——" The words broke off suddenly, and Frieda Edmonds's eyes and mouth widened. She stepped back abruptly; the paper was unheeded in her grasp. "Now I know. Always I've thought I knew you from somewhere. You're the one. The little girl who brought milk to my baby. Now, with your child your face is the same as it was that day on the awful immigrant train in Wyoming." Short and hurried steps brought her near Caroline to encircle her arms about this friend from the past. Frieda Edmonds cried. As the tears coursed her cheeks the paper slid unnoticed into an open and half-packed box.

It lay there when footsteps sounded outside, and Olga's husband led a stranger into the room. He spoke in an excited and hurried tone. "It's arranged, Mrs. Herndon. All arranged. There's a freight train about to pull out for Glenwood Springs." He turned to his companion. "This is Mrs. Herndon and her baby, George. You explain what we've arranged."

There was reassuring warmth in the stranger's words. "You don't know me, Mrs. Herndon, but you know my wife and kids. I'm a brakeman on the D and RG. I'm going out on this run to Glenwood. We've already fixed it with the conductor. You can ride in the caboose, but you'll have to hurry. We're due out right away."

Caroline rose as she answered, "How can I thank you—all of you. You're doing so much. Risking so much."

The trainman opened the door. His voice was gruff but failed to hide emotion. "Did you ever ask for thanks when you carried grub and hope here to shacktown?"

Caroline smiled into Frieda Edmonds's face. "You'll get to Cascade. You'll get *him* there and nurse him to health. Frieda, will I ever see you again?"

"Our ways have crossed twice. Who knows? Perhaps ... perhaps."

When daylight came to the valley of the Roaring Fork, the jolting and swaying freight train was already far from Aspen, had picked up an empty gondola at Caroline Station, and moved slowly toward Glenwood Springs. After a time the brakeman squatted on a seat close to Caroline. "Will you head toward Denver, Mrs. Herndon?"

She was silent a long time. She had given her destination no thought. The brakeman watched her intensely, then asked, "Do you need money? Is that bothering you?"

Caroline eased the baby to the seat beside her. "I've got enough money." She remembered the strangely compelling force that had urged her to borrow an extra thousand dollars at the bank only hours ago. Had a lifetime, a century, passed since she stood before the questioning cashier?

"Will I have long to wait for a train at Glenwood Spring?" she asked. "A train either way?"

He pulled a watch from his bibbed overalls and studied it. "We should pull into Glenwood ahead of Number Eight. It's the westbound passenger."

"Are you sure we'll be on time?"

"We can if we skip picking up some empties down-line." He stood up, moved to the conductor's table, and spoke briefly to his fellow trainman. Then he returned to Caroline's side. "We'll make it all right," he said, grinning.

Already she had folded money in her hand. She pressed it into his palm. "Can you get a ticket for me? Help me onto the passenger train without people in the station seeing us?"

"Sure. We'll handle it. But the ticket—where to?"

"Any place," she replied. "Any place a long way from here."

They left her in the dingy caboose until the westbound passenger train had drawn into Glenwood Springs and halted before the depot. When they came down the caboose steps and hurried through a maze of tracks and sided cars, Caroline had drawn a scarf about her face.

As she reached the station platform, Caroline did not know that she was studied by a well-dressed and valise-laden youth who had descended from this train and stood uncertainly near the station entrance. His gaze ran over her and studied the urgency of her steps, her veiled face, and the baby clasped tightly in her arms. She mounted the vestibule steps of the westbound, and its conductor was already signaling the train from town when he turned to go into the depot. A perplexed frown gathered on his brow.

The train gathered speed, and laced the walled canyon of the Colorado River, when she was shown to a small, but comfortable, compartment. She busied herself for a time caring for Freddy. Then, when the conductor entered, to pick up and study her ticket, she scarcely heard or noted his mention of her destination or time of arrival. The door closed behind him. She sat near the window as an endless panorama of widening canyon, valleys, and of sun-sparkled river slid by. Her head dropped forward and she slept.

Later, she awakened and fed her baby. Then she slept again. Later she peered outside. There were no mountains now. Over far reaches of arid, stunted vegetation a setting sun cast long and shafted shadows.

It was darkening when a trainman knocked at the compartment door. He entered and looked anxiously at her. "Sorry to annoy you, ma'am. You've been so quiet. Haven't been out to eat. Are you all right?"

"Yes." She smiled. "Only tired. Very, very tired."

"I'm glad you're not sick. We've got a sick girl—a mighty sick one—up front in one of the coaches."

"I'm sorry," Caroline murmured. Then noting the anxiety of his face, she added, "Can I help? What is her illness?"

"Nerves mostly, I guess. I'd never have let her aboard, back at Glenwood, if I'd known her condition. She's pretty well out of her head. Talking about Aspen. And a mine. And a ranch."

Her words brought an instant tightness to Caroline's throat. "From Aspen—a girl. May I see her? I'll go with you."

He glanced at the sleeping baby beside her. "You've about got your hands full, lady. Them up front can watch out for her."

Caroline's decision was swiftly formed and spoken. "A young girl from Aspen in a chair car alone among strangers. Bring her back here. Do it now."

The conductor's face took on grim relief. "Do you reckon you know her?"

She shook her head. "I don't know. Probably not. But she's sick. Needs a bed. Needs care. Bring her."

She was gazing from the compartment door, tensely expectant, when they carried the girl to her. A single glimpse of the pained and tormented face drained blood and feeling from Caroline's lips. Her first impulse was to slam the door. Lock them out. Bar herself now and forever from the figure and the face she had glimpsed. Instead, she clenched her teeth and stood aside as the limp form was carried into the compartment and laid on a quickly prepared berth.

Caroline turned to moisten and wring a towel. She

moved closer to the berth. She leaned over. Her numb hands lifted the cloth to wipe it softly across the pale forehead, the shrunken cheeks, and the closed eyes of Ellen Bradley Corlett.

Much later the girl stirred, tossed painfully, and opened her eyes. At first her gaze was vacant and unheeding. Then Ellen's blue eyes widened as she shrank back. "Where am I?" she cried. "How did you get here?"

"It's going to be all right, Ellen. Everything's going to be all right. You're on the train—remember? This is my compartment. I asked them to let you stay here with me."

Eventually Ellen Corlett slept. The outer desert was dark and unfathomable, and the lights of the compartments subdued, when she opened her eyes again. Caroline pressed a glass to parched lips. "Drink this, Ellen. Then lie still and rest."

Instead, wretching sobs tore the girl's face and shook her body. "He's dead, Caroline. Hardrock is dead. They took his mine, our house, everything. He couldn't bear it. He hung himself in the carriage house."

Caroline smoothed the wild disarray of yellow hair against a pillow.

"Who robbed you?" she asked, even though she already knew.

"It was the Shaners. I was a fool. They looked rich and talked rich. I fell for it and put Hardrock in their hands. Everything he'd worked for. Everything he had." Her words became a wail. "I want to die too, Caroline. They told me to leave, leave Aspen. Gave me fifty dollars. Let me be, Caroline. Let me die."

Caroline lifted the glass again. She spoke slowly and calmly. "You won't die, Ellen. Neither of us will. My husband is dead, too. So is Mrs. Jorgenson, who cared for me so long. Perhaps they and Hardrock are the lucky ones. But you and I are alive. Whatever is ahead we must face."

Ellen struggled to sit up. "Where's your baby, Caroline?"

Caroline pointed to the sleeping child.

"Lift him up, Caroline. Let me see him. I've always wanted a baby." She looked long and hungrily into the child's face, then sank back onto the berth. "Caroline," she

283

said. "Why couldn't I be like you? Proud and capable? I've always been jealous of you. Wanted to be like you, walk like you, and talk like you—not just a guttersnipe. A nobody. A fool." She was crying again, a tired broken crying, that gave way to sleep.

The trainmen came again to the door. Anxiety was stamped across their faces. Caroline sent them quietly away. She sat very still. Underneath was the endless clicking of railheld wheels.

Far up front of the train a whistle sounded. Caroline Ainsley Herndon heard a mournful dirge for the past and all of the loneliness of the unknown into which she rode. Lance would be home now, perhaps with Jim and Maude Daley at his side. The town, spread between towering peaks, would have again darkened. The town would be buzzing, aghast, shock-ridden by what she had done.

PART FOUR

1891–1894

Chapter 15

As the train rushed westward, carrying two women ever farther from Aspen, an air of tenseness and shock lay across the town on the Roaring Fork. There was only one topic of discussion among those gathered on the streets and in homes, hotels, and saloons. News of the destruction of the Buccaneer mine had come slightly before dawn. Men from the Castle Creek area rode sweat-lathered horses into town and told how the explosion had wakened them with its reverberating roar and how the dazed guard had sought them out with news of the disaster.

During the morning an attempt was made to enter the tunnel and to evaluate the extent of damage. Within minutes it had become apparent that the effects of the blast were catastrophic. Only a new tunnel could give access to the area that had once been a large room containing the pumps and the shaft head. It would be difficult, dangerous work. Perhaps it would be impossible. Could heavy timbering hold the shattered and shifting rock? Could pumps contend with the water that dripped and ran in ever-increasing amounts? Only time, endless work, and heavy redevopment costs would furnish an answer.

Lance Ainsley was eating breakfast in Ashcroft when word of the explosion reached him. His first reaction was amazed disbelief. It was followed quickly by a searing premonition, and the urge to get to Aspen and to Caroline's side. At a livery stable he arranged for the fastest horse available. Even as he left the small, peak-bound camp, the creek road was crowded with men afoot, on horseback, or with varied vehicles headed down-canyon toward the Buccaneer.

He kept his mount at an urgent gait, hardly able to resist the consuming desire to spur the horse into speed that he knew would bring exhaustion far short of Aspen. Excited queries were yelled at him, but he neither comprehended nor answered.

Could Caroline have done this? For damn sure he himself could have under stress of the torment she had endured. But she must have had help. Jed Curry? He shook his head. Curry had already left town, talking of Montana and its lure.

The canyon access road to the Buccaneer was crowded and choked with men and horses and wagons as he rode past. He gave it only a minute's scrutiny, then continued homeward. More and more people recognized him and attempted to halt and question him. He rushed past both friends and strangers. He rode on heedlessly and blindly. The Shaners would be swift in their attempt at revenge. Caroline would need him. Perhaps even now at home——
He dug spurs into his mount's flanks. God, how slow a good horse moves at such a time!

It seemed hours, agonizing hours, later that he slid the horse to a halt, swung from the saddle, and entered his house. He gave no heed to a small, excited crowd gathered in the street. Inside, Olga waited. Her husband was with her. Foreboding swept him as he gazed into their faces. "Where is Caroline?" he demanded.

"Mr. Ainsley," Olga answered unsteadily, "she isn't here. She has gone. Left Aspen."

"What do you mean?" Lance's face whitened. "Where? When? Lord Almighty, please speak up. Tell me."

The young husband laid a steadying hand on Lance's shoulder. "Of course we'll tell you, tell you all we know. But first you'd better read a letter she left for you. It's in your bedroom."

Later, after a silent and tortured time alone, Lance reappeared. Tired and shaken, he muttered, "Tell me all you know."

"Caroline went horseback riding yesterday," Olga began.

"Yes. Yes I know about that," Lance answered. "Then what?"

"She came home an hour or so before sunset. She acted strange. Quiet and grim and mad, awfully mad. She went out alone after it got dark, and was gone an hour or so. Then she came back. She looked wild and determined. She asked us to stay with the baby. Then she left again before midnight. She didn't say anything—just took her horse and rode off."

"And then?" Lance leaned forward and searched her words.

"She got back a long time after midnight. Then she wrote the note to you." Olga paused. Her words were stifled by broken sobs.

"I can tell the rest of it," her husband said. "Caroline told us she had blown up her mine and had killed a man. She asked us to help her hide and to help her get out of Aspen."

"Kitten, kitten, why didn't you wait for me?" Lance Ainsley's words were haunted.

"Mr. Ainsley, I don't think she was afraid for herself. She was afraid for the baby and for you. She'd gotten the idea she had ruined your life. She couldn't face you."

Lance lifted apprehensive eyes toward them. "But where is she, now?"

"I was coming to that. We took her over to Freida Edmonds's house in shacktown. She has friends in that part of town, more friends than even she realized. I left her there and looked up some fellows I know. We put her and the baby on the caboose of a freight pulling out for Glenwood Springs. That was about three o'clock this morning. She wanted it that way. That's all I know. Honest to God, Mr. Ainsley, we did what Caroline wanted."

Lance came slowly to his feet. "I'm sure you did. If I only knew where she——"

Olga had quieted. Now she peered steadily into his face. "The trainmen will know more. They'll be back in town sometime tonight. We'll ask them to come here and tell you."

For a long time Lance was silent, studying the sight and

289

sounds of the group in the street. Determination grew in his face. "No, don't bring them here. Talk to them quietly tell me later. There's going to be hell to pay for a time. Keep quiet about what you know. You'd better go home now and rest. And thanks for doing what she asked you to do."

Lance later reentered his bedroom, picked up the single page of the letter, and read it again and again. Suddenly the house was lonely and ghastly and unbearable. He went outside to the stable, where he fed and curried the sweat-stained black mare. He tried to reconstruct the events of the night and to make sense of chaotic fragments. Somewhere, somehow, Caroline had happened upon the truth and had sought out the identity of Bob's killer. But where? How? Why had she returned from her ride and then gone to some unknown place in the night?

He was still brushing the mare, intent in his search for facts, when a form darkened the barn door. He wheeled about and managed a soft, relieved smile for Maude Daley, who rushed to throw her arms about him.

"Lance, is it true? We just heard downtown."

"Heard what, Maude?"

"That the Buccaneer mine has been destroyed. That likely Caroline did it. Either she or Jed Curry."

He held her tightly, managing to extend a hand to Jim Daley who followed her.

"Yes, it's true. She dynamited the mine."

"Christ alive," Jim Daley whispered. "I shoulda known my spunky partner would fix Shaner's plow. Where is she, Lance? Speak up. We've got to see her. Help her."

"You're too late," Lance said dazedly. "We're all too late. She got out of town. I was in Ashcroft last night. She blew the stinking hole to smithereens, rode back here, then got some friends to help her clear out. She left a note. Come along to the house. Read it."

Later, when they had read the letter, and Maude Daley had laid it down with a shaking hand, she turned to Lance. "How awful. How she must have suffered. And we left the ranch so sure this would be a happy day for her." She turned to Jim, and added, "Tell him, Jim. Tell him the surprise we had for Caroline. What we came into town to tell her."

Jim Daley choked on his words. "Just that the little gal's our partner now. More than ever. That confounded bill of sale she gave me. Maude and me tore it up. Burned it. Caroline still owns her half of the Lazy Seedy."

"And why not?" Maude murmured. "She found the ranch and put it together. She saved it by outwitting Shaner in court when he tried to pollute the creek. Lance, wherever she is, she's our partner for life."

"That's wonderful, wonderful," Lance said. "The Lord must have forseen trouble for kitten. He gave her so many friends."

"She made a heap of friends by her own doings," Jim said.

"And enemies," Lance sighed. "Damned vicious enemies."

"What are your plans, Lance?" Maude Daley's words were anxiously urgent. Are you going to look for her? Can we help?"

"I haven't had time to plan or to think. But just now, until this all cools down, I'll stay put here in Aspen. She wants it that way. Besides, there's a chance I'd just be leading the law and those same enemies to her."

"Could be you're right," Daley answered reluctantly. "But about you, Lance. Today. This ruckus the town's in. Them people standing and gawking out in the street?"

Lance shrugged. "They're curious and looking for excitement. Wondering if Caroline really did it. If she is here. If the law, or the Shaners, will come for her." He paused, brushing a tired hand across his forehead. "Right now I'm going downtown and act downright unconcerned, walk around as if nothing had happened. The Shaners are bound to make a move as soon as they know for sure a fortune's been blasted from their hands. I'd as soon they look me up where there are a few witnesses and less opportunity for dry-gulching."

"I'll drag along with you." Jim Daley's words were brittle. "Want to go downtown, Maude? To a hotel? Do some shopping?"

"No," she answered. "You go along with Lance. I'm tired. I can rest better here. There's something of Caroline here. Always will be. Get along, I'll be all right."

After they walked down the street and beyond her sight, Maude Daley sat for a long time in a soft chair near the window. She wiped tears from her eyes. A kaleidoscope of the years turned before her, strangely sharp and clear, as it fastened on the house in far-off Evans, and the room in which a beaten child had fought back to life and health. If only I could be with her through this travail and this agony of loneliness, she thought. Instead, she is by herself. No, she isn't by herself. She has her child, her boy. Maude closed her eyes. A child. Perhaps before she would again see Caroline she, too, would have a child. Jim's child. Caroline, you brought that about too. If they hadn't brought you to me, that night when Jared Swope used a brutal whip on you, I would never have left Evans and gone to San Francisco. I would never have come to love and to marry Jim. Thank you, Caroline. Oh, dear God, thank you.

Near noon the inevitable move of the Shaners got underway. For a long while Lance and Daley had walked the downtown streets and made their presence known by stopping and talking with all who hailed them. Time after time, Lance reiterated that he knew no more of the explosion than those who questioned him. Rumors were widespread. It would take hours or days to sift out the facts. As for his daughter's whereabouts, he answered only that he had not seen her since the previous morning when she had gone riding. Upon some faces, his words brought doubt and furtive grins, but the general feeling was one of sympathy and friendship.

The two men paused for a time in a Durant Street saloon. They had scarcely reached the sidewalk when they were approached by the city marshal, by Matt Shaner, and by an older man whom it took Lance awhile to recognize as the prospector Gagnon. The marshal's manner was grim and reluctant. "Lance, can you arrange to have your daughter come down to the office right away? Mr. Shaner has sworn out a warrant for her arrest."

Deliberately, Lance propped an elbow on the brick saloon wall. "You mean you're going to jail her?"

"I'll have to. She can have a hearing today. Arrange for bond."

"Interesting. Very interesting." Lance's tone was cool. He thoughtfully pushed back his hat. "I suppose Shaner or Mr. Gagnon have plenty of evidence to substantiate the charge. By the way, what is Caroline charged with?"

The marshal's face grew uncomfortable. "Hang it all, Lance, I'm just doing my duty. She's charged with destruction of the Buccaneer mine. The evidence is something for the judge, not me. I'll have to bring her in. You can make it easier for her and for me."

Lance shook his head. "Sorry, Marshal. I have no idea where Caroline is. I was in Ashcroft most of the day yesterday. She went for a ride before I left. I haven't seen her since."

"He's lying!" The words broke from Matt Shaner as he pushed forward. His face was twisted in anger.

Lance Ainsley's arm suddenly dropped from the wall. His gray eyes narrowed and darkened. He stepped forward, his face inches from Shaner's. "Listen, you conniving bastard. When you call me a liar be ready to back it up with your fists or a gun! I said I hadn't seen her. Now, make something of it."

There was a tense shuffling in the crowd. Without turning, Lance knew Jim Daley was standing with his back against the wall, ready to take a hand if necessary.

Seconds passed; Shaner's gaze shifted to the marshal.

"You've got your warrant. Bring her in."

The marshal straightened. "Mr. Ainsley says she ain't around. That's good enough for me." Lance detected relief in the statement.

"Maybe," Shaner answered. "I'll have to take men and do your job for you. Drag her from his house!"

"You'll play hell doing it," Jim Daley cut in. "My wife is alone at Ainsley's house. If you bother her it'll give me an excuse to put a .45 slug between them weasel eyes of

293

yours." He paused, studied the group with a sardonic grin, and added, "Besides, Ainsley would have to burn the house down to rid it of your stench."

The laugh of the gathering crowd tore self-control from Matt Shaner. "You talk big, both of you, but we'll get her."

Lance stared at him. "How? Like you got her husband? At night. On a dark street? From a safe distance?"

Shaner's face purpled. "She can't crap on us. Blast our mine, cuss out me and Len———" His words broke off. In his face was self-staggering realization of what he had uttered.

There was the lightning strike of fact in Lance's mind. "So she saw you, saw your brother, cussed you out—she knew, Shaner. Somehow she found out which one killed Bob. Was it you? Was it Len?" He shook his head. "No. Neither one. Just some gunslinger you slipped whiskey and money to gun down a man."

As Lance's words ended, Jim Daley seemed to take off where he had stopped. "Marshal," he said, "I've lived down on Wilderness Creek quite a spell. Aspen ain't had any trouble from me or my outfit. Don't count on it lasting. If anything happens to Ainsley, now or later, we'll be riding in to ferret out every damned Shaner, dog or pup."

Lance's hand fell on the rancher's shoulder. "Whoa up, Jim. The marshal ain't looking for trouble or wanting it. He'd better go with us and search the house and the town. I hope he can find Caroline somewhere about. I can't."

"Hell," Jim Daley said, and spat vigorously onto the walk at Shaner's feet. "My partner's too smart for the whole pukey crew." Without a backward glance, he followed Lance homeward.

Aspen had been shaken throughout the day by the news of the Buccaneer blast, but with evening quiet again spread across the town. Other affairs, daily and routine, were resumed. A mine and a girl had vanished. Now there were other mines, other girls, other problems.

The warm summer night closed in upon the Roaring Fork Valley. Through this soft darkness, the evening passenger train moved steadily upgrade from Glenwood Springs. In the middle of a crowded, uncomfortable coach, a boy sat stiffly erect and peered from the window. For a time he had listened to the animated and wonder-struck conversation of several rough-clad men. By their words and their clothing he guessed them to be day la-borers heading toward the promise of jobs in Aspen's mines and mills. The urge had been upon him to question them, to find out something of this strange, mountain-locked country that lay ahead and hidden by darkness. In-stead, he peered from the window, seeing little except the dim reflection of his own face in the smoke-stained glass.

The talk among the men was clearly audible, but he could comprehend little of it. There was talk of a disaster. A mine explosion. He caught such names as Buccaneer, Shaner, and Herndon, but the names and the events were alien. He stared into the darkness. A sprinkling of lights came finally into view as the train slowed and whistled.

People about him stirred and retrieved coats and lug-gage. He came to his feet and reached for his own valise when a door slammed and the conductor's voice sounded through the coach. "Aspen. End of the line. Aspen."

The lights outside thickened. The train jolted to a halt. He had not spoken to any fellow passenger as he dropped to the station platform.

He stood quietly on the platform as the activity of the train's arrival subsided. A lopsided moon crept above shadowy mountains off to the east, and the valley was bathed in a luminous and revealing glow. He studied the distant vistas in wonder. The land seemed to reach ever skyward and was so different from the level miles and dis-tant horizons that had for so long formed the boundaries of his world. Although it was summer, a chill permeated the thin air. He shivered a little as he picked up his valise and went into the depot.

He approached the ticket window and came under the gaze of a balding man wearing a green eyeshade.

"I've never been in Aspen before," he said unsteadily. "Can you tell me where I could find Caroline Ainsley?"

His question drew a startled glance from the ticket

clerk. "Kid," he answered, "there's plenty of people who'd like to know where that girl is right now." The clerk would have said more, but the troubled aspect of the boy's face caused him to become momentarily silent, and then to say more gently, "She's been living with her father lately. You'll find their house about four blocks from here." With a stubby pencil he drew a rough map of the street and marked the location of Lance Ainsley's home. "Follow that, young fellow. You shouldn't have any trouble. Just ask anybody downtown."

"Thank you, sir," the boy said, and turned quickly from the window. As he left the building, the clerk stared after him. He was vaguely stirred by the somber intensity of the youth's manner. It wasn't until a chattering telegraph instrument summoned him that he could rid his mind of the memory of blue eyes beneath a shock of unruly brown hair, or of the tight-lipped and quietly concealing manner of the boy's words.

The boy hesitated at a white-picketed gate, opened it, walked slowly up the graveled walk, and mounted Lance Ainsley's porch. Lights burned within the house, and he caught the sound of men's voices. He started to knock, then hesitated. His breathing quickened; his fist was tightly clenched as he rapped on the door.

It was opened by a middle-aged and pleasant woman whose smile was reassuring and kind.

"Is this Mr. Lance Ainsley's residence?" he asked, and the words seemed frightened and desperate.

"Yes, yes, of course it is."

"Are, are you Mrs. Ainsley?" he stammered.

"Heavens, no," Maude Daley said, laughing. "I'll call him. Please come in."

The boy crossed the threshold; the valise was clamped in his trembling hand.

"Lance," the woman called, "there's a young man here to see you."

The boy's gaze fixed in fascination on the tall, well-groomed man who rose and moved toward him. His mind registered awareness of this man's black and silver-touched hair and his gray, worried eyes.

"I'm Lance Ainsley. What can I do for you?"

The boy panicked. He would have retreated, but his hand was caught in the firmness of Lance's grasp. "Mr. Ainsley," he choked, "don't you know? Don't you remember me? I'm Shawn. I'm your son."

For a moment Lance stiffened in a frozen stance. Then he pulled the boy into his arms, and his cheek lay against the brown riot of his hair. "Good god," he said at last. "Can it really be?" He held the boy at arm's length. "Let me look at you, son. Why, you're almost a man." He turned toward the wondering gaze of Jim and Maude Daley. "Come over here. My boy has come. My boy, Shawn."

Shawn Ainsley acknowledged their greetings, but his gaze roamed the room. "Where's my sister," he asked. "Where is Caroline?"

Jim Daley caught the desperation of Lance's face, and said, quietly, "Lance, let me tell him. Let me explain." He pulled Shawn toward a sofa. "If only you could have got here a day or so sooner. I hate to tell you about this right off, but here goes——" His voice sounded in the room a long time as Lance sat alongside his son. Maude Daley retreated from the room and sat pale and shaken in the kitchen.

". . . that's the story," Jim Daley finished. "We have no idea yet where Caroline went, only that she caught a westbound train this morning at Glenwood Springs."

The boy rose, paced the length of the room, then faced Lance and Daley. "I think I saw her, Caroline, down at Glenwood Springs. She was hurrying along with some railroad men. Carrying a baby. She had a scarf across her face. I'm sure it was she, Caroline. My sister."

"Then you've seen her since I have," Lance answered dully. Immersed in thought, he was silent for a time and did not notice as the boy moved quietly toward the door and picked up his valise. His hand was on the doorknob when he turned, studiedly ignoring the surprise on Jim and Maude Daley's faces, and said to Lance in a strangely impersonal tone, "Thank you for telling me about Caroline. I'll be going now."

Lance was stunned as the boy's words jerked him erect. "Be going? Son, what do you mean? You just got here."

"I'll get a room at a hotel. Likely I'll see you tomorrow before I leave."

Bewilderment and terror gripped Lance. "Shawn," he murmured unsteadily, "don't you want to stay? This is your home. We've so much to tell each other. There are years to make up for."

Shawn's eyes grew coolly appraising. "How do I know you really want me here? Maybe you are just thinking it's your duty to take me in because you're my father and people would talk."

For an instant anger gouged Lance's face. "What a hell of a thought. You're my son, Shawn. I love you. What people think or say doesn't mean anything." He paused. His face and tone became wistful. "Right now I want you here more than anything else in the world. One child is gone; I can't bear losing another." He strode to his son, put an arm about him, and led him from the door.

Shawn still doubted. "You never cared shucks for me or my mother, not as long as you had Caroline. You never came to see us. Not once. You never came to Greeley, ever."

The withering impact of his son's words whitened Lance's face. He struggled to form a reply, when Maude Daley broke the silence.

"Shawn," she asked firmly, "if you feel that way, why did you leave Greeley? Was there trouble between you and your grandfather?"

"I just wanted to come," the boy said evasively. "I wanted to see my sister."

Time would be needed to search out the truth of Jared Swope's place in this boy's life and mind and heart. And so Maude said, very softly and very kindly, "Shawn, stay with your father for a while. Give him a chance. Right now he needs you more than Caroline might, or anyone else. Get acquainted. Talk things over. Then come down to the ranch and see Mr. Daley and me."

Shawn's face brightened suddenly. "You've got a ranch? A real ranch? Is it a big one?"

Jim Daley had taken the valise from the boy's hands and carried it into Caroline's bedroom. "Sure it's a big outfit. A 'helluva' big ranch. That's what your sister says. And she ought to know. She owns half of it."

Disbelief and wonder livened the boy's face. "My sis owns part of a ranch? Has it got cattle? Horses? Real bronc horses?"

"Some of the saltiest broncs west of Denver," Jim Daley confirmed, grinning. "Just stick around Aspen awhile. There are lots of things to make your eyes bug out. Ask your dad about them or come down to the Lazy Seedy and throw questions at me."

"The Lazy Seedy?" Shawn's words and face grew puzzled.

"Sure," Daley explained and squatted on the rug to draw huge figures. "That's our cattle brand, the Lazy CD. The Caroline and Daley outfit. Couple of weeks from now we could use an extra hand about your size."

Shawn Ainsley looked at Lance. "Maybe it'd be better if I slept here tonight. Tell you about my mother, and grandfather and grandmother."

Maude Daley glanced from father to son, from face to face. Suddenly she laughed softly. "Men can be so stupid. What Shawn needs right now is pie and milk or even some heftier food." She clutched her husband's arm and drew him toward the kitchen. Clear of the room, she shook her head. "He's got Ainsley pride, stubborn, unrelenting pride. It'll take them a long time to get to know each other and to love each other."

"Anyhow it looks like the boy will stick around, Maudie."

"I'll pray to God he does."

The first gray of dawn touched the sky before Lance Ainsley slept. Every sound of the night seemed to press in upon him. With each whistle of a switch engine he sat tensely upright. Where, in some far-off place, was another engine speeding Caroline ever farther from him? How many nights, how many lonely whistles before he would be able to search her out and bring her home? Occasionally there was a sound from the adjoining room where his son, this baffled and troubled boy, slept. How could he attack the barrier between them? Would he ever have both children at once?

He awakened to sparkling early morning sunshine. There was a note on the living-room table, in Maude Daley's flowing hand, explaining that she and Jim had left early to return to the ranch, but would see him in a few days. He peered cautiously into Caroline's room, where Shawn still slept.

Later, he went to the stable to turn the black mare out into a small corral. He stood with an elbow propped on the horse's rump, watching the activity of encircling mines and mills, as his son came out of the house and walked to the corral.

"Good morning, Shawn. Sleep well?"

"Pretty well," the boy said, eying the black mare.

Lance swept an arm that encompassed industrial Aspen. "Ever see a sight like this? Maybe a million dollars a week come out of all the smoke and ruckus. Silver mines. Some of the richest on earth."

The boy followed his pointing hand. "They're a mess," he said flatly. "But the mountains. They're the highest, prettiest mountains——" His words broke off as he again watched the mare. "Is that your horse? She's pretty old."

"She belongs to Caroline. Jim Daley gave her to Caroline a long time ago."

Shawn reached a hand to stroke the mare's muzzle. "What is Caroline like, Dad? Is she like my mother? Did she really own a ranch and a mine?"

"Whoa up." Lance grinned. "How about our drifting downtown for some breakfast? Then we can talk. After that, we can saddle up and ride around awhile."

"Both of us on this old mare?"

"Of course not. I've got other horses out on pasture. Or we can try a livery stable."

"Don't you have to go to work?" the boy demanded.

"Most of the time. We'll make today an exception."

Shawn's answer was cautious and laden with doubt.

"You don't have to do anything for me. I don't want any favors."

Lance glanced sharply toward him. "Listen, Shawn, let's get this straight. I don't curry favors or give them unless I enjoy doing it. I'd like to show you the town and the country hereabouts. If you want to go, just say so. Otherwise we'll forget it."

The black mare edged closer, and the boy put his arm about her neck. "Can I ride this one, Caroline's horse?"

"All you want, son, provided you're gentle with her. When you get back you'll have to feed and curry her."

Their ride lasted most of the day, taking them from Hunter Creek to the lake-studded base of the Maroon Bells and then homeward along the Roaring Fork. Lance avoided direct questions, although snatches of conversation told him that his son had come to Aspen in search of self-direction. He sensed that Jared Swope had offered the boy too much, and expected even more in return.

It was only when he spoke of his grandmother that the boy's face softened. *Grandma* was an endearing word as Shawn spoke it. There was no doubt that Florence Swope had devoted her life to this boy.

Of his mother, Shawn said nothing throughout the day. It wasn't until they returned to Aspen and rode past a small clapboard church that Emily was mentioned. Shawn stared at the building. "How many churches are there in Aspen?" he asked abruptly.

"I don't know, son, never counted them. I've always gone to the Community Church."

"Greeley sure has a scad of them."

"It has always been a religious town," Lance said cautiously.

"I know. Outside, they call it Saint's Roost. Some churches are fine. But in some towns any half-baked fanatic can call himself a preacher and drag in followers." The boy's face twisted bitterly. "My mother married one of those off-breed preachers. A shouting and jumping fanatic."

"I heard she remarried," Lance said quietly.

The boy's voice quickened and took on a rebellious pitch. "She wasn't the same after that, Mom wasn't. First, that preacher Gartrell converted her. He said she'd have to be cleansed of her sins. What sins? Then he had her going from one store and restaurant to another asking for donations and handouts. After that, everyone but the braying asses in Gartrell's church was full of sin. Full of lust. Gartrell said so. Mom seemed to lap up his brand of zeal. It was a sin for Grandma to play anything but psalms on the organ. It was sinful for me to say 'golly' or 'gee whiz.' Dad, Mom went sort of crazy after she'd been with the preacher awhile. She said her mission was to help purify children. How can a little kid that can't even talk need purifying?"

Lance shook his head sadly. "I don't remember her like that. She was always gay, pleasant, laughing."

Shawn's face was twisted and bitter. "She ... sure isn't any more. I haven't seen her for a year. They moved to some dry-land town out east of Greeley. I don't know what preacher Gartrell will find to purify out there on the prairie. But he will sure as hell find something. Anyway Mom can detect sin in a meadowlark's song." The words ended, strangled by a sob, as Shawn turned his face away. Lance could not see the nakedness of his hurt.

"Maybe Jim Daley has the right slant on things," Lance replied after a time. "He says the Lord is in pine trees and soft rain and little white-faced calves, but mostly in a person who faces up to doing what is right and honest even though it's tarnation hard to do."

"Dad, would it be all right for me to go down to Mr. Daley's ranch, Caroline's ranch, tomorrow? Stay awhile?"

Lance reined his horse closer and tousled the boy's hair. "Sure. I'd hoped you would want to, but not quite so soon. But come back, Shawn. Come back to Aspen. Come back home."

"My home is in Greeley," the boy said defensively. "With Grandma and Grandfather."

"Your grandfather can offer you a lot, Shawn. He's pretty rich. Powerful."

"I don't want him giving me anything," the boy flared. "I don't want anybody pushing me ... making up my mind. He wants me to be a banker, go to college, and then start in with him."

The studied penetration of Lance's glance was smothered in the dusk of twilight. "And you haven't made up your mind, son?"

"How can I? He wants to think for me. He thinks he owns me."

"You'll have time to decide down at the ranch. But tonight you'd better write a letter telling your grandmother where you are. She'll worry."

"How did you know I ran away and didn't tell them?"

"It's hard to say how I know, son. Maybe just because I'm an Ainsley, too, and your father."

They rode in silence for a long time and were nearing home when the boy said, "Dad, see if you can find me a job in Aspen. Do it while I'm down at the Lazy, the Lazy Seedy."

"Sure thing," Lance agreed, and grinned for the first time in many hours.

The days sped by. Knowing that his son was at the ranch with the Daleys, Lance was content to await the boy's return. Now he could give full time to the thing he had determined to do. Regardless of cost, the Shaners must be exposed, discredited, and driven from Aspen. Only then could arrangements be made to seek out Caroline's whereabouts and arrange for her safe return to Aspen. Word was already about town that upon expert advice the Shaners had ceased their efforts to reopen the Buccaneer. The cost would be prohibitive, even though the shattered depths held rich ore. Men could not be hired to work in the dangerously shattered tunnels and shafts. Water was even a greater menace. A flood of water filled the mine and seeped from every crevice. Whatever mystery and telltale evidence the Buccaneer held would likely never be seen. The past had buried its dead.

Word was brought to Lance of the Shaners' guarded inquiry as to what had become of their hatchet-faced gunman. It was evident they did not wish to press the matter by letting it be generally known how integral a part of their group and their activities this man had been.

When the first subtle tinge of approaching autumn rode the darkness, Lance sat at a poker table in the Roaring Fork Club. He had reserved the private room. Jim Daley had come into town at Lance's asking and was there with him. H. A. W. Tabor came in from Denver and brought Eric Duane with him.

With swift, decisive words, Lance bared his determination to see an end of the Shaner outfit in Aspen. "I asked all of you to meet with me because I'm likely to need your help—not that the Shaners have much left to keep them here. Caroline whipped their hind ends completely as far as placering on Wilderness Creek is concerned. They swiped the Buccaneer. I'm darned sure that if Bob Herndon had lived he had proof of that. But the mine's done for now."

"Seems like they'd better look for new territory," Tabor said.

"Not just yet—unless they're forced to. They'd like to stay. They hope Caroline is coming back. Besides, they're trying to ferret their way into some other properties. They can get enough gold out of Hardrock Corlett's diggings to make it pretty well worth their while."

Daley nodded. "They've got a few men up there. Shawn rode up that way a day or so ago and saw them."

Lance's face tightened uneasily. "What'd he do a fool stunt like that for. If they'd known who he was——"

"Luckily they didn't. He didn't ride in close or stick around. The kid's got sense, Lance."

Tabor grinned reminiscently. "Maybe he'll put together another helluva big ranch somewhere up there," he said, laughing.

"Nope. Not that boy," Daley replied. "He's cut out for something. But it ain't ranching. He just wants to take a horse and a dog and ride into tall timber. Then he sits and stares." He glanced at Lance. "Don't get me wrong. He's a good boy and willing. He's just trying to figure something out. When he does, he'll make you proud of him."

"When is he coming back into town?" Lance asked. "He

wanted me to find some sort of a job for him. I've got something spotted. A job in a grocery store. Not much future in it, but maybe it'll keep him busy until he gets over the thing gnawing at him."

"I'll tell him when I go back tomorrow," Daley answered. "We'd sure like for him to stay on at the Lazy Seedy. Maude and me have taken a shine to him. But if he wants to try lugging groceries, that's all right too."

Throughout the discussion, Eric Duane sat in silence. His chair was tilted back as he gazed at the blankness of the wall. Now, he wheeled to look at them. "Likely there's little I can do about this cutthroat crew you want out of Aspen, but I'm certain of one thing. I'm going to find Caroline. I'll find her if I have to travel a year." He paused, and a wistful smile marked his face. "I think all of you know I'm completely in love with Caroline, and I have been ever since school days in Denver." He hesitated. "I know this isn't the time to talk of how I feel or how I've always felt."

"You're wrong, Eric," Lance said steadily. "This is the time to talk of everything. It's time to clear the air and clear the town."

H. A. W. Tabor riffled a deck of cards and smiled at Daley. "How about a little game as we talk? A long time back, Jim said he was damned sure we'd just be talking instead of playing cards at train time. Now he's gabbing. Time sure deteriorates a cowman."

Jim Daley glowered. "You're old and plumb garrulous, H. A. W., my friend. Name the stakes; cut for deal."

Tabor grinned eagerly. "How about the loser paying all the costs of Ainsley and Eric traveling to find the little gal, Caroline?"

"Now wouldn't that be a bitch of a game?" Daley snorted. "Everyone wanting to be the loser, discarding aces till hell wouldn't have 'em."

"You and I could buck heads," Tabor offered. "Your ranch for my Ashcroft holdings."

"Not any more," Jim Daley said softly. "One scare about losing the Lazy Seedy was enough before Caroline

305

pulled it out of the mud. Besides, she owns half of it. Maude——"

"Speaking of Maude," Lance cut in. "Have you told H. A. W. and Eric you're to be a daddy?"

"What?" Tabor exploded. "You mean this broken down old cowpoke is still enough of a man to——"

Eric Duane shoved out his hand. "Congratulations, Jim."

Suddenly H. A. W. Tabor snapped cards onto the table. "One hand, all down," he said. "Eric, you don't play this game of sin and skill. Makes three of us left. Winner of this hand passes his first name on to Jim's boy, God help the little tyke."

There was skillful poker that night in the Roaring Fork Club. And thus it was foreordained that Jim Daley's child (Maude must cooperate by production of a boy) would carry throughout life the name James Lance Horace Daley, Jr!

It was late when they left the club. With the momentous decision made as to what Maude Daley would be told to name her son, the talk reverted to serious discussion of driving the Shaners and their henchmen from Aspen. Lance had given days and nights of planning to the problem. The moves he outlined would be legal, intricate, and time-consuming.

Eric Duane restlessly paced about. "All that will take weeks, maybe months, Lance. I can't wait that long. God knows where Caroline is; maybe right now she needs help."

Tabor glanced up and threw an enigmatic look at Jim Daley. "Jim," he said slowly, "could you delay getting back to the ranch for one day? Meet me at the Jerome Hotel for coffee in the morning. I've got a deal to talk over with you. I won't go into it now; it'd only bore Eric and Ainsley to listen."

Lance, intent upon the details of his riddance campaign, failed to see the slow wink that accompanied Tabor's words and the crisply acknowledging nod of Jim Daley.

The dew of earliness was still on the grass, and an unsuspecting Lance Ainsley had hardly awakened, when Jim Daley and Tabor lifted steaming coffee cups and stared at each other.

"That's the way I see it," Tabor said. "Ainsley's plan to chase the bastards out of town would work, but it'd take an eternal long time. You and I like action—quick action. I've gotten hold of an interesting fact. Both of the Shaners dealt the girl her crappy hand. Len has faded out of town. But Matt's still here handling things. Let's look him up. Talk turkey."

Daley gazed at him in admiration. "Sometimes you talk sense, H. A. W. If you were half as pretty as Caroline I wouldn't mind being partners with you in a deal or so."

Discreet inquiry and a couple of helpful bribes brought them an hour later into the small upstairs room that served as Matt Shaner's office. He had a disarming and affable grin for Tabor. It dropped off sharply as he recognized Jim Daley.

"Mr. Tabor," Shaner said cautiously, "it's a pleasure to have you look me up. I worked for you once. A long time ago. Remember?"

H. A. W. Tabor dropped, unasked, onto a chair. "I remember, Matt. Remember real well. That was before Lance Ainsley fired you."

Shaner's face bleakened. "Ainsley wanted my job. Cut my throat for it."

"Seems you're pretty good at throat-cutting yourself." Tabor's voice changed to brittle authority.

Matt Shaner glanced from face to face with quick awareness of trouble ahead. "I'm pretty busy," he said. "What can I do for you gentlemen?"

"You can be out of Aspen in twenty-four hours," Tabor answered flatly. "You and your whole cutthroat crew. Likely your brother Len has something going elsewhere where your questionable talents will be valuable."

"The hell I'll leave," Shaner retorted angrily. "I've taken more from the Ainsleys and from your friend Daley now than——"

Jim Daley edged forward, but Tabor waved him back. "Matt," he said almost sociably, "you haven't a damned thing left worthwhile in Aspen or Pitkin County. Old Hardrock Corlett's diggin's are small potatoes without placer operations. You may as well seal the Buccaneer and kiss it good-bye."

"The devil I'll seal it. I'll be around waiting for the bitch that blew it up."

"Can you prove she did it? You've double-crossed half the people on the Western Slope, Shaner. Anyone of them could have blasted it."

Matt Shaner's face was pasty. "When I get hold of Ainsley's daughter, she'll be glad to own up she did it."

Tabor laughed harshly. "How do you propose to find her? Her father can't. Daley can't. I can't. Matt, you won't be in Aspen if she should come back."

"Why?" Shaner asked sullenly. "Nothing is going to put me out of this town except a bullet through my head."

Jim Daley's laugh rang scornfully through the room. "Likely such an end ain't far off, Shaner. We just left Lance Ainsley. He thinks you had a hand in the disappearance of his daughter. He's about convinced himself you killed her. Maybe today he'll look you up and gun you down."

"Bullshit," Shaner raged. "Ainsley's just a tinhorn surveyor, a business slicker. He's no gunman."

H. A. W. Tabor grinned knowingly. "You think so. Find out for yourself, Shaner. It's about time your luck runs out. I don't know why I'm telling you. Act of mercy, maybe. Lance Ainsley spent years on the riverboats from Memphis to St. Louis to New Orleans. He was known as the best pistol shot on the river. He's still the damnedest, fastest."

Jim Daley squatted on the corner of a desk. His face was scant inches from Shaner's. "And if Ainsley don't get you, I'm coming after you. Me and my cowhands. Think it over."

H. A. W. Tabor moved to the door and added with finality, "Sure, think it over Matt; think it over today. Then get out of Aspen tonight." He paused at the door and looked back. "By the way, Matt. Tell Len that Arizona lawmen are sure on his tail. There's extradition papers at the statehouse in Denver."

It was a tribute to Matt Shaner's efficient and persuasive handling of his men that not a single resident of Aspen saw them depart. During the rest of the day they were in and about town, but by nightfall they had faded into oblivion.

Chapter 16

In the fall and winter of 1892, Aspen had unknowingly come to the zenith of its growth and wealth. Even as endless smoke lifted from the smelters and increasingly large and valuable shipments of silver bullion were outward-bound from the town, a catastrophe was in the making. Political maneuvering was underway across the nation. A swiftly mounting campaign was designed to bring about the repeal of the Sherman Silver Purchasing Act. The new president-elect Grover Cleveland prepared his ultimatum for Congress. Silver purchasing by the federal government must be discontinued. The nation must return to the single monetary standard—gold. Silver must go!

As the rumors and news reached Aspen that winter, Lance Ainsley foresaw the coming of the town's decline. There would be unemployment, poverty, business failures, and widespread misery. He was not concerned for himself. He had long before diversified his interests, specializing more and more in acquiring forest tracts from which lumber could be cut, milled, and shipped to distant markets. Industrial minerals, plentiful on the Western Slope, caught his attention, and he spread his holdings.

More acute and personal than the ominous shadows moving westward from Washington, D. C., was the utter futility of his search for his daughter. No single word had come from Caroline since her predawn flight from Aspen. Clues led only to Salt Lake City, but she was not there. His own trips, and those of Eric Duane, had been of no avail. A westbound train had carried her from him and from the town. There was no trail to follow, no definite fact upon which a meaningful search could any longer be based. Now, he could only wait and mark the passing weeks and months with hope that someday a letter would come or that she might return.

For the first time Lance Ainsley acknowledged that he was whipped. The flashing smile and jaunty manner that had marked his years was a rare thing these days. The graying of his hair and the deepening furrows across his face gave evidence that worry and years took their toll.

He took some comfort from the fact that Shawn remained in Aspen, even though it was comfort tinged with doubt and apprehension. Shawn put little enthusiasm into his job at Coulter's grocery. The boy seldom spent spare time at home or in Lance's company. Shawn had developed into a lone wolf with an attitude that led him to spend endless hours roaming the forests astride the old black mare. Somewhere he had acquired a mongrel dog and its adoration. There was scarcely a work-free hour when this trio could not be spotted along an ice-bound creek or plowing through the snow of a mountain slope.

Lance Ainsley watched and worried and kept silence. His son's attitude toward him was respectful and aloof. Not once since the evening of Shawn's outburst of bitterness about his mother and her marriage had he allowed Lance to penetrate the barrier between them. He was adamant in his demand that Lance accept part of his meager earnings in payment for board and room. Shawn seldom was at home before darkness for he had taken on a second job. He nightly cut and stacked wood at the home of Vern Coulter, the newly married son of the store's proprietor. How long would this sort of thing continue without ambition or plans for the future, either here or with Jared Swope? Shawn had received letters from both his grandfather and grandmother in Greeley. Those from his grandmother he read and tucked carefully into his pocket; those from Jared Swope lay unopened and unnoticed on a table beside his bed.

With the deepening sense of impending panic and ruin upon Aspen, Lance was called upon more and more often to consult with businessmen who planned to avert the utter collapse of their own enterprises and the city's economic life. It was well that he was busy as winter marched its way toward spring; his home was silent and hardly to be endured.

On February 11, 1893, *The Aspen Times* carried the comforting news that nine votes had sent back the Silver Repeal Bill to the Committee on Rules. This temporary reprieve was hailed with relief and wishful thinking by mine operators, merchants, and all concerned with the welfare of Aspen.

Lance attended a meeting at the Roaring Fork Club to discuss future strategy in the fight for survival.

That winter evening his son finished a late delivery for Coulter's grocery and walked the few blocks to Vern Coulter's house. Coulter had left earlier in the day on a trip to Denver. The corpulent and easygoing young man had frequently gone alone to Denver during the few weeks of his marriage to the bride he had brought to Aspen.

Shawn sat on the woodpile as darkness swiftly approached. The chopping and stacking job was done. Presently the open door of the house spilled out light, and Laura Coulter called to him. Shawn had wondered about Vern Coulter. How could a man marry such a beautiful girl as Laura and then, within a scant three months, leave her alone time after time while he trekked off to Denver? Why had he not stayed home? Why had he not taken his wife with him?

He responded quietly to her call, slid from the log pile, and piled high his arms with split wood. Mrs. Coulter stood in the doorway. Her full and graceful figure was outlined by lamplight.

She latched the door behind him after he entered.

"You've worked so long and so hard tonight, Shawn.

311

While you chopped the wood I baked a pie. I'll cut it. How about a glass of milk?"

He gazed soberly toward her and nodded. It was hard for him to speak to her. Her loveliness, the dark chestnut curls tumbling over her shoulders, and the mystery of her blue eyes always stole words from his lips. In seventeen years he had never met such a woman, softly rounded with lips that carried a subtly lurking smile when she spoke.

She placed the pie and milk before him. Then she left the room and returned wearing a maroon-colored robe, tied at the side and reaching to the tips of small and dainty slippers.

Separated from him only by the width of the small table she sat and stared toward the yellow glow of the lamp. Her eyes were distant and veiled. "Damn him," she said. "I'm sorry, Shawn. Thinking. Just thinking. I didn't mean to be rude. You're probably still hungry. More pie?"

He rose slowly to his feet. He wanted to stay here, continue to look at her, and to hear the low melody of her voice. He was still hungry, but politeness warned him not to show it.

"Thank you, Mrs. Coulter," he managed. "It was very good pie." His words died off and he stood uncertainly before her. Suddenly he was aware of himself as he had never been. Of his denim jeans and work-stained jacket. Of his soiled hands and of the unruliness of the hair dropping onto his forehead. At that moment he wanted desperately to be different ... someone of the world from which she must have come. If only now he was as carefully groomed and as much at ease as his father.

"I'd better go now," he said, and added swiftly, "Thank you, again."

Laura Coulter's gaze searched him intently. Her breath quickened. Then her hand moved across the table to grasp and hold his fingers. "Wait, Shawn, wait just a little while. It's so lonesome here I can't stand it. He'll be in Denver two or three days. Why? For God's sake why? He says it's business, but what business takes him so often and so long? It's another woman. And a drinking, helling good

312

time while I wait here and shrivel from loneliness and boredom."

Her white perfect teeth gleamed in the soft light as she clenched them and fought back frustration and tears. "To hell with him. To hell with the high and mighty Vern Coulter, where ever he is tonight."

She rose swiftly and moved around the table toward him. Suddenly her arms were about him, and her head bent as her lips held his in a long and hungry kiss.

After she drew back he stood rooted in mingled fear and fascination. Within him was the first stirring of a small, growing hope. His eyes widened as he watched her reach out to the lamp and turn it off. When she again moved toward him, there was only the flickering light from the grate of the kitchen stove, light that was sufficient only to outline her face, her throat, and the smooth rose-tipped breasts from which she had drawn the robe.

Laura Coulter's hands quickly grasped his arms. She leaned back, closed her eyes, and breathed softly.

He shook as he cupped his hands over her elbows and drew her toward him. His kiss on her throat was light and inexperienced and told of unsureness that such as this could be. His hand stroked the soft cleanliness of her hair. "Mrs. Coulter," he said brokenly, "you're so pretty. So awfully——"

She placed a finger on his lips. "That's the nicest thing anyone could say to me. But I'm not Mrs. Coulter any more—not to you, Shawn. I'm Laura, just Laura from now on."

The boy's eyes stirred with excitement and turned again to her breasts. He was sure that nothing could be more perfect, could offer more than was revealed by the stove light and the stirring, unknown flames within him.

She watched smilingly and said, "Would you like to touch them, Shawn?" Her hand guided his fingers softly across her nipples. At the cautious, embarrassed lightness of his touch, she laughed gently and tightened his fingers across the fullness and roundness that entranced him. "They won't break, Shawn. Really they won't. Hold them tighter, tighter."

Then she was in his arms again, and he was kissing her. No longer frightened kisses, but urgently demanding lips that swept her eyes and her mouth.

She later moved from him and broke his grasp with gentle suddenness. For a moment her hands were at her side. The robe slid from her. The soft glow revealed the complete perfection of her body with its sheen and its curves and its promise.

Her voice was low and compelling as she led him into the darkness beyond the stove and the kitchen. "Shawn," she whispered. "Oh, Shawn, hurry."

In the high country days of late winter are enticed by brilliant sunshine and warm breezes; it seems that surely tomorrow will mark the end of winter's harsh rule and will be a time of ice-free waters, budding flowers, and green hillsides. For those who have wearied of deep snow and relentless cold there is subtle promise in dripping eaves or the sight of a garden furrow peeping from beneath a white and crusted drift. The creatures of the wild quickly react to ageless change. There is new vigor in the bouncing steps of a deer, in the frisking of horses, and the whir of a mountain grouse. Already the white drifting clouds portend the imminent coming of a storm that will lash white fury across the wilderness, but now winter is battling with only a delaying action. Perhaps only a single storm separates today from the caressing touch of spring.

Well after sundown of such a day Maude Daley gave birth to a child. She wanted to remain on the ranch for the event, but Jim knew the isolation of the Lazy Seedy and insisted that she stay in Aspen, close to the Citizens' Hospital and its medical facilities.

She could well have remained on Wilderness Creek because her labor was brief, terminating with a suddenness that caused Jim Daley to comment proudly when he met Lance in the Jerome bar: "Cripes, Ainsley, wasn't no trick a-tall the way Maudie handled it. I've had more problems with a cow dropping her fourth or fifth calf. She just doubled up her fists, cut loose with a yell, and there he was."

Lance's glass clicked against Jim's. "I'm delighted for

both of you." He paused and added, smiling, "How did Maude take to the long-handled name we shoved at the boy from that poker game?"

Jim Daley squinted at his emptying glass. "She mulled that one over quite a spell, Lance. Let them three names, James . . . Lance . . . Horace, spill from her lips several times. Finally she said it was like loading a little colt with three saddles. Then she agreed it might work out—providing——"

"Providing what, Jim?"

"Providing the boy grew up having your manners, my lovin' ways, and H. A. W. Tabor's knack for money-making."

The following evening Lance left home after dinner for a walk to the hospital and a visit with Maude Daley. Throughout the day he found himself thinking eagerly of the visit and of a chance to see the day-old child. The weather still held a warmly serene promise of spring.

Shawn had been at home for the meal, but had eaten little and had spoken less than a dozen words. It seemed to Lance that his son was becoming more and more a stranger and an enigma. Lately the boy's movements had taken on a secret manner that at times seemed alarmingly furtive.

Half a block from his house, Lance paused on the street and studied the moon struck silhouette of mountains. He had never ceased throughout the years to marvel at the beauty of night as it enfolded the Roaring Fork Valley.

The sound of hurried steps across the street broke his reverie and caused him to look up. He immediately recognized Shawn and realized that the boy had left the house as soon as he thought he would not be seen. Lance watched the hurrying boy approach, pass opposite him, and trot on. Shawn had not looked about and had not seen him standing quietly and observantly.

Something half-curiosity and half-premonition caused Lance to move along after the retreating form. He never questioned his son's coming or going or been struck with desire to pry or to spy. Tonight, the urge was undeniable.

As the boy moved onto a side street, Lance kept a silent but safely distant step.

Within minutes he was sure of the boy's destination. Down a darkened and almost deserted street lay the home of Vern Coulter. Coulter would not be there. Lance knew that he was off on another long trip to Denver. Laura Coulter would be there—young, lonely, lovely, a neglected bride with deeply brooding eyes, with lips pensive and passion-curved.

Abruptly Lance halted. He stared after his son until the hurrying figure became part of the unfathomable night and then wheeled about and walked rapidly to the hospital.

Maude Daley was radiant in a blue-lace bed jacket. Propped up in bed, she squeezed her husband's hand. Lance knew as he entered the room that already plans were being made. The plans reached into the years when young J. L. H. Daley would pick up the reins of an empire along Wilderness Creek. Their son is one day old and they can chart a course for him, he thought. Mine is nearly grown, and what can I do? How can I interest him? Mine—how can I reach out to him?

He forced the agony from his mind, and threw a kiss to Maude Daley. "Hello, Mama. You're loafing. Just loafing. You look well enough, beautiful enough, to go dancing. How about it? Just you and me. We'll leave Pa Daley to mind the young'un."

Despite Lance's banter and the gayness of his approach, Maude Daley watched him with a puzzled face. When Jim was out of the room she dragged the matter into the open.

"Lance, thanks for being kind and good company. For wanting to see my baby, but something's wrong. Now, what is it? Something about Caroline?"

"No," he said tiredly.

"Then it's Shawn, isn't it, Lance?"

"Yes, it's Shawn all right."

Maude seized his hand and pulled him to her side. "Poor Lance, you've never been able to have your boy. Really have him, as a son, a companion."

"It's hopeless, Maude. I shouldn't be bothering you with my troubles tonight."

"Any night, Lance. Any night or any day." She paused and then said firmly, "Lance, ask Shawn to come and see me. Sometimes it helps a boy just to talk to a woman."

"That's the hell of it," he grated. "Right now he's talking to a woman. Doing more than talking with a woman who can mean only disaster for him."

"Just the same," she said firmly. "Please send Shawn to see me right away. Tomorrow, Lance."

After leaving the hospital he walked down the hill toward town. His steps were measured and trancelike. The lights of the Jerome bar beckoned, and he entered. He was at the bar until almost midnight, but whiskey offered no solution of the problems pressing about him. Reluctantly he walked home. The night would offer little sleep or rest. There would be no friendly, family bound discussion with his son.

His steps led him past Bob Herndon's locked and shuttered assay office. He seldom walked this way because the white frame building and the neglected mineral case near the gate were potent with memories.

Suddenly he stopped. Where there should have been but blackness across the building, his eye caught a narrow band of light. Someone was or had been inside the assay office.

He touched the reassurance of the pistol that lately had been his constant companion. Then he opened the gate and walked with silent steps along the walk and onto the porch. He touched the door and found it unlocked. Inch by inch he pushed it open, then entered. The light was coming as an intermittent thing from the back room, from Bob Herndon's old workshop. Lance edged cautiously toward it.

He peered in. The intermittent light was no longer a mystery. The beam of light was off now, but a different radiance held one corner of the workshop. In an eerie glow, cast by a shaded lamp, dozens of mineral and rock specimens had taken on wondrous and lovely hues. Of

317

course, Lance nodded silently, he's turning the black light on and off to see the minerals' florescence. He studied the head and shoulders of the form hunched over the display and knew it was his son. Shawn had come here and sought out the wonders of a strangely beautiful world that could be revealed only through darkness and the mystic glow of black light.

Lance watched silently. At last the boy straightened, touched a switch, and cut the room into normal light. He straightened suddenly and turned. The father and son looked squarely into each other's face.

"I saw a light in here," Lance said quietly. "Thought it was a prowler. Don't let me interrupt you."

Shawn shrugged. "Doesn't matter. I was leaving."

Lance stepped forward and switched the lamp back to black light and the dazzling rainbow shimmer of color.

"It's a beautiful sight, isn't it? It always has seemed a trifle haunting and out of this world to me."

"It's all right," Shawn said, shrugging. "Just a bunch of rocks." The deliberate words were unconcerned, but Lance wondered how long his son had been entranced or how long he would have remained had he not been interrupted.

"I'm no minerologist or mining engineer," Lance said. "But I've wished many times I was. There's fascination and fortunes in ores. There could be a fine career for you."

Shawn's face twisted. His words were ironic and biting. "Yeah, I suppose so. A fine future crushing rocks to pieces. The stink of acids. Maybe two dollars a day for work in a slimy shaft."

Lance Ainsley's face darkened and his temper rose. "Yes. A future. A hell of a lot more future than you're going to find screwing Vern Coulter's wife."

Shawn's face slackened in surprise and guilt.

"I might have known you'd find out, spy on me. But I don't care. Sure I go to Laura's house. She wants me there. It's not like your place and your charity."

Lance struck the boy across the cheek. "Shut up, Shawn," he demanded.

He touched his reddening cheek. "I'll not shut up. Why should I? Why should I do anything for you? You deserted me and deserted my mother. You ran away. All you wanted was Caroline. I'm, I'm glad she's gone. Likely you ran her off."

Coldness crept across Lance. "I'm sorry I slapped you Shawn. Maybe I had a drink too many. I've tried to break through to you. Gain your respect. Your love. Perhaps I don't deserve them. I've a feeling now is the time for both of us to call it quits. As things are, there's no reason in anything. Tomorrow I'll buy you a ticket back to Greeley and Swope's mansion." His voice was low and unsure as he wheeled to the front door, then paused. "Do just one thing for me. For yourself. For common decency."

"What?" the boy answered, and his voice was dazed.

"Go up to the hospital tomorrow and say good-bye to Jim and Maude Daley. Maude has her baby, a boy. She wants to talk to you. Will you do it?"

"Sure."

"Good. Lock the door when you leave here. Bob Herndon and Caroline put a lot of their lives and their hearts into what's here."

Shawn came down the hallway to Maude's open door, peered in, and hesitated. For a moment, seeing the mingled anger and bewilderment enshrouding him, she wavered in her purpose. Then she clasped her hands onto her elbows and steeled herself. She had a job to do. She called him to her side and reached out to press him into a chair beside the bed.

"Shawn, it's nice to see you. Jim and I have missed you since you left the ranch."

"I've missed you too, Mrs. Daley. I'm awfully glad about your baby. Will they let me see him?"

"I'm sure they will. But first, let's just talk. Perhaps you'd better close the hall door, Shawn. There are some pretty sick people here we might disturb."

When he was again seated, she firmly fastened her hand about his fingers. "Shawn," she asked, "are you unhappy here? Would you like to come down to the Lazy Seedy again?"

A guarded wariness crept into his eyes. "I'm all right, Mrs. Daley. But I can't come to the ranch. I'm leaving Aspen tonight or tomorrow."

"So soon, Shawn? You've been here so short a time. Your father will miss you terribly."

The boy said with a scowl that mingled anger and bitter resentment, "A fat chance of his being lonesome. It's his idea to get me out of town. He told me to get out. He's shipping me off back to Greeley to my grandfather."

Maude's eyes widened. "I can't believe that, Shawn. I know Lance so well. I know how happy he was when you came here."

"He'll be a whole lot happier when I leave. He's tried to act as though he wanted me. But I know different. It's Caroline he wants. She's all he ever wanted. He took her away from all of us, from me, and my mother, and Grandma."

Maude Daley listened with growing understanding. She caught the terror of a little boy too long certain that he was unwanted and rejected. It was a voice from the narrow, twisting labyrinth between a lonely boyhood and the encroaching demands of manhood. Maude Daley wanted to put her arms about him and to draw him tightly to her. Instead, she said calmly, "Shawn, do you know your grandfather well? Do you feel close to him? Do you want to be with him? Be like him?"

His answer was perplexed. "I don't know. Grandfather took good care of my mother and me after my father deserted us and took Caroline away. It's just that Grandfather wants to boss everybody and everything. He tells me what to eat, what to wear, what I've got to study and whom I can be friends with."

"Yes," Maude murmured, "Jared Swope would demand his dollar's worth."

Shawn's curiosity quickened. "What made you say that? Did you know my grandfather?"

Maude Daley knew the time had come.

"Did I know Jared Swope? You bet I knew him. I knew

him for what he really was—and is—the most brutal, black-hearted, old scheming hypocrite in that colony or any other. Did I know old Sunday-praying, weekday stealing Jared Swope? Oh, Lord, how I knew him!"

Her words brought Shawn to his feet. His eyes narrowed angrily and his teeth and hands clenched as he yelled, "Stop it! You can't talk about my grandfather like that. He never left his kid and ran off. He's, he's a businessman, not a crooked tinhorn like my father."

"Sit down," Maude Daley said. The intensity of her demand dropped him back to the chair.

"Now, Shawn Ainsley, it's time you knew a few things. Maybe a man would half-beat your brains out and then tell you. I'm different; I'm a woman. A woman who happens to love every Ainsley, including you. Did your mother or your grandmother ever tell you why Lance took Caroline and left Swope's mansion? For damn sure Jared Swope never did. Never will." She leaned toward him. Her face was stark and her grasp a vice on his arm. "He left because Jared Swope gave Caroline a cruel and horrible beating. A beating so needless and so horrible I can't stand even now to think of it. She crawled out of that house and started across the hill afoot and without a coat for Evans. You know where Evans is, how far it is. In a blizzard a man found her on the road and brought her to my place in Evans. She was about frozen and half-dead."

The boy fixed dazed eyes on her. "To your house? You lived in Evans."

Maude spared no one now, neither Jared Swope nor herself. "Yes to my house, Shawn. To a sporting house, a whorehouse to be exact. Ask Jim Daley what happened then. Ask H. A. W. Tabor. Caroline nearly died. For weeks she was the sickest person I ever saw. But did anyone from Swope's mansion come to her? Not one. Not your mother. Not your grandmother. Not the man who had been the rotten cause of it—not Jared Swope!"

Shawn's head dropped onto her arm. "Why didn't my father tell me?"

"I think I know, Shawn. Your father's a proud man, a

fine man. He wanted to gain your respect by his own actions, not by dragging in dead cats. There's something else; Lance wouldn't for the world have destroyed your respect for your grandfather by telling what I've told. He'd die before he'd do it."

"But why didn't he bring us with him—like he did Caroline? Why did he leave us?"

Maude Daley was tiring and close to tears. "Because your mother wanted it that way. She couldn't bear to get beyond the security of Swope's mansion and Swope's money. You were so little you had to be left. Besides, your grandfather always seemed to love you as much as he hated Caroline."

Eventually the boy lifted searching eyes to her face. She caught a quick breath as she saw the calming wistfulness of his gaze.

"Mrs. Daley, can I call you Maude? I know Caroline did."

She smiled cheerily. "Why not make it Aunt Maude ... and Uncle Jim?"

"Aunt Maude," he murmured slowly. "If I'd only been told all of this before last night. Before me and my father had the row."

She drew him to her and kissed his forehead. "If I know Lance Ainsley, you'll find him at home about ready to kick a hole in the wall or get drunk. Get out of here and go to him, Shawn. Tell him you know and that things will be all right now."

He moved toward the door. "Things *will* be different. They sure will. Dad and I will see to that." He went a dozen steps down the hall and returned. "Aunt Maude, can I come back tonight and see the baby?"

"Of course, Shawn. Anyway, Jim wants to be the first one to show off the boy."

When his son burst through the door, Lance Ainsley looked up in amazement. "Did I hear you whistling as you came up the walk?"

Shawn's grin was abashed, but his gaze fixed steadily on

Lance's face. "I guess you did. I felt like singing. That would have been a lot worse for you to listen to."

Lance fumbled the railroad ticket in his pocket, reluctant to pull it into view. "It's the first time I ever heard you whistle. The idea of getting away from Aspen must have given you a lift. Son, there's a train——"

"Dad," the boy interrupted, "what are you going to do with the assay office and all that equipment?"

Lance strove for an answer, but he thought suddenly, He called me *Dad*. It's the first time he has made it sound that way as though we belong together.

"Shawn," he answered slowly, "I don't know what to do about the assay shop. Don't know what Caroline would want me to do. Hang onto it. Rent it. Sell it. Honestly, I don't know."

Shawn drew a deep breath and let it escape in urgent and tumbling words. "It would make a dandy laboratory if a fellow was studying engineering, mining engineering. It'd be quiet for study and experiments." He paused, frowned and said, "But I'd need a teacher. No one here——"

Lance stared into his son's face. Unconsciously, he crushed to a small wad the ticket in his pocket. "There are a couple of men here who would beat any professor at school. The way times are getting, one of them might jump at a chance to stay in Aspen as a tutor."

"It would cost an awful lot," Shawn said doubtingly.

"A good engineering education costs money. Don't worry about it. In a couple of years they'd have you ready to do advanced work at the School of Mines down at Golden."

Shawn squatted on the carpet. "I could move the desk over by the window. That'd make room for another——"

His father listened intensely. His face gleamed enthusiastically with each of Shawn's words. After a time, he said, "We'll get busy on it right away, just as soon as you go see Maude Daley."

The boy looked at him unwaveringly. "Dad, I've already been there. She told me about a lot of things. About why you and Caroline came to Aspen, and how Grandfather beat Caroline and why Mother didn't want to come

323

with you." He stopped and was silent for a time before he asked, "Dad could a good mining engineer be as successful as a banker?"

Lance squatted beside him. "Mining will go on as long as people need things. Maybe the silver boom is bust for a while. But how about copper? Iron? Nickel? Dozens of others? Shawn, success can be in any line of work. Mostly it's doing what you're cut out to do and doing it better than you have to. Real success is enjoying what you chose for a career. There's an extra desk gathering dust in back of my office."

The name of Laura Coulter never passed between them again. Shawn never knew that the following morning his father called on the elder Coulter, painted a glowing picture of the need for a grocery store in the gold camp of Cripple Creek, and bought the building occupied by Coulter's grocery in Aspen. There was one emphatic stipulation. Old man Coulter must agree to have his daughter-in-law, Laura, and his son out of town within forty-eight hours!

PART FIVE

1894-1912

Chapter 17

The windswept garden was surrounded by weird battlements. He looked southward along a three-mile stretch of breakers rolling in from the Pacific. Below him was the Cliff House and Seal Rocks. On the autumn day in 1894 it was clear, and the sharply folded hills of Marin County loomed across the bay. To his left, the few and scattered homes of San Francisco's Sutro Heights gleamed white and shining in the afternoon sunlight.

His favorite redwood bench nestled beneath twisted cypress trees. There was the splashing hue of geraniums in spots where they were not hidden by rose bushes growing luxuriantly in the cool and damp ocean air. He had been here often; time hung heavily on his hands these days, and the walk from his own home, sometimes with a detour through the newly developed Golden Gate Park, was a pleasant way of passing the hours.

He sat stiffly upright on the somewhat uncomfortable bench; perhaps a retired man should be allowed the privilege of slumping, or even napping, on the bench, but he surmised his reasons for not doing so were valid. Asleep, he might miss sighting the ships bound in and out of the Golden Gate. Slumping was alien to him. His years of military life had instilled in him the need to be alert and erect. There was no time for slumping and little time for sleeping in the old days at Fort Fred Steele, or at Fort D. A. Russell. He'd kept his time occupied at the Presidio until the inevitable day of mustering out and retirement had come. He was no longer in cavalry uniform or longer in command, but even here in the quiet of Sutro's Garden he was still a military man, Colonel John Brenton, U.S. Cavalry, Ret.

The sound of light footsteps and a child's voice caused him to give up scrutiny of a sluggishly moving freighter and turn to smile at the little boy who bent over the graveled walk to pick up smooth pebbles. He noted the child's long, almost flame-colored hair. The wind-tumbled locks fell onto the wide collar of the child's white-linen suit. John Brenton smiled as the boy dropped hoarded pebbles into a pocket and then wiped grimy hands across his face and blouse-front.

Moments later the child moved closer, forgetful of the rocks. His interest was now ensnared by the riotous glow of the geraniums. He darted toward them. Abruptly he let out a howl, and Brenton knew that the boy had backed into the rosebushes and come afoul of their thorns.

Brenton rose from the bench and strode to the child's side. "Those stickers hurt. Let's see the damage." He knelt, pulling the child toward him. "Now back up. Easy now. There it is." He plucked a broken thorn from the seat section of the boy's pants. "You'll be all right, young man. It'll quit hurting in a minute or so."

His words swung the boy curiously about, and Brenton looked into eyes that were either blue or gray, depending on the slant of light toward them. He judged the child to be almost four years old.

"What's your name, young man?"

"Freddy. What's yours?"

"Mr. Brenton—John Brenton. Now, Freddy, perhaps we'd better take a walk together and find whoever was looking after you. Was it your mother?"

"Mother's up at the big house. I was playing with them."

John Brenton cast his gaze at Sutro's rambling palatial home and then over a group of older children toward which Freddy pointed a fist.

Brenton folded the child's hand into his own. "Let's go over to the big boys and girls."

Freddie tugged solidly backward. "I don't want to. I want to stay here until Mommie comes."

Brenton studied the situation. Apparently the child had

been temporarily put in the care of the older children, who found more exciting things to do and had promptly forgotten about him. "Maybe we'd better stay together, Freddy, until your mother comes. Now let's see ... what can we do?" His eyes roved the distant reaches of the ocean. "There's a ship." He turned. "And over there's a mountain. Mount Tamalpais."

The child looked into Brenton's face with sudden interest and pride. "My mommie knows where there's big mountains. Big white mountains. With snow."

"Really? With snow? Where, Freddy?"

"A long way off. Clear across the world. In Aspen."

The words brought Brenton to a halt. His weather-lined face tightened with expectancy. "Where did you say they were—the snowy mountains?"

"In Aspen. You ought to know that."

Brenton stooped down, lifted the child, and set him on the edge of a marble sundial. "Of course ... of course. Anybody should know where the white mountains are." He studied the little boy's face with searching intentness. "Freddy, what's your other name, your last name?"

The child's name was hurried and indistinct. Still, Brenton had listened almost with bated breath. For a moment he matched sound and memory.

"Freddy, did you say *Herndon?* Is that your name?"

The boy nodded his head. "Yes." He looked about the garden; his small feet beat a restless rhythm on the marble.

Excitement welled within Brenton. He lifted the boy to a standing position on the sundial and brought the child's face close under his probing stare. "Freddy Herndon. That's a fine name. I'll bet you I can tell you what your mama's name is."

The boy caught the zest of a game and laughed with delight. "Bet you can't," he challenged.

Brenton carefully grasped and counted his fingers as he tolled off names, "Let's see now. Your mother's name isn't Ruth, or Betsy, or Anna. I know. *It's Caroline!*"

Freddy Herndon eyed him with reproach. "You knew all the time."

Brenton moved the boy to the ground, and pulled at his hand. "Can I wait here with you, Freddy, until your mother comes?"

The boy eyed a tall, fragile-appearing piece of statuary nearby. "If you'll put me up there on that."

Brenton made quickly sure there was no garden attendant in sight. "Right now," he murmured, "I'd set you on top of Mount Tamalpais," and added with sheer joy, "Caroline. Caroline Ainsley Herndon. Here in San Francisco!"

Half an hour later she came through the door of Sutro's mansion, descended a long stone stairway, and approached. John Brenton, watching her quick and sure steps, was lost for a few seconds in nostalgic recollection of the past. He clearly remembered the day he saw her. He had lifted her to his shoulders and carried her piggyback across the long, narrow bridge spanning the North Platte River, while the garrison flag of Fort Fred Steele moved listlessly in a rising Wyoming breeze.

In the small lapse of time before he could discern her face, he smiled approvingly at the stylish mode of her serge suit and the simple fur piece which accentuated it. "Beautiful," he muttered. "Downright beautiful."

She caught sight of them now and hurried along the graveled walk. Brenton's gaze fastened on her face. He sensed that Caroline's attention had fastened on her son and that she would not be aware of his appraising stare. She's older, he was thinking. A mature woman. Somehow, somewhere, she's gone through some hell of agony. It has left her quieter, more subdued, stronger. I remember a pretty girl. She's more than pretty now. Something about her face. Yes—that's it. Her face. Only courage, and indomitable spirit and pride, can shine through with that sort of radiance.

Beside them, she reached for the boy. She paused, glanced swiftly into Brenton's face, and gasped.

"Caroline," he asked quietly, "do you remember me?"

Her answer was short as she rushed forward to encircle him with her arms. "Captain Brenton, how could I ever forget you?" Her face rested for a while on the rough

330

weave of his shoulder. Later she peered into his face. "You haven't changed a bit."

"The army is more discerning, Caroline. They saw my wrinkles and white hair. I'm retired. Out to pasture." His hand tilted her chin and he grinned broadly at her. "I won't say you're the same, Caroline. A long time ago you were belle of a ball. Now you're lovely, Caroline. Lovely indeed."

"How did you happen to be here?" she asked.

Brenton turned to nod toward young Freddy, who scampered along the walk and was eying the nude figures of a fountain. "Your boy lost a fracas with rose thorns. I happened to the rescue. He's a fine fellow, Caroline. A lively one. And that red hair is just like Bob Herndon's."

Something in her face forecast her words. "Bob has been dead almost three years. Papa must have written and told you."

His face was sad. "No. I didn't know, Caroline. Lance hasn't written to me. There's so much I want to know. About Aspen. About Lance and about you. What brought you to San Francisco? Are you visiting or living here? I want to get really acquainted with Freddy."

Brenton's arm was about her as they strode slowly along the walk. They had almost caught up with the boy when Caroline's grasp on the cavalryman's arm tightened. "There's another Herndon you'll have to meet. I have a little girl. Annette. Almost two years old. She was born after I left Aspen. After Bob died."

"Two children," he marveled. "A boy and a girl. Wait till I get home. My wife is going to be so excited——" He became abruptly silent for a time, then asked, in a bewildered tone of voice, "Caroline, why haven't you ever looked us up or gotten in touch with us?"

When she answered, she had drawn him onto the redwood bench beside her, and turned a pale, determined face upward. "I had no right to seek out friends. I wanted to. Lord, how I've wanted to. Captain Brenton, I was hiding when I came to San Francisco. I'm still hiding. Even my father has no idea where I am."

331

"Lance doesn't know?" His words were low and incredulous.

"No. I've never written. You see, I ruined his life and my own. I dynamited a mine, and I killed a man. I meant to kill him." She was shaking, and her gloved hands lay clenched against her cheeks. He drew her firmly into his arms. "Do you think that would have made any difference to me or my wife. Caroline, Caroline, if you blasted a mine likely it needed blasting. And it's for damn sure the man needed killing."

"It's not killing him I'm sorry about," Caroline said slowly. "He tried to kill me. He murdered my husband. Shot him down on a lonely street at night. He was the same man who shot old Mr. Jorgenson, the storekeeper, that night in Rawlins."

"Then why did you panic, Caroline? Run away? I'd say you should have had a medal."

"I had to get out of town, fast. At night. He was only a hired killer for more ruthless men. They'd have found me."

Brenton fit obscure pieces together. "You're not the kind to run. Besides, Lance would have——"

"I couldn't face Papa after I'd done it in a town where he was successful and esteemed. I had ruined him and his name, his work."

Brenton kicked a pebble and sent it soaring over the head of Freddy who circled a lawn sprinkler. "Bosh, Caroline. If I know Lance Ainsley he was proud you reared up and fought. But to run out on him, and not to write, that was cruel." He sat silently beside her until the storm of her revelation had subsided and calmness returned to her face. "And so you came to San Francisco. What then? What since? How did you manage here? A stranger. Alone. With a small child. With another expected."

"But I wasn't alone, Captain Brenton. There was another woman with me. She was fleeing Aspen too. A woman named Ellen Corlett. She needed me; maybe I needed her more. Ellen's got no schooling or training, but she has a talent that pulled us through here in San Francisco. She's an absolute genius at designing and making

332

women's clothing." A smile that mingled pride and relief touched Caroline's voice as she nodded toward Sutro's mansion. "That's the reason for my being here today. Ellen is designing gowns for a ball Mr. Sutro's daughter is planning. I act as Ellen's messenger, her business agent."

Brenton's gaze swept Caroline's lithe form. "Did your Miss Ellen make the outfit you're wearing?"

"Every stitch," she said smiling.

"San Francisco will be at your feet," he said and added firmly, "right now you're going home with me. If I went home and told my wife, and didn't fetch you——"

Caroline noticed her son's proximity to the sprinkler. "If you'll rescue Freddy, I'll tell Mr. Sutro's carriageman I'm ready. I'll have to stop by and explain to Ellen."

Brenton moved quickly to Freddy's side. "Young man, sprinklers can soak you hide and heel. Let's leave it alone. How'd you like to see a fort? A real fort——with soldiers."

The boy cast him a dubiously interested glance. "How? Are you a real soldier?"

"Freddy, that's a point that's been debated on about every cavalry post west of Abilene."

Even before a Presidio bugle sounded reveille the next morning Brenton was out of bed and bent over a small writing table. He concentrated on the swiftly penned words:

Dear friend Lance,

During nearly fifty years in the cavalry I've had some exciting things to do. But what I'm about to write, and the privilege of being the one to write it, will prove the thrill I shall remember above all others.

You will be so glad, and so relieved to know. . . .

The letter was short and revealing. Brenton was determined that it go forward in the first eastbound mail.

Aspen in the fall of 1894 was strangely quiet. Although Indian summer arrived with blazing colors and delightful temperatures the sounds and sights of the city took on a melancholy and embittered air for Lance Ainsley. Stricken by repeal of the Sherman Silver Purchasing Act on November 4, 1893, and by the resulting panic, the economy and business life of Aspen collapsed. Stores failed and closed; mines and mills shut down. A majority of those with money had already moved to more promising locations. Many miners, without funds or hope, walked out of town or rode the boxcars of the few trains still moving to and from the silver city.

The city had been beautifully and solidly built. It was designed to endure throughout the decades, but within a single year it was dealt a death blow. The mine and mill structures fell into disrepair; neglected industrial buildings seemed to brood silently and cry out their desolation across empty streets and lonely, unoccupied stores. Few people moved along once proud residential streets. The windows of homes that had been the pride of their builders now stared vacantly onto untended lawns and untrimmed shrubbery. The glass would go. The paint would go. Only the empty and haunting shells would remain and some would perish mercifully under the ravages of fires with which the city no longer had means to effectively cope.

Some people remained. There were those who would never leave, who would remain always as a backwash of the proud and pulsating boom days. Their every year would be made endurable by bitter-sweet nostalgia, and by their unflagging certainty of the miracle of the town's rebirth.

Lance chose to remain in Aspen. He was far too practical to be deluded by rumors and wishful thinking. As the queen of silver camps Aspen was dead.

Aspen would nearly perish. Yet the mountains would stand serenely tall and the forests would be alive with elk and deer and bear. Trout would swim in pure, cold streams. Life would be quieter, but that would be all right for Lance. From his diversified and scattered interests he derived ample income. Jim and Maude Daley were down on the beautiful and prosperous Lazy Seedy. There were enough of his friends for a poker game, for quiet drinks at the hotel bar, or for forming a hunting party upon an hour's notice.

Perhaps most conducive to his remaining in Aspen was his son's progress through tutored study at Bob Herndon's assay office. Other youths had asked the privilege of studying with Shawn, and Lance had given quick approval. He was sure now that Shawn had found his field and his future; his son would be a mining engineer. Additional study at a university would be required, but the basic studies progressed in the quiet town that so recently and so successfully built its short-lived prosperity on a single, gleaming metal.

Lance Ainsley was content to have it so. Sometimes, though, he wondered what course he would have taken, or whether he would have chosen to remain in a dying town, had not Caroline been swept from his life.

As he strolled toward the post office on the clear, crisp October morning, he had no idea or premonition that soon his life would again merge with his daughter's.

The daily arrival of mail offered respite from hours that could become dull and lonely and monotonous for those who so well remembered the vibrant and pressingly busy days of other years.

Already half a hundred men, women, and children gathered at the post office. Lance knew them all by face and name. He acknowledged their greetings, and spent time to talk with those who wished to talk. He knew their need to discuss the small events of the week and to reminisce upon the hazing, unforgettable glory that had once hovered upon the city.

When the mail had been sorted and passed out, and the crowd had reluctantly thinned, the postmaster smiled at Lance from behind an iron-grilled window and shoved a folded bunch of mail toward him.

"Here's your mail, Mr. Ainsley. Seems you get more than almost anyone left in town. It's getting so this job sort of haunts me. Used to be I'd shove out scads of mail—invoices and billings for the stores, social invitations, whopping big checks from smelters up at Leadville

335

and Denver. Nowadays it's a few seed catalogues, circulars from stores down at Glenwood, and returned letters written to friends who've left without proper addresses."

Lance puffed at an unlit cigar and nodded his understanding. "It's rough all right. Every day I look around here, sort of thinking I'll see a face, hear a voice but I know confounded well they won't come this way again. I suppose next you'll be pulling stakes and transferring to some post office in a roaring gold camp."

The postmaster shook his head and grinned wryly. "Not me. This job pays enough to get by on. At least me and my wife own a home here. She's got her flowers and a cantankerous tomcat. I've managed to buy up a couple of claims that'll surprise people when the mines get going again. Shouldn't be long. They're saying up at Leadville. . . ."

The rest of his words were lost to Lance. He unfolded a newspaper and began sorting the letters it held.

Abruptly he studied a letter which carried a San Francisco postmark and the return address of Colonel John Brenton. A sense of guilt descended on Lance as he opened the letter. From Brenton, bless his blue-clad old bones. I never answered his last one, years ago!

He began reading. Within seconds his eyes darted along the lines. His breath quickened. His pulse pounded. He came quickly to the end and reread the letter. He dashed from the post office and left the rest of his mail in the lobby.

The postmaster came from behind the dividing wall and retrieved it. "Wonder what's got into Ainsley? He must have sewed up another big deal. He's lucky as sin, that fellow. Well, my time's coming. In a year or so them claims of mine. . . ."

Lance's time in speeding to the assay office was likely the best he ever achieved. He pulled open the door and stepped purposefully inside. He was the object of instant attention of a circle of teenaged eyes, and the startled glance of the tutor who stood chalk-smeared at a blackboard containing a problem in quantative analysis.

Lance flashed the teacher an excited and persuasive

336

smile and turned to his son. "Shawn, you'll have to come along with me right away. Hurry!" He helped his son gather up papers and books. He swung about to face the tutor. "I'll explain later. Shawn will miss a week or so of classes. Keep right on with the other boys. I'll see that Shawn studies while he is away."

"Away?" Shawn said with amazement. "Where?"

"In San Francisco, son. You and I are leaving on the next train—passenger, freight, or cattle."

As they cleared the door, the tutor turned uncertainly back to the blackboard. "Let's resume," he murmured. "The theory behind this problem is ... why in kingdom come is Ainsley heading for San Francisco?"

Had Caroline's black mare been endowed with the magic hoofs of Pegasus, or been akin to the steeds of the Valkyries, Lance would have chosen her swiftness for the journey to the city beside the Golden Gate strait. Instead, he settled for railroad passage for himself and his son. He had never been west of Grand Junction. His memory of the sea, as he had seen it from Louisiana coastal towns, seemed that of another world and another life.

Shawn was alert to the changing scene of every mile. The trip westward through mountains and desert was vastly exciting. The boy struck up acquaintances with those who could tell him of the Utah and Nevada towns and of the scarcely touched reaches of wilderness that separated them. He stood beside the car window and peered out with an intensity that Lance surmised did not miss a single distant butte or even the succession of telegraph poles that paralleled the track.

Brenton's letter had been brief. Its wording was in the mode of a military dispatch and disclosed only the salient facts of Caroline's presence in San Francisco and her address.

He told me just enough to entice me, just enough to whet my curiosity and make certain I'd come a running, Lance reasoned. He could have at least mentioned how she's been getting along. How she has supported herself the last couple of years. Maybe she has remarried. With the thought came a disturbing likelihood. If she has married, she may not wish to leave San Francisco and may not be able to return home.

As the train labored up the eastern slope of the high Sierras, and twisted through mountain passes, Lance caught himself pacing impatiently about the car. The expectance had become an engulfing thing as they descended onto the green and wooded Pacific slope and came at last to the East Bay terminus of the railroad.

The boat that would ferry them to the San Francisco side was delayed. The day was clear and fog-free, and the widening bay rippled in the same mellow sunlit sheen that fell upon the distant, fabled hills of San Francisco.

At last the ferry cast its mooring and chugged slowly on its outward course toward San Francisco.

A wry smile touched Lance's face. This was another city with a destiny entwined with men's lust for the wealth of mines. Aspen was born that way. It lacked only the strategic location. San Francisco had grown and prospered. Likely it would become a proud and wealthy and immense city. His town of the Roaring Fork was also proud and wealthy, but it was doomed. Already some of the wealth of her mines had come this way and built homes and businesses in a city that would not die.

His thoughts and his mood carried Lance into unusually silent reverie. He was glad that Shawn was eager to attend to the details of handling luggage and of hiring a cab for the short part of the trip before them.

To Lance the thick, horse-drawn traffic and trolley cars through which they threaded Market Street seemed but a delaying irritation. They had turned toward Parnassus Heights when he realized his son's delight and excitement. "The town's built on nothing but hills, Dad. Some of 'em are steeper than Red Mountain back home. If Caroline lives up here she's a mountain goat by now."

On Edgewood Street they stopped before a pleasant two-storied house with white walls and tile roof. The cabbie pointed his whip. "That's it, mister, the address you're looking for."

Lance paid him and said, "Wait here a few minutes and

338

help us with the bags." He alighted. Shawn's eyes were wide as he looked across the bay, the Golden Gate strait, and the green symmetry of the Presidio off northward where the land fell away. "Come along, son. We'll meet her together."

Suddenly Shawn Ainsley tensed. He muttered with agitation, "You go ahead, Dad. I'll wait here. I haven't seen Caroline in such a long time."

Lance gripped his son's arm. "Nothing doing; you've looked forward to this moment as much as I have. She's your sister. It's time you got to know her."

They paused before a heavy and intricately carved door. Lance's gloved hand twisted a bell knob. Half a minute later the door opened, and Lance stared in wonder at the face peering into his. "Ellen," he whispered. "Ellen Corlett!"

Momentarily her composure fled, and she uttered a strange cry. She silently struggled for control. Lance had time enough to glean revealing facts. This was an older, more subdued, and quieter woman than the Ellen who had been Hardrock Corlett's wife and who had ruled his mansion. Lines traced her face; graying strands were woven into the corn-flower hue of her hair.

She stood aside and motioned for them to enter. "Caroline and I live together here. She's upstairs. I'll call her."

"Please do, Ellen. First though, may I present my son, Shawn? Don't tell Caroline about him. It's a surprise."

She acknowledged Shawn's presence with practically unseeing eyes, then turned quickly toward the first step of a curved stairway. "Caroline," she called, "come down. Right away. You have visitors." When a muffled reply reached her, Ellen Corlett turned, smiled vaguely toward Lance, and quickly left the room.

Caroline Ainsley Herndon was halfway down the stairs when she caught sight of her father. He awaited her at the stairway. In that moment her steps became the same rushing, half-falling descent that so long ago had brought her to his arms at Swope's mansion. His arms swept her up and held her. He had rehearsed words for this moment, but they were gone. "Kitten," he whispered. "Kitten."

Perhaps a minute passed before he felt her stiffen, and knew that her gaze had found Shawn.

"Know who's behind us?" he murmured.

"Yes," she answered. Within her was a memory of a boy peering at her amid the Christmas gaiety of Daniels and Fisher's toy department. "Yes," she repeated slowly. "I know. And I'm glad ... so glad. It's my brother. It's Shawn. Shawn Ainsley."

As Lance watched them cling to each other, he realized that life offered few moments of fulfillment and content. His children were with him and together; for a time at least he had them both.

Later, he threw an arm about each of them. "You've got lots of time to get acquainted. Give me a break. I have a grandson I'm aching to romp. One time when I did it, he wet a diaper and soaked me."

"He's a little old for that now," Caroline murmured laughing. "Even my other one had grown——"

"Your other?" Lance said.

"Yes, Papa. My younger child, Annette."

"Your . . . your dau—— Well, I'll be damned." His words quickened. "What's holding you, kitten? Round them up for Grandpa."

An hour passed as he claimed them for his own. A red-headed boy named Freddy. The auburn-tressed and solemn-eyed two-year-old girl that was Annette. At last their allegiance wavered toward Shawn, who sprawled on the carpet and devised a game.

Lance took time to look about the spacious rooms and to note the simplicity and comfort of their furnishings. "You have a beautiful place here, kitten. Just right for the kids."

"I have Ellen to thank for it and for so much," she answered.

Lance shook his head studiedly. "I couldn't believe it when Ellen Corlett came to the door. Back in Aspen you and she hated each other's guts. What happened?"

"We met on the train the night both of us ran away. Ellen needed me that night. Within days I needed her more.

We stuck together. Perhaps at first it was necessity—the lame carrying the blind."

"And now?"

"Now there's understanding and respect. We've managed to build a business because Ellen is such a genius at designing and making women's clothes. San Francisco is a wealthy town with cosmopolitan ways. The women can't resist Ellen's garments and the magic of her needle."

Lance's eyes roamed about. "She sure managed to get away from Shawn and me in a hurry. I suppose she's busy sewing."

"No," Caroline said. "She's probably crying. She'll be all right after a while. Seeing you brings back too much. Too much of Aspen. Too much of the past. Too much of gentle old Hardrock."

He sat beside her and was content to cradle her hands and look hungrily into her face. She was twenty-six years old, the mother of two, and caught up in a business, but not remarried.

Lance and Shawn became skilled at finding reasons why they should tarry in San Francisco. The days lengthened to one week, and then another. Shawn encountered a city that challenged him to explore its streets and beaches and hills, and although Lance was adamant that his son continue the studies that had been interrupted, he knew that San Francisco offered experiences unparalleled in any textbook.

· He came to know and to respect Ellen Corlett and the dignity of the partnership that linked her to Caroline. There were parties and tours in which Mr. and Mrs. Brenton joined.

Lance glimpsed the aimlessness that had overtaken the old officer since his retirement and voiced his concern about Brenton to Caroline. "It's a crying shame about Brenton. He's fit and capable as ever. Just wearing down from nothing to do. Wilting on the vine."

Caroline puckered her lips pensively. "Strange that you should mention vines, Papa. They're just the thing that could be the answer for him. He's got his eye on a vineyard over in the Napa Valley. He could organize it on brigade schedule, but an army office doesn't buy much land on retirement pay."

Lance looked from the window. He was lost in the wonders of the blue-tinged bay. "Speaking of land, kitten, you ought to know you're still a partner in a lot of land, the Lazy Seedy ranch. Jim and Maude Daley tore up the bill of sale you gave Jim. They said they'd have it no other way after you skinned Shaner's hide in court over the water-pollution deal."

Caroline's eyes glowed softly. "That was wonderful of Uncle Jim and Aunt Maude. I can't accept anything. They've worked years to build the ranch."

"Wasn't work all the time," Lance said grinning. "They've a husky boy, a son named James Lance Horace Daley, Junior."

"Named what?" Caroline gasped.

"You heard me. Jim and H. A. W. and me played poker all night working out a name for the tyke."

"I suppose Maude knew all about it?" Caroline said doubtingly.

"Not exactly. Not 'til the boy was born. But she agreed."

"I'd love to see her and Uncle Jim."

Lance shot her a quickly assessing glance. "No reason you shouldn't. You'd be mighty welcome on the ranch and in Aspen. There'd be no trouble. The Shaners pulled out—disappeared—a long time ago. Fact is, kitten, I came out here to take you home."

She drew close and leaned her head on his shoulder. "No, Papa. Here I am. Here I'll stay. What is there in Aspen now for me except memories? What is there for our children, Bob's and mine?"

Suddenly Lance recalled the deserted streets and crumbling buildings. "Maybe you're right, kitten. Aspen is already pretty much a ghost town. It'd make you weep to see it. Empty houses. Stores gone broke. Mines shut down. Common sense would tell anyone to steer clear of the silver city these days."

"Papa," she said unsteadily, "it isn't because Aspen is in trouble. You know I wouldn't desert the town or the

Roaring Fork just because of that. Back there I'd be living too close to the past, too close to all I had and lost—a husband, a home, a mine. Besides, I've got my children and Ellen to consider."

"Don't try to explain," Lance said numbly. "I've known ever since Shawn and I came that you wouldn't be going back with us. And the hell of it is, kitten, is that you're right. You should stay here." He fell silent, searched out his hat, and left the house.

It was very late at night when he returned. The day was a busy one. Perhaps Caroline wouldn't return to Aspen, but that wasn't any reason why he shouldn't have looked up Brenton, driven over to Napa with him, and arranged for the old officer to buy more land and more grapevines than he probably should be working at his age.

Lance would help. He'd have to keep an eye on things, on the business end, on Caroline, on Freddy and Annette. It could mean several weeks, or months, in California every year, but dang it, Caroline wasn't the only Ainsley that could be stubborn or successful at scheming.

The appearance of her father and brother brought to Caroline a happy contentment that she had despaired of ever knowing again. During their stay, the tortured, self-condemning thoughts that had been part of her flight from Aspen, and that had kept her from revealing her whereabouts, dropped into oblivion.

She knew few regrets for destroying the Buccaneer. She had struck back in the only possible way at those who had sought to achieve their greedy ends with treachery, robbery, and murder. The man she had killed and left in the shambles of the mine wanted to murder her. Had she not acted swiftly, she would have died, instead, that night. She was at peace with herself. Now, at last, had come the sureness that her acts had not ruined her father or shaken the firmness of his life and his place in Aspen.

After Lance and Shawn left there was a steady and comforting flow of letters. Messages came with the unexpected and delightful arrival of Jim and Maude Daley and their young son.

The Daleys had scarcely left when another unheralded

visitor arrived. Eric Duane had learned where she lived and lost no time in journeying westward. From the day of his arrival, Caroline knew that she would be called upon for a decision. Eric would ask her to marry him and return with him to Denver.

His renewed courtship gained intensity and fervor with each passing day. Caroline found herself caught up in days sightseeing and nights when they visited clubs and restaurants and theaters that she had not entered during the time she had lived in the city.

The hour was late. Eric had escorted her through an enchanting evening and then returned her to the quiet of her home on Edgewood Street. She knew that the time had come when she must give her answer. It must be honest, honest for Eric and honest for herself.

He lingered in the house and stood before a window that caught a jeweled and panoramic sweep of the city's lights. When he turned to her, she knew the adoration of his gaze. His face was more firmly molded now than on that night in Denver when he had asked if she must run off to the mountains. There had been Bob and the call of Aspen then. But now—

She walked slowly toward him. The lonely way of her days seemed an unendurable cloak about her. Then she was in his arms and the flames of tumultuous passions kindled within her. She lifted her face toward the yearning of his blue eyes, the freckle-ridged nose, and the sandy, unruly shock of hair.

"Caroline," he said desperately, "I've waited so long. There's never been anyone else. Never can be. I love you, Caroline, want you and want your children. Denver can be a wonderful home for all of us."

She answered the crush of his arms and the demanding crush of his lips with an abandon that cried out her pent-up longings and desires.

Then she pushed him from her with gentle firmness. "Eric, please go now, even though I want you to stay more than I want you to go."

His reply came as a groping, protesting whisper born of

scarcely controlled emotion. "Which does your heart tell you, Caroline?"

"My heart, Eric? It's pounding, now, now, now! Would to God I had only it to listen to, but reality cries out too. My children, Ellen, and the business we're building, my need to prove I can build success from failure. Eric, I've no right to ask you to wait longer. But if you will, if you'll give me time to do the things I must, I'll come to you. Heart. Soul. Body."

She was in his arms again. But now the urgent onrush toward an abyss was passed. There was understanding and comfort and a dawning promise.

When he had gone, she sought out her children and stayed beside their beds for a long time. When she returned to gaze out the window, crimson streaks of dawn flamed through the eastern sky.

Chapter 18

Lance Ainsley saddled a rangy gray gelding. The lines of his face were taut as he slid a rifle into the saddle scabbard, gave a final yank at the cinch, and mounted. It would be a disagreeable day to ride the high country. It was late February, 1897, and after a series of heavy snowstorms, the weather warmed. It was not the brisk and welcome warmth of sunshine, but a muggy and soggy warming that had been brought about by unseasonal rain and a night of intermittent wind squalls.

He rode westward from town, skirted the Roaring Fork, and was soon enveloped in the mist and low-hanging clouds that obscured the valley and mountains. He kept the roan to the ridges and hillocks because the lower areas had thawed into a muddiness that plagued and slowed the horse's progress. The river was swollen, fast-moving, and turgid. From the creeks, broad floods joined the Roaring Fork. Melting snow that shouldn't be moving for several weeks was going to waste. The water would be needed by the valley ranches when summer came and the mountains had dried.

Two hours later he left the river and rode northward up a gorge that would bring him atop a heavily forested plateau. He shouldn't need to go into the foggy gloom of the heavy timber on such a day. Nobody should be up there on timberland Lance had acquired almost a dozen years ago.

If he hadn't been in San Francisco the last couple of months, checking up on Caroline and her kids, he immediately would have known about the trespassers. Word of their presence on his land had come from one of Jim Daley's riders who had happened onto the plateau, observed what was taking place, and then ridden into Aspen to warn Lance. The warning was terse. "There's a loggin' outfit squatted in your prime timber, Ainsley. Maybe a half dozen men. Cuttin' and skiddin' about every tree sizable enough for a two by scantling."

Lance pondered the report in almost unbelieving silence and said, "Are you sure? There wasn't a sawed tree within miles last fall, I spent a couple of days up there. I rode the whole section."

"Last fall ain't now. Like it or not, Ainsley, you've got timber pirates on the plateau."

"But where would they haul the logs?" Lance demanded. "They wouldn't show up in Aspen with timber. There's no clear way down to the railroad. No spur for loading."

"Nope." The cowhand shook his head. "I've thought about it. Calculate maybe they have some way of getting sawed lumber over the divide up north, then down to a siding on the Colorado River, maybe around Gypsum."

Lance rode along a steadily ascending trail toward the north. As he gained altitude, the denseness of the shrouding clouds lessened. A momentary shafting of sunlight fell onto the narrow ravine through which the trail was twisting. The mountain slopes were precipitous and heavily blanketed with slushy snow. He allowed the horse to choose his own gait and his own footing.

At the plateau he paused and gazed back along his course. Only a billowing whiteness of clouds far off and below him marked the fog-hidden valley of the Roaring Fork. Off to the west were high and cloud-ridden peaks. He thought it would clear and be miserably cold before night. Only a slight change of weather could renew the clamp of winter.

It was half an hour before he rode into a small clearing well within the boundaries of his property. His anger deepened as he halted at timber's edge, and he probed the wanton destruction ahead.

Across the clearing a single quick-built and shoddy cabin thrust a tin stovepipe and sullenly hanging smoke into the air. Alongside the cabin was a donkey engine and a frame-mounted saw. He caught the whine of its blade as it bit protestingly into a log being fed to it by half a dozen workers.

The area beyond the shack and the saw riveted his attention. In late October it had been a beautiful and mature stand of Engelmann spruce. Now there remained only a desolate and slashed wasteland. Only a few broken saplings, too small for the saw's havoc, remained.

Lance reached down, withdrew the rifle, and lay it across the pommel of his saddle as he spurred the roan into the clearing and neared the laboring crew.

He was almost upon them when they noted his approach. They turned, shifting uneasily about and waiting. "Which one of you fellows in is charge here?"

A tall, broad-shouldered man pushed a leather-billed cap high above twisted black hair, before he answered brusquely, "If you're wanting to buy lumber, I can talk the deal."

Lance swept the group with appraising eyes. "I'm not," he said frostily, "in the habit of buying what already belongs to me."

The stranger scratched at the open neck of his shirt. "I don't recollect you ever bought any of this lumber."

347

"I sure didn't," Lance agreed, then added quickly, "I haven't sold any of it either. These logs belong to me. These logs and this land. You're a quarter mile into my property."

His words were greeted by a bland grin. "I suppose you've got a survey and a deed. That you blazed trees along your property line."

Lance took his time in answering. Of a certainty no property markers had been allowed to remain. The blazed trees would have been the first to go through the saw. Despite the intensity of his anger, his mind was fast working and wary. "You've known all along that this is private property and you're trespassing. Now let's get down to facts. I'll be back tomorrow. I'll expect you to have cleared out and left."

"If we ain't?" The logger's words were accompanied by an almost imperceptible turning of his head that brought his companions to an expectant stance.

With deliberate slowness, Lance swung the rifle to cover those staring at him. "If you're not gone, I'll have the law with me. County law and law of my own kind. Enough to throw you out—dead or alive. Take your choice."

He edged the roan carefully from them, riding at an angle that would keep them in view and within the quick sweep of his rifle. He rode in this manner until he reached the shelter of the timber.

Had he not been so intent upon the happenings of the moment he would have noted two things. He would have heard a distant murmur that grew and thundered and receded. And he would have seen two of the loggers squat to fasten snowshoes, to cram objects into small back-toted packs, and then strike out into the timber along a course that roughly paralleled his own.

He had descended again into the murky dimness of the narrows of the ravine when the sound smashed against his ears. He glanced quickly upward, then spurred his horse to escape the gorge. The sound became an engulfing roar. The first white spume of cascading snow smashed with blinding, sudden force against his face and knocked his hat from him. Then the cascading fury, the avalanche, was

348

upon him. Tons of sliding snow and debris knocked the horse from his feet. A scream of terror broke from the animal. Lance threw his arm against his face, in a vain attempt to ward off the towering, tumbling white wall that was upon him. He could not move again. From high and steep slopes, the snow crashed relentlessly down.

Minutes later it had stopped. Silence hung over the gorge. The gorge was snow-filled. Silent. Lonely. Devastated.

With the coming of night, the weather turned colder and cleared. The morning dawned with cloudless skies and renewed sunshine. The sogginess of the ground had firmed under freezing temperature, and the creeks already ran lower and clearer. The day wore on, calm and brilliant and frigid.

At mid-afternoon Jim Daley had strewn hay for a bawling herd of cows. Now he forked manure from his horse stable. The pungent stench of the refuse shed a warm vapor into the cold air. He paused to wipe a red bandana across his sweated face and to watch one of his riders approach along the icy bank of Wilderness Creek.

The rider reined in beside him. Daley ran an appraising hand over the horse's sweated withers. "You've been riding hard, Mike, to lather a horse in this cold. I expected you in yesterday."

The rider crooked his knee over the saddlehorn and stretched tiredly. "I'd a been in last night, except I went into town to warn Lance Ainsley."

"Warn him? About what?"

"Plenty. Plenty of trouble for Ainsley. You know that half section of timber he owns up on the plateau? There's a logging crew up there slashing hell out of it. Won't be a tree left come spring. I looked Ainsley up yesterday morning, and tipped him off."

Daley nodded his approval. "Lance'll sure raise thunder with them. Nobody steals from him and gets away with it." Daley thrust the fork deep into the manure pile. "Maybe you and me better get into Aspen. Ride up to the plateau with Lance. I'll tell my wife we'll—"

"Wait, Jim," the rider interrupted. "You ain't heard it all yet. Ainsley is already up on the plateau. He saddled up and rode out five minutes after I told him. Took a Winchester and a handgun. Damn but he was mad. Mad. Quiet. In a hurry."

"You mean he went up there alone?" Daley's face was tightening, as he added, "How about his boy, Shawn? Didn't he go along."

"Couldn't. Shawn's down at Golden for a spell studying at the mining school."

"Why didn't you ride with Ainsley, Mike?"

Mike tugged worriedly at his hat. "My horse was done in from riding into town to tell him. The mud made the going plenty rough. Besides, Ainsley didn't seem to want company." He paused and spat tobacco juice at the dung heap. "Jim, I'm bad worried. Ainsley didn't get back into town last night. I stayed up most of the night waiting, then headed back here. Knew you'd have the best idea what to do."

Jim Daley cocked an eye at the westering sun. "Suppose we can get up onto the plateau before dark?"

"Not a chance, Jim. Them gulches will be sheet ice."

Jim Daley was already heading for the house. "We're going, anyhow. You get down to the corrals and fetch every man that's about. Get yourself a fresh horse. Tell the men to dress warm and get armed and be ready for anything."

The February night closed in upon them before they were scarcely a dozen miles from the Lazy Seedy. With the going of the sun, and their slow ascent from the valley, the thin air took on a piercing bitterness. They hunched in their saddles to ride silently in single file. Mike led them up a series of hillsides where the hooves of their horses brought protesting squeaks from the frozen snow. The breath of the six men and their animals lifted as a white and hanging vapor.

Three hours passed before they entered the gorge that wound narrowly upward onto the plateau. The going became rougher along the sharp and ice-sheathed embankments upon which a horse could slip and fall or slide into the tangle of brush along the boulder-strewn creek.

Half a mile farther they reined to an abrupt halt. Ahead of them there was no longer the open course of the stream and the steep, encroaching slopes. Instead, they stared at a tangled and snarled blockage of ice and snow and uprooted trees, the towering, earth-stained residue of an avalanche. As far as the meager light of the night allowed them to see, the gulch was buried beneath tons of snow that formed an ominous resting place for broken trees and tumbled rocks.

They could not continue or reach the plateau except by a long and hazardous circling of the snow slide.

Daley swore in frustration as he dropped from his horse and kicked a splintered, half-buried fir tree.

"This does it. We'll have to hole up here until daylight." He beat numbed hands against his thighs. "We'd better rake up plenty of firewood. It'll be a long, cold night."

They listened in quiet agreement, knowing that Daley's appraisal of the situation was correct. A rider thrust out an arm and pointed upward toward a broad, black gash marking the downward patch of the avalanche. "I'm right glad it ain't thawing tonight. More of that snow might break loose and come roaring down. We wouldn't stand the chance of——"

Jim Daley failed to hear the rest of his words. A thought had struck him. A possibility swept grayness into his face and a chill within the deep recesses of his mind. . . .

In the frost of dawn the men were up and moving stiffly about the warming edge of the fire. They waited impatiently for daylight to seek out and light the depths of the ravine. Mike climbed part way up the hillside to get his bearings and to assess the length of the havoc ahead. He returned and said, "We can go back about a mile, veer to the east, and skirt around the slide. It'll be heavy going, but I can't see any other way of getting onto the plateau."

Daley listened gravely; he shook his head. "Later on maybe. Right now we're going to tether the horses and

351

climb onto this snow and rubbish. Take a look around the whole length of it."

The grimness of his words and the set of his face stirred uneasiness among those about him.

"You think that maybe——?" someone said.

"I don't know what to think." Daley's words were a short and barking sign of his growing apprehension. "Let's get at it. Start climbing."

The search was a slow and difficult thing for the unevenness of the cascaded snow and the snarl of wreckage demanded laborious climbing and constant alertness.

An hour went by. And another. They had fanned out almost the length of the buried gulch when Mike's yell echoed along the slopes.

"Jim, look here. Christ Almighty—look! It's his hat—Ainsley's hat." He had lifted the black, misshapen object above his head. "Get over here, all you guys. Fast."

They stumbled, waded, and slid toward him to form in a frozen-faced knot as Mike thrust the hat into Daley's hand.

Jim Daley's hands were clenched and corded as he grasped the hat. His words mirrored the agony of his face and eyes when he spoke. "We'll dig here. Get poles and start probing. Maybe it'll be a foot or so. Maybe a hundred." He turned from them and covered his face with his hands. "Lance," he whispered. "Lance, old friend. Oh, God . . . God . . . God."

They came down from the high country into the valley of the Roaring Fork. Six weary and silent men rode horses whose tired dispirited gait seemed in tune to the somberness of their thoughts. Two men were mounted on one horse. Upon another was the stiffened body of Lance Ainsley. They had found him where he had fallen, pinned beneath his dead gray gelding under the snow that had cascaded upon him with its fast-moving burden of rocks and broken trees.

When they neared the river and the railroad, Jim Daley waved them to a halt. He nodded to his two oldest, most dependable riders. "Take him into town," he said quietly.

"We'll ride down to the ranch. Maude and me will come up to Aspen and handle the arrangements. Don't try to send word to his son or to Caroline. Maude will do that; she'll know what to say." He turned in the saddle and gazed for long moments at the burdened horse. Then his eyes swept the length of the sun-drenched valley and the guardian mountains. He'll be part of the valley and the town, Jim thought. Now. Forever. Except maybe the part of him we'll all have in our recollections and in our hearts.

Jim Daley touched gently reluctant spurs to his horse. He was going home to the Lazy Seedy and to Maude, but his stare was beyond the rise of the mountains and the distant, shadowed horizon.

On the morning after they had come sadly home from Aspen, Jim Daley went heedlessly and methodically about the few chores that he had never turned over to the hired hands of the Lazy Seedy. In the house, he made an awkward try at being gay, but Maude had sensed its pathetic thinness and that it had been only to comfort her. For many days to come, Jim Daley's thoughts would be with the friend on a snow-spotted cemetery hillside.

After a time he saddled a horse, rode close to the kitchen door, and called Maude onto the back porch. "I'm going to give the meadows a once over. Maybe fix some fence or ride down to the river. I'd be pretty poor company for you today, cooped up in the house."

"I'll fix you some lunch to take along," she agreed. "Just in case you're not back by noon. Wasn't for the baby I'd go along, Jim."

He stooped in the saddle as she stood beside him, his lips touching hers and gleaning the comforting assurance of her kiss. "Don't bother with any grub, Maudie. Likely I won't be hungry before night."

She watched him wheel the horse and ride out of the yard. When he had gone, she wiped away the tears that she had managed to conceal from him. "Perhaps," she murmured, "being out around the ranch and the valley, he'll find something to comfort him. Sustain him. Somehow he's got to accept what has happened."

Even as her thoughts rode with him, Jim Daley settled his horse to a steady, purposeful pace. He knew before he cleared the ranch yard that this could be no day of aimless dawdling and moping about the Lazy Seedy.

That snow slide, he told himself, doesn't add up. Doesn't make sense. I've seen a hundred of them. It wasn't natural. Lance wouldn't have taken fool chances; he knew these mountains and the weather. The warning signs before a snow plunge. Them things start slowly and gain momentum.

He rode on, frowning in his inability to pinpoint the reason and justification of his thoughts. All too many men had died beneath cascading snow upon the precipitous mountain slopes. But those fellows weren't Lance Ainsley, or in that gulch at that time of day.

He was aware of the revolver at his side and the saddle rifle sheathed nearby as he straightened in the saddle. There was one way to know and make sure. He had to make peace with himself and the memory that rode with him of Lance Ainsley. He would ride up to the slide area and climb the slope where the avalanche had broken loose. He'd do some snooping and searching. Maybe there would be enough of the day left to see if the loggers were still on the plateau and learn whether Lance had ever reached them.

At the hour Daley gained sight of the avalanche-blocked gorge, Shawn Ainsley dropped from the single, dingy coach of a mixed train that stopped momentarily at Caroline Station. He welcomed the two-mile walk along Wilderness Creek to the Lazy Seedy. The town and the house had become unbearable. Caroline and her two children were spending the day with friends. She had asked him to go with her, but the urge and the need had been upon him to seek out the quiet of Wilderness Creek and the sustaining strength of Jim and Maude Daley. There would be days enough in Aspen before he would return to Golden and his studies. He and Caroline must give time to the somber task of closing up his father's house and his business and planning for the future when he would be in

Golden and his sister would have returned to San Francisco.

As he walked to the ranch house, he paused to look across the meadows, study the livestock, and view the familiar miles. It seemed that he saw the ranch and its majestic setting more clearly than ever before. They call it an empire, he thought pensively. That says it better than a dozen fancy phrases. That's what this Lazy Seedy is—a high, clean, wonderful empire.

He came finally to the ranch house, and found Maude Daley with a kerchief tied about her head as she vigorously scrubbed the kitchen floor.

"It's nice you came down, Shawn," she said, and offered him hot coffee. "Jim and I and this ranch need someone about to cheer us up."

"I'm the one needing companionship. You and Uncle Jim are part of the family as far as I'm concerned. Caroline feels the same way. Likely she'll bring the kids down here tomorrow or the next day."

"This is where they belong," Maude answered. "Here with room to scamper about." She swung the mop expertly under his feet as he lifted them and added, "Most of the men are up the valley hauling hay and doing odd jobs. Maybe you'd like to join them."

"I was hoping that I could work with Jim today," Shawn said. "I'm sort of lonely."

She gazed at him with quiet sympathy. "Of course. Jim would like that too. He rode off earlier this morning, saying he'd probably fix fence or ride down to the river. There's a couple of horses in the corral. You can take one and go look him up."

He stood up and threw his arms about her. "Thank you, Aunt Maude. Why is it you always have the right answers for me?"

"Maybe I'm trying to get in practice," she answered and gave him a warm smile. "One of these days my boy will be old enough to need some right answers."

Jim Daley neither repaired fence nor loitered along the river. It wasn't until Shawn had ridden a couple of miles upstream, following the mud-imprinted tracks of the rancher's horse, that he sensed Jim Daley was riding with a steadiness of a man intent upon reaching a definite objective. After a time the trail veered northward, beginning a sharp ascent from the valley.

The tracking was harder now. When he came upon the half-devoured carcass of a deer, pulled down by a panther, Shawn Ainsley knew for sure that he was following Jim Daley. Hoofprints told that the rancher had paused to scrutinize the scene. He had also dismounted. In a small barren spot lay a stick with sharp and muddy point, a stick with which Jim had absently scratched small concentric circles.

Only Jim would do that, Shawn reasoned. He remembered the countless rugs and tablecloths and graveled walks on which the rancher had drawn or carved such rings. Faint, but discernible, tracks bore northward and headed into the lower reaches of a ravine. Shawn set his course to follow and rode patiently on.

He had never been in that direction. Ahead was an unknown solitude, yet he became increasingly certain that Jim Daley was heading into the area where an avalanche had roared down to claim the life of his father. Somewhere ahead was a snow- and rubble-heaped gulch. Beyond it was the timbered plateau toward which Lance had gone to protect his timberlands.

The ride became increasingly hard for Shawn. His thighs and rump had never become saddle-callused, and during the past months he rarely had been astride a horse. He moved restlessly in the saddle as he tried to lessen the growing discomfort of tender and aching spots.

He was within sight of the white and jumbled snow-slide that blocked the gorge when he noticed that the trail of Jim Daley's mount had veered from the stream's course and started a long, sharp climb to the dark slash that marked the upper reaches and the beginning of the slide's path.

Tracking became easier now because there was deeper snow on the mountain's slope. He hung tenaciously and painfully to Daley's trail as it zigzagged its way upward through timber and around menacing ledges and boulder-strewn clear spots. He could follow the trail, but could not judge or even guess its age. Perhaps Daley was two or three hours ahead of him; perhaps it was only minutes. He peered upward and scanned the slope. There was only the dazzling brilliance of sunshine across mantled snow, only the dark spots that were trees and exposed rocks, and only the sullen raw gash left in the wake of white and cruel fury that had engulfed the gorge.

It took him a long while to gain the vicinity of a small, sharply dropping ledge that marked the upper limits of the snowslide. A hundred feet from it he paused to read the signs about him. Jim Daley had also halted his horse here, then gone afoot to the ledge. There were returning footprints too.

Shawn Ainsley sought out a small pine tree. Then he got down carefully from the saddle and tethered his horse. Step by step he moved in Daley's footsteps to the protruding rock of the ledge.

And then he knew that this avalanche had not come about through sun or falling snow or through rain or freeze or thaw. Men had been here. Men had fused a charge of giant powder and blasted off only a small overhang of the ledge. No more had been necessary. The falling rock and the reverberation of the blast had done the rest and shaken the lightly clinging snow masses into motion. Rock and snow gathered ferocity and volume down the slope and into the gorge. This had been time for the passing of a rider far below. This had been time for the murder of Lance Ainsley.

A consuming anger was upon Shawn as he knelt to study the mute evidence about him. His eyes narrowed and took in every detail—broken rock, the faint but undeniable trace of powder, and off to one side, where Jim Daley had squatted, the inevitable circles in which the old cowman had scratched his agony and his wrath.

With faster and less cautious steps, Shawn Ainsley went back to his horse. Now he must find Jim Daley. He must hurry to join forces with his father's friend.

The tracks of Daley's horse left the scene to plod even

higher on the mountain slope, to circle above the ledge and continue northward.

"He's going after them," the boy murmured aloud. He's going after them alone. His impulse was to urge his horse into rushing, headlong speed. His tiredness and the gall of the saddle were unheeded and forgotten. Only time mattered now—time to come to Jim Daley's side. The hazard of the steep slope, the dangerous footing his horse must tread, kept him to a steady and plodding gait.

Nothing slowed his spiraling anger which surged and tore within him and then leveled to cold, relentless fury.

He never knew how many miles he rode, or the exact course he rode, as the footprints of Jim Daley's horse led him from the slope and into the heavily timbered levelness of the plateau. He could make better time here, and he whipped his horse into a gallop.

Minutes later he reined to an abrupt and sliding halt. Ahead of him was the sound of a shot. Then another. The passing of half a minute brought a burst of gunfire that could have been three weapons speaking almost in unison. They were muffled, and he could not discern whether they came from rifles or revolvers.

He rode ahead again, but his movements were cautious and his eyes watchful. He carried no gun on this trip. The stark reality of this fact caused him to scowl. Now, as he moved on, he was swept by a sense of utter helplessness and futility. He had only his horse, his hands, and his thoughts. It was so little, so damned little.

Through scattered timber, he sighted a clearing. Another shot crashed out, unmistakably that of a rifle. He listened, tense and waiting, but there was no answering sound. There was only a deep and urgent silence.

To ride farther and reveal himself would be idiotic. He swung to the ground and edged from tree to tree. Unknowingly, Shawn had approached the clearing at an angle different from that his father had ridden in days before. He walked a short distance farther and dropped to the ground. He edged his way carefully to the edge of the clearing. A muddy, broken log offered refuge, and he slid against it. He was on the back side of a cabin that loomed fifty yards ahead. Off to his left were the acres of despoiled timberland. Closer at hand were piles of discarded brush and branches, a dozen racks of piled lumber, the donkey engine, and the silent and motionless saw.

His eyes widened and his face became grimly pale as his gaze fastened on the saw frame. Across it a man sprawled in the limp and grotesque posture of death. Another lay midway between the donkey engine and the open door of the shack. There were moments of raking fear as he stared at the bodies. He was certain that one was Daley.

Before he could know, a sound came from somewhere among the piled timbers and caused him to hug closer to the ground, to hold his breath, and to wait.

A warning sense of movement caused him to jerk his head about and stare at the piled lumber. A man had slid into view and aimed at the saw frame with a revolver. There was a crash, the sound of a slug striking metal and ricocheting into space.

A man's derisive laughter cut the air. A rifle barrel glinted momentarily over the timbers and the railing of the saw frame. As its blast shook the air, splinters jumped about the head of the hunched form amidst the lumber.

Other shots poured at the saw frame from hidden men and hidden positions among the brush piles and the raw sawed timbers.

Shawn was certain that Daley was squatted in the scant protection of the saw rig, that he had shot down the men whose bodies sprawled within a dozen feet of him, and that this was the battle of one vengeance-driven man against hidden and ruthless enemies.

There was a minute of silence broken by Jim Daley's voice which spilled challengingly through the thin air. "Come on you cowardly, murdering bastards. Come and get me." Retaliatory shots, prodded loose by his words, banged the heavy saw frame. Daley laughed strangely. "Try sliding them timbers down. Blast 'em—like you sons of bitches blasted snow and rocks on Ainsley. Then I'll shoot your eyes out and riddle your guts into your hands. Come on. What's holding you?"

Shawn Ainsley lay still and watched in self-condemning

359

agony. Why was he here without a rifle or a pistol? Why was he here at all—useless and helpless?

His inner rage gave way to watchfulness and to studied appraisal of the movement of two men from brush pile to brush pile as they retreated toward the timber. He knew that a third logger was still crouched within the protection of the sawed lumber.

A sudden desperation came to Shawn. They're going to move through the timber and flank Uncle Jim.

His mind flashed about in blind torment. A minute passed. Another. Already the two crouched and slinking loggers were well on their way as they circled toward the unguarded and unprotected side of Jim Daley.

"Oh, Christ," the boy whispered. "I can't lie here and let them get around there to shoot him in the back." Suddenly he reached out. His hand tore the soft earth and loosened a flat, fist-sized rock. Then he was on his feet. He arched his arm backward and hurled the rock at the form poised with drawn pistol in the sanctuary of the piled timber. The rock struck a scant two feet from the hiding man's head and caused him to jump forward in startled wonder. The revolver swept toward Shawn Ainsley. He knew, even as he was dropping against the log, that he would not have time.

But time was given to him as Jim Daley's rifle slid quickly over the saw frame and spit out the bullet that spun the logger backward and pulled the handgun from his grasp. Within an instant Shawn was again pawing to his feet, then running with desperate leaps toward the lumber pile. His blind rush caused him to stumble over the logger's still-writhing body. But the pistol came into his grasp. He snapped it open, clawed shells from the dying man's belt, and shoved them into its chamber.

"Look out, Jim," he called softly. "They're getting behind you."

He saw Jim Daley leap across the saw frame. The powerful thrust of the rancher's body held one hand on the metal rail and the other clutched his rifle.

Daley's head suddenly jerked. A rifle shot had sounded from the timber's edge and a puff of smoke rode the air.

Even as Daley crashed to the ground, Shawn raced toward him. He knelt at the rancher's side. His eyes were transfixed and awful. Jim Daley was already dead.

Shawn never knew how long he crouched and stared into the rancher's face. He would have been there, unmindful and unprepared, when the two timber pirates closed in from the woods had not their steps warned him.

They moved cautiously to circle back to the protecting brush piles when he saw them, a small, wiry man and a taller broad-shouldered one with twisted black hair. He knew they were unaware of his presence and had not heard his low warning call to Daley.

He waited with frozen stance as they came closer into full view. His movements were strangely gentle as he laid the revolver on the ground and picked up Jim Daley's rifle. Then from the same kneeling position he lined the rifle sights on the larger, bulkier form and squeezed the trigger. He felt the gun jump in his hand. He jerked the lever action and fired again and again until a dull click told him the rifle was empty. The two loggers lay slumped and quiet in the line of his fire. Only the silence and loneliness and his own heartbreak were about him.

Chapter 19

On an April afternoon Caroline and her brother were deep in discussion with Eric Duane. The shock of their father's death and of Jim Daley's violent passing, and of the ordeal surrounding both, were over. Sometimes the memory lingered in their saddened eyes and in the loneliness of the little house where Lance's smile had so often flashed and where Jim Daley's laughter had cheered the rooms.

Today was the beginning of the summing up, of fitting

pieces together, of striving to gain a clear and workable picture of the many facets of Lance Ainsley's business ventures and affairs.

When H. A. W. Tabor had come from Denver for the sad rites, they had asked him to throw light upon their father's financial status, but he shook his head in a rueful manner. "Your dad's work for Elkins and me back in the early days won't call for much explanation. He was capable and honest, made a lot of money for us. You pay a man like that well. He earns it. Later he branched into a lot of things on his own. Some of them I suggested. Lance was tight-lipped about his business affairs—even with me."

Tabor had been able to give them only a sketchy and shadowy outline. "You best get together with Eric Duane," he suggested. "Duane handled things in Denver for your dad."

Lance Ainsley's children realized that Tabor's suggestion had indeed been valid. For an hour they studied papers that Duane laid before them. They were aware that into Eric's hands, and the investment section of his bank, Lance had placed the handling of funds and property far greater that they had even surmised he possessed.

"How could he have done it?" Shawn asked in disbelief. "I always thought this house, his sawmill, and a few claims were the extent of it."

Eric looked up with a quick smile. "He provided pretty well for you, Shawn, here in Aspen and down at the college at Golden."

"I never gave it a lot of thought," Shawn explained. "Didn't ask for much. And Dad sure never handed money out recklessly."

Eric's gaze searched the faces confronting him. "A man dedicated to one purpose isn't apt to throw money around." He paused, as though searching out words for strange and revealing facts. "Lance had one purpose. One goal. It stayed with him from the time he came to Aspen until——"

Suddenly Caroline leaned forward. "I think," she said, "that I already know that purpose. He wanted to get hold of Grandfather's house in Greeley. To buy Swope's mansion."

"That's part of it, Caroline, but not all. He could have bought that old house years ago. There was something else, a greater consuming passion. Your father wanted to get hold of every property, every holding, every interest Jared Swope owned or controlled. He swore to Swope that someday he would break him. Ruin him." Duane's voice was little more than a whisper as he added, "And he's done it—absolutely and irrevocably."

"How?" Caroline murmured. "Eric, how? What do you mean?"

He studied her quietly. The tenseness and wonder of the moment brought color to her cheeks. Within Eric stirred the old, but never-lessening love that tore both his heart and mind. He plunged into swift words that would lay bare a mystery, and that he hoped would mask the stark reality of his emotions as he watched her.

"Caroline, do you recall, just before you married Bob, I told you Lance wanted to talk to me. Wanted me to handle something in Denver?"

Caroline nodded, mindful of the morning and the table at the Clarendon and all that had been said.

"It started that day. Lance knew I'd gone into investments. He was frank with me. Told me a lot, then counted on me to keep quiet. He wanted to get at Swope's throat for something the banker had done to you, to your mother, and the family. He said *undermine* Swope. Buy up every obligation he commits himself to. Put prospects and lures in his way. Do anything legal. But get him. Get him good. Smash him."

"It'd have taken money. Lots of money," Shawn said in wonder. "Grandfather was no fool. He made a pile in banks and mortgages and farms around Greeley. He could smell out anything likely to turn up a profit. I know. I lived with him."

"Indeed he could," Eric agreed. "It was that very thing that enabled us to trap him and bring about his undoing."

"You mean he's broke? Grandfather is broke?" Shawn gasped.

"Yes. Only he doesn't know it. Lance had him against the wall months ago if he'd wanted to close in. Why he didn't, I don't know. Maybe he was enjoying a cat-and-mouse game, savoring the kill before he made it."

"Eric, explain the details," Caroline said slowly.

"It'll take time, but I'll make a start," Duane answered. "You have to know the whole story. It's your problem and your responsibility now. You two are Lance's only heirs. He saw to it that was iron-clad."

Duane paused and shifted into an easier posture. "The big opportunity came for your dad when Swope got interested in a railroad promotion. Greeley and the farm business began to seem limited to Swope. He was striking for new fields. Greater opportunities. A couple of years ago a new railroad was proposed. It would run from Denver to Yellowstone Park and then on to Portland and Seattle. British and French capital became interested. Bonds were issued and a lot of right of way bought or leased."

Shawn Ainsley stood open-mouthed. "You mean Grandfather bought railroad bonds?"

"No, Shawn, they weren't offered on the open market. But he sensed opportunity in getting town-site land along the proposed right of way. He plunged into that. Bought in Colorado, Wyoming, even Idaho. Those town sites stood to make him millions."

"Didn't they?" Caroline breathed.

"No. They ruined him. The railroad never got started. Not a single rail or tie. The Union Pacific saw to that; it brought pressure on the capitalists in the East and even in Europe. The deal folded. Swope had a tremendous amount of land, practically worthless land after the railroad promotion collapsed, land he wished to the Lord he'd never seen. He'd mortgaged about every property he could, even borrowed a lot of money." Duane stood up and stared at them. "Land. Acres of land. Sections of land. Miles of land. Bought with money from loans and mortgages. And your father bought up every mortgage, discounted, and got hold of every loan note. That's it. The story."

364

Caroline's head dropped for a time onto a table. When she lifted it, her face and eyes were tired and troubled.

"You mean, Eric, that now it's to be our decision, Shawn's and mine, whether to foreclose on our own grandfather. Make a penniless and broken man of him?"

"Yes," Eric answered thoughtfully. "The decision must be yours."

Shawn threw his arm about his sister. "It was Dad's money. His plan and ambition. Sis, what would he have wanted us to do?"

"I don't know, Shawn. Honest to God I won't know until we stand face to face with Jared Swope."

"You mean you're going there? Back to Greeley? To Swope's mansion? When?"

"Within a week or so, maybe sooner, if Eric can get papers in order."

"They'll be ready," Duane said. "Be ready very soon."

Within hours of Eric's shocking revelation, the urge was strong upon Caroline to once more visit the wide, tranquil acres of the Lazy Seedy and to seek Maude's advice.

Far into the night they sat by the great stone fireplace. Earlier, the children had played about them. Jimmy, the child that was now Maude Daley's closest link to the rancher she had loved and married and lost, played with Freddy and Annette.

Caroline's hands caressed the worn cowhide of the chair. "I'll always remember him here, Maude. In this room. In this chair or squatting down to draw those circles." She hesitated, then asked, "Maude, will you stay here on the Lazy Seedy? Can you endure staying?"

Maude's reply came with a pensively soft smile. "Yes, I'll stay. Caroline, this home isn't something to be endured. Not when there's so much of Jim about me. Everything he believed in and loved is here. The house. The livestock. The ranch. He'd want me to stay. He'd want me to raise his son here." Maude paused, anxiety creeping into her words. "But perhaps you want to sell the ranch. You know half of it is yours."

"No, Maude. No. The ranch is yours and Jimmy's forever. I had hoped you would want to stay on Wilderness Creek."

"Half the income belongs to you," Maude said firmly. "With growing children you'll need——"

"Wait, Maude," Caroline interrupted. "Our business in San Francisco—Ellen's and mine—would assure plenty for the children. But Maude, there's something beyond that, far beyond that. Papa was wealthy. I never realized it, nor did Shawn."

"Jim used to wonder about that," Maude reflected. "He'd say that likely Lance had enough stashed away somewhere to make a lot of people sit up and whistle. I'm glad, Caroline. Glad for you. Glad for Shawn. But I'm happier that you're here with me tonight. This is where you and the children should settle down and live. You don't have to go back right away, to San Francisco, do you?"

"Before too long," Caroline answered. "First, I have an ordeal to see through."

"An ordeal?" Maude's words were worried.

"Maude, let me tell you. I knew when I came down from Aspen that I must talk it over with you. Perhaps you won't believe it. I scarcely can myself. Most of Papa's money was invested in such a way, and for the one purpose, of ruining my grandfather. Papa waited and worked for years just to accomplish it. He bought up every mortgage and note Grandfather contracted."

Disbelief marked Maude Daley's eyes. "Jared Swope never borrowed money that I knew of. He loaned it. Loaned a dollar and took a pound of flesh."

"Not always, Maude. Not recently. He wanted to spread out. Wanted to be a capitalist. He put huge sums into land along the route of a proposed railroad. It didn't materialize. Papa had Eric Duane watching and waiting. Maude, today Shawn and I hold the power to break Jared Swope. I wish to heaven we didn't. It's as if we've become Papa's avenging hand, as though he is depending on us to complete this ruthless thing."

Maude Daley leaned forward; her face was strangely eager. "Wait, Caroline," she said abruptly. "Wait and listen to me. You say it is ruthless, something you hesitate to carry out." She stood before Caroline. "It's time for you to know—to know that I would give anything to be in your shoes, to be the one to deal with Jared Swope."

Caroline stared at the older woman's agitated face. "Why?" she gasped.

"Why? I'll tell you why. Caroline, when you were sick and they brought you to my house in Evans did you realize what sort of house it was?"

Caroline's eyes held levelly to Maude's flushed and troubled face. "Not then, when I was sick. Later, I think I knew. But Maude, what difference could that possibly have made to me. I loved you then, Maude, and I love you now."

Maude Daley's hands clasped Caroline's in an ever-tightening grip. "That sporting house was bought for me by your grandfather."

"He bought it for you?" Caroline's tone was incredulous.

"It's about all he ever did buy me. Jim Daley knew what I was, what I had been. Jim's great love was the one wonderful thing of my life. Now he's gone. Perhaps I deserved only a few years of such happiness and such love. Maybe I don't even deserve my boy. You see, Caroline, I lived with Jared Swope. I was his mistress." She paused, studying the disbelief of Caroline's face. "Oh, yes, it is true. Jared and I grew up in the same town back East. I thought I was madly in love with him, and he with me. I didn't know his true love, his consuming love for money and power. I could offer him my body; your grandmother could offer him her father's fortune. Guess which won out."

For moments Maude Daley stared into the fireplace. With a tearing sigh she continued. "Jared Swope wanted both. When he moved West and joined Greeley's colony, he had to be very careful, furtive. Swope's mansion was his showplace. A house where Florence could uphold his dignity and his prestige. But my house could be easily reached at night over the hill in darkness. After a time even that was too risky. My house was just another piece

367

of real estate from which rental and a percentage could be collected on the sly. That went on until I looked him up in Greeley, at his bank. I told him to deed the house to me or I would have a talk with Florence. I think he could have killed me then, but he signed. He signed and ranted and hated."

As Maude Daley finished, Caroline looked at her with infinite softness and pity. "Maude, he did that to you?" Her words firmed at sight of the older woman's face dropping tiredly into her hands. "You're going to Greeley with me, Maude. You're going to be the one to tell Jared Swope that he's through. Whipped! Broke! Cleaned out just as Papa vowed to ruin him!"

"Of course I'll go with you, Caroline. But your brother must know. Shawn must know everything that I've told you tonight."

Caroline's arm swept proudly about Maude Daley. "Don't you imagine, Maude dearest, that somewhere tonight Papa and Uncle Jim are chuckling about this?"

"Probably they are," Maude said and smiled through welling tears, "If Jim isn't too busy scratching circles around a star."

In the summer sunlight of the following day, Caroline answered a knock at the door of the ranch house. A pleased smile brightened her face. It was Eric Duane, clad in neatly creased tan trousers, riding boots, and a plaid woolen shirt. "Come in, Eric," she said. "Maude will be so glad you came down. So am I."

"I couldn't stay away, Caroline." He lifted a sheaf of wrapped and tied papers. "I've been telling myself I had to bring these papers down to you. It's a lie. Caroline, I had to see you. Aspen grew lonely the very minute you left. So did I."

She looked at him with understanding quietness. "You need to be out of doors more, Eric. After lunch we can go for a ride. I'll show you the Lazy Seedy."

She had turned to search out Maude when his low-spoken words reached her. "I'll enjoy riding, Caroline—with

368

you. You'll be looking at cattle and mountains. I'll probably see only my mountain princess."

Near sunset they rode hand in hand through a greening grove of aspen. Eric Duane's face was thoughtful. "I'm glad you told me about Maude and why she's going to Greeley with you."

"You must go too, Eric. It couldn't be handled without you."

He nodded. He was quiet as he tightened his clasp of her hand and drew his horse to a stop.

"Caroline, can it be *now*—for us? I've loved you so long, waited so long."

"Eric, do you still feel that way? I'm not a young girl. I'm a widow. With two children and a face that's beginning to have etchings, lines."

"Stop it," he whispered. "It has always been you. Perhaps, perhaps, Caroline, if you had let me stay, stay that one night in San Francisco, I could have come to terms with myself. Perhaps I could even have forgotten you, but since then I've been chained by my love of you and my need for you. I'll be that way every day of my life. Caroline, make today our *now*. Say that we'll be married."

"Eric, our *now* is close. Very close." She leaned toward him and her dark hair caressed his cheek. "Let me get this business in Greeley over with. Get my mind at ease. Then come to me in San Francisco, Eric. Come very soon."

Chapter 20

As one town dies, another prospers and grows.

When spring 1897 gave way to early summer, the verdant greenness of a town, and an ever-spreading checkerboard of productive farmland, bore evidence of the good judgment with which the pioneers of Greeley's Union Colony had chosen the location for their settlement.

It was a far different city from the prairie-ringed village through which Caroline Ainsley had walked toward her grandfather's house on a December evening seventeen years before. Water, rich soil, and hard work had already transformed the valley of the Cache la Poudre River into an agricultural area surpassing even the hopes of Greeley's founding fathers.

Abundant water was carried through canals and laterals onto the wide prairies and transformed into productive fields of potatoes, alfalfa, grains, onions, and sugar beets for the factories already being planned.

The day of vast herds of range cattle was past, ended by plows and barbed wire. Livestock, carefully bred and fed on the farms, had become a profitable segment of the economy of this growing farm territory.

The town had become the hub and the trading center of a large segment of the state. As farm products flowed out of the town, money flowed in. The state Normal College had come to Greeley and brought an educational and cultural stability that would endure through the years.

Jared Swope was aware of all this as he looked from the window of his red-brick bank on Eighth Avenue and watched the movement of people and vehicles along the wide, solidly built street. It was Saturday afternoon, a time when folks from the farms were in town for shopping and relaxation. Few of the people on the street were strangers to Swope or to his bank. It had always been good business to know these people from the countryside. It was expedient also to know their habits and their short-comings. Many a loan had been called and saved through knowing a man's foibles as well as his credit rating.

His attention fixed on a black-clad, heavily veiled woman who alighted from a livery rig and approached the bank. Something of the manner of her firm, unhurried step brought a perplexed frown to his forehead. This woman was a stranger in town, but the sight of her stirred some strange, unknown emotion deep within him. His aging, heavily jowled face slackened under the thrust of something akin to terror.

He forced himself to shrug away this thing that clutched him. He tried to swing his thoughts to plans of a new company he was considering promoting. Sterling and Camfield were doing well by themselves with such ventures. He needed something with the scope and possibilities of a new land and irrigation development. Only such an undertaking would enable him to recoup the losses he'd incurred when the Denver to Seattle railroad had floundered.

He assured himself that he would regain for himself and his bank the solid stability that he had jeopardized to gain funds for the railroad town sites. He knew vaguely that the mortgages and notes he had given had found their way into the hands of a Denver syndicate, but they had not gotten in touch with him; they probably wouldn't, for the paper carried excellent security and interest. Much of it was already overdue, but the interest would go on. Besides, wasn't his own prestige and that of the bank behind the indebtedness enough to guarantee payment?

His eyes turned again to the woman in black. She crossed the street and approached the bank. Suddenly he sensed that she would enter and that she was coming to see him. He turned from the window and dropped heavily into a swivel chair. "I'm a fool, an utter fool," he muttered savagely. "I don't know her, probably never did. It's just that I'm tired. Jumpy as hell." He fell silent, knowing that a knock would sound at the door of his private office. He was uncomprehendingly and completely scared.

Time seemed unending before a clerk rapped at the door and thrust his head inside. "There's a lady here to see you. A Mrs. Daley."

Jared Swope's mind savored the unfamiliarity of the name. "Tell her I'm busy today," he said.

"I did. She says it's important. She said to tell you her name is Maude Selby Daley."

"Show her in. I'll squeeze out a minute or so for her," Swope answered. He drew a deep breath, scornful of the irrational and stupid fear that he had allowed to play upon him. After all these years, she's come back, he thought.

Well, that's all over. She will get nothing from me except a damned blunt warning not to come around here again.

She walked into the office and closed the door quietly behind her. Swope did not rise from his chair. For a moment he ignored her as he shuffled a sheaf of papers on his desk. She sat stiffly upright on an oak chair when he turned to face her.

His self-confidence became a lessening armor as he studied her form and tried to get a clear glimpse of the face obscured by the heavy veil. She's held herself together pretty well, he thought, and suddenly Jared Swope was keenly conscious of how the years piled on him and worked their unalterable way about his body and his face.

"Well, Maude," he said finally. "You've come back. Let's see, how many years has it been?"

"Enough of them, Jared. Enough for you to get mighty well established and build a fine bank. Enough for twigs and saplings to grow into wonderful shade trees. Your town is beautiful, Jared."

"I don't imagine you came here to talk about buildings and trees, Maude," he answered abruptly. "You've had time to get around a bit yourself." His voice took on a viperish twinge. "In your business you have to get about. You get run out of one town and get set in another. The law and the married women see to that."

"Jared, I'd just as soon not talk about myself or my life," she said, and her voice was studiedly humble. "I came here because of your family, your grandchildren Caroline and Shawn."

"What about them?" he rasped.

"Perhaps you've heard," she began patiently. "Their father—Lance—was killed this spring."

"I read that in the paper, about his getting trapped in a snowslide up at Aspen. Then Shawn wrote of it to my wife. What's that got to do with me?"

Maude Selby slowly lifted the heavy veil and studied him calmly. "At a time like this, Jared, they have nobody to turn to except——"

Jared Swope braced himself firmly back in his chair. At that moment the old hatred surged in his face. "Stop right

372

there, Maude. Shawn left my house and the future I'd planned for him. Chose his own bed to lie on. The other one, the girl, Caroline——"

"She's a widow now, Jared. A widow with two children."

"It's no concern of mine," he snapped. "They had years to try to do something up there in Aspen. Likely Ainsley spent all he made on liquor, on gambling, and whores."

At his words Maude Daley bit down on her lip in desperate effort to mask the revulsion and the anger within her.

"They're here in town, Jared. Both of them, Caroline and Shawn."

He came heavily to his feet and leaned across the desk. "I had an idea this would happen, someday," he said. "I figured they'd come begging." He laughed aloud. "Know what, Maude? Just before Lance Ainsley left Greeley, he did a lot of bragging to me. He said someday he was going to break me, clean me out, ruin me." Memory of the moment reddened Jared Swope's face as he continued. "Now his kids expect me to take them in, provide for them."

"You never thought Lance could make good, did you?" A lurking smile came onto Maude Selby's lips.

"Expect it? Hell, no, Maude. I sure didn't hold my water waiting. Waiting for that cheap surveyor——"

She raised her hand in an oddly silencing gesture. "Perhaps you *should* have listened, Jared. Perhaps you should have *held your water*."

He looked at her amused face. Again the strange twist of fear cut through him. "What do you mean by that, Maude?"

The smile dropped away from her face and gave way to a look that mingled anger and contempt and infinite satisfaction.

"Jared, I've waited a long time for this. I never hoped I would have the God-given privilege of telling you. Lance Ainsley made good his vow to you. Every word of it. Jared Swope, you're through. Broke. Cleaned. Plucked. And Lance Ainsley did it."

373

"You're crazy, Maude," he yelled.

"Am I? Just listen. Listen and judge for yourself. Those notes and mortgages you gave, all those debts you took on thinking you'd reap a harvest on railroad town sites: know who bought them up? Lance Ainsley did. He had a strangle hold around your rotten old neck. Now his children have it. He saw to it they would have."

"You expect to come in here and make me believe this?"

"Jared," she laughed vengefully, "did you ever hear of Jim Daley, the cattleman who used to operate down the Platte?"

He stared at her wordlessly, realizing the potency of her words.

"Yes," she went on, "Jim Daley. My husband. He died soon after Lance's passing, but he left a ranch, the finest ranch on the Western Slope. Clear of debt. Clear of any mortgage. I own half of it. Know who owns the other half? Caroline. Caroline Ainsley Herndon—your granddaughter."

Jared Swope slumped across his desk, but doubt lingered in his eyes. "I'll look into all this," he murmured.

"You sure will, Jared. Right now. This morning. There's a man waiting for me across the street. A man with papers that will tear your cozy and scheming little world apart. He's waiting for me to send him here, Jared. He has the papers to strip you of this bank, of Swope's mansion, of your farms and your business buildings, and your town-site lands." She rose to look down at his crouched body and his ashen face. "Don't take it too hard, Jared. You've done this same sort of ruthless thing to a lot of people. You won't starve. Caroline and Shawn were too soft-hearted for that. They probably were thinking of Florence more than of you. You're still to have enough for a living. You're to keep the small bank in that little town toward the south end of Weld County."

Maude Daley moved toward the door, then glanced back. "Good-bye, Jared. I've an idea it's good-bye forever this time. God rest your bastardly old bones."

She walked through the bank and heaved a huge, re-

374

lieved sigh. A sudden and sobering thought was upon her. There's not much satisfaction or fun in felling an old and towering tree, even though you've contemplated it for a long time and know it's a rotten, worm-ravished tree.

Upon their return to Aspen Caroline and Shawn gave the matter long and thoughtful reflection. Once more Eric Duane was called from Denver and sat with them far into the night preparing documents to implement the decision they had reached. One third of their father's fortune was immediately to be transferred into an irrevocable trust for the lifetime benefit of Florence Swope and Emily Ainsley Gartrell. Thus, their grandmother and their mother would always have a steady and protecting income, from funds upon which Jared Swope could never place his hands or use for his own devices.

Caroline realized that the days of her stay in Aspen were shortening. She must soon return to San Francisco with her children and resume the routine life from which she had been taken by the double tragedy. It would be a lonely life, but a busy one, without the visits and the letters of her father.

Eric Duane lingered in Aspen, and she knew that he would not leave until she was on her way westward. He would come to her in San Francisco, too, but would she be able to tear up her roots again, dispose of the business she and Ellen had built, and return with him to Denver?

She considered the enigma as she rode a slow-moving train to the Lazy Seedy for a parting visit with Maude Daley. Her children were eager to romp about the ranch yard with Jimmy Daley.

Maude was in the small office, her face tired and baffled as she studied papers and records. Caroline adamantly urged Maude to forget the paper work and relax with coffee and chatter. The three children played outside, under stern warning to keep away from the cattle, the horses, and Wilderness Creek.

"Maude, about the ranch records," she said. "I have all day and tomorrow, too, if it will help. I used to keep all of Uncle Jim's records; I'd be glad to help."

Maude Daley lifted her feet onto a kitchen chair and sighed. "Caroline, this ranch is too big and complex. Jim always seemed to take it in his stride, but he'd spent his life with cattle. He knew how to handle them. How to handle men, too."

"You've got dependable men here, Maude. Some of them have spent years on the ranch. They can help you."

Maude listened, but her hazel eyes fixed an oddly disconcerting gaze on Caroline's face. For a time she was absolutely silent, then she said, flatly, "Half of this ranch is yours, Caroline. Jim and I have always wanted it that way, and I still do."

Caroline started to protest, but Maude's hand lifted to silence her. "Let me have my say, Caroline. Half of all this is yours." Her sweeping nod encompassed the miles along Wilderness Creek. "Half of the ranch. Half of the profits or the losses. Half of the responsibility and the work of running this sprawling shebang. How can you take care of what is yours by running back to San Francisco?"

"But my millinery business, mine and Ellen's," Caroline gasped. "I just can't drop that either."

"The devil you can't," Maude answered firmly and leaned forward to cup her hand under Caroline's chin to bring the girl's troubled gaze with her own excited eyes.

"About that dress shop and Ellen Corlett. She'll manage by herself, perhaps better than you think. Likely with you away, she'll get married."

"There is a man she——" Caroline began slowly.

"There's always a man, Caroline. Unless you dawdle too long and let the years and happiness pass you by."

Caroline's eyes widened as she gleaned the deeper meaning of Maude Daley's words. But what she might have said, the protest she might have uttered, was lost as Jim Daley's widow said, "Don't mistake fool's gold for the real thing, child. Take your happiness while you can. While you're young, able to live, to love, to dream. Sell that dratted San Francisco thing to Ellen or give it to her. Then marry Eric Duane. He loves you and he loves this Roaring Fork country. Then the two of you settle down here and run this ranch for yourselves and for me. I happen to know Eric has dreamed of living here. Caroline, throw away that blind reason and logic of yours. Come to Wilderness Creek. Build yourself a home in this valley. Raise your children on this vast and clean empire. It's their heritage."

Caroline rose to her feet. "Maude," she whispered. "Oh, Maude, thank you." She glanced at a ticking clock. "It's just about eight hours until I can catch a train back up from Caroline Station to Aspen. Maude, I want to be on that train. May I leave Freddy and Annette here for the night? I want to go to Aspen and Eric. I want to tell him our *now* is here."

She moved to embrace her friend, but the softness of her face, and the youth flooding into it, told that already her thoughts were hours ahead of her, and searching out the arms, and the comfort, and the love of Eric Duane.

PART SIX
1912–1919

Chapter 21

The girl sat for a long time in the quiet of her bedroom. She studied the small, leather-bound diary on which her name had been embossed in gold letters—Annette Herndon. She had never been zealous or regular about writing in the book, and now, after ten years, there were many blank pages left. She picked up a pen and tapped it reflectively against her teeth. She chose a blank page and wrote words at its top:

MRS. JAMES DALEY, JR.

The strange unfamiliarity of the name stared back at her. By this time tomorrow, that will be my name. I'll be married and on a train taking me back East for a honeymoon with Jimmy. How odd that we could live next door to each other, practically grow up together, fall in love, become engaged, and yet now, only hours before becoming his wife, I'm pondering his true nature and the years stretching out before us.

She rose and looked pensively out the window. Nothing seemed changed in the view before her. How could the Lazy Seedy remain so calmly solid while the hours carried her toward a moment when surely everything would be changed and different?

She could scarcely recall a time when she had not lived here in the house built by Caroline and Eric Duane. A quarter mile up tree-fringed Wilderness Creek was the older, sprawling ranch home of Maude and Jimmy Daley. Across the creek were the vast alfalfa fields that were replacing the meadows. The log stables and pole pens that she could remember from girlhood gave way to a complex of red barns, surrounded by symmetrical cattle and horse corrals of solidly placed and gleaming white posts and boards. Only the mountains, rising with forested slopes toward jutting peaks, seemed changeless.

She knew that this ranch, which she and Jimmy Daley would return to, had become a valuable and prospering business.

Presently Annette's thoughts were on the meeting that had brought together all of them—her mother, her stepfather, Jimmy and his mother, and her. A firm pride had been in Eric's manner of speaking as he summed up the details of ranch management. "Jimmy," he had said, "I've always felt that this ranch was merely entrusted to me for safekeeping until time for you to take hold. That time is here. You and Annette will do all right. Both of you have grown up here. Both of you know what has to be done and how to do it."

Something in the finality of Eric's words had caused Annette to turn questioning eyes toward her mother. Caroline looked toward Eric with gentle pride, then explained. "When you youngsters get back from your trip, you're to have this house. Even a Lazy Seedy isn't large enough for too many bosses and too many women."

Annette ran to Eric and dropped into his lap. "Daddy, there's plenty of room. Isn't there, Jimmy?"

Jimmy Daley lifted his lithe thin form from a chair and grinned persuasively. "I've tried to tell Eric we'll need him here more than ever."

"I'll be close enough to help out—in a pinch," Eric said. "You can look us up in Aspen. There's a house on Hunter Creek, about a mile from town, we've had our eyes on."

"You mean the Gregg place?" Annette asked eagerly.

"That's the one," Eric replied.

"It is lovely, old-fashioned and wonderful," Annette breathed. "Not all that fakery of scrolls and gingerbread. Large rooms. Fireplaces. So much lawn and garden space. And that little stream that goes pell-mell through it." Annette ended her enthusiastic burst and turned to Maude

382

Daley. "You're not going up there to Aspen, anyplace, are you, Aunt Maude?"

Maude Daley shook her head. "No, Annette. I'm staying here on the ranch. I wouldn't fit in anywhere else, but I'll have my own house and keep out from underfoot. Maybe I'll travel some. Visit your Uncle Shawn down in Arizona or look up Freddy in San Francisco."

And now, with the whiteness of the diary still challenging her beneath this name she would carry, Annette thought how brief had been her brother's stay upon the ranch. Suddenly the urge grew within her to go downstairs and ask endless questions of her mother. There's so much she can tell me, Annette mused.

Her mother was outside, snipping rain-freshened lilac blossoms from a hedge and dropping them into a basket. Annette paused before speaking, and watched the swift deftness of her mother's movements. She's forty-four years old, Annette marveled. She's still as graceful and alert as can be. Even the boys in Jimmy's crowd, and my friends, say that she is beautiful and so much fun to be around. Most of them would rather dance with my mother than with me. She's had a wonderful life with Daddy here on the ranch. Perhaps she has never known any real trouble, except maybe when my own father died. I hope I can be like that—like her—when I'm getting old.

Caroline gathered another handful of flowers and turned when she saw her daughter studying her. She smiled a welcome that did not reveal the sudden memories roused by the flame glint of Annette's hair and the wide candor of her blue eyes. She's so like him, she silently told herself. So like Bob, the father she never saw or knew. His hair and eyes. His flashing smile and impetuous ways. Jimmy will be enraptured. Puzzled. And exasperated. They'll have to learn to give and take. To match her impulsiveness to his quiet and plodding ways. Thank God for his good nature and good sense. One minute he'll want to smother her with kisses. The next he'll have an urge to smother her—with a pillow.

Annette crooked her arm about the flower basket.

"Mother," she asked suddenly, "why didn't Freddy stay here? Grow up on the ranch with me?"

Caroline stood silent for a time, aware of the chatter of Wilderness Creek and the pleasant warmth of spring sunshine beating against her back. At last she said wistfully, "How I wish it could have been that way; how Eric wishes it." She moved to a flowering apple tree and leaned against a heavy bough. "Annette, do you remember when we lived in San Francisco? Friends we had there . . . Colonel and Mrs. Brenton?"

"Just barely, Mother. I was only five or six."

Caroline nodded. "And Freddy was two years older. Old enough to become enamored of the Presidio and military life and uniforms. Colonel Brenton was his hero and a father to him, too. When we came back here——"

"Why did we come back?" Annette demanded.

"Your grandfather and Jimmy's father were killed the same week. I had to come back and take care of things, I and your Uncle Shawn."

"Then you met Daddy, Daddy Eric, and married him." Annette was summing up for herself. "But I still don't understand why Freddy went back to San Francisco."

"It was his choice," Caroline explained softly. "Love of a military life and of soldiering was deeply instilled in him. Ranch life wasn't. He chose a military academy close to the Brentons." Caroline looked at her daughter. "Why didn't you ask Freddy about this when he was home on leave?"

"I don't know, Mother. Maybe it didn't seem important then. But now so many things are suddenly important." Annette's arm linked her mother's. "Tomorrow, when I'm married, perhaps family history and such won't seem too important. But right now——" She broke off, then asked suddenly, "Mother, how long did you know my father before you married him? What was he like? Where did you go for *your* honeymoon?"

Caroline pulled Annette down beside her on the lawn swing. "We'll have to begin a long time ago, Annette, when I was twelve years old. There's an old fort in Wyoming. It's deserted now and a river flows past it."

An hour later Caroline rose from the swing, clasped her daughter's hand, and moved with her toward the house. "Annette, come with me up to my room. I've pondered when the time would be right to give something to you. Today—right now—is the time."

They sat together on a bed. Caroline's black head was close to the red-tinged curls of her daughter. She probed a dresser drawer and removed a small box. From its velvet lining she removed an object and laid it in Annette's hand. "It's my engagement ring, the one your own father gave me."

Annette studied it. "It's lovely, Mother. But different. I never saw one like it."

Caroline smiled. "At first it was only a flower stem. Your father twisted and slipped it on my finger. Later, I had it encased in the glass and mounted on the white gold band and the jewels set alongside. But that brown inside is the old, old flower stem." Caroline's breath quickened as she went on. "Do you know what your father said when he slipped it on my hand? I remember so well, Annette. Remember his face, so much like yours. And his voice: *'It's not much, but maybe it will last until we can get into town—to a jeweler. It says one thing: Caroline Ainsley belongs to me. My god, how lucky can one man be?'*"

"You mean, Mother, you want to give the ring to me? Want me to have it?"

Caroline nodded. "He was your father, Annette. He would want it this way."

Annette Herndon rose from the bed and looked out over the sunlit serenity of the ranch. Then she turned to drop to her knees at the bed's edge. "Mother, I want to go find Jimmy. I want to find him right now. Tell him that this is the ring I want him to use for the ceremony tomorrow. Then I want to keep it forever."

Chapter 22

Eric and Caroline Duane weren't always at home. They traveled a lot. But the white house on Hunter Creek was kept always ready for them and for the crowds that gathered for parties and social events when the lights that gleamed softly across the river signaled the return of the Duanes to their favorite spot.

Automobiles made their way frequently into Aspen now up the valley from Glenwood Springs on a twisting and dusty road or climbing laboriously over Independence Pass from the towns of the Arkansas Valley. Each year the town knew a burst of activity when hunters from far-off cities roamed the hills by day and congregated in the Jerome Hotel at night.

It was during hunting season of 1918 that Caroline's world was torn asunder by a telegram from the D and RG depot.

The message was brief and carried a Washington, D.C. date: THE SECRETARY OF WAR IS SORRY TO INFORM YOU ... KILLED IN ACTION ... MAJOR FRED HERNDON.

She first read it as she stood beside the white gate of a picket fence. Later, the tears would come, but now she stood white-faced and very erect. She lifted her eyes to distant snowfields.

Spring of 1919 came to the Arizona desert with a profuse burst of wildflowers born of strengthening sunshine and of gently persistent rains carried far inland from the Gulf Coast. It was the land of the thorn-bristled saguaro cactus, and of ghoulish wolf spiders and scorpions. Vast heat-tortured slopes and ridges reached toward the coolness of encircling mountains.

The land was rich in copper, and men fought distance, heat, and loneliness to establish mines and towns dedicated to wresting the rich ore from the earth, putting it through smelters, and shipping it out to meet the needs of a growing nation.

Shawn Ainsley loved this country. It had not happened overnight for he had brought with him as a young mining engineer his memory of Aspen nestled in the cool and lush valley of the Roaring Fork. His mind's-eye picture recalled forests that swept through blue-hazed infinity toward the grandeur of peaks where summer and winter differed little.

In Arizona he found a challenge, a career, and a wife. With them had come contentment and growing awareness of the beauty of this desert land.

As the sun drifted toward a harshly serrated range of distant, westward mountains, he lifted his gaze from the paper spread on his desk and studied the twisting, canyon-locked town and the white drift of smoke from smelter stacks a mile beyond.

At forty-four his steady blue-gray eyes were set in a tanned and purposeful face. His reddish hair, still somewhat unruly, grayed at his temples. He moved toward a bookcase. About him was an air of confidence. Men respected his judgment and his thoughtful, fair decisions.

His face was puzzled and thoughtful as he thumbed the yellowing pages of an old, seldom-used notebook. He searched out a few handwritten pages, sat down again, and read with concentration. He laid the book beside the paper on his desk and drummed his fingers on the wooden arm of his chair.

Memories surged within him. He recalled the days and nights he had studied in Bob Herndon's old assay office, and the field trips he had taken while at the Colorado School of Mines.

He remembered other faces, other times, incidents of long ago.

He sat for a long time in a reverie that encompassed the strange, unrelenting way Lance Ainsley had sought revenge upon Jared Swope. He spent years working and building and saving to destroy a man. Caroline's beating probably touched it off. But there was something else, something deeper. There had to be. He never remarried. He never seemed much interested in women.

Shawn Ainsley's eyes widened. That was it! he breathed. His greater obsession was the loss of my mother from his life. The cruel fact that she chose Swope security and wealth instead of what Lance Ainsley could offer—love, devotion, adventure.

An evening whistle echoed through the canyon slopes as he walked to the office of the general superintendent. "Gordon," he said, "I'd like to take some time off for a trip to Colorado. It may take ten days, maybe longer."

The older man waved him to a chair. "Likely it can be arranged, Shawn. Lord knows you're due for a vacation or some rest." He studied Ainsley's face and added, "Is something wrong up in Colorado? Someone sick?"

Shawn shook his head and leaned forward to place a folded, blue-penciled paper on the desk. "Look at this, Gordon. Does it make sense to you?"

The superintendent scanned the half column, then whistled sharply. "I'm not familiar with that particular mining stock. Right now, though, I wish I had a bundle of it. Do you happen to hold shares, Shawn? Are you that lucky?"

"Gordon, this thing is crazy. It's impossible. Less than a year ago that stock was worthless or next to it. It's been done for for twenty years at least. My grandfather, the banker in Greeley told you about, invested moderately heavy in it. When the big showdown came, the shares were turned over to my sister, Caroline, and me."

The older man grinned wryly. "I wish my folks had bought some of it instead of land down on the Salt River flats around Phoenix. Damned if that'll ever pay off."

Shawn Ainsley retrieved the paper and rolled it in his hands. "It doesn't add up," he insisted thoughtfully. "This outfit, this Sangre de Cristo Mining Corporation, seems to be headquartered in New York City. They're asserting claim to valuable gold discoveries in the San Luis Valley of Colorado. At Cascade. Gordon, it's phony. It has to be phony. I know the Cascade area well. If there's sizable gold deposits there, I'll eat my——"

The superintendent smiled at him. "You've seldom been wrong, Shawn, to our good fortune. But you might be this time. You'll likely know when you get back. Will you take Barbara and the boys to Colorado with you?"

"They would hang me if I didn't," Shawn said, laughing. "Caroline has a big house and scads of yard room at Aspen. The kids can make like cowhands on the Lazy Seedy."

"The Lazy Seedy?" The superintendent's words were puzzled.

"A helluva big ranch," Shawn answered. "Someday you've got to see it, Gordon. You won't believe it till you do."

Caroline termed it a clan bivouac when her brother and his family arrived from Arizona. Annette persuaded Jimmy and Maude Daley to join them in Aspen. The days were exciting and fun-filled when the house on Hunter Creek rang with gay, excited voices, and when it seemed the place was alive with almost as many people as lived in the deserted and decaying town across the river.

Dinner was served late on the second evening. Caroline was buoyantly gay as she smiled down the long table lined with the faces of her family and her close friend. She acknowledged Eric's prideful and reassuring wink. Before them was an evening to be enjoyed, prolonged, remembered.

The day had known its moments of nostalgic sadness. They had gathered earlier in the hillside cemetery and stood beside the simple stones bearing the names of Lance Ainsley, Jim Daley, Robert Herndon, Mrs. Jorgenson, and a newer one inscribed Fred Herndon. She laid her son beside the father he had never remembered. The alchemy of passing time had eased her anguish. She walked from the carefully tended place with her hand nestled in Eric's with the bitter-sweet memories of yesterday receding before the cheer and warmth of a gathered family.

She sat proudly erect with all eyes turned toward her as she lifted a quieting hand. Her shining silver hair caught the soft glow of a chandelier. Across her face was the fretwork of lines seared by passing years. Yet, its eager smile and intense gray eyes seemed those of the child who had ridden pigtailed and wonder-struck into an Aspen of slab-sided shacks and of tents.

She bowed her head in a short, but meaningful, prayer. Then she said, "Before we eat, I have something special to announce. All of you know how badly Jimmy and Annette have wanted a child. They've been married seven years and no little tykes have arrived on the Lazy Seedy." She took an eager and deep breath. "All of this is about to change. This fall, in September, I'll be a grandmother. Annette is going to have a baby."

Maude said to Caroline, "I told them it would happen someday, Caroline. Things always work out down at the ranch. It takes time, but things work out. It's Daley magic."

Caroline suddenly laughed and reached out to clasp her daughter's hand. "I don't know about the Daley magic, honey," she said. "I've an idea you should credit nightly persistence!"

A crimson glow swept Annette's face. "Oh, Mother," she gasped. "You're, you're impossible." Then as laughter swept the table she buried her face in Jimmy Daley's shoulder.

"I suppose, Jimmy, you're set on it being a boy—a son," Shawn said.

Jimmy Daley pushed back his chair and rose to his feet. "We'll welcome either a boy or a girl. The desperate can't be choosers." His gaze fastened on Caroline's uplifted face. "But we really want a girl." He paused a moment, lifting a glass. "Yes, a girl. A girl who'll grow up as tall and as proud, as beautiful and as compassionate, as Caroline Ainsley Herndon Duane."

His hand beckoned them to their feet. "I propose a toast," he said. "A toast to Caroline. To Aspen. To the

390

Lazy Seedy. And even a mine called the Buccaneer. Destiny touched them all. Let none of us forget."

The next morning Shawn broached the subject that had brought him so hurriedly from Arizona. He and Caroline sat in a veranda swing, and Eric pulled a chair close to them. John drew the blue-penciled paper from a portfolio and handed it to Eric.

"Read this, Eric," he said, "and see if it makes sense to you."

At Caroline's questioning glance, he turned to explain. "Sis, when Aunt Maude cracked down on Grandfather there were some stocks and bonds he had to fork over. Remember?" She nodded, and he continued. "Among the stuff were shares in a mining company, The Sangre de Cristo Mining Corporation."

Eric scanned the paper and sat with it on his knee. He said, "As I remember, it was one of the few stocks we sized up as worthless. Jared Swope didn't have many investments that weren't shrewdly come by."

Shawn picked up the paper and underscored a market quotation with his finger. "Look at that figure, Caroline. There's something fantastic about it. Fantastic and fishy! Years ago I studied the very area where this outfit claims to have made a gold strike. It isn't there; it can't be there. I'm pretty familiar with gold-bearing stratas and ores. I'll stake my reputation that there's nothing sizable at Cascade. Nothing could warrant a stock jump of this kind."

Eric leaned forward to reply, but became silent at sight of Caroline's face.

"Where did you say, Shawn?" she whispered. "Where is the mine?"

Her brother turned to her with a surprised and curious gaze. "At Cascade. Over in the San Luis Valley, at the base of the mountains. It's an old forgotten settlement in the grass country beyond the irrigated farmland."

Caroline's eyes had widened with memory. "Cascade," she murmured. "Yes, that's it, the name of the place. It's where she went, and took Dr. Miller."

Both men were staring silently at her, amazed by her words and the rapt interest of her face.

Moments later Caroline smiled quietly. "You must think I'm daffy. Talking to myself, remembering." She rose, and her words grew agitated as she gazed down at them. "Cascade," she repeated. "It's a name from a past and buried time. I'll explain. Both of you know how I left Aspen after Bob was killed and I destroyed the Buccaneer and how I stowed away on a D and RG caboose. Perhaps I never told you the details of that night, and why the name Cascade is familiar."

They stared open-mouthed as she continued.

"When I rode back into town that night, Papa's housekeeper and her husband were waiting. They took care of Freddy while I was at the mine. I asked them to help me, help me hide, and get out of town. They took me to a house in shacktown. Frieda Edmonds and her little girl lived there. She was a practical nurse who worked for Dr. Miller and helped him on cases about town."

"Was she the one who helped you escape?" Shawn asked.

"No, others did that. I know Mrs. Edmonds and her daughter. That night she was frightened, almost hysterical. She told me that Dr. Miller had been found alive. That she was hiding him in her house, and that before morning she was leaving with some friends, some miners, for the San Luis Valley and Cascade."

Eric's eyes coursed his wife's face with wonder. "You never mentioned that Dr. Miller was found alive."

"Scarcely alive, Eric. He was beaten, terribly and brutally beaten. His memory was gone. He was a helpless, mumbling child."

Shawn's mind delved into words and facts from the past. "Wasn't he the one that had the office where Bob crawled and was murdered?"

"Yes, Shawn," she answered. The horror of that long-ago night echoed in her words. "Bob was killed and Dr. Miller beaten insensibly within the same hour. Bob told Dr. Miller something. I'm sure of that. Papa was sure of it, too." Caroline's words dropped off. The men on the

veranda beside her were silent and waited for the vividness of her memories to diminish and for composure to
return to her.

"Shawn," she said at last, "I want to go to Cascade if
you do. Perhaps Frieda or her daughter . . . ?"

"Caroline, it's been almost thirty years," Eric protested.
"Surely you don't expect——?"

"I don't know what to expect, Eric. But I want to go.
Perhaps there will be some trace of Frieda or Kathleen or
someone who knew them."

Shawn reread the stock-market quotation. "I'll be going
to Cascade all right," he said. "That's what brought me to
Aspen this time, sis. I'm going to look into this mining
thing. Find out what is going on and who's behind it. I'll
be glad to have you along. There's a narrow-gauge railroad from Salida. We can——"

"Not this time," Eric cut in firmly. "I'm going along,
too. Nowadays there's a passable auto road over Independence Pass into the Arkansas Valley and down to Salida.
We'll drive over."

Caroline watched the sun-glinted ripples of Hunter
Creek. "Frieda said our paths had crossed twice," she
murmured. "Let's go over to Cascade this week."

Chapter 23

The San Luis Valley was high, wide, and beautiful. It
reached northward almost a hundred miles from the New
Mexico boundary. Through much of its mountain ringed
vastness flowed the Rio Grande River, the El Rio Del
Norte of the Spaniards.

Eastward, it was shielded by the towering and rugged

Sangre de Cristo Mountains. On the west there were high, forested, and snow-capped mountains.

As Eric turned the car from the graded road that threaded the valley's center, their way became a rutted trail. Eastward and above them lay Cascade. Fences were left behind them, as was a constant and choking dust plume from the wheels of their car. The thickening herds of range stock were different from the stubby-legged Herefords of the Lazy Seedy.

They sighted buildings toward the north. The sprawling ranch buildings were half-obscured in a grove of ancient cottonwood trees.

When they came abreast of the distant buildings, reaching a point where wagon tracks diverged from the road, a rider spurred his horse from a grassy knoll and halted in the middle of the road to block their passing. When the car halted, he reined in closely. He was a thin, black-bearded man, clad in faded denims and wearing a holstered gun.

"Ain't you folks lost?" he asked.

"I've about decided we are," Eric answered wryly. "This road would confuse Jim Bridger."

His jest was lost on the grim-faced rider. "Better turn around and head out," he said. "You're trespassin' on private property."

Eric eyed him quietly. "Isn't this the road to Cascade?"

"Sure. But this is a closed road. Private. Cascade is private property, too. Now wheel around, fellow."

At his words, Caroline would have objected if Shawn had not shot her a warning glance, and said to the rider, "This isn't the way I was told we would be welcomed." He turned to Eric. "All right, we'll do as the man says. These people don't want capital invested; we'll find something for our money elsewhere."

The remark brought a quick change to the rider's face. "Maybe it'll be all right. Go ahead into town. You'll find the mine office about a block west of the store."

As the car rumbled ahead, Shawn spoke urgently. "I've seen a setup like this once or twice before. They stink to the moon. I've an idea you should go easy about mention-

394

ing anyone you know. From now on, we're capitalists. Better yet, suckers aching to be plucked. Try and see everything. Then say nothing."

The ghostly appearance of the old town, struggling against the forest and the oblivion that sought to reclaim it, seemed upon first sight to be but an extension of Aspen. On a main street there was nothing more than a short road slashed through the pinion woods and across a swift-running creek. Already the mountains were a precipitous and guarding barrier scarcely half a mile beyond. Rusting steel topped a narrow-gauge railroad bed. A depot tumbled into decay.

Despite the town's forlorn aspect, there was activity with more people about than they had expected. Their arrival brought quiet stares from people who looked them over and then turned, tight-lipped and unsmiling, to go their way.

"The place gives me the shivers," Eric commented. "There's something hanging over it."

Shawn peered down the street. His survey was studiedly casual but penetrating. "We'll be watched," he said. "Nobody comes into this sort of place without having a tab kept on him."

They halted finally before a two-story house set well back from the road. It was adjoined by a half-acre lot strewn with pipe and equipment. A high fence of tightly strung barbed wire encircled it. Shawn ran a critically appraising eye across it. "There has been money, lots of it, put into that stuff. It's hydraulic equipment. New, powerful, and expensive."

Nearby a small sign acknowledged the building as the mine office. They left the auto, mounted plank steps, and entered. They paused momentarily in a hallway leading toward the open door of an office.

"Mind if I do the talking?" Shawn whispered. "I have an idea."

They agreed and walked down the corridor to a spacious, well-lighted room. A young man met them. His affable smile was fixed; his eyes swept their clothes and faces in a calculating manner. "Good afternoon," he said briskly. "What can I do for you?"

Shawn's eyes and mind coordinated many things. "My name is Swope," he said and thrust out his hand. "This is Mr. and Mrs. Duane who are traveling with me. We thought you might be able to recommend a suitable place for us to spend a night or so in Cascade."

The clerk's face bleakened. "I'm sorry, Mr. Swope. We can't offer overnight accommodations in Cascade. The houses are occupied by our workmen. We have no hotel."

Shawn allowed his face to show regretful annoyance. "We had hoped to stay. The Duanes are looking for suitable investment possibilities. I recommended they come here. My family already holds considerable stock in your company."

The clerk's gaze moved uncertainly toward the closed door of an office behind him. "I'll ask Mr. Fenton, our office manager. Perhaps he can discuss our property with you right away."

Shawn turned from him. "It doesn't matter. Mr. and Mrs. Duane have other properties in mind to visit. If there is no place for us to rest, we'll return to Salida."

The clerk lifted a staying hand. "I'm sure Mr. Fenton wouldn't want you turned away. Have a seat, please. I'll talk to him."

When the inner door had been closed behind the young man for several minutes, Shawn leaned toward Caroline with whispered words. "Right now I'll wager the dusty stock records of this shebang are getting a frantic once over. Swope is my name. Don't forget!"

After a while an older man appeared from the back office. "Mr. Swope," he said in greeting, "I'm sorry if our clerk was abrupt. We have so many sightseers with so little space and time for them."

"I'm sure you do." Shawn smiled. He wondered if a single curious sightseer had ever gotten past the mounted guard three miles down the road.

"It so happens," Fenton said, "one of our officials is away on business. I'm sure he wouldn't mind our offering you his quarters for the night."

396

Shawn's answering grin was wide and guileless. "As a stockholder, I appreciate your thoughtfulness, Mr. Fenton. In the morning I'm sure I shall want to urge Mr. and Mrs. Duane to invest in corporate stock."

Fenton lifted a key from a hook board and donned his hat. "I'll show you to the cottage. It's small but comfortable."

"Thank you," Shawn answered. "And about meals? Do you have a restaurant in Cascade?"

Fenton's eyes grew wary. "No place you folks would care to eat. We can arrange to have dinner and breakfast brought to the cottage."

When they were in the car and moving down a cottonwood-lined side road Caroline voiced a question that sprang from her seemingly careless observation of the village. "Mr. Fenton, the mines must be quite large. Do all of these people in town work there?"

"Not all," he answered guardedly. "There are ranches about. Some of the men are employed by them; their families live here in Cascade."

He's lying, Caroline thought quickly. There is one ranch and one mine. Nothing else within twenty or thirty miles. Somehow they're linked together, the ranch and the mine.

The cottage proved to be a four-room house far better kept than those about it. Its modern conveniences and furnishings caused Eric to chuckle after they were sure Fenton was well on his way back to the office. "Being a potential investor has its advantages. This must be the royal suite."

"It's more likely the shearing pen," Shawn muttered.

Caroline gazed thoughtfully from the window. "I wonder on which street and which house Frieda lived. It's possible she's still here, but she would be very old."

Shawn pulled off his coat and stretched comfortably on a couch. "You've got to remember it's been well onto thirty years since she came here, sis. That's a long, long time. Perhaps she moved. Or died."

Eric joined his wife at the window. "We're being watched," he said presently. "Don't stare. But that man down by the corner among those cedars has his eye on this house."

"I expected it," Shawn said, nodding. "That about rubs out any chance of looking for your friend Frieda or word of her. If we go looking or asking questions, they'll know their investors are up to something."

Caroline sank into a chair and sat silently for a long time. "I've a feeling," she said at last, "that I'm going to be terribly, terribly sick."

Their startled and concerned faces caused her to smile. "Two of us can play a game, Shawn. Mine is a long shot. I doubt there is a doctor in this settlement. Who would be called if I suddenly needed medical attention or help?"

A dawning comprehension marked Shawn's words. "It might work. It might just possibly work if she's still here. You said Frieda Edmonds was a practical nurse. But she's so old——"

"Her daughter isn't," Caroline answered. "Kathleen probably learned nursing from her mother. There's an outside chance——" She paused and shrugged discouragedly. "Oh, I'm doing idle scheming, wishful thinking."

"Any kind of thinking beats none," Eric said slowly. "Do you suppose you could make it seem real? Real enough they wouldn't wise up?"

"I can get awfully sick." Caroline laughed softly. "But I'll wait until after they send our dinner over. I want to be comfortably ill."

The town lay in deep twilight, and far above a fading rose hue across the ice fields marked the end of day. Shawn Ainsley slammed the door of the cottage behind him and loped swiftly toward the nearest house a half block down the street. He ignored a barking dog and rushed onto the porch. His pounding at the door was frenzied and brought quick response from a slatternly, middle-aged woman. She eyed him in dismay.

"I hope you can help me," he panted. "Is there a doctor in town? Mrs. Duane has taken ill. Very ill."

"Mrs. Duane?" The words fell uncomprehendingly from the woman's slackening lips.

"I'm sorry, ma'am. Sorry I startled you. But we need a doctor. Quick. We're staying at the cottage."

"There's no doctor hereabouts. Ain't been for years."

"But there must be someone who can help us. Perhaps Mr. Fenton could send someone. Some woman. . . ." Shawn paused, aware that mention of Fenton's name had kindled assurance in the woman's face. He was sure, too, that a figure had detached itself from the cedar clump and moved within earshot.

"What ails your wife?" the woman in the door was asking.

"Mrs. Duane isn't my wife," Shawn explained in jerking and worried tone. "Mr. and Mrs. Duane are here on business with me. Her husband is with her now. He's helpless, so am I. I'm afraid she's desperately ill."

The woman glanced quickly beyond him. Shawn surmised that a sign reached her from the man out in the street. She peered abruptly back into her house. "Tommy," she yelled, "get down to Kathleen Bishop's house and tell her there's a sick woman up at the mine cottage. Hurry now. Scat!"

In that moment Shawn Ainsley could have laughed triumphantly aloud. *Kathleen,* his mind tolled. Damned if Caroline hasn't come up with the right idea. He managed to keep his face agitated. "Thank you, ma'am. You're very kind. I'd best be getting back to the cottage. I hope the lady hurries."

The calm woman who minutes later came swiftly up the path was nearing middle age. She wore a light jacket against the evening chill. Her gingham dress was clean and neatly ironed. Eric met her at the door.

"I've been told there is a lady here who is ill." As she entered, her gaze searched the room and the men awaiting her.

"It's my wife," Eric explained. "She's lying down in the bedroom. I'm afraid it's stomach trouble; she's susceptible."

"I am Kathleen Bishop," she answered. "I hope I can help. I'm not a doctor." She moved quickly into the bedroom.

Caroline uneasily awaited her. The risk now was enormous. Even a practical nurse would quickly detect fakery. She twisted her face in pain. "I'm so glad you're here," she panted. "Men are such a helpless lot." As she spoke, Caroline peered into the woman's face and steady eyes. She strived to match them to a memory of the solemn-faced child she remembered so vaguely as Frieda Edmonds's small daughter. Her decision was sudden, gauged to the possibility that they would be given little time alone. "Please close the door," she said and added, as the woman turned back to her, "I'm Mrs. Duane. What is your name?"

"I'm Kathleen Bishop. Was this a sudden seizure, Mrs. Duane?"

"Kathleen Edmonds Bishop," Caroline said softly.

The name and the manner of its coming caused the woman to stiffen. Her blue eyes grew large. "How did you know that? Who are you? What do you want?"

Caroline struggled into sitting position. "Kathleen, don't be frightened. Try to remember me. I'm the woman your mother and her friends helped escape Aspen on the night she brought you to Cascade. Kathleen, is your mother here? Is she still alive?"

"Yes," Kathleen Bishop murmured. "She lives here in the village." She paused, her practiced eyes intense on Caroline. "You're not ill," she breathed softly. "Not ill at all. Why did you summon me?"

"It was my only way of finding out, Kathleen. I came here to see your mother. Here in town we've been watched, guarded, treated like spies. There was no way I could seek your mother out."

"How do you know I won't tell them now?" Kathleen asked slowly.

"Because you couldn't; you're Frieda Edmonds's daughter."

There was the sound of the outer door opening. Fenton's voice was sharply questioning in the adjoining room.

"Yes," Shawn's voice cut through. "Mrs. Duane has been taken very ill. Perhaps because of the water or something in the food. Mrs. Bishop is with her now."

With deft hands Kathleen pushed Caroline down and

drew a blanket over her. She leaned forward, her words lightly whispered. "You were foolish to come here, Mrs. Duane. This is a dangerous, deadly town."

"Why do you stay, Kathleen?"

"My mother is here. She needs me. I buried a husband here. Where else would I go?" The almost inaudible words gave way to a louder, briskly professional tone. "Here, I'll give you these, Mrs. Duane. They should ease the pain."

Caroline clutched her companion's hand. "Kathleen," she murmured, "can you bring her here? Bring your mother to see me?"

There was long hesitation. Kathleen's lips moved to form whispered words. "I'll try. Since you're so ill, or will be tonight, I'll need her help, her advice."

Caroline's grasp tightened in silent thanks. Then she turned to the wall. The groan of pain that escaped her carried convincing agony to the ears of Mr. Fenton.

Ten minutes passed before Kathleen Bishop came gravely into the room where Eric and Shawn sat silently waiting. Fenton still lingered.

"Which of you," she asked, "is Mr. Duane?"

The question brought Eric upright, suddenly not entirely sure that all of his wife's restless tossing and her cries of pain were sham.

"I'm Eric Duane," he said quickly. "How is she?"

"She's very ill and needs medical attention at once." Kathleen turned from him and walked to Fenton's side. "Mr. Fenton, we must send for a doctor."

Fenton's face grew troubled. "A doctor? Is it that bad? There's no doctor nearer than Monte Vista or Sacuache. It would be hours, perhaps morning, before one could possibly get here."

"I know," she said. "And there's no one in Cascade, except . . . no, it's out of the question."

Fenton was impatient. "What's out of the question, Mrs. Bishop?"

Kathleen's reply was reluctant. "My mother has taken care of such cases. She knows the symptoms and complications. She's familiar with drugs and remedies that doc-

401

tors used years ago." Her voice trailed off. "But mother is old. So very old."

Shawn sensed there was a cue in the woman's words. "If your mother can help Mrs. Duane she must come." He turned to Fenton. "You have a telephone at the office. Is there an outside line to Salida, or Alamosa, or Saguache?"

"There normally is," Fenton answered, "but the line's out of repair."

Shawn sensed the man was lying. Probably Fenton was under orders to use it only for mine affairs. He allowed annoyance to mark his reply. "Mr. and Mrs. Duane are quite wealthy and influential. Everything possible must be done at once, Fenton."

Fenton's face was a mirror for his thoughts. These people were strangers. They were annoying. Yet one is a stockholder who must be mollified. The others seek investments. Obviously, they're monied people. He turned slowly to Kathleen Bishop. "Bring your mother over here," he said curtly.

She shook her head and moved toward the bedroom door, which scantily muffled the sounds of Caroline's ordeal. "I must stay, Mr. Fenton. Mrs. Duane is too ill to be left alone. Could you send someone to bring my mother?"

"Yes. Yes, of course," Fenton said. At the door he paused. "I can stop by and tell her myself; be glad to."

Caroline lay very still and wide-eyed when Frieda Edmonds pushed open the door and came quietly into the bedroom. There was but a single window in the room. The carefulness with which Kathleen had drawn the shade brought memory of another window that had been blanketed, and the time she had last seen this woman.

Kathleen waited for her mother and led her quickly aside to whisper urgent words. During these moments, as incomprehension gave way to wonder in Frieda Edmonds's aged face, Caroline noted the snowy whiteness of her hair, the sparseness of her stooped figure, and their contrast to alert and questioning eyes. She's old, Caroline thought. Very old. But thank God she isn't crippled or

402

senile. She will remember me. Remember Aspen. Perhaps even Fort Steele and the time the train stopped there.

When at last Frieda came to the bedside, it was with outthrust and trembling hands, with a troubled but joyous face. "Caroline," she said softly, "at last. At last. The years are so long. So many of them."

"Frieda. You said—that last night—our paths might cross. I had to see you. This was the only way."

Momentary mischief lighted Frieda's eyes. "Let me look at you, Caroline. You're the healthiest, loveliest, dying woman I ever saw."

A warning gesture from Kathleen muffled Caroline's laughter. "Tell me," she said. "About yourself. About Kathleen. About Dr. Miller."

"We're here, Caroline. We're alive. Thirty years hasn't done us in."

"Even Dr. Miller is alive," Caroline marveled. "How is he, Frieda? Did he really recover?"

"His body did, Caroline. It took a long time. Years. But he's still spry. Sprier than most sane people."

"You mean——?" Caroline whispered.

"His mind went the night he was beaten. His memory never returned. He's still a child."

"And you still take care of him? You've done it all these years?"

"Who else was there?" Frieda Edmonds answered simply, and then asked, "But about you? Why did you come here—into danger?" The concern in her words and her eyes caused Caroline to sit up quickly. "Frieda, what is wrong here in Cascade? What frightens the town and the people? What has brought it about? Who?"

There was the swift, unbelieving intake of Frieda Edmonds's breath, the dismay and wonder across her face. "You mean you came here not knowing, Caroline? You didn't know that this town, the mine, and even the ranch are in the scheming, bloody hands of *Len and Matt Shaner?*"

Caroline's reply was so shock-ridden that it dulled her words and tore her face. "The Shaners. You mean they are here in Cascade?"

403

"No, Caroline. Not in town. They have men like Fenton in charge here. They stay at the ranch and at the mine. The mine's on ranch property."

"They've been here all these years?" Caroline asked.

"Only about three years. Before that, the town was quiet, peaceful. It died down years ago when the mine petered out."

"But the mine didn't play out, Frieda. It's owned by a New York company. They are planning heavy and costly expansion. The company shares have gone sky high."

"The mine is owned by the ranch," Frieda persisted stubbornly. "Owned by the Shaners. I know they have plans of some sort afoot. They've brought men and machinery in. But there is no gold ore. There never was any of value."

Sudden concern was upon Caroline. "Do they know you're here, that you live here, Frieda? Do they know about Dr. Miller?"

"Yes, they know. They knew from the first."

"And they leave you be? They don't harm you?" Caroline was incredulous.

"They visited me, Caroline. It was one of the first things they did in Cascade. I was ready for them."

Caroline leaned forward, panting. "Ready for them? How?"

"I had already mailed letters to the newspapers in Denver. I told Matt Shaner that those letters were to be opened if anything happened to Dr. Miller. That the letters told of the murder in Aspen. They believed me. They had to believe me. We've been safe."

Caroline spoke decisively. "Frieda, one of the men here is my brother. He came here to investigate the mining company. May I call him in? Will you tell him what you have told me?"

The retelling was swiftly done. When it was over, Shawn Ainsley's face was angry, perplexed, and purposeful. "You mean the men who killed Bob Herndon and stole your Buccaneer are here? That they're behind this stock deal?"

404

Caroline nodded. "But why? What can they accomplish?"

Shawn turned to Mrs. Edmonds. "Do they own the ranch?"

"I don't think so. It seems it used to belong to a family in Boston. They hired men to run it. It is terribly large ... thirty or forty miles long and from the peaks clear out into the valley. It would cost a fortune."

A dawning revelation surged into Shawn's face. "What a scheme," he murmured. "Bold. Daring. Ingenious. Take a worthless mine with traces of gold. Salt it. Salt it good. Then form a Wall Street company and boost the stock clear to heaven. Buy hydraulic equipment. Bring the lambs—the unsuspecting—out West and let them see high-pressure jets washing away a mountain. Sell the stock. Sell it quick. Sell it high. Then buy a ranch." His face twisted in unwilling, almost unbelieving, admiration. "The fantastic idea of it. The sheer guts."

Kathleen Bishop had remained quiet for a long time, nervously watchful and listening. Now she peered shrewdly at Shawn. "Mr. Swope, you know mining. It is a hydraulic development, the pipe, the equipment."

He smiled broadly at her. "I should know something of it. I'm a mining engineer."

Her face tensed. "If they find that out, they'll kill you."

"Probably," he agreed. "They're playing for fast, high stakes. They wouldn't be easy losers."

"They never were," Caroline said. Her face was white and worried.

"I should leave now," Frieda muttered reluctantly. "If both I and Kathleen stay too long, Fenton may get suspicious." She stood quiet a moment then added, "Why couldn't it have been different? So that we could have visited a long while?" She grasped Caroline's hands again. "We have so much to remember. So much in common."

Caroline clung to her. "Don't leave. Not just yet, Frieda. Where is Dr. Miller? Tell me about him."

"He is safe, Caroline. For a long time I had to keep him in the house and in the yard. I built a high board fence around my house, my yard. But people knew he was

405

there. Gradually they accepted him. Now he is free. Free to roam the village, night or day. They give him scant notice. They call him the old crazy man, the harmless imbecile."

Through her words, Shawn quietly listened, his hands shoved in his pockets, and his face remote and thoughtful. Now he wheeled about. "Mrs. Edmonds, I know this area. Years ago I plodded about every acre of it. Where is the mine? For a hydraulic operation it would have to be on a creek, a swift one. But which? Where?"

"I've never been up to the Shaners' development," she answered. "No one from town is allowed past the guards. Likely though it is near the old gold site five miles from here up Glacier Creek."

Shawn's eyes closed as he struggled to trace a mental map. "Glacier Creek," he said at last, and spoke his thoughts aloud. "Go north. Climb the first upthrust. Detour around the hogback and through Gannett Park. Hit the headwaters, then drop down." His face grew eager. "It would work. By God, it would work. It'd bring one in smack behind their playhouse."

Caroline lifted a protesting hand, then abruptly let it drop. Already she knew his plan, and the desperate chances it involved. She listened spellbound as Shawn laid his hands on Frieda's shoulders. "Mrs. Edmonds, is there a chance we could get hold of horses? Tonight?"

Her furrowed face gathered confidence and a lurking adventurous gleam. "It might be arranged. But you'd have to get past the man they have watching outside on guard."

Kathleen glanced at the beaten leather bag her mother was grasping. "I detest Fenton. Detest what they've done, he and the Shaners, to our town. To Cascade. Mother, is it in there? You usually carry some—some chloroform."

Frieda chuckled softly as she handed a small bottle to Shawn. "Not too much of this," she warned. "Unless you want to put him out of the way for good. A few whiffs on a cloth."

Shawn looked at her in fascinated wonder. "Why are you doing this? Why are you risking so much?" he demanded.

"Fiddle," she snorted. "I risk nothing. Your sister was resting easier. I went home. Kathleen went home. You stole the bottle. Slipped it from the bag." She straightened, then added, "Besides, get your sister to tell you about the first time we ever met. Have her recall an immigrant train in Wyoming. A baby. A baby named Kathleen."

Kathleen moved to Caroline's side. "Can you ride a horse Mrs. Duane? Ride well?"

"Yes. I've always ridden."

"Then you should go. All of you should leave. I'll manage about horses. You'll have to leave your auto. It's better to lose it than your lives. There's a pass and a trail up on Glacier Creek. It'll take you across the range into Wet Mountain Valley. From there you can reach the plains around Pueblo."

For long moments Caroline clung tightly to both of these courageous women. "Come and see me. Come to Aspen," she pleaded.

"I'd like that," Frieda managed through tears, and turned to the door. She opened it to the night, and said in a louder tone, "Remember, Kathleen. The medication. Every hour. Call me if she doesn't improve." Then she was gone.

Chapter 24

The hour neared midnight as Kathleen Bishop slipped into her jacket. "The town will be asleep now, except for the man they have stationed to watch. He'll see me leave. Possibly he will ask how things are here. It may be half an hour before I can have horses."

"How can you get them at night, alone?" Eric asked. "One of us could meet you, and help after the guard——"

"No," she answered firmly. "I have friends. Friends who trust me and will help. Some of them will be happy to trick Fenton and the Shaners."

Eric and Shawn waited until she disappeared into darkness. The time had come. Their searching out of the guard must be swift and silent. Through the rear door of the cottage they came into the night and a raspberry patch. Their way lay along a rutted and trash-strewn alley. There was the possibility of rousing barking dogs. They crept the length of the block with agonizing slowness. The street must be crossed now before they could approach the cedar thicket and the man they had sighted there so many hours before.

"He could have moved," Shawn whispered. "He could be anywhere about."

Eric's answer was a sudden thrust of his hand over Shawn's lips. He moved closer. His words were scarcely audible. "Over there," he said, and pointed. "He must have walked away with Kathleen." As they crouched in watchful waiting, the guard moved closer, angling across the deserted street. They knew then that he was headed toward the cottage, intent on a closer survey of its silently looming form and the pale streak of light leaking past the insufficient cover of its blinds.

As the dark figure drew nearer, Eric stooped, tugged at his shoes, then stood sock-footed in the dewing grass. He leapt and his arms encircled the guard's face; his hands clamped the man's mouth with silencing, smothering force. It was Shawn's cue for action. His low onrush swept the guard's feet from beneath him and brought him sprawling into the dust of the roadway. Even as the stranger's hand sought urgently for a weapon, they were upon him and pinned him in helplessly struggling silence.

The work of the rag and the bottle was swift if not expert. Their prisoner's breath deepened to a gasping, choking fight for air. The power of his struggling dropped away. He lay silent and limp beneath them.

When later they lifted him, tied and gagged, his limpness and the manner of his breathing caused them to look at each other in speculation as to whether consciousness would return.

They carried him back into the gloom of the alley into tall and tangled grass beside a dilapidated rail fence. They lowered him into it, knowing that it would hide him, but that if he should again come to his senses he could roll into the alley, where at daylight he would be seen.

As Shawn and Eric rose to leave him, the menace of noise brought them tensely erect and quiet. There was the sound of rapidly shuffling footsteps approaching along the alley. There was no time nor chance to hide or to get away. One moment there was only the enveloping gloom of night. The next an old man whose white hair and stooped form belied the quiet ease of his movements. He brought his face within inches of Eric's and peered silently upward.

He was clad in miner's boots, worn black trousers, and a denim jacket. His face held them motionless and silent. Upon it there was neither anger nor friendship. The eyes were those of a staring, uncomprehending child. He spoke. The words were a babbling, incoherent murmur.

A thrust of intuitive wonder cut through Eric Duane. "My God, Shawn," he whispered. "It's the old doctor. Dr. Miller." He reached out a cautious hand, but the old man shied back from it. When at last they moved cautiously toward the cottage, the stranger followed and matched his gait to their uneasy progress.

When they reached the raspberry patch Shawn watched with amazement the expert sense with which the old man kept clear of entangling branches. "He moves like a squirrel," Shawn marveled in a whisper. "I'm half-blind and awkward. But look at him, Eric. Cat-footed and owl-eyed. He must roam half the valley or the mountains at night."

His words caused the stranger's gaze to move toward him, but it was a vacant stare, void of knowing and of understanding.

Kathleen waited at the darkened door of the kitchen with Caroline. Their desperation, born of the appearance of this eerie stranger and of the possibility of his crying out, or bringing others upon them, was etched across their faces. She sensed it as she spoke reassuring words. "It's only the doctor. He's harmless. Curious and harmless. You are someone new in town and in the night. It attracts him."

Her voice brought the old man quickly to her side, and she threw a protective arm about him. "Carry the man," he said in halting words. "Throw the man in the grass."

Kathleen glanced inquiringly at them, and Shawn said, "The guard is out of the way, tied up in the alley. Did you manage about the horses?"

"Yes. We have horses for you, good horses that are used to mountain trails. There are saddlebags with a few provisions. And rainslickers, if you should need them." Kathleen motioned them closer, then continued. "There are three horses hidden in a pinion grove a quarter mile north of town. A man you can trust is there with them. He is masked and will not speak aloud to you. Don't try to thank him or to learn who he is."

"Thank you, Kathleen, for everything," Shawn said in relief. "How do we reach the pinions, the right grove?"

"Walk north along the alley," she explained. "It ends in a couple of blocks, then two small trails branch off. Be sure to take the left one; it veers westward just a little. And be very quiet."

They briefly stood silently. The desperation of their planned escape was upon them. They thought, too, of how much the daughter of Frieda Edmonds had risked to aid them. Caroline drew Kathleen into her arms. The "thanks" of Shawn and Eric brought a wistful smile to their friend's face. "You had better go now," she said. "Hurry."

As they came to the kitchen door, the old man glided from the shadows to stand at Kathleen's side. He would have followed Shawn and the Duanes had not Kathleen restrained him. "Stay here," she said softly. "Stay with Kathleen."

It took only a few minutes to pass along the darkened alley, seek out the left-forked trail, and to climb upward and abreast of the silent, masked stranger. They mounted the horses he held in waiting.

Shawn studied the narrowing canyon, and the swiftly

410

climbing escarpment before them. "It's coming back to me now," he said. "In two more hours with luck we will be in Gannett Park. We'll come onto Glacier Creek there and can follow it down to the Shaners' bonanza."

"Must we?" Caroline asked in a tired and worried voice. "Kathleen said we could ride out into Wet Mountain Valley, out of this accursed country." She scanned her brother's face. "What have we to gain by taking the risk? Meddling around the mine? Shawn, I have had enough of mines and their damnable doings for a lifetime."

Her words brought stubborn, unyielding response as Shawn urged his horse ahead. "You're forgetting, Caroline, who's behind these shenanigans. The Shaners, the men who killed Bob and pirated the Buccaneer."

"No," she said, "I haven't forgotten," and then was silent.

"I wasn't in Aspen when they were on a plundering rampage," Shawn continued thoughtfully. "Later, when I used Bob's office for a classroom, I wished to heaven I had been around in the old days, that I could have taken a hand." He quieted and reined his horse clear of an alder thicket.

When they had followed, he spoke again. "Something else has always plagued me, haunted me. Those loggers that brought about Dad's death—and Jim Daley's—on the mesa. I don't know for sure, probably never will know. But I've had a hunch they were tied in with the Shaners. Who else would have killed an Ainsley over a patch of timber?"

There was determination in the touch of Caroline's heels to her horse. "If you believe that, Shawn, if there is a chance it's true, we're riding down Glacier Creek. We're going to look over Len and Matt Shaner's handiwork."

They rode a long time in silence, and descended a rock-strewn slope into Gannett Park. Eric, who rode in the rear, checked his horse abruptly and called out, "Stop a minute. Wait and be quiet. There's someone following us. Horseback."

They drew together, listening to the plodding hoofbeats that marked another horse's descent of the slope. A min-

411

ute passed. Another. Then suddenly the rider was beside them and they sighed in relief and amazement. It was Dr. Miller who peered blankly at them. Eric reined closer and reached out. This time the old man did not shrink back, and he allowed Eric's hand to lie on his arm.

"Go back," Eric said patiently. "Go back to Kathleen. Back to Frieda."

The old man's response was but a childish murmur. "Ride the horse," he said again and again.

Anger, resurgent across the years, tightened Caroline's face. "The Shaners. The bastardly Shaners. They did this to a fine surgeon. Beat sanity from him. Ended his career."

Shawn stared worriedly at Dr. Miller. "What can we do with him? We can't send him back or make him understand to go back. We can't take him with us away from Cascade."

"I've an idea he's been up here often," Eric answered thoughtfully. "Probably he knows every inch of these mountains. When we leave them and get into strange country, he'll turn back. We're something new, something different, and we attract him. It'll wear off in time."

"We've little time to find out," Shawn fretted, "and we're wasting it. He'll have to ride along." He urged his horse forward on the trail.

The four rode through the night. They cut across Gannett Park, sought out the narrow and swift course of Glacier Creek, and swung westward down its course. Within a hundred yards they were in a narrow, twisting gorge. Shawn swore at the dimness and uncertainty of the scant trail.

He paused to search its way when Dr. Miller let his horse move forward. They watched in curious silence. Then they followed single file as the strange old man held his mount unerringly to the narrow, obscure path that led downstream.

They could only guess how many miles they rode—perhaps three, perhaps five. Then the canyon widened to spread between high walls and offer the smoother footing of a heavily grassed meadow.

412

They traveled its length and came again into a sharply descending canyon. Moments later Shawn checked his horse. An amazed gasp prefaced his words. "Pipe! They've put in large-enough pipe to carry almost the whole creek." He studied the pipe and its swift fall before them. "With that volume and pressure they could wash a mountain away. They'd need heavy mechanical jets to control it. The modern ones."

His words reminded Caroline of Wilderness Creek and the turgid flood it had carried when Hardrock Corlett's claims had been placered.

"They've always liked to wash gold, not dig for it," she commented tersely.

"They're not washing gold," Shawn answered abruptly. "Not in this area. This's strictly a sucker setup. For show. For selling their worthless stock."

Eric stared at the overhanging stars. "If we intend to make sure tonight, let's get moving. Daylight comes early this time of year."

"It won't be far now," Shawn reasoned. "They couldn't have more than a half mile of pipe with this fall. The pressure would rip it apart."

Caroline lifted an anxiously warning hand. "If we're so close, shouldn't we leave the horses here and go afoot? Sound carries far in this thin air."

While they tethered their animals in the denseness of a spruce clump, Eric probed the night with anxious eyes. "We're shy one traveler," he muttered. "The old man, your Dr. Miller, must have ridden on ahead when we stopped."

They listened, hoping for a clue of his whereabouts, but there were only the sounds of mountain darkness and their own breathing.

"If he rode on down there," Shawn worried. "I wish he were here or back in Cascade."

They inched cautiously to the side of the pipe, then crept its course as it dropped through a sheer-walled, narrow canyon. After the walls of the canyon had lowered behind them, they came into another meadowed park. Encircling hills were silhouetted against the sky. Shawn

413

paused and scanned the area. "I remember this spot. Years ago, during the gold rush days at Cripple Creek, prospectors drifted down this way and honeycombed every ridge. There were sizable shafts and a few traces of gold and lead."

Eric listened with diverted attention. "I still wish our confounded old doctor would loom up. I'd feel more comfortable, safer."

Caroline's answer carried more hope than assurance, as she said, "Probably he rode on through down the creek. He may be halfway to Cascade by now."

Her brother scanned the eastern horizon and the faint tinge of light marking it. "Let's get on. Daylight isn't an hour off. Let's take a look and get out of here."

"Look at what?" Caroline demanded. "You've seen the pipe and know what sort of setup this is. Why go farther?"

Shawn shook his head. "I've got to know," he answered. "I must see the wash area and get hold of some ore specimens if there is any ore. I have an idea it will be clay, plain worthless clay, instead."

They had gone less than a hundred yards farther when they glimpsed Dr. Miller's horse on the trail before them. An instant later they realized that the animal was riderless, that the old man had slid from his saddle and kneeled close to the animal's left foreleg. His hands encircled the horse's leg and were tugging it upward as they drew nearer.

"His horse is lame," Caroline whispered. "Probably a stone bruise."

Before she could say more, or they could come to the strange, old doctor's side, a snort of fright and pain broke from the riderless horse. Suddenly he reared. A wild and twisting leap brought him about and over the old man. His rear hooves lashed in a frightened, vicious kick.

It was abruptly over. There was the dull thud of a hoof striking against Dr. Miller's head. He spun from his knees and sprawled in the dust of the trail, where he lay limp and quiet. A nervous whinny broke from the horse as he trotted a few yards from them to stand nervous and heavy-breathed.

414

Caroline broke into panicked steps and knelt at Dr. Miller's side. Her hands stretched quickly out to lift his face from the dirt. Her sleeve wiped across his forehead.

Shawn and Eric came to her side as she said, "He's bleeding. Look! It tore his scalp, above his ear."

Eric dropped to his knees, his head lowering to the sprawled man's chest. "He's still breathing. Could be a concussion. Fracture."

Shawn looked quickly about. "We'll need water. Maybe there's still a trickle in the——"

His words were cut off by a groan passing from the doctor's lips. They hovered quickly over him. There were moaning sounds, and a pained struggling, as his head broke from Caroline's hand and jerked upward. Words formed on his lips. They were groping and uncertain yet strangely audible, words. "Don't, Shaner, For Christ's sake, don't do it. Don't shoot him again. He's gone. Dead. Bob Herndon is dead I tell you!"

A small cry of realization and wonder broke from Caroline and seemed to draw Dr. Miller's stare as his eyes came slowly open. "Who are you?" he murmured. He shoved a wildly strong hand against her. "Go get him. Get Lance Ainsley. Matt's brother has killed Herndon."

Caroline gathered the old man's white, dirt-streaked head into her arms. Her head fell forward, heedless that blood stained her scarf. "It's all right, Dr. Miller. I'm here. I'm Caroline Ainsley and I'm here."

He was quiet a long time as Shawn Ainsley sought out water and they bathed his wound. Finally he looked up again, and now reason and awareness rode his gaze. "Where am I? Are they still waiting in my office? They'll beat me again."

"They're gone," Caroline whispered. "They've been gone from Aspen a long time."

His eyes fixed on the faintly coming dawn that streaked the east. "It is nearly morning. Take me to Lance. Don't let Frieda go to the office until Lance——"

Shawn's hands sought out the old man's palms and clasped them. "Dr. Miller, can you hear me? Understand me?"

"Yes," the word came as a gentle sigh. "I hear you. Who are you?"

Shawn strove for words that would carry comprehension, but not shock. "I'm Shawn Ainsley, Lance's son. You've been ill for a long time, a very long time. Now you're better. We're in the mountains, looking for the Shaners."

The doctor shook free of their hands and elbowed his way to sit up. "I'm going with you. They beat me. Pistol-whipped me. Wrecked my office. Lance will want me with him."

A firmness, born of desperation and fleeting time, marked Shawn's answer. "Dr. Miller, you must know and realize a long, long time, years have passed since that night in Aspen. Lance died years ago."

"You mean I've been——" The terror of full realization crept into Dr. Miller's words and face. He thrust out a hand and gazed at it. "I'm, I'm an old man. What has happened to me? What stole my time, my years?"

"Amnesia," Eric said quietly. "Amnesia brought on by a vicious beating."

The doctor gazed about him in bewildered unbelief. "But you said the Shaners are in these mountains. That you're going after them?"

"They have another mine close to here," Shawn explained, then added, "We want to see it. We'll be gone but a little while. One of us will stay with you."

"I'll stay and care for him," Caroline whispered.

He stood erect, pushed them from him, and stood spraddle-legged on the trail. "None of us will stay. If the Shaners are hereabouts, I'll go. I can walk. Maybe, maybe I can get close enough——" His hands swept out in a gesture of rending, tearing passion. They could only yield and take him with them.

They crept along the pipe and out into the flatness of the park. Presently before them was a dark cluster of buildings that stood off northward a hundred yards from a sharply overhanging cliff. There was no sign of movement or of habitation. There were only the buildings, the cliff, and the predawn quiet.

416

They moved cautiously along the pipe. Abruptly it was no longer at their side; instead their way was blocked by the solidness of a timbered structure upthrusting to a tower a dozen feet above them. Shawn studied it carefully. "It's their jet station," he murmured. "Inside, the water forces up into mechanically controlled jets." He faced the cliff in wonder, then turned again to the looming jet mounts. "My God," he whispered, "with this setup, the size of the jets and the fall of the creek and the pipe, they can tear the cliff apart."

Dr. Miller peered at him with pale but comprehending face. "You mean they mine with this? Mine silver?"

"No. Not silver. Maybe gold. Traces of gold. Mostly mud to make a big splash for the investors, the suckers."

The doctor's face mirrored his struggle with distant memories. "I saw something like it once. They use a control valve to turn loose the water and a lever to direct it."

"That's the general idea," Shawn answered, then turned to Eric. "I want to get over by that overhang, the cliff. See what they've washed down. New York may be surprised."

In the moment they stole silently across the intervening meadow to reach the slimy, washed mud tailings at the cliff's base, a voice was hurled at them from the lessening darkness. "That's far enough, Ainsley, far as you'll ever go!"

Suddenly men bore down about them. The menacing circle of men with lights and drawn guns tightened. A blinding, glaring light fell on Caroline's face. A voice tore at her and swept her back to a smoke-hazed room of the Jerome Hotel.

Then she saw the hate-ridden face of Len Shaner.

"It's her all right. The Herndon woman. The bitch that blew our mine to hell."

Matt Shaner's voice sounded then. "Len, we've got 'em at last. Thirty years, but we've got them. Good thing you and me ransacked that car and figured this out. If it'd been up to that idiot Fenton, they'd have got away."

Matt Shaner's words broke off, lost in the vicious and stunning slap his brother crashed against Caroline's face.

"This is a starter," he rasped. "You'll wish to hell it was all."

The blow staggered her to her knees. She stared upward in silent contempt and loathing. If she spoke, the words were lost. Eric swung about with a wildly lashing blow at Matt Shaner. It was futile and useless as men jerked him backward and a fist smashed against his face.

Len Shaner's gaze shifted to Shawn Ainsley. "So your name's Swope, you miserable, lying bastard. You're an engineer, a snooping, mining engineer."

Shawn faced him, rigid and frozen-faced. His arm swept the park. "You've quite a deal going here, Shaner. Too good to have it exposed for what it is—worthless and rotten." He slumped tiredly. "The move is up to you now, Shaner. You're in the saddle."

Even as Shaner's glare of hatred and triumph was upon him, Shawn probed the darkness. There would be no chance of escape.

There was a moment of quiet as Len Shaner towered above Caroline, yanked her to her feet, and stood staring into her face. Shawn heard a far-off sound and an unreal whispered hope. It grew upon him as his gaze again swept the encircling faces. Dr. Miller was not with them. His slight and bent form was nowhere within the glow of the lights nor revealed by the creeping dawn.

Shawn's hope became a flaming thing as Len Shaner said, "Take them up to the bunkhouse. We'll deal with them inside."

Shawn Ainsley waited five seconds, then his yell tore the dawn and the park. "Caroline, Eric! Down! Fall! Roll!"

Even as his words sounded, he flung himself to the ground, moved with blurring speed that sent him crashing into Caroline's legs, and knocked her down to sprawl beside him.

The suddenness of it and the seeming idiocy of his movements caught the encircling men unaware. For a moment they stood shock-still with wordless and wondering faces.

Then it came, the tearing, drenching, chilling, surge of water that was upon them. "Crawl," Shawn screamed at

Eric. "Crawl away to the meadow. Keep going," he gasped. "Roll. Crawl."

He was aware that men no longer stood in their way. The jet force struck full upon Shaner's group, staggering them back against the cliff, dazing them, beating them into insensibility. Even as he tugged at Caroline's clothing, his mind was strangely alert and fast working. *He waited at the jet station. Dr. Miller waited. He saw the lights, the men, the Shaners.*

Shawn's thoughts were momentarily shattered by a gunshot that spoke above the roaring hiss of the jet stream. He moved with faster, desperate motions toward the meadow and away from the menace of the cliff. For a moment he glanced back toward the group that lay flattened and struggling at the cliff's base. *He's got them all in his wash stream. Every damned man, the Shaners and their gunmen.*

Shawn knew that he should crawl farther and keep moving after the fleeing forms of his sister and of Eric into the protecting and hiding grass. Instead he stood up and gazed at the searing, tearing stream that knocked the men about like chips at the base of the cliff. *Their loins torn to pieces; that force can knock a man's head off.*

Shawn stared with fascination. Momentarily the jet's force was raised and washed dirt and rocks downward to shower on the men behind him. When one or two of them struggled to rise, the lashing surge of water was lowered to bowl them about. When at last they all lay silent, the rush of water again lifted and held to the cliff's sheer wall.

Then there was no wall. The caving and falling face of the overhang became a rumbling crashing mass piling at the cliff's base and upon the men beneath it.

As the water continued its menacing arc, Shawn Ainsley crept to the jet station and peered about. Far off, in the meadow, he saw Caroline and Eric struggling to their feet.

His gaze turned from them as he mounted a wooden ladder to mount the jet controls. Abruptly he knew why the roar of water and the crumbling of the cliff continued. Dr. Miller lay dead at the levers. Blood spread from his

419

side. "One shot," Shawn whispered. "One shot, and they killed him. Perhaps it was meant this way. Had to be."

He stared eastward, seeing but not heeding the red flame giving birth to another day.

They came back into the old, tension-ridden town near mid-morning. There were men on the street who watched their coming as their horses emerged from the canyon of Glacier Creek and down the juniper-studded slope. They paused near the store, and Eric spoke quietly to a handful of men whom he called to their side. "I don't know who among you are Shaner's men. It doesn't matter now. Both Matt and Len Shaner are dead. So are Dr. Miller and several others." At the doubt in their faces, he added, "Ride up the canyon. See for yourselves. Bring the old doctor back to Mrs. Edmonds."

"He's lying," someone shouted.

Shawn looked them over tiredly. "Would we have ridden out of that canyon unharmed otherwise? Make what you will of it, but prepare for a different day and a different life. This town is free of the Shaners and their vengeance. Likely it'll be free of fear too." He reined his horse beside a young boy, and asked, "Where does Frieda Edmonds live? Show us to her house."

The crowd parted, clearing a way for them as they rode on.

Hours later Frieda Edmonds drew Caroline aside. "God has mysterious ways and mysterious avengers. It is over. At last it is over. Now Kathleen can leave Cascade and really live again. And I, I can visit you, as you asked, in Aspen."

"Come soon, Frieda," Caroline said softly, "and bring Kathleen. We've a big house and——"

She became silent as Frieda moved to a table, opened a book, drew an old and yellowed slip of paper from it, and handed it to her. "Here," Frieda was saying, "this belongs to you. I meant to give it to you once before, on the night you and your baby hid at my house and then left Aspen. Kathleen found it the night your husband was killed."

Caroline looked at her in wonder. "And you've kept it all these years?"

"Yes. Not that it is anything valuable. Just a receipt of some kind. At first I meant to send it to your father, but it didn't seem important. Then I forgot. I didn't think of it until last night after you left Cascade."

Eric and Shawn crowded close as Caroline's fingers spread the old and brittle paper. She studied it momentarily. A cry of disbelief broke from her. "Look," she said. "This is an assay talley sheet. One that Bob wrote for old man Lorentz in 1881." She was silent a moment; her breath came in short, tearing gasps. "This must—it has to be—what Bob found that last night and was bringing home. Don't you see? Don't you understand?"

They looked at her with bewildered eyes, as she said dazedly, "This would have saved the Buccaneer mine for us. Would have meant so much, so different a life for so many of us if Bob had brought it safely home."

"How do you know?" Shawn murmured. "How can you be sure, Caroline?"

Her finger trembled as she pointed to the bottom of the old paper and the marks it bore. "See that? See that 'X'? Lorentz couldn't write. Couldn't write his name. He made the mark and Bob attested it."

"But what does it prove?" Eric urged.

"So much. Oh, so much." Her voice neared a sob. "When the court decision went against us and we lost the Buccaneer, Matt Shaner and Gagnon produced a bill of sale *signed by Lorentz. Signed with his full name*. It was forged. Their bill of sale to the claims was forged. It had to be. This paper would have proven it."

Frieda Edmonds sat down weakly, her hands clasped and white. "If I'd only known, had only given it to you that night."

Caroline turned to drop to her knees and encircle the frail old woman and to peer with steadying eyes into her wrinkled and worried face. "No, Frieda, even then it was too late. Bob was dead, the Buccaneer destroyed."

Eric gazed silently out the window. After a long time, he said, "The men are bringing Dr. Miller's body."

421

Caroline looked up at him. "We must stay here now, Eric. Stay and help until after——" She paused, hearing the sound of a dog barking and the playful shout of a child. People would come slowly, almost fearfully, into the sunlight of security and freedom, but time carries both understanding and healing.

PART SEVEN

1938

Chapter 25

As Caroline Duane entered her seventieth year, the home on Hunter Creek enshrined tranquility and comfort. The years had surged by, years that had given so much and asked so much in return. Maude Daley's laughter would be heard no more, for she had died in 1928. A sudden heart attack four years later took Eric from Caroline.

After Eric's death, Caroline traveled and sought out countries and cities whose names carried the mystery of strange sights and strange languages.

Of these distant countries, she best remembered Austria and how an athletic and pleasant young man had come often to visit her. His questions about Aspen, the Roaring Fork Valley, and Colorado were endless. All she could tell him was of a town with wondrous natural beauty and a silver-hearted past. She reluctantly told him about the silent, deserted Aspen still so close to her heart.

"Your town will live again," he said confidently. "Austria and Switzerland have many such mountain towns prospering as tourist and recreational centers. Yes, and cultural centers too. Mrs. Duane, you must have magnificent ski slopes on your mountains. I'm certain your lovely Aspen has another destiny to fulfill."

The days of 1938 marched their destined way. August merged into September with but a mellowing of sunshine and a riotous burst of color across the flower garden.

It seemed to Caroline that every blossom had reached a deeper hue this year. Early each morning she quickly stepped out of bed. There was rich satisfaction in being out of doors in this quiet time. The sound of Hunter Creek gave a clear chuckle through the warming air, and dew provided a diamond sheen across the green expanse of lawn.

The entire yard could be watered by merely sliding a board into the concrete head-gate of an irrigation ditch, but Caroline seldom made use of the device. By hand sprinkling with the hose, she could prolong the hours in her green domain. Birds made her trees a haven. She knew where some nested and might return another year.

Later, when the garden tools had wearied her, she would go inside and prepare breakfast for herself and for her collie dog Gwain. Gwain held a special place in her heart, for he was the son of an equally magnificent dog that had been Eric's gift to her.

Until noon she busied herself with the dusting and cleaning that kept both floors of the house clean, and lent them the air of being used and needed. She never considered closing off the upstairs or any part of her house. She had seen others do this, limiting their living to two or three rooms. To her, it seemed they closed off part of their lives and their past. She insisted on having each room open-windowed and open-doored when the weather permitted for it brought a subtle blending of living space with the outer yard and the rise of encircling mountains.

Visitors came less often now for upon the town in its lonely desertion was a new day and a new generation. Jimmy and Annette had long since insisted that she live with them at the Lazy Seedy, or at least keep a companion constantly with her. She would not have it so. This was her home and her world.

She had consented that a car be kept at the single Aspen garage, ready at all times to carry her to Wilderness Creek, through the imposing gate and up the long driveway of the ranch. She had gone to the Lazy Seedy only once within the past month. The wide, smooth highway offered no challenge and little interest to one who had plodded these long miles astride a horse and over narrow, twisting trails. The ranch, with its huge and immaculately landscaped colonial house, seemed to Caroline of a foreign place and of a time with which she was strangely out of tune.

426

It was mid-September before the first heavy frost came out of a cold, still night to lay white and killing crystals upon the yard, the valley, and the mountain slopes. The days remained warm and sun-filled, but the ageless sorcery of autumn worked swift changes on high aspen groves and the shrubs and flowers of her garden.

Suddenly a mystic and smoky haze filled the valley. The days of Indian summer passed one by one.

In late October the first heavy snow fell. There was little wind with the storm, and on the second morning the sun broke through to reveal a white blanket nearly a foot deep. On the mountains, the snow was much heavier, and the peaks seemed to draw fleecy blankets about their shoulders and settle into hibernation akin to that of the bear, the chipmunks, and other animals of their snow-laden forests.

With yardwork a pleasant memory for the year, Caroline found it rewarding to spend much of her time before the fireplace, with her tawny collie. She required little sleep, and even now daytime naps were not a part of her routine. There was sewing to be done, books to be read, letters to be answered.

The letters proved hardest to handle. Often the name on a letter would bring a perplexed frown to her forehead; she studied a while to recall just who the writer could be.

She decided that memory was an unreliable and tricky thing when one aged. It seemed easy to remember places and people and happenings out of the distant past. But the events of yesterday could quickly become veiled or forgotten. Her memory of the Hugus store at Fort Steele as she had seen it more than a half century ago seemed more detailed than that of the new department store in Glenwood Springs to which Annette had taken her in early spring.

On a day in late November another snowstorm raked the valley and the town. Downward spiraling temperatures followed. Winter came to the Roaring Fork.

The storms came in quick succession with deepening snow and enduring cold. The first flakes of such a heavy,

427

windswept storm were falling on an evening as she reread a letter from the young man in Austria. He would visit Aspen soon if the rising tide of war did not delay his journey.

She folded the letter and laid it aside. The collie, Gwain, was beside the door and asked to be let out. She moved with him to the porch and watched him run quickly into the yard. Inside again she stood near the warmth of her fireplace.

Half an hour passed. She listened for Gwain's scratch and whine. But there was only the crackling of the fire and the sound of a rising gale searching the eaves of the house. She waited a few more minutes, then wrapping a shawl about her, she went again onto the porch.

"Gwain," she called. "Gwain, come in. Here, Gwain, here." She waited, then called again. When no furry, tail-wagging form came out of the darkness, she walked into the yard.

She found him beside the picket fence, stretched and already stiffening in a death that had come with the agony of poisoning. She stooped and ran unbelieving hands over the silken softness of his head and throat. Then she stood up, heedless of the cold, as she stared down at the quiet form on which already snowflakes were gathering.

Her gaze turned, lifted. Far off and not yet storm-enshrouded was a moonlit peak from which a snow plume trailed in silver sheen. It would disappear soon in a sweep of the approaching storm.

Caroline Ainsley Duane slowly opened the gate, moved beyond the picket fence, and came onto the quiet road. Her breath lifted as a white vapor in the searing cold of the night. Suddenly she moved ahead and walked more and more swiftly. Her breath quickened; her eyes were distant and fixed.

She must hurry now. Hurry to escape this place of tragedy and of horror behind her. *She must escape Swope's mansion.*

Dark, storm-laden clouds raced across the sky, but the distant peak still glowed as a beacon to guide her in the moonlight.

At that moment the snow plume became for Caroline a billowing whiteness that haloed a wistful face. Lance Ainsley's smile drew her down the lonely, frozen road. Somewhere, somewhere beyond the hill in Evans he would be waiting.

She began the ascent of a slope. Her breath became panting gasps, her steps an eager, headlong rush. Beyond the hill were warmth and comfort—and the reaching arms of her father. Others wait beyond the hill. So many others.

Surely and eagerly she moved on. And her heart sang in tune to the winds of the blizzard that quickly closed in to engulf her.

GREAT WESTERN ADVENTURE
FROM AVON

Packed with all the action, color, and adventure of the Old West, these Avon Great Westerns are guaranteed to blaze a never-to-be-forgotten trail across the discriminating reader's memory. The Avon brand means Western excitement with the kick of a .44!

WILLIAM COLT MACDONALD

☐	BULLET TRAIL	20875	.95
☐	GHOST TOWN GOLD	20560	.75
☐	POWDERSMOKE RANGE	20065	.75
☐	ROARING LEAD	20198	.75
☐	SIX-GUN MELODY	19745	.75

TODHUNTER BALLARD

☐	APPLEGATE'S GOLD	17525	.75
☐	OUTLAW BRAND	19232	.75
☐	TROUBLE ON THE MASSACRE	19364	.95

RAY HOGAN

☐	LEAD RECKONING	18069	.75
☐	THE MOONLIGHTERS	18879	.75
☐	NIGHT RAIDER	18549	.75
☐	REBEL IN YANKEE BLUE	18432	.75

Available at bookstores everywhere or use this handy coupon for ordering:

AVON ◭ THE BEST IN
BESTSELLING ENTERTAINMENT!

THE BIG BESTSELLERS
ARE AVON BOOKS!

☐	**Aftermath** Ladislas Farago	25387	$1.95
☐	**Lionors** Barbara Ferry Johnson	24679	$1.75
☐	**Dark Fires** Rosemary Rogers	23523	$1.95
☐	**Creative Aggression** Dr. George R. Bach and Dr. Herb Goldberg	24612	$1.95
☐	**Aton** Irving Greenfield	24844	$1.75
☐	**Chief!** Albert A. Seedman and Peter Hellman	24307	$1.95
☐	**Endgame** Harvey Ardman	24299	$1.75
☐	**Alive: The Story of the Andes Survivors** Piers Paul Read	21535	$1.95
☐	**The Rosemary Touch** Lois Wyse	23531	$1.75
☐	**The Wall Street Gang** Richard Ney	23549	$2.25
☐	**Teacher and Child** Dr. Haim G. Ginott	24414	$1.75
☐	**Watership Down** Richard Adams	19810	$2.25
☐	**Devil's Desire** Laurie McBain	23226	$1.75
☐	**Having a Baby Can Be a Scream** Joan Rivers	23234	$1.50
☐	**Autopsy** John R. Feegel	22574	$1.75
☐	**Shifting Gears** George and Nena O'Neill	23192	$1.95
☐	**Working** Studs Terkel	22566	$2.25
☐	**Jane** Dee Wells	21519	$1.75
☐	**Theophilus North** Thornton Wilder	19059	$1.75

Available at better bookstores everywhere, or order direct from the publisher.

AVON BOOKS Mail Order Dept., 250 West 55th St., New York, N.Y. 10019

Please send me the books checked above. I enclose $_____(please include 25¢ per copy for mailing). Please use check or money order—sorry, no cash or COD's. Allow three weeks for delivery.

Mr/Mrs/Miss_____

Address_____

City_____State/Zip_____

BB 8-75